I0665814

Worlds Apart

By

S.L. Gape

2017

Worlds Apart © 2017 S.L. Gape
Triplicity Publishing, LLC

ISBN-13: 978-0999737002
ISBN-10: 0999737007

All rights reserved. No part of this publication may be reproduced, distributed, or transmitted in any form without permission.

This is a work of fiction. Names, characters, places, and incidents are the product of the author's imagination and are used fictitiously. Any resemblance to actual persons, living or dead, business establishments, events of any kind, or locales is entirely coincidental.
Printed in the United States of America

First Edition – 2017
Cover Design: Triplicity Publishing, LLC
Interior Design: Triplicity Publishing, LLC
Editor: Miranda Campbell - Triplicity Publishing, LLC

Acknowledgement

This was the first book where I've found inspiration on holiday. I arrived on vacation in Cancun and realised that sun, sea, and sand (and a Margarita or two) was my muse. Finding a comfort and ease to spend each morning viciously typing on my phone by the pool, as I formed the beginning of Worlds Apart. I have no idea where the inspiration came from, but those quiet mornings from sun up through to my battery dying, is what got us here today. I've since realised that vacation is definitely my motivation and so, of course, I now need to spend more time with a cocktail in hand and by the pool.

However, thanks not only goes to Mexico, but equally, a huge thank you to all the team at Triplicity Publishing, in your editing, marketing, cover designing and bringing it all together. Miranda, you have the patience of a saint when it comes to my questions, and here's to working on Nautical Delights together. And my two 'fave' gals, Lisa and Sarah, who always find the time to proof for me.

Dedication

For all the Country lovers out there...

Chapter One

"Buenos Margherita," Dawn said, kissing her on each cheek. "Como estas? Donde esta, Heidi?"

"Ay ay ay, s'no Bueno. S'no Bueno," the greying, Hispanic woman said hurriedly, rushing them towards the large door in front of them, and shaking her head erratically.

"Heid's, come on it's me," she said. "Shit!" She swiped back her long, black hair. "Jesus, this heat is excruciating. You'd think I'd be used to it now," she said to nobody.

"Ow!" Dawn rubbed her hand where the small, Mexican woman slapped her, listening to her ranting. She picked up on the words "God" and "name," clearly being scorned for saying Jesus or something. "Lo siento, mamacita," she smirked and winked at the crazy lady, laughing as she toddled off down the vast hallway.

"Heid's come on, mate. It's too hot out here. Why isn't your AC on? This is insane. *Heid's!"* She said, harsher this time. "For fucks sake," she whispered, checking Margherita wasn't around. "Heidi, come on, it's me. We need to talk about this. It's been seven days, mate. Come on!" she whined. "Seriously, we've been best friends for 37 years. We've lived in L.A. for 12 years. I was there when your parents told you that you'd be getting a baby brother, and there when gramps died. You've been my wing woman whenever I'm out to get lucky. We went to the caravan together as kids, the farm. Oh, you remember the farm? With my cousin, Anna? Ah, those were good times," she said reminiscing, sliding down the door to get more comfortable.

"Aqui?" Margherita asked, handing Dawn the ice-cold Voss.

"Aye perfecto. Muchos gracias, mi amor." Dawn took the water from the housekeeper and gulped it down.

"Que esta loco," Margherita ranted pointing fiercely to the door.

"I'm not loco, Margherita." They heard from the door and quickly looked around.

"Heid's, you're alive! Great stuff. Come on. You *are* acting loco," Dawn said, pleading with her best friend.

Once again, silence filled the air.

"For the love of God," Dawn said, looking up at Margherita apologetically. "Lo siento, lo siento, lo siento."

Too late. Margherita was off again ranting about them both being loco. In her defence, Dawn wasn't acting crazy at all, but Heidi was.

"Alright, last chance saloon buddy." Dawn waited. Clearly Heidi had no intention of engaging in any type of communication, and continued to ignore her.

"Heidi Jayne Rita Edwards!" she stormed, knowing how much Heidi hated her full name being used.

Suddenly the door was yanked open, and Dawn fell into a backward somersault, doing what could only be described as giving the U.S. Olympic gymnastics team a run for their money. She felt the cold, liquid seep into her blouse, and quickly darted up, wiping water from her New Gucci handbag.

"For fucks sake, Heid's, this is brand new!"

"Dawn, it's a handbag. And this..." she said, snatching the bottle of Voss and holding it under her nose "...is water. Seriously, what are you going to do when it rains?"

"We live in L.A.; it *doesn't* rain!" Dawn spat.

Heidi hated when Dawn was right. She could feel her lip giving her away.

"Don't fight it. Nope, don't you dare! I can see it..." Dawn said smirking. "I know that little curve too well. I can see it. Yup here it comes... in one, two, oh she's playing hardball, two and a half... and there we have it," Dawn smiled, ducking out of the way of the cushion flying towards her.

"Jesus, you could've taken my head off," she said, walking towards her best friend.

"You know you really need to stop cursing in front of Margherita; it's disrespectful to her culture and beliefs."

"I know, I know. I do try. I just don't know what comes over me when I'm here. On the plus side, she loves me; I mean look at me, who wouldn't?" Dawn smirked, posing like an 80's game show model.

"You *are* looking hot, lady, I must admit," Heidi weighed up her best friend's long black hair, her athletic body and tall frame to match. *She was so L.A.*, thought Heidi. And yet *she* was the movie star.

"Although, you need to stop with the exercise and the one-lettuce-leaf-a-day diet. You really are getting too thin. Your mum will kill me next time she's over." Heidi looked at her seriously.

"Don't sweat it, I'm all good. I like to stay in shape. Plus, we're in L.A., the place where even a size zero is considered overweight!" She rolled her eyes.

"Hmmm, that doesn't make it right. Anyway, what do you want? I'm fine, I just want to be left alone. You've seen me. I'm alive. Margherita is here; should I kill myself, she'll smell the rotting body," she said sarcastically.

"You're an idiot! That's not even funny," Dawn said annoyed. "Plus, with 16 rooms, it'd take her a while, especially considering how slow she walks. Come on." Dawn stopped walking, assessing the anarchy before her. "Oh Heid's, why are you doing this to yourself?" Dawn dropped her bag and water to the floor, slowly picking up the hundreds of tabloids laid out in front of Heidi. They covered the entire floorspace of the smallest of her three sitting rooms.

"Don't!" She shouted, grabbing Dawn's arm. "Leave them, I haven't finished reading them yet."

"Babes, we *aren't* doing this. It's not healthy."

Heidi gently pulled the magazine from her hand and began to read.

"The world mourns as Hollywood's '*dream*' couple is no more. The nation's sweetheart's marriage crashes and burns. No hope for any love story now, as Everett Brady cheats on his leading lady, Heidi Spencer-Brady. Everett found love in a hopeless place.
Hei—"

"Stop already! What are you reading this nonsense for?" Dawn said, ripping it from Heidi's hands. "Heidi it's bullshit. You need to ignore it."

"How can I, Dawn? Jesus. Last count, I'm up to 57 tabloids. It's on every radio station, every TV station. You know how many TV stations I have in this house?"

"Well that depends as to whether you're counting them in each room of the house." She smirked.

"This isn't funny, D; this is my life!" Heidi snapped.

Dawn grabbed her best friend's hand and took her to one of the couches. "Babes this isn't your life. This is Hollywood making it your life. Heid's, you remember what happened on March 12th, 2012?"

"Of course, I do!" She spat, pulling her hand away.

"And have you slept with Everett since?"

"You know fine well I haven't," Heidi snapped again.

"So then, this *isn't* your life. Well, outside of the press being all over it. Give them a couple of weeks. It'll be old news, babe," Dawn said realistically.

"It's already been a week." Heidi sniffled. "I can't believe he's done this," she said sadly. "He's such a jack ass!"

"Babes he's always been a selfish ass. I don't know how you've lasted 12 years. He's self-obsessed to a fault. Sleazy, over the top, and a self-righteous cheating bastard. "We know of four times, and as I said back in 2012, you deserve way more than someone treating you this way. C'mon look at yourself. *Look!*"

Dawn pulled her to the full-length mirror. *They were a prerequisite for each room in their lavish mansion, required by the Prince of Cheaters himself,* Dawn thought. She pulled the hairband from Heidi's long, dirty blonde hair, allowing the very slight waves to sleekly fall over her shoulders. She wiped away a fallen tear, and allowed her best friend to assess her.

"You have blue eyes the color of the ocean. You have skin that few fair-haired people have, far more relatable to dark haired and Latino people. Geez, if Margherita had bonked James Dean, I guarantee you'd be the secret lovechild," she said pointedly.

"You're an idiot," Heidi laughed.

"Yes, but an incredibly sexy and lovable one," she winked. "Come on, babes, we've gotten through much worse than this. You don't like all the press anyway. On the plus side, at least one part of the 'influential' couple will be destroyed," she pointed out. "And what's left? The

5

beautiful, leading lady scorned by her elusive, leading man, having damaged her trust in people, and her faith in love, feeling and fearing that there will never again be the opportunity to feel the way she once felt—a feeling that could only be likened to a distant memory."

"That's my press release, isn't it?" Heidi questioned her best friend, agent, and publicist.

"Wonderful, isn't it? I figured that would get us a couple more million through the lawyers. Oh and of course your ever growing followers, which is becoming even more significant. I know you hate all of this, but sweetie it comes with the territory. Remember at school in drama class when Mr. Price said you would never be an actress, that you should lower your sights? Remember what you said?"

"Nope!" She stomped.

"Yeah you do, behind the bike sheds having a sneaky cig... come on, play ball, Spence?"

"Sod you, Price! I'll show you who'll make a good actress!" she giggled turning to Dawn.

"And that you did beautiful girl, that you did," she said, pulling her into a hug.

"What am I gonna do, D? He's pretty much all I've known over here."

"Babes, you hit the big time back home before him or even Hollywood. The offers flocked in before he got his big break." She eyed her best friend carefully. "You got yours years before him. He didn't make you. You were already made, Heid's. Well and truly. He grew because of you and your relationship. You have been an unstoppable force, but this isn't going to change things. For you, it will mean bigger things. He's done this. You guys haven't made love in over 4 years," she confirmed. "You will be the scorned wife, they'll pull him apart, and her career will be over before it's begun. No director will want to touch a young, unknown tramp that has destroyed America's idea of the perfect marriage. But you need to face it. We've been holed up here for too long.

"Look at this," she said, pulling her to peek behind the blinds. "The press aren't going to leave until we've faced it. I know you don't want to, but just give them what they want. I'll give you the words and then hopefully they'll disappear."

"I really don't think I can."

"Si bambina, puedes. Of course, you can my baby," Margherita said in her broken English.

"Gracias mama," the two women said in unison, smiling at her.

"Right. We do this, we do it properly," Dawn said bluntly. "Get rid of all this rubbish," she pointed to the tabloids littering her house. "Get the guys in to…"

Dawn stopped looking her friend up and down. "Well, to um... freshen you up, shall we say. We can go out to lunch. I'll sort the press release saying that you need to be left alone through this difficult period. You would appreciate some time and privacy to digest and when you are ready you will do an interview. That way we can try and get you back to some form of normality and you won't need to hideout," she finished.

"You don't actually buy that do you? Please tell me you aren't that naive?" Heidi quizzed.

"What alternative do we have? Send you into outer space?" Dawn pulled her iPhone out of her Gucci handbag, heavily pressing the numbers.

"Hi, it's me. Project runway is good to go. Get here ASAP."

"Project runway?" Heidi asked.

7

"Don't you worry your pretty little head, just go and get a shower. The guys will be here in ten," Dawn said, feeling a sense of accomplishment.

*

An hour later, Heidi was hyperventilating at the front door. Margherita ran in circles panicking like a Benny Hill comedy sketch, and Dawn tried her damnedest to calm both women down.

"Seriously? What is the alternative? Hide out here forever? Come on, we're going for lunch is all. I'll ensure they all keep away. We have privacy in the restaurant, so it's literally here to the car, which is *on* the driveway," she huffed. "Come on Heid's, we have to do this."

Heidi finally calmed her breathing, knowing Dawn was right. She took another deep breath before taking charge.

"Okay, come on," Heidi said, opening her front door, feeling the combination of California heat, flashes, and shouts coming from the bottom of her driveway. "Thank God for gates; the press are like animals," she said to Dawn as they got into the car.

*

A short ride later, they were outside the private entrance, otherwise known as the "celeb-trance" of their favorite restaurant. Heidi wasn't hungry, not in the slightest, but equally she couldn't recall the last time she'd eaten. She managed to get inside without too much hassle. The manager, Susie, ushered them in within seconds to a private part of the restaurant as she hugged and kissed Heidi, proffering her apologies and acts of kindness.

Worlds Apart

It's amazing how in situations like these, nobody ever liked your husband in the first place, Heidi thought. It's a bit like your mum when your first boyfriend breaks your heart. Suddenly he said and did things which make it clear he wasn't right for you. Yet nobody speaks of this.

Well, except Dawn.

She'd told her numerous times. Constantly told her, in fact. In their ten year relationship, she'd frequently informed Heidi that he was a lying, cheating asshole and she should dump his sorry ass. Heidi ignored that though. She'd loved Ev—his big, blue eyes, and sturdy frame, his blonde curls falling sheepishly across his chiselled features. God, he was a beautiful man. But as Dawn always said, a beautiful man in this industry would never keep it in his pants. She always thought it was kind of a sweeping statement, yet her best friend turned out to be correct.

It wasn't all bad. In the beginning, it really was perfection. The Hollywood fairy-tale everyone wrote about. He'd won her over, eventually. After the chemistry on their first movie together grew, she realized he was everything she'd ever wanted. The protective, loving husband, the funny, dashing, loveable sweetheart. The princess's fairy-tale prince. And of course, with all his very public declarations to 'woo' his very own princess, they quickly became the talk of Tinsel town. Everett had a complete buy in. Everyone was on board, and everyone was waiting until the day the real-life love story got its perfect ending. But it wasn't the perfect ending, was it? No, the perfection lasted about two years before she started questioning where he was and who he was with. The drinking became worse. The flirting. The womanizing had become an everyday occurrence, and soon after, the love of cocaine had become way more than an indulgence. Likened much more to an

S. L. Gape

addiction. Heidi never succumbed to the celeb lifestyle of drink, drugs, and anything else money could buy. She enjoyed a nice glass of wine as much as the next person, but she had always been conscious of it becoming a pain killer or a deterrence from the lack of life and privacy that came with the job.

"You doing okay?" Dawn asked bringing her back to the here and now.

"Yeah, fine. Sorry, just thinking about stuff. What're you having?"

"Probably just the caesar salad. Shall we get a bottle of Dom since we aren't driving?" she asked her friend speculatively.

"Actually, I'd rather not if you don't mind. While I'm riding the storm it's probably best I'm not seen with a drink. You know what it would be like. *'America's sweetheart eases the pain of heartbreak with the bottle'* or *'is this the reason our fairy-tale prince looked elsewhere?'* It's not worth the trouble. I'm good with some Perrier and lime. I will most definitely give them a show where foods concerned though. I haven't eaten in days, and the smell has completely awakened my senses," she said, looking keenly through the menu.

"What are you thinking?" Dawn asked as she glanced over at her friend again.

"I'm torn between the spaghetti and the salmon. God, what I'd give for mum's Sunday lunch right now," she said distantly.

"Well, why don't you consider going home for a couple weeks? We have nothing going on for a bit. You've been saying you need a vacation and, well, this is probably the perfect time. I can monitor stuff here for a while, and I'm in talks with Disney about shooting. We don't want to do anything until we know for sure the dates. I can hold things together here and you can relax and spend some time with your folks," she said, stopping to order her food.

"I'll have the honey glazed duck with green beans and a Perrier please?" Heidi said politely.

"Of course, Mrs. Spencer-Brady. Um, Mrs. Spencer, um...Ms...um...sorr—"

"Heidi is quite alright," she nodded politely to the young server.

"Sorry madam," he said, walking away and checking the vicinity to ensure no management heard the error. Most definitely that kind of error would result in him losing his job.

"And so it begins. You know what? As much as I like the idea, I don't think I can handle the fuss. My mum will go on and on about how I've brought it on myself. Why didn't I settle for a normal life and normal husband? How I've sold my soul to the devil with my choices. And then, of course, the, 'I can't even go to church anymore because everyone acts like it's me that's famous and asks for my autograph!' Yadda yadda yadda." She rolled her eyes.

"You know she loves you. It impacts everyone around you is all. Whether they want it or not. You know they went to bingo the other night, and she was telling Mum that you're likely to get the lead in the new Disney movie," she said seriously.

"Did she?" Heidi asked, surprised.

"Yes, she's ever so proud, Heid's. She just struggles that her only daughter is as big as Madonna. I'm sure Kate Middleton's Mum felt the same when her daughter came home from Uni and said, "I'm marrying my boyfriend. Oh, and by the way, he'll be the King one day so you and dad will be parents of a princess."

"I'm nowhere near as big as Madonna, idiot. And Kate Middleton is a very different situation," she said, rolling her eyes.

"Babes it really isn't. From a couple of years old, you wanted to be an actress. From 5 to 15 I went from hairdresser, farmer, air hostess, TV host, footballer... well, the list went on. Yours never changed. So, can you imagine when you went out and achieved that goal? That pride from your parents? But babe, that wasn't their dream. Suddenly, their beautiful, little girl goes from a school play to the star of the biggest soap on TV. Before you know it, you're winning awards and creating mega Hollywood stardom. Your mum suddenly couldn't enjoy church. They had people camping on the doorstep, friends begging for money for this, that, and the other. She couldn't nip to Asda for her monthly shop. She loves you Heid's, no doubt about it, and they're both incredibly proud of you, but she's famous by association, and for someone so incredibly private and chilled, that's a shit load to deal with. Of course it stresses her. It would stress me had I not decided to come with you and abuse this fame hungry town." She winked.

"We really are opposites. I don't know why you love it so much; it's painful. I can't even have a wee in peace. You literally eat it all up. It's rubbish! I mean, there were probably about 700,000 people in the world that got divorced last week, and I had 79,000 tweets, 12,000 Facebook messages, 53 phone calls, and features on the front page in about 150 countries—that I know of. It's barmy. I'm me, just me. This is my life. Let me just deal in peace for God's sake!" She snapped, as the server put the drinks down in front of them.

"Oh, I'm sorry, I didn't mean you," Heidi said apologetically.

"No problem," he said, showing off his award-winning smile. Missing only a 'ding and flash,' he replicated a Colgate advertisement.

"You aren't going to eat that are you?" Dawn asked, pointing to Heidi with the bread in her hand.

"Too sodding right, I am," she said taking a huge and very un-ladylike bite, smirking to her friend.

"Fair enough," she backed down. "Look, it will blow over, honestly. They'll get bored. You know what Hollywood's like. Just ride it out and ignore it. But you can't keep hiding away. If you're going to do that, then go away, and do it somewhere away from here. What about a cabin in the woods? Oh or that lovely place in the Poconos?" she said, moving her hands so the server could put their food down.

"Why should I have to leave, D? He did this, not me. Why can't I just enjoy some free time at home? Spend some time in the sun by the pool." She knew full well that in theory it was all well and good, but the drones of helicopters hovering above to get snap shots of her, or people breaking in to try and get the next million-dollar snap of the broken-hearted princess was a much more likely situation.

Chapter Two

"Mum, I'm fine, honestly. Please don't worry, you know what the tabloids are like; they make stuff up. I'm not dead, I haven't been in rehab, nor do I need sectioned. They will just try to get some info from you. I'm sorry you're being put through all this," Heidi sighed heavily in the phone. "It's been a month. I really thought it would've died down, but clearly they have no better stories."

"Don't be so silly, darling. I just wish I could see you in person, rather than in every paper and magazine I walk past. We're worried about you. I really thought you may come home to see us, or maybe even move back," she said sadly.

"Oh Mum, we've discussed this before. I'm sorry, but I love my job and one day this very materialistic and shallow industry is going to eat me up and spit me out for being too old or too grey or too fat. So, I just want to make the most of it while I can. Then I promise I'll do the whole normal thing for you."

"Heidi, you don't need to do anything for us. We love you and we're both overwhelmingly proud of you. It's your life. Do what *you* want. What makes *you* happy. We're your parents, and we worry that's all," she said sadly. "Look, Dawn's mum will be here any minute. I'll tell her you said hi. Look after each other and know we both love you dearly. If you want to come home for a few weeks, you know we'd love to see you," she said optimistically.

"Thanks Mum, good luck at bingo. I love you, see you soon," she said hanging up.

Maybe her mum and Dawn were right; maybe she should go home for a bit. These vultures were still obsessing all this time and they didn't appear to want to let it go. But would it be any better at home? Mum was getting stalked in the house, at bingo, even at bloody Asda. Dad had to avoid the golf course, which infuriated him to no end. So what was the actual solution? Just ride it out? For how long though? When would they give up? A press release and two interviews on the biggest TV shows around and it still wasn't enough. She was still on the front page of every tabloid known to man.

"Bambina bambina!" Margherita frantically wailed throughout the house.

"Margherita, que pasa? What's wrong? What's wrong? Calm down and slow down," she said as her phone started ringing.

"Hang on," she said to Margherita. "Hell—"

Before she could finish, Dawn's frantic words cut her off.

"What the bloody hell is up with the pair of you!?"

"I'm turning down your road," Dawn said. "Open the door."

Heidi rushed down the steps to the front door with Margherita following her every move, still wailing "dios mio" over and over. *Why the bloody hell did she keep saying 'oh my God' over and over? And what was up with Dawn?*

She opened the door, and Dawn bounded in, knocking her to the ground.

"Shit, D, what the hell's the matter with you?"

"TV," she said out of breath and rushing past her.

Margherita was now on Dawn's tail shouting '*dios mio*' to the TV.

When Heidi reached them, she saw her husband and his mistress as their faces filled the TV with the headline: "Breaking News: Leading man expecting his first child with new love."

Heidi needed to sit down, but before she could find her sofa, she fell. She read the words scrolling across the bottom of the screen:

"Just weeks after Hollywood's leading couple split up, Everett Brady announces his first child is expected next year and that he does not want their first child born out of wedlock. Everett Brady proposes to his new leading lady while still married."

"He popped the *fucking* question? The slime ball, bastard, wanker head is still married!" Heidi shouted at the TV, the *'dios mio'* wails still coming from her housekeeper.

Dawn sat next to her. "Babe, I'm *so* sorry. I don't know what to say. Heid's, we need to do a press release," she said sincerely.

"I'll do a sodding press release! How about I ain't divorcing your sorry ass, you low life, lying, cheating coke habit, alcoholic, lying alcoholic... shit, I said that already. Well, selfish ass. Then see how you can't have a baby out of wedlock," she screamed at the TV. "Liar, cheater!"

*

Margherita poured more liquid in to the crystal glasses for all of them. A present from an 'A-lister' who attended their wedding years ago. It'd been around three hours since the announcement. The phones were pinging and ringing, texting off the hook. If Margherita said *'dios mio'* once, she'd said it a million times. Dawn in true fashion, finally calmed down, got her professional head on, and drafted the press release to provide to the world.

She was pushing Heidi to go on vacation for a while, knowing full well that if it was bad before, it would get a whole heap worse now. Plus, she felt it was the perfect opportunity to get payback on her cheating, lying husband. If he couldn't locate her, then how could he possibly serve her?

Heidi didn't play dirty—she never had—but because of the recent treatment from her low life husband, she was seriously starting to consider it.

*

"So, what are your thoughts?" Dawn asked.

"Honestly, I don't know," Heidi responded. Why the hell should I have to, you know?"

"You shouldn't, and you don't. But it's been four weeks, and it's not settled down. And now this? We could easily send you to a discreet resort, or see if you can borrow someone's place for a few. I just think if you get out of the thick of it, it may well just die its death a little. No pun intended."

"What about home? God, I'd murder a proper curry and a real, home cooked roast dinner," she said sadly.

"Babes, that's going to be the first place they'll expect you to go. Your mum may just have a breakdown. If you wanna see your folks, why don't you fly them out somewhere? Get a villa in the middle of Spain," she said, raising her eyebrows. "They always did good curries. Get Mum to bring out some bisto. She can make you roasts every day."

"I don't know, let me think about it. I'm all over the place," Heidi said. "I need to digest. I'll see you tomorrow, yeah?"

*

For 40 minutes, Heidi allowed the hot, sharp water of her shower flow freely over her body. She was beginning to reflect a prune. Admitting defeat, she removed herself, got into a freshly pressed pair of silk pajamas, and climbed into her oversized bed. Her and Everett's bed. She switched on the TV, hoping she'd find something easy going to watch. Maybe a movie or a comedy TV show. Still, every single channel she searched through featured them—Ev and her. *Look at him with his hand on her stomach,* she thought.

"There's not even anything there, dickhead. She's just a child herself. You're a 43-year-old bloody man you…you… weirdo," she said shouting to the TV. *Well that wasn't healthy,* she thought, putting the remote back on the stand and opting for her book instead. Something easy-going and relaxing to take her mind off everything for a bit.

*

Heidi woke startled. "*What the...*" she thought erratically, lifting her eye mask up, and checking the time. *Who the hell was calling now*?

"Hello?" she said groggily.

"I've got it."

"Dawn? What the hell? Are you pissed? It's four a.m."

"No, I'm not pissed."

"Are you dying, or have you got a limb falling off? You best be dying or have a limb falling off because it's four a.m, and if one of those two aren't happening, I'm driving over there to actually rip one of your limbs off," she said seriously.

"Bloody hell, when you're tired you're still as dramatic at this age as you were when we were kids. Listen, why don't you go to Anna's?"

"Who the bloody hell is Anna?"

"My cousin. You know, the farm we went to as kids? It's remote; nobody will find you. It's quiet. I bet she doesn't even have a TV. It's brilliant. *I'm* brilliant! Plus, you can have as many roasts as you want. You may be cooking them all yourself as she works like 20 hours a day, but you'll be entirely alone. It's genius."

"Dawn?"

"Yes?"

"Have you *really* just called me to tell me about this idea?"

"Yes, I really have. It's come to me, and I genuinely think it's genius. He'll never find you. More importantly, you can find *you* again... hello? Hello? Heid's?"

Dawn heard the phone line go dead. "Night then." She smiled back to her pillow thinking of her idea.

Chapter Three

"Good morning," Dawn said, walking into Heidi's kitchen. "Mmm delicious, what's that?" Margherita batted Dawn's roaming fingers away from the food preparation.

"Is it a good morning, really?" Heidi said sarcastically. "Maybe it would have been had I had a full night's sleep. As opposed to being awoken mid-way through," she eyeballed Dawn.

"Oh, come on. You pay me to protect you, keep you safe, and keep you out of the public eye in damaging situations. This is perfection."

"Que, que?" Margherita asked.

Dawn put her arm around Margherita's shoulder.

"So, given everything that's been going on, how we're four weeks on and there's still no let up with the press, and now Ev has decided he wants to marry his mistress *and* have their baby in wedlock, it's clearly gonna get worse before it gets better in the coming months. We have nothing going on while waiting for Disney. My family has a farm back home. It's holed away—no TV, no paparazzi, no cheating husband. She can enjoy some time out alone and wait for the storm to pass. Plus, Everett will have no idea where she'll be, so he won't be able to file for divorce." She grinned wickedly and snatched some bacon from the pan, feeling the wrath of Margherita. "Come on, it's ingenious. You loved Anna, and you loved the farm."

"This be good idea, no?" Margherita said, handing her the plate of scrambled eggs and bacon.

"I last went there when I was six years old—35 bloody years ago. You love *everyone* at that age."

"Look, Anna is there alone. It's her job. So ultimately, if you have nothing in common, who cares? You don't need to like her, and vice versa, so you both can go about your normal days. I.e., her working and you hiding." Dawn smiled again.

"You're forgetting one very important factor."

"What?"

"I hate animals!"

"You do not hate animals. Nobody hates animals."

"Um yes they do, and I'm one of them. I've never liked them. They smell, they never like me. They're always eyeing me up, ready to pounce or bite... or spit. Remember that spitting camel in Morocco on the film shoot? When it finished spitting it nearly bloody well killed me."

"Heid's, that's a *bit* of an exaggeration. I think they just didn't like the attention and the flashes of 700 cameras. It wasn't you; it was clearly the situation. Anyway, you aren't there for the animals, you're just there to hideout. It will be complete and utter perfection. You can read. You love to read. Anna won't need anything in terms of the animals. She has worked there alone since her dad left 15 years ago."

"Her dad left? It was her folk's farm," Heidi said confused.

"Yeah, he did, but she took it over. Aside from some young guy who's her farm hand, she has it all under control," Dawn confirmed.

"Hmm young ranch man, maybe he be like young, strong cowboy." Margherita smirked, lifting her eyebrows up and down erratically, causing them both to laugh.

"That's okay, Margherita. I'm off men for good," Heidi said while seriously considering the idea. "Okay, okay. Just say, and this is purely hypothetical, I considered it; what is your plan exactly? When? For how long? What will you tell the press? Because clearly it will be that I've been sectioned or gone to rehab. What are the finer details?" she said seriously.

"I'm not too sure; I can't make those decisions for you. We would sit down and discuss all those things, establish how long realistically you can be away for, get details booked without the press finding out, and figure out a way to get you out of this goddamn country and into that goddamn country privately.

"What I would say is, it could be beneficial to bring your folks to London for the night, put them up somewhere swanky and hidden, spend a night with them so the press just follows you in and thinks you're there, and then we can smuggle you out to Surrey. We can't risk having them find you. Not only for your sake, but for Anna's and the business. Then once we have a plan we can roll with it. Oh, and I'll call Anna when you've decided," Dawn finished.

"Ay ay ay," Margherita said, shaking her head in her hands, prepared for what was coming.

"You've not *spoken* to your cousin yet? For God's sake! Why bring all of this up if you haven't done the most important thing? What if she doesn't want me there or it's too taxing for her? She'll feel that she needs to babysit me, firstly. I don't need babysitting. It isn't fair to put that on her," she stormed.

"Will you just calm down? Heid's, she won't care. I will ensure she knows you don't need babysitting and that we won't impact her life in any way. You're not going to be seen or heard. Plus, she loved you too. She'll be fine," Dawn smiled happily.

"Again, to reiterate, I haven't seen her since we were all six. She's a farm girl who doesn't even have a TV, and I'm a world-famous movie star. What the hell could we possibly have to talk about? Oh, and again, I hate sodding animals!" she shouted.

"Margherita busy. Margherita busy," she said, running from the kitchen.

"Will you chill…the…hell…out? You're going to spontaneously combust. Just stop. Stop for one bloody minute with your whining!" She held up her hand to quiet Heidi as she scrolled through her iPhone, and pressed call.

"Hello you, how's it going? No, no-no, calm down, everyone's fine, hun," Dawn said into the phone, ignoring Heidi's erratic head shaking. "How's Dad?

"Really? Oh, that's good. Yeah, they're all okay, thanks. We're trying to get them out for Thanksgiving, but you know what they're like... All 'why would we do that, when we aren't American. We don't celebrate it.'" She giggled.

"Yes, she's fine, thanks for asking," Dawn said, pointing winningly to Heidi. "Actually, that's kind of why I'm calling. Look, Anna. I'm sorry for doing this, especially out of the blue, but you know how you always say, 'come visit me?' Well, I was wondering if I could call in that favor? Well, in a manner of speaking, it's for Heidi." Dawn giggled again.

What was said that made her giggle? Heidi thought.

"Yeah, well we have a few problems and she kind of needs to go into hiding. No, nothing like that. No police, or mafia have anything to do with this. Just maybe her husband trying to divorce her. And some press. Also, her husband is unlikely to do too much because he's too busy with his adolescent mistress! Well, yes actually, that's exactly what's happened. Yeah, he cheated on her last month, and unfortunately now he's got the girl he cheated with pregnant! *And* he wants a divorce so that they can have the baby in wedlock." She laughed.

"Yeah, I know, what an asshole. As you can imagine, the press are stalking her and having a field day. Now he's acting like he has morals and values," she said, squeezing Heidi's hand. "Well that's the thing; it would just be Heidi. She and I both want to confirm she isn't a gibbering wreck. She doesn't need babysitting; she isn't going to be sat in your house crying constantly, making you feel you can't do your work and need to look after her. She'll come armed with a load of books, some new manuscripts to read over, and will simply be hiding out, getting away from the press, and, to put the icing on the cake, hiding from him so he can't get the divorce he's so urgently requiring!"

Dawn was quiet for a brief period, listening to Anna on the other end.

"Oh good God no, she has way more sense than that. I think she just wants a hideout. She's a way bigger person than I am. I want major payback. I give her a week and she'll be on the phone to her lawyer telling him to sort it. I'd make the cheater suffer until at least after the baby was born... well, this is true. Maybe why I thought your hospitality may be the right way to go."

Heidi tried to work out what the conversation was about.

"Are you absolutely sure? Ah, you're a lifesaver. Thanks so much, Anna. Well, we've not got quite that far yet, but I'll call you as soon as we do. I'm thinking go to town with her folks when she first lands. The press will get her at LAX and social media will be all over it; she'll be bombarded at Heathrow. I reckon if we put her in a private place in London, she can have a day or two with her folks, and then we can try and get her an escape route to your place.

"Really? What day? That's only six days away. Well, I suppose. Nothing like spontaneity is there? If we can get the details of your car, then we can tell the hotel. Or maybe a cab will be better to come and meet you? That way, if the press are on her tail, they'll never keep up with a London cabbie. Excellent! You're a star. I assure you, I'll get your butt out here after all this, even if I must pay for a farm sitter for a couple weeks. Oh, and I'll just warn you, you may wanna lock away your farm hand. Margherita thinks that she can have some fun with a young, strapping cowboy. That's Heidi's housekeeper. Nooooo, don't worry. She knows that you don't have a housekeeper; she won't expect to be waited on. And if the farmhand is only 24, even better. I hope he's cute. Maybe we can get him pictured with her at a London premiere in the coming weeks," she giggled again.

Heidi sat uncomfortably with her arms folded, not looking the least bit impressed with her agent. *Dawn was no longer her best friend; she was her agent right now*, she thought, annoyed.

"Done. We have a plan. She's in London next week. She said she can pick you up. I know it's short notice, but what's the alternative? Allow you time to change your mind?" Dawn asked seriously.

"When next week?"

"Tuesday."

"Dawn, that's *six* days away!" She shouted.

"I know, I know. But look, I'll get your flight booked for Saturday."

"Dawn, its Thursday now."

"Yes, I know. Look, calm down. What do you need to do? You don't need clothes; you can pack in an hour. We'll book your flight for Saturday evening to land Sunday morning. Go meet your folks, stay with them, and Anna will come get you on Tuesday. We can get an open ticket. When you're ready, tell me. I'll book the flight, and have you picked up before you can say 'Surrey farmers market,'" she said simply.

"I don't know, D. It all sounds very unprepared and unorganized," she said seriously.

"Ms. Spencer, you go. I look after here. Dawn can check. We keep everything good. You go, and leave horrible people and have sexy, sexy time with young cowboy," Margherita said, oddly wiggling her eyebrows again.

"Look babes, what do you pay me for? I know I'm your best friend, but I'm bloody good at what I do; you can't deny that. I've an established agency to ensure that I have the best staff on hand to all the big guns in this town. Part of that requires us, and me specifically, to make sure that everything runs perfectly, smoothly, on time, and without any undue stress for you. This is probably the most amount of time I've been given on a project, so how about you go pack, and I'll arrange a car to pick us up to have lunch in Santa Monica," she said calmly.

Dawn walked out of the kitchen, leaving Heidi completely dumbfounded by the whole situation.

*

"Are you sure this is going to work? I feel completely unorganized," Heidi said, biting into her pizza.

"I do, and we've gone through the list three times. She's only a half hour from some shops so if you need anything, shop there. She can hire you a car if need be. Or get the cute farm hand to take you out. On a serious note—"

"Will you please *stop* with the farmhand stuff? I don't want to get involved. Unlike you, jumping from one body to another, isn't the way I do things, okay? And serious note? What's wrong?" she asked concerned.

"Well, you know I love you..."

"What have you done?" Heidi stormed, pissed off again.

"I haven't done anything,"

"Dawn, you always start with, 'I love you' when you've done something wrong."

"Oh, be quiet for God's sake. Listen, I love you, and you're beautiful. Painstakingly so. It's really pretty annoying."

"Dawn!" she shouted.

"Well, babes, I know you're looking forward to home and stuff, and the hiding out will be great, but Heid's this is LA; you'll get that contract ripped straight from under your nose if you come back... well, fat," she said bluntly.

"Dawn!" she spat. "I'm a size four!" She was completely appalled at her best friend's words.

"Heid's, it's Hollywood. There are many who would class a four as fat. Look, this isn't school anymore. Back home a size four, or our size eight, was *too* skinny, you know, like when we were growing up. Now, they're trying to say people those sizes are too big. Any slight tummy bulge would be seen on every tabloid here. Look, all I'm saying is you're naturally beautiful, and movie star pretty, not to mention you have a body to kill for. But when you get to Anna's, you aren't going to have Troy and Nina

27

coming at five am to do your three hour morning workout, or people monitoring your every meal. So please don't go and binge eat, and try to get in some exercise, even if it's a run around the farm or something."

"It's sodding October; it'll be bloody freezing," she said, still shocked.

"I know, even more reason to work hard and keep yourself warm," she said with a winning smile.

"Un-*believable*! If Hollywood can't accept me for who I am, maybe my mum's right and it is time to quit," she said.

"Don't be so daft. Go have some time out; worst case, we can check you into a boot camp when you return. Heid's, I'm doing this as your manager and best friend. We've been here twelve years babes, this shouldn't be a surprise to you," she said quietly, taking a bite of lettuce and pushing her other food away.

"Oh God. Come on, let's just get out of here," Heidi said, unable to enjoy her last decent pizza before returning to the UK.

It's the only meal she'd preferred in the states, along with the burgers and steaks, but by God she could do with some spice, a proper roast. She refrained from telling her best friend that. Although, Dawn's no doubt already been on to Anna to warn her of said L.A. rations.

One cucumber and one lettuce leaf are all she's allowed. Oh, and iced water. Nothing else, darling. Heidi amused herself. *Dawn didn't even speak like that,* she thought.

"What are you smirking for?"

"Nothing, just thinking about this young cowboy," she said facetiously, flashing her very best Hollywood smile.

Chapter Four

Nigel, Heidi's bodyguard, had done a full sweep and communicated to the Virgin Atlantic staff that they would wait until the last minute to cause undue fuss. Thankfully, they were accepting of this and happy to assist given the celebrity, and of course, the nature of the situation. Dawn managed to get her as close to complete privacy as she could without a private jet—her chosen method—but Heidi was happy of this route. It was rare, but she was fortunate enough to catch the buzz and excitement of the airport. After numerous debates on whether Nigel would escort her, it was conceded by way of a compromise that he would accompany her to her parents and then return to the U.S. For that, Heidi got normal travel, if you could call it that. World Class and more seats purchased afford her the luxury of that.

Moments later Heidi said goodbye to her best friend, arranging to call once she landed. She put on her baseball cap and sunglasses, and followed Nigel and her luggage to the virgin desks.

LAX was great. It wasn't unusual to see a celeb or two, so people tended not to really look. She managed to get all the way to check in, where a polite TSA agent offered words of sympathy and welcomed her to the impending flight with her company. Heidi smiled curtly and followed Nigel as he picked up their hand luggage and passports, ushering them through the gates, and straight to the VIP lounge. Thankfully, it was still empty. Having recognized a few people from the industry, offering their acknowledged, experienced nods, she and Nigel found themselves a quiet corner to blend into. That had always been the major plus of LAX, which meant they could relax here until she made her way back to her homeland.

Chapter Five

"Mum, Dad," Heidi lovingly greeted her parents when she arrived at the hotel.

"Sweetie, it's so good to see you. Gosh, you're so thin! Haven't you been eating?"

"Mum."

"Sue, leave her be. We've discussed this already," her dad said. "Hello darling. We've missed you. How are you bearing up?"

"I'm good, Dad. Honestly." She smiled sincerely. "And don't question me," she pointed to her father who smiled back at her. "I know you always say, 'I'm your baby girl,' but I promise Dad, although I may be 41, I'm not lying. I'm okay. Just the press…" she said, perfectly timed, as the sudden barrage of flashes and calls of her name cried out.

Ordinarily, she wouldn't have ignored it, but it had been eight months since she last saw her parents. More importantly, she really felt she wanted and needed them right now, so she became oblivious to everything else.

"Come on, let's get out of here," Heidi said.

"Where are we going to go? We desperately wanted to take you for an Indian; we know how much you miss them when you're over there. We'd had it all planned, but…" Sue stopped, looking around her. "Well, look at it here," she said, pointing to several press surrounding them. "It's impossible. Has it been like this since Everett left? We saw his new bit of stuff."

"Sue!" Her father reprimanded.

S. L. Gape

"Dad, calm down! Mum, leave it for now, eh? We're fine; Dawn sorted it all. Of course, would we expect anything less? Have you checked into your room yet?"

"Yes, just before you arrived."

"Great, let me sort my bags, and then we'll go," she said.

"Hope that fear of not being able to go for a curry hasn't put you off one," she smirked at her parents. They didn't do the whole celeb thing, or even the plush thing. They begrudged living in the 700,000-pound house she bought them with her first pay check. *But she was sure they'd buy into tonight,* she thought happily, especially after her mum seemed so upset that they couldn't take her for an Indian. Heidi knew she'd be accepting of this little treat. Dawn was forgiven for everything.

Heidi walked outside and successfully managed to get into the cab with only one or two, "can we have your photo taken?" interruptions. Her parents got into the cab and left the door open as the icy rain hit their daughter. After the pictures, she got in, gave the address to the cabbie, and quickly called Dawn to ensure everything was on. With a quick confirmation, they were soon back in central London at her favorite Indian restaurant in the world.

"What are we doing?" Her mum asked, concerned. "You can't just walk into an Indian. You'll get mobbed and pestered the entire time. We won't get a chance to speak to you," she said, sadly.

"Come on," Heidi smiled excitedly. "There's lots of perks with fame—none of which I intend to abuse—but on this occasion, it seems appropriate."

"I don't understand!?" Her mum said, questioningly.

"Sue, just go with it for once. Trust our daughter," he said, squeezing her hand.

32

They paid for the taxi, rushing in to the restaurant opening, and heard the people behind them being turned away due to a private function. Wandering in, the aromas of the spices and food satisfied her senses.

"God, how I've missed this," Heidi whispered to her parents.

"If America has everything, why don't they have Indians? And why is there nobody here?" Her mum asked seriously.

Before Heidi had a chance to answer, the owner of the restaurant greeted her. "Mrs. Spencer-Brady, good to see you again. It really is a pleasure to have you here," he said kindly.

Heidi had known the restaurateur from the occasional premiere that often brought her to London. Visiting this Indian was always a necessity for them. On the last visit he had insisted anything she wanted he would provide because of his daughters' love and adoration for Heidi to the extent that Dawn had near enough asked the guy to come and be a live-in cook. Dawn was fantastic at making people feel special, and like they did with Heidi, those unimportant things really did count to people. "These are my parents." She smiled softly.

"Very nice to meet you," he shook their hands. "And these are my—" the owner continued. "—your two beautiful daughters. Well I'm guessing you're Aisha," Heidi said to the elder of the two girls who looked completely smitten.

Dawn said she was 13 , and no doubt would want every form of evidence of their meet and greet: social media, autographs, the works.

"And you must be Priya," she said to the seven-year-old who looked somewhat more introverted and shy, remaining very close to her father."

"Thank you so much for doing this. We will happily pay whatever we need to for the rental of your restaurant this evening," Heidi said, sincerely.

"Nonsense, you will not. This," he said, pointing to his daughters' faces and the beautiful woman who sat by the bar, "this is years' worth of a busy restaurant. No amount of money can buy this. I'm truly honored that you've chosen my restaurant," he said sincerely.

"Are you kidding? You know it's my first port of call when I get back home. If Dawn and I thought we could work it, we'd have you as our live-in chef," Heidi said, laughing, noticing the look of bewilderment on his elder daughter's face.

"Dad?" Her look questioned seriously, causing them all to laugh.

"Come, I got the staff to move this around a bit, so we have plenty of room for you and your family to enjoy and spread out. Will it just be the three of you dining?" he asked politely.

"You and your family can join us. It's the least we can do when you've gone to so much trouble for our daughter," Heidi's mum stepped in.

"No, thank you so much for the offer," the owner's wife said. "I'm sure it's rare you have the opportunity to actually spend time as a family. We'll also take this opportunity to have some family time. We'll be just over there. We'll try not to disturb you too much," she said, sincerely.

"Don't be silly. It'll be incredible to just have a normal night with no interruptions, combined with the amazing food, of course." She smiled noticing the disappointment on the eldest daughter's face.

"You wanna get out a few Instagram's and tweets before we eat?" Heidi said to the eldest daughter. "You on Facebook? I don't use it often, but I have a work account and my own personal one. If you're on it, and wanna be friends, I'll add you. It'll kind of have to be our secret though as nobody knows my real one," she said, noticing the little girl's eyes light up.

"But Mummy, I don't have Facebook," the youngest girl said sadly, walking to her mum.

"Hey, don't worry," Heidi said seriously. "How about you get a signed autograph, and you know what? I'm doing a Disney film soon. How about when I come here for the premiere, you come with your family. Maybe a couple friends?"

The little girl smiled expectantly to her mother, as the beautiful woman nodded to her daughter and mouthed "thank you" to Heidi.

"Cool. So, you want to take a photo with me? We can tweet it on mine if you don't have one," she said, tapping next to her.

"Really?" she said apprehensively.

"Sure thing."

The little girl left her mum's hand and sat on Heidi's lap, smiling widely into the camera. She leaned over Heidi's shoulder, reading her Twitter account name, and watched as the photo was broadcast to the world.

"Thank you," she said quickly, running back to her mum and dad. "Mummy, does that mean I'm famous now too?" she asked, innocently beaming.

"Why, of course it does," Heidi winked to her.

"So, what would you like to eat?"

"Oh my god, what *would* I like? What *wouldn't* I like! Just please don't tell Dawn when you see her next?" Heidi responded, rolling her eyes. "What're you thinking?" She turned to her parents to advise her of her favorites.

They opted for a tapas style dinner, which overjoyed Heidi. With a seven-course dinner her parents would be able to taste almost everything, which they were more than happy with.

*

Heidi reacted to the constant pings of her phone, knowing they were likes and comments of the tweets, posts, and Instagram's she'd posted earlier. Since she only had a brief period with her folks, she switched the phone to silent and slipped it back into her bag. She had no idea what she was going to do with them tomorrow. While she would have loved to return home, especially now that the secret of her being back in the UK was out, there was no chance. The press would be all over it.

Heidi was glad that when she bought the house for her parents, she'd ensured there was a private entrance. The press would believe she was with her folks; she arrived here to meet them, after all. Having left the hotel and gone to the Indian with them, the press would be outside waiting where they'd follow them back to the hotel. Tuesday morning they planned for the first car to leave, her parents visible inside. The press was sure to follow the car all the way. Heidi would sneak into the next car to go meet Anna, which would take her to her farm in Surrey.

God, she hoped it all worked. She didn't know what the hell she would do if it didn't. Where would she go? She shook the thoughts from her head, not allowing her reservations and negativity to unfold.

*

"This is an obscene amount of food. What the bloody hell did you order all this for?" Her mum asked.

"Leave her alone, she never gets to do this," her father said. She's eating her favorite food with no eyes on her. She's relaxing with her parents. Just us, no interruptions."

He turned to his daughter. "It's lovely, darling, and so good to see you. How you holding up then?" he asked his daughter seriously.

"I'm fine honestly." Heidi noticed her parent's indignant stares. She didn't really want to tell them the whole deal, but she knew she should. If anything, it meant they'd worry less. Although, they seemed overly happy that she was getting away and going to the farm. At least they knew where she was and who she was with.

Heidi had stunned her parents by confirming everything—the truth. Not what the papers wrote. She knew even if Everett came back on all fours, begging and pleading, there wasn't a chance in hell she'd take him back. That she had no issue with telling them, but they were stunned to have learned the details. Both confirmed they didn't know what a public marriage would be like, but neither had ever envisaged that their daughter wasn't blissfully happy, which of course, saddened them deeply.

Heidi didn't want them to be sad by the news. She wasn't a parent—she could only imagine how they felt—but she ensured that their daughter was good.

They finally finished discussing her marriage, or lack thereof, because she wanted to enjoy some normality for a while, and more importantly, enjoy their time together.

First, she had to do a little tormenting. "You have to wait a minute. I need to let Dawn know I'm still keeping her on her toes, that she isn't just on vacation," she said smiling.

"What do you mean?" Her mum eyed her suspiciously.

"Just watch! Oh, and get your cell...mobile," she corrected herself. "out."

Heidi smirked and took photos, snapping away happily at the 12 different dishes on the table.

"Heidi, what are you doing?" Her mum asked, watching her daughter's smirk grow.

"Give it five minutes," she said, sending the pictures and switching her cell back off.

"So how you guys—"

"Sorry to interrupt Mrs. Spence—"

"—Please, seriously, call me Heidi. It's really unnecessary, especially after all this incredible trouble that you've gone too," she said sincerely.

"Of course, Heidi. I just wanted to move a little space," he said turning around to see loud sizzles going off before him.

"I know this is your favorite, so I figured I would get you a little more than a "taster" portion." He grinned widely.

"Oh my god that isn't... Oh, you didn't. Oh my gosh, Mum this is the most incredible thing you'll taste in your life. Dad, you'll love it. Bloody hell, is that a whole rack?" she asked, watching the served food sizzle away noisily.

"It is indeed, a rack of Tandoori lamb," he said simply.

"Oh! I'll never leave if you continue with this," she said, already trying to grab a piece before the chef even cut it.

"Well, I'm sure the country would welcome back our queen of the screen," he said sincerely. Slowly, he walked away with words to the chef, causing him to work quicker and leave with the slightest nod to Heidi and her family.

Heidi looked around, touched by the experience. She was convinced this was the most incredible thing she'd ever tasted. Heidi could hear Dawn whinging about eating with her fingers.

What if people see? What will they say?

She picked up a piece of the lamb, noticing her dad's easy smile. She could tell his concerns had been washed away. His little girl was back, and that's exactly how he'd see it, regardless of her age.

As if by magic, the moment she bit into that beautiful, spiced, tender lamb, her mother's phone rang, alerting the whole restaurant.

"Bloody hell, Sue, what you got it that loud for?"

"I don't know, I don't know," she said flapping. "I didn't know it was that loud. Quick, what do I do?"

"Bloody answer it," he said back.

"I can't."

"Why not?" Heidi and her father asked simultaneously looking around at the family grinning at the comical spectacle in their restaurant.

"Give it here." Heidi grabbed it. "Well hello, Dawn. How are you? Apologies, my mum can't come to the phone right now, she's eating... one, two, three, four... wow, 13 appetizers. Can you imagine how many mains will arrive?" she said, laughing giddily.

"Dawn, I told you I'm on vacation. I just got a whole rack of lamb. Mmm I know, amazing, right? Switch to FaceTime, so you can watch me eat it." She ate noisily for added effect. "Hello? Hello?" she giggled.

"Come on, you need to try these while they're still spitting," she offered her parents, placing a few pieces on a plate. "Seriously, they're incredible."

*

They said their goodbyes to the owner and his family, followed by promises of contact and regular visits when she was about. He was even kind enough to offer her the opportunity to come by and collect some food to take and put in the freezer. Never had Heidi been so tempted by an offer. She was almost certain she would snap off his hands for that offer.

The girls were satisfied with their autographs and pictures, along with of course, the off-scale interest they were getting from likes, retweets, and friend requests. All in all, Dawn had well organized an incredibly perfect evening. She would make sure when she returned to the states she'd treat her to something expensive to thank her. Even her mum was relaxed. A little tipsy, but relaxed. She'd had such a wonderful evening that she couldn't stop going on about it. Ultimately, Dawn had hit the jackpot, but that didn't stop Heidi worrying about how her parents would be when the time came to leave again. They seemed very accepting of the situation, though, both appeased from seeing their only daughter face to face.

They made their way back to the hotel again, and the relaxed evening was soon amiss with crowds formed outside of their hotel. She knew the hotel wouldn't allow neither the press nor the public in unless they were staying, so she was happy that the beers with her meal had relaxed her somewhat. She felt at ease and able to handle the short walk across the herds before her.

"What are we going to do?" Her mum asked.

"Just keep your head down, walk in, and *don't* bloody forget my takeout," she said smiling, paying the cab and letting her parents out first, seeing the pings of bright flashes before her.

Her mum hated this part of her job, and truth be known, it wasn't her favorite part either. She grabbed her mum and rushed through as her dad carefully guided his wife and daughter inside. All remained completely silent until the concierge quickly stepped out and barricaded the people from entering. A stark difference came as they entered the lobby area, where very few people paid attention to her, and those who did merely made discreet comments to their partners, friends, and agents, then continued with their own lives. This had really been a spectacular evening, and she couldn't have asked for anything more than a perfect night with her family.

"Do you need to go to bed, love? I'm guessing you're jet lagged?" her dad said to her.

"Nope, I'm kind of buzzing, so all good. I don't know how long Mum's gonna last," she said to her dad knowingly.

"What? I'm fe-yine," she slurred.

"Not quite, darling," he raised his eyebrow to his daughter. "That looks like a nice, private, little piano bar in the corner. How about I take your mum up and get her to sleep and I'll meet you in five. Mine's a scotch on the rocks, Heid's." He winked to his daughter.

Her father and her never did this. God, she missed normality. The problem was she loved her job. It was fantastic, but there was also a downside. Unfortunately, like Dawn had confirmed on so many occasions, she *was* Heidi Spencer-Brady. Even if she gave up the job, she'd never lose the fame. People stopped working all the time in Hollywood, and they were still constantly in the public eye. They were still recognized or asked for autographs, unable to just nip to Walmart or Costco's. Or to her favorite Indian, even if it was on the other side of the Atlantic!

No, this was the life she chose, and unfortunately, she was now stuck with it.

*

Heidi and her dad spent the best part of four hours in the bar. The hotel manager had come over and asked if they wanted to be left alone, but the very few people in and around the room had either not recognized her, or clearly didn't care. Which was again, perfectly blissful.

"You had a good night, sweetheart?"

Heidi smiled enigmatically. "Honestly, I've had the best night I've had in... forever actually. It's been amazing to see you guys. I forgot how...what's the word I'm looking for?" She pondered for a moment. "I forgot how respectful the Brits can be compared to the, well, compared to L.A. They don't let up, you know? Everything's for a story. Don't get me wrong, you guys know the whole story now, as does Dawn and Margherita, but nobody else does. As far as the eye can see, we really were this loved up perfect couple and they still feel the need to pry and push. I mean, Jesus, he cheated on me and weeks later he's announcing he wants a divorce to the world and that he's having his first baby. And they're all there camped outside my front door? I can only imagine what your house looks like right now," she said sadly.

"Listen, darling," he said seriously, leaning back and sniffing his whiskey. "When you were two years old, you learned the words *'look at me.'* You spent a lot of time saying it around people you felt comfortable with. 'Look at me,' 'look at me, Daddy,' that's what you used to say," he smiled. "Then you'd perform for us, and them, whoever it was. You learned to read, and you'd act it all out to the family and make us mark you out of ten. It wasn't until you reached about nine or ten that you suddenly became quite self-conscious. Strange really, I never knew why," he said contemplatively. "That was when your mother hoped you'd change your mind, but in true Heidi fashion, it didn't change your mind at all. It made you more motivated and driven and suddenly you had this air of maturity. The drive and love for your acting and performing made you desperate to show everyone that you could be modest *and* do your job. We're ever so proud of you, Heidi. Just because Mum doesn't say it much, don't thing we aren't."

Heidi had never really heard her parents say that, nor was she aware of this story. More importantly, she'd never really remembered a time her parents had told her they were proud. She absolutely knew they were from the looks in their eyes and the comments Dawn would tell her, or the men's poker and pizza parties her parents attended, filling everyone in on the latest Hollywood movie or chat show. But she couldn't recall a time since moving to L.A. that her parents had told her they were proud. Maybe it was the Jim Beam taking over, but she'd never felt more emotional and loved in her life.

"Thanks, Dad. I can't say I've ever really known that, and so it genuinely means the world to me," she said seriously.

"Oh baby, don't ever think that. You're our pride and joy. Both you and Tony are. Tony, Meg, and the kids all feel the same too. They're actually really disappointed they didn't get to see you," he said convincingly.

"Well, when the press finish stalking everyone, you'll all have to come over to the farm. Although, I'm sure Tony and crew can come before that. I'll speak to Anna when she collects me," she said, wanting to see her niece and nephew.

"Good, well we're playing golf during the weekend and taking Ashton with us. He's a right little golfer. We may end up with a second, famous kiddie at this rate," he said smiling proudly. "But I'll mention it. I think they'd all love that. I know we have. It's not the same just doing that Skype thing as it is to spend some good, wholesome time with you, sweetheart."

"I know, Dad, I'm sorry."

"Don't ever be sorry for following your dreams and your heart. Proof is in the pudding, sweetheart. You do it and you succeed in it. It's what life's all about, and there's so few of us that manage to get that. If you're lucky enough then grab it with both hands and cling on for dear life until you've got no option, but to let go." He squeezed her knee. "Anyway, you have been up far too long now, as have I." He looked at his watch. "I think it's been a couple of decades since I was up until after three drinking," he said, winking. "Come on, let's hit the hay and we can meet for breakfast in the morning to see what the plans are," he said nodding to the lifts.

Heidi brushed her teeth and got into the large, oversized bed in her room. She could hear the hustle and bustle of London even now. Switching her phone back on, she watched as the notifications came chiming in. 17 missed calls from Dawn. She left three voicemails and 12 texts, telling her off. They ranged from "you best not be eating all that" to "you'll get fat and Hollywood will drop you; it's happened before to other celebs, you know this." She must have gotten bored as by the end they were "bloody hell, go and enjoy yourself. I'll move Troy in when you return, and you can do full workout days." There were thousands of likes, loves and retweet notifications from the pictures with the young girls earlier that evening. She was glad she'd turned it off, as it really had afforded her some quality time with her parents.

Chapter Six

Heidi woke on Tuesday morning feeling relaxed and refreshed after spending the previous day at the hotel spa. The hotel manager really couldn't do enough for them; he'd even obliged in reheating their leftover Indian and sent it up to the room with complimentary champagne. She relaxed from day to night, watching movies in the lounge part of her hotel room, and eating leftover Indian. Over a bottle of pink Moët, they had discussions of how exactly they could get her out of the hotel.

The hotel manager explained the hotel had underground parking, which nobody could get in or out of unless they were a guest. Unless the press had booked a room and were sitting in the car waiting, which was a possibility, then nobody would see her. It was decided that two cars would come, each with blacked out back windows. The security would go down and physically check every car for people sitting inside them. Luckily it was a boutique hotel; it only held around 15 cars. The first would house her parents, putting her mum in the front to be seen and would carefully drive them back home in the hope that the press would spot her and follow them. A short while after, Heidi would leave in the second car, hiding in the back of the blacked-out car to be taken to meet Anna.

In theory, it was genius. Whether it worked though was a whole other matter. Fear and apprehension took over. She had no clue what she was going to do if the plan didn't work. Go home and face the music? Move back to her parents and stay hidden there? She shook herself out of the negative thoughts.

"Let's do it. Or at *least* try. Thank you so much for all your help through this," she said to the hotel manager.

"It isn't the first and won't be the last time, madam," he smiled kindly and wandered off, talking quietly to some men around him. They watched the men who suddenly rushed off, each carrying out the roles assigned to them.

*

"Hello?" Heidi said into the phone.

"Hi, honey. I think the eagle has landed."

"What?" Heidi asked confused.

"Is that not what they say in the movies when a plan works?" she asked seriously. "Oh no, your dad has just told me they only say that when somebody has arrived. Hmm, I guess that makes more sense. Well, what about 'they have taken the bait?'"

"Well it depends on if they actually have," Heidi responded.

"Well I think so love. We came out and they were all there trying desperately to consider my car window and I waited until they saw me, and then pretended to hide my face so they were all snap snap snapping away, and chasing us. Hang on. Mr. Driver are they following us?"

Heidi and her father both told her she couldn't call him "Mr Driver."

"I most certainly will. He keeps telling me I must call him Mr. Rogers. He's my driver and his name is Mr. Rogers. Well, *I'm* not the celebrity. *I'm* not the movie star. So, if he won't let me call him by his first name, as though I'm just getting a lift, then I'll keep calling him Mr. Driver.

Seriously, I'll be in Asda in an hour getting us chops for dinner tonight. When was the last time you've done that, Heidi?" She ignored her response and spoke elsewhere. "Oh really? Okay, thank you, Mike. It's okay, it's Mike Rogers. He says I can call him Mike. So, Mike, do we have anyone following us?"

Heidi rolled her eyes. Her mother could be so painful at times. It's where Heidi's strong will came from.

"Well?" Her mother chastised, waiting for a response.

"About six cars, a cyclist, and four motorbikes. Houston, we have lift off," she said proudly.

Heidi rolled her eyes again, refusing to correct her as she heard her father already doing so. "Okay mum, I'll call you when I get there. Love you," she said hanging up.

"Are we ready, miss?" She heard the driver say.

"Would you mind giving it another five, just to be completely sure?"

"Of course, miss."

Heidi sat in the seat before getting back up and leaning over to the driver. "Excuse me, what's your name?" she asked politely.

"Mr Clarke." He smiled back to her.

"And your first name? If you wouldn't mind, could I call you by that?" she said to him.

"Um, well it isn't normal practice for the company, miss. We are your drivers and are therefore referred to by our surnames."

"Well how about I don't tell if you don't." She smiled. It was her winning smile, a smile that Dawn always said had gotten her where she is today.

The nation's sweetheart's award-winning smile.

"Graham, miss. My name's Graham," he winked.

Heidi smiled back at the older gentleman. "Lovely to meet you, Graham. My name's *not* miss. It's Heidi. I think we can go now, Graham, if you're ready."

His eyes twinkled at her. She had won him over easily. She figured he was around her dad's age, and they were always easy wins.

"Of course, Heidi. Let's get you out of this place as discreetly as possible. You going to lie down while we exit?"

"Maybe so for added precaution," she said seriously.

"Good stuff. If you go down low enough, I can lower the windows so they can inspect the car. Then they'll never think you're in here," he winked.

"You're a professional at this aren't you, Graham?"

"A wonderful 39 years, Heidi. And I must say, I feel very privileged to have taken today's job," he said as they made their way out of the car park and onto the street. Worked a treat, miss, um, sorry, Heidi. We're good. They bought it hook, line, and sinker. You can get up now and sit more comfortably, and I'll get you out of here," he said kindly and turned the CD on. "You mind?" he asked, pointing to the music. "I'm a huge fan of jazz."

"Don't mind at all, Graham. This is your vehicle and that sounds pretty good to me." She smiled, adjusting herself to a more comfortable position, and enjoying the flow of jazz throughout the car.

*

"Heidi? Excuse me, Heidi? Miss?" She heard as she woke up and adjusted her eyes.

"Shit, sorry. Oh, bollox, sorry for swearing. Jesus!" She slapped her head. "Oh, I give up," she said sitting up sprightly. "I'm very sorry."

"Heidi, just because your face is all over the papers or in the biggest movies around, I don't assume it means that you don't do the things the rest of us do, like fall asleep or swear. As I said earlier, I've done this job for almost 40 years," he smiled. "Don't panic, it's our little secret." He winked again. "We're here, love. I believe this is the car I needed to be next to. A nice, young lady is in the front and I've done a check and there's nobody around. I believe our plan worked and this is where we say goodbye."

Heidi looked around her. There wasn't a car in sight other than the dirty, old Land Rover next to her. "Bloody hell it actually worked. It bloody well worked!" She said stunned as she leaned over and kissed his cheek.

"Thank you so much, Graham! Thank you!" She gave him 100 pounds and asked for his card, advising that she'd call him in the future.

"I can't accept this, it's far too much."

"You bloody well will. You know the last time I fell asleep in a car? Never. Thank you for a wonderful journey and experience, and I promise you I'm going to see you soon." She smiled her smile again and grabbed her luggage.

"I'll get that for you."

"What and let my agent admonish me even more for the weight gain and lack of exercise? Nah, I'm good." She winked back and rushed from one door to the next.

"Hel... oh, um hey." She smiled, stopping as she saw the woman before her.

Anna smiled to her slightly. "Hi," she said questioningly. "Are you okay? You seem surprised?"

"What do you mean? She asked inquisitively. "And yes, thank you."

"Well you jump in all excitable and like '*ohhh heeeeyyyy*,' in your fresh, part Yankee accent, but then see me and stop. Obviously, I've changed; it's been 30 odd years," she laughed. "Although, my attire hasn't really. I'm pretty sure I used to dress like this when you came to visit." She pulled at her sweater. "Jeans, boots and a sweater. True farm girl attire," she winked. "Oh, and the cap was for *your* benefit. In case I was going to be all *undercover driver,*" she smirked. "It's good to see you again," she said, maneuvering the car and its chugging exhaust out of the car park.

"I do not have a part Yankee accent," she said seriously. "And I didn't stop, nor did I become less excitable. I guess I just didn't know what to expect after all these years. And FYI, in case you didn't notice, I'm also wearing jeans, boots, and a sweater," she said simplistically.

"Yeah of course, Heidi. You're..." she stopped, looking down at the boots. "Um, your Louboutin's or whatever they are, white diesel jeans, Gucci belt, and Armani jumper are the same as my cats, Asda jeans, and Nike sweater. All of which have seen better days," she smirked.

"Does Asda really sell jeans?"

"Oh my God, you're such a princess," she laughed heartily. "Yes, they do, and I was actually winding you up. They're "next" jeans—not quite Armani, or Gucci, or Diesel or whatever. Unfortunately, the joys of being a farmer." She smiled softly.

"For the record, they're Alexander Wang," she said smirking.

"Excuse me?"

"My boots. They're Alexander Wang. So, how are you?" She smiled at Anna. "You've aged well," she said kindly. "Very well, indeed. Clearly, it's correct what they say: Brits do age better since they're not in the sun 24/7."

Anna laughed heartily. "Thanks, I think?" She raised her eyebrow. "I'm not sure what I'm more complimented by—the fact I still look six, or that I'm pasty." She turned to face Heidi whose face was a picture.

"Oh crap. No, I, I didn't mean it like that." Heidi noticed the loud laughs from Anna. "Oh, you're winding me up."

"Sorry, yes I was. Thank you for the kind words. I guess the arduous work of a farmer keeps me somewhat youthful, and if I don't look 41, then I can assure you I'm happy." She smiled. "And likewise, but I guess you can pay to keep things that way," she said, concentrating on the road.

"I don't pay for anything. I'm completely natural, thank you very much," Heidi quipped.

"Sorry Heidi, you've misinterpreted me. I wasn't talking surgery. What I meant is you can pay for trainers, health experts, and sun care experts. All the things that essentially normal working-class people can't pay for. I'm sorry if I offended you."

"Oh, sorry. I guess I'm just not used to people ... um, well I don't know, I guess everyone in L.A. is so blasé about surgery and Botox and stuff that everyone automatically assumes we all do it. But thanks, and yeah, you're right to a degree. In fact, I wouldn't be surprised if Dawn hasn't already got a PT waiting at home or gave you a list of foods we can and can't have," she said aimlessly.

"PT?"

"Personal trainer. She's warned me; I'm not allowed to get fat."

"She's done what?" Anna asked exasperated.

"Oh, don't worry. She's just looking out for me." Heidi looked back at her.

"Really? Well last time I checked, friendships didn't consist of people telling each other they are fat!" She said pointedly. "I've got to say, I'm annoyed she's done that; we weren't brought up like that."

"Seriously, don't be pissed. The point is, she's my best friend—always has been. She loves me like a sister. She's been there through the entirety of my marriage breakdown. She's phenomenal at her job and has made an incredible living from it. She's right in what she's saying. Ordinarily, I would be up at five am for two, maybe three hours, depending on sessions with two PT's. If we go out to eat, the paps are everywhere, so you can't eat badly, or they'll be all over you with the next headline of your being obese. Unfortunately, L.A. and the industry really are as shallow as you hear or read about. If I get fat here because of a lack of exercise or eating badly, chances are I won't work again. Well, at least not until I get back to my normal size. She's worried about Disney pulling the plug, that's all," she said smiling.

Anna nearly lost control of the car. "Disney!?"

"Yes, I just signed to be the lead in a new Disney movie. It's called *Crystal*. I can't say anymore, but—"

"—Let me guess, you're Crystal?"

"May-be," Heidi said drawing it out with a smile. "So, you see, that's why she's worrying about me gaining. I'll be fine. I've had two Indians; I'm desperate for a home cooked roast and then I'm done. I'll find some way or another to exercise." She smiled.

"Wow, you really are a princess…a Disney princess no less," she said sarcastically. "There's plenty for you to do on the farm," she smirked.

"I see you have a sense of humor," she rolled her eyes. "And um, I'm sure I can find some form of exercise *not* involving animals."

"It's okay, I'm messing with you again. Dawn warned me. I don't have to babysit you and you don't like animals. Odd place to come visit, I must say. We do have one real problem," she said seriously.

"What?" Heidi asked concerned.

"Well, I work on a farm, a place full of animals, some of which have been around since before me. Heidi, I'm a vegan. I don't—can't—eat meat. You'll have to go into town to have a roast I'm afraid," she said.

"Oh God, of course. I'm so sorry. I'm very... how completely inconsiderate of me. Sorry Anna, Dawn didn't mention it. I won't have meat in your home," she said, already feeling the disappointment of being back home without the chance of making the most of "Roasts." Clearly it was a somewhat stupid thing to think that a farmer would eat meat.

"Can I ask you a question, Heidi?"

"Yeah, sure."

"Are you always this gullible? Do you not remember Dawn bringing home bags of meats, amongst other things after she'd been here?"

"*Really*? You are such a windup merchant! I vaguely do, now you say it."

So how have you been? Husband? Kids?" Heidi asked her.

"Neither, just little ole me. The farm keeps me busy to be fair. And as it's only me and Jack, I'm working almost around the clock. Plus, there's nothing near me, so it's not like even if I wanted to, I could start dating," she said, keeping her eyes on the road.

"Not even Jack? You say you guys spend so much time together."

Anna laughed fully. "Jack," she spluttered. "God, I'm old enough to be his mum, and most of the time feel like it. He's only 24. He's a good kid and a hard worker, so for that, I'm very thankful. But, no, he's far too young." She smiled. "Don't worry, he's incredibly good looking and I am under strict instructions to get you '*laid.*'" She winked to Heidi. "FYI, he'd be happy to oblige."

"She did not!" Heidi gasped.

"Oh, but she did," she laughed.

"I'll bloody *kill* her. She thinks that me having sex with a young, gorgeous guy is going to make it all better. What the bloody hell is wrong with her? For the record, I have no intention of sleeping with your farm hand or anyone else for that matter. The point of coming here was to hide away, and I'll be doing exactly that. Plus, if I wanted to get laid, I'm perfectly capable of going and finding a guy by myself," she responded.

"You know our Dawn. Thinks like a man. Everything is good if you have a good shag. She keeps telling me I need to come visit so she can get me laid. Like seriously, why would I want to go all the way to L.A. just to have sex?" she laughed.

"She's obsessed!" Heidi said, relaxing back in her seat.

The rest of the journey was quiet. They made sparing chit chat, but mostly just listened to the radio along the way, allowing Heidi to hear news outside of what was going on in her own life.

"I forgot what it was like to listen to real news as opposed to idle celebrity gossip," she said distantly.

"It must be hard. Living through these things is hard enough, but to have it be so public for everyone, everywhere to comment and have an opinion? That must be the worst of it. I really don't know how you deal with it," she said in wonderment.

"I don't. I mean, I'm not, am I? I've run away to someone's house that I haven't seen in over 30 years. It's why I'm here, remember? It is hard, and if it wasn't for Dawn and Margherita I don't know what I would have done," she replied.

"Ahh Margherita, the housekeeper, correct?"

"Yes, my housekeeper. She's wonderful, she's probably the only person outside of your Auntie Janet that can keep Dawn under control too," she smirked.

"Bloody hell, I must meet this incredible woman. Um, Heidi?"

"Yes?" She turned to face her.

"Have you thought this through properly?"

"What do you mean?"

"*This*? Coming to my house? I don't have a housekeeper. These clothes will be trashed in minutes," she said, pointing to Heidi's clothing. "I have animals wandering around everywhere you look. Don't get me wrong; I'm very clean and tidy and I like that, but I do that myself, in between the farming. Additionally, it probably has to do with how little time I get to myself to mess it up. I simply don't have time to, well, wait on you. Like you've become accustomed to," she said seriously.

"Anna if this is or was an issue for you, you really should have mentioned that to Dawn. I have a job like you. Albeit a job that's very much in the public eye, but like you, I have very little time to myself and to be alone. I haven't forgotten my roots and Dawn would never allow me to. She keeps me grounded. I have no clue how as she's the one who needs to keep being reigned in, but somehow, she

56

manages it. The housekeeper is simply because we live in a ridiculously large home. I'm not saying it's the right thing, but unfortunately, it's the normal thing to do. There are many things I push back on. Gosh, so many. And I'll continue to do so because it's who I am and most likely why people tend to like me. But there are some things you would get totally obliterated for, and not living in some great mansion in Beverly Hills, with a housekeeper, are some of them. So yeah, having such a large home and spending so little time there requires someone to maintain it. In fact, your cousin was the influencing factor on it. I was adamant. I didn't want it when I first started out. Why would I? I didn't need it, but there was Dawn saying it's a requirement for Hollywood. It was only a few days later that a realtor went to the press and allowed them to see what I'd been looking at. It was right after my first big lead, and they basically pulled me apart because I was looking at small places. They dug out my parents, the home we lived and grew up in. All sorts. And that kind of transformed my thinking.

"Anyway, my apologies. I'm digressing. I bought a bigger house up in the hills. It was perfect for me and it had the exact amount of Hollywood sass. Dawn released a press statement about the places I was looking at being a thank you gift for my parents—no doubt a major contributing factor to the adoration that soon followed—but when the housekeeper conversations came into play, it was a definite no for me. I was adamant that I was pushing back on this. I didn't want to:

A. Forget my roots

B. Become one of '*those*' people.

"She told me not to look at it as getting a housekeeper—like someone to pick up after my shit—but to look at it as getting a Hollywood mummy and helping someone. Get a live-in housekeeper, and don't put them in little living quarters or granny flats outside. Have her inside with you, she said. You'll be out and filming so frequently. You're giving someone the opportunity to live in a mansion with a pool 70% of the time," she said distantly. "Dawn has her faults. I mean, don't we all? But she made that right. We met with a load of people and for the most part, they were actresses trying to get into the industry or fame hungry press feeders, anyone who could get their faces in the paper, and make a few bucks from it. We had all but given up hope and then we met Margherita. Her small, Mexican features were so cute. She worked as a cleaner in the same hotel for many years and her granddaughter, who she was primary care for, was a junior in high school and desperate to become a doctor. God, by the end of the conversation, Dawn and I were nearly in tears. But Dawn was apprehensive, concerned that it was all a story. The thing with Hollywood is you can make so much money for a decent story. There are so many people who are prepared to do just about anything for it. So many rats. I, on the other hand, instantly loved her. I knew in her broken English that she would be a great 'second mummy.' Then Dawn said something like bloody hell or God's sake and completely went off on her. She told her off in Spanish and English about taking the Lord's name in vain and I just sat there laughing the whole time. I mean seriously, who does that? Tells your interviewers off in the middle of an interview. I knew right then I had to have her. Her granddaughter lived in a complex and Margherita did everything since she'd taken custody to ensure she had the very best upbringing she could afford to buy. Sofia wanted to go to med school, so Margherita knew she had to get a job in the hills and earn more cash to be able fund as much of it as possible. We had her in the living quarters on site while she was on her month trial period and she was perfect.

"So, to cut a rather long story short, she *is* my housekeeper, and yes, she will always make sure I've eaten or will make me something when I get home late et cetera, but she doesn't necessarily clean up after me. I still do that. I was brought up with manners. I wouldn't leave plates lying around at my parents' house, so why would I do it there? Or here? She is kind of like my housemate; we both live there and clean up after our mess. She just does a little more because she's there far more than I am. To answer your question, yes, I've thought about it, and in great depth. I don't need you or anyone else to clean up after me, I don't need babysitting, and I'm super excited about having some time to myself without interruptions. No press on my tail. Don't panic, all's good," she said.

"I'm not panicking, I was just concerned you were going to have the shock of your life when the reality kicked in that you're going to be living almost on top of me, with animals—which you don't like—roaming around, and having to clean up after yourself. Anyway, just so you're aware. So, what about Sofia?"

"Huh?"

"Sofia? Did she get into university?"

Heidi laughed proudly. "She sure did. She kicked butt in high school, medical school, and is now just beginning a three-year residency at Baylor University Medical Center. It's a large hospital in Dallas. She's done amazingly well. We had a massive graduation party for her and her close friends at the house. Margherita couldn't have been prouder," she said lovingly.

"She sounds like a wonderful woman."

"Yeah, she's awesome. Dawn pretends that she tolerates her and nothing more, but she loves her too. She really does look after us both so well," she finished.

"Well, your long ass story shortened the journey," Anna said. "Here we are. Home for the next, well, however long." She pulled up next to the house.

"Wow, it looks so different," Heidi said, grabbing her bag and getting out of the car.

"Well, the last time you visited the farm was 30 years ago. You didn't really think it would still look the same, did you?" She laughed. "Come on."

Heidi walked in taking in the structural work that had been done. "Wow, this is new. When you think of a farm, it's hard not to imagine Emmerdale Farm—a big wooden shed in the back filled with hay, a small area for the kitchen and lounge, and animals just walking around in the kitchen. Which by the way, was my main concern—eating in a kitchen with animals," she said slightly distressed.

"Right, well I moved them out of the way until you got in, but they do roam freely I'm afraid," she said seriously.

"Oh, um, sorry I didn't mean to be rude," she stopped, noticing the smirk on her face. "Are you gonna quit winding me up?" She shoved her a little.

"Yes, when you stop making it so easy. Jesus, I'm not some fodder that lives in a slum. And yes, I like animals, but I do have some standards. Equally, as I keep saying, I make my living from animals." She smiled. "But thanks, I think there was another compliment that was maybe hidden once again in there." She smiled. "FYI, there is no such thing as Emmerdale Farm anymore."

"Shut up, it's not on TV anymore?" she said incredulously.

"It is; it's just Emmerdale now though," she laughed.

"Idiot! Look, I didn't mean to offend you. This is beautiful, I love the open plan kitchen, dining room, and lounge. Wow, do these doors open all the way?! Oh, look at this view!" She walked towards the bi-folding doors. "Gosh this is incredible," she said, looking out to the miles of greenery, the fields and mountains in the distance, and a twinkling lake at the bottom.

"Thanks, and yes, they do open all the way. Great for summer, but not so much this time of year," she began, cut off by Heidi's screams. Anna turned rapidly to see Heidi lying on the floor.

"Shit, what happened?!" She rushed over to help. "Are you okay?"

"No, there's a bloody camel at your window," she turned around, seeing only the view before her again.

"A camel?" Anna laughed. "Have you been drinking, Mrs. Spencer-Brady?"

"No!" She snapped. "There was a big, bloody camel. It came at me. It was there." She pointed slowly, moving forward to peek outside the window. "There! Quick!" She grabbed Anna's hand and pulled her to the window. Heidi erratically pointed out the window to the brown and mustard colored animal that was rushing around near the window. "See, I told you!" She said hysterically.

Anna laughed. "This is gonna be a long ass holiday for you, H." "That's Lola," she said, walking back to the kitchen area. "You want a tea or coffee?"

"Lola? That camel's yours?" she said exasperatedly. "What the hell?"

"It's not a camel. It's a llama. Tea or coffee?" she asked again.

"A llama? Are they even real? It looks like a camel. Well, maybe a camel with a slightly stunted growth. Since

S. L. Gape

when do camels live on farms? I thought they lived in the desert. Sorry, I'd love a tea, please. If you have zero percent cream, then white, if not, I'll have it black."

"I have plenty of cream; I live on a farm. However, if by cream you mean milk, then I'm unsure what zero percent is. I have full fat, semi-skimmed, or skimmed if any of those will work. And I assume that camels most likely do live in the desert, however, to reiterate, Lola is a llama. Many farms have them. They are great guarding animals. And she laughs!"

"She laughs?" Heidi said, looking between the llama and Anna.

"She laughs," Anna said seriously.

"Really? Like *laughs* laughs?" she said.

"You wanna make your own tea?"

"Shit, sorry. I was just caught off guard by the camel," she said walking toward Anna. "Awesome, I'll have skimmed please."

"Again, there is no camel. That is Lola, the laughing llama," she said as Heidi leaned against the cupboards and raised an eyebrow to her.

"Are you messing with me again?"

"No, you'll see. Do you want something to eat?"

"No, I'm good thanks. I ate breakfast. I'll wait until dinner."

"Good stuff. Well, I'll show you to your room. It's got an en suite, so you have a shower, but the main bathroom has a bath if you want to use that. Just make yourself at home. I need to do a few bits on the farm. If you wanna get settled and then write me a list of what you need from the supermarket, I'll go later."

"It's okay, you don't have to do that."

"You wanna risk going to Asda to shop for yourself? Have people following you back here? Come on, honestly, I purposely haven't shopped this week knowing that I'd get everything all together," she said, walking them up the stairs.

"I'm sorry, this really is an inconvenience for you," Heidi said sadly.

"Don't be daft. It's not like I'm doing anything out of the ordinary. I need to go anyway. I just need to check on Jack and do a few things first. So, this will be your room. I have an office over there." She pointed to the end of the hall with a door leading to a smaller room. "If you need a computer, or printer, or anything you can use that room. Make yourself at home. There's drinks et cetera downstairs. The shower's very easy to use and same goes for the bathroom, which is the room next to the office. I've left some towels on the armchair there and some pen and paper on the table. When you're finished writing the list, just leave it on the dining table downstairs and I'll grab it on my way out."

"Thank you so much for everything, Anna. You really are the kindest. This room is beautiful, and the views here are perfect." She smiled.

"Anytime. Hey, Heid's, if you randomly decide to take a walk please watch out for the camels and elephants and giraffes. You may wanna change your clothes unless you're happy to throw them all away after," she said seriously.

"Wait, elephants and giraffes? Really?" She chased Anna from the room who walked off laughing loudly.

*

S. L. Gape

Heidi unpacked her clothes and put on her pajamas. She realized nothing she brought would be sufficient. *What the bloody hell had she been thinking?* She thought to herself as she saw the pen and pad left on the table for her shopping list.

Heidi finished her list, pulled 250 pounds out, and left it all on the side table. She had no clue what things cost in the U.S. let alone in the UK, so she figured that would be sufficient. If not, Anna could tell her the difference, and she'd pay her later.

Heidi ran the bath, grabbing her kindle and set out for a long, hot soak without any interruptions, something that was somewhat of a novelty to her. She wasn't used to it, but she wanted to make the most of it.

Chapter Seven

Anna rushed in and grabbed the sheet of paper on the side. Not wanting to mess up the house with her mucky clothes, she shoved it in her pocket, and ran out the door to go shopping.

A short drive later, she grabbed the trolley, and made a point of going up and down each aisle so she didn't miss anything. She opened the list and read it three times unsure whether she'd read it correctly the first time around.

"Hmmm," she said aloud, smirking, as she made her way to collect the Hollywood superstar's shopping list.

*

Back at the house, Heidi decided to take Anna's advice and relax in the bath. She was still concerned over the money she'd left for Anna, especially given the amount of alcohol she'd asked for; she didn't know why she'd done that. Another thing Dawn had probably told her about. Equally, she didn't know how long she would be here for, so she needed to ensure she was stocked if she wanted something. Anna would most likely think she had a drinking problem. She shook the thoughts from her mind as she relaxed in her bath, and smoothed the mud mask around her face. *It was bliss*. She laid back, enjoying the peace. She couldn't remember a time it was so quiet. Just as Heid was relishing, the bathroom door flew open, and all she heard were screams. There was her own, and then the more masculine of the two.

"Who are *you*?" a man shouted.

"I could ask *you* that? I'M in the bath," she said covering herself with more bubbles. "Who are you and what are you doing here?" She scorned.

"I can see that. And I asked you first! What are you doing in Anna's house?"

"I'm staying here; we're old friends," she said. "And you?"

"Well, if you're old friends, why didn't I know anything about it? She would have told me if that was the case. I work here," he said sternly, standing taller. Proving his masculinity, and protecting his surroundings.

Heidi smirked at the young man. No wonder Dawn had wanted her to sleep with him. He was what she would consider a ten. Gorgeous, big, brown eyes, messy but cute, deep-brown hair, standing at an easy six feet two. Jack had a rugged jawline, and at this moment he reminded her of Simba from the Lion King, acting all tough, but not quite there yet.

"I don't know why you didn't know, but I can assure you, if I was trespassing and not supposed to be here, then I wouldn't be in the bath, would I? I'd be doing something wrong, like stealing or ransacking the joint. Anna is just at Asda, collecting my groceries." She smiled this time, watching the cogs roll in his brain.

"Hmm, yeah I suppose. I'm still surprised she didn't mention it to me. There's no plausible reason. She always tells me when her mates or family are here," he said confused.

"Well how about you let me get back to my bath and ask her when she gets back?" she asked, still covering her breasts from the young guy.

"Shit, yeah, sorry. I'll use the en suite," he said. "So, what's your name?"

"Um... it's Heidi."

"Right. Well nice to meet you, Heidi," he said still adding up in his head before turning with a cheeky smile. He leaned against the doorframe, tensing his muscles. "Oh, and if you fancy some company while you're here, Anna has my number." He smirked, shutting the door behind him.

"Dear God, he's about 18," she said to the room, before hearing him shout "24!" through the door.

"Goodbye, Jack!" She said harsher this time, trying to kerb the smile sneaking across her lips. It felt nice to be paid a little attention.

Chapter Eight

Heidi woke later in bed, her kindle beside her, and noticed it was dark outside. She didn't miss this about the UK, how she felt so lethargic and yucky when it was night time and already pitch black at six pm. She could hear the wind on the window as she checked her phone, surprised that she had slept in the middle of the day. She *never* did that. Either way, it was time to get up or there was no chance of her sleeping this evening.

Oh God, what *was that smell?* Her tummy started growling heavily. She needed to investigate. She checked herself in the mirror. Amazing—sleep lines down her cheek, her hair a complete mess. She tied her blonde hair back into a high pony and smoothed down her pajamas. She really hoped that Anna had done her shopping for her. She would never ordinarily walk around in her PJ's; Everett didn't like it, said it was a lazy British obsession. *Should she get changed*? *Yes, she would*, she thought, not wanting to sit around in this. That smell was killing her. She couldn't remember anything smelling so delicious. It smelled like vegetables, like a nice, delicious hearty soup. Hmmm, she could eat just about anything now.

Heidi threw on a pair of dark, diesel boyfriend jeans and a Calvin Klein oversized jumper. It was the most casual outfit she had, despite still looking thoroughly overdressed.

Going barefoot wasn't an option. Wearing heels or riding boots was stupid, *especially to sit indoors eating soup,* she thought. What would they do? What would *she*

68

do? *It was all very surreal now,* she thought as she opened the door and faced Anna.

"*Shit!*" They both said in unison, jumping backwards.

"Sorry, I was coming to see if you were hungry. Dinner is ready." She looked Heidi up and down. If she had any thoughts on what she was wearing, she certainly didn't say anything.

"Hungry? More like hangry," she laughed. "Sorry, I crashed out weirdly, but the smell woke me. It smells incredible," she said kindly. "Sorry about sleeping all afternoon, especially when you went out shopping for me," she said awkwardly.

"Hangry? What the hell is that? And Heidi, I went shopping for me. I just got your stuff too."

"You don't know what hangry is?" Heidi laughed. "It's when you're angry because you're so hungry…thus, hangry," she laughed. "And thank you, seriously."

"It's fine, honestly. Clearly you must have needed it, but you don't have to apologize to me. You're here to relax and hide, not to entertain me in any form. I just figured you were reading one of your scripts or something." She smiled, walking into the dining area and offering Heidi a glass of red. "Come on Miss Hangry, let's get you fed before you go all Kathy Bates on me. I figured with *all* the alcohol you requested, you'd be okay with red." She laughed.

"Oh, I knew you'd think I was an alcoholic," she said seriously. "And Kathy Bates really? I would have at least thought I'd get a Sharon Stone, basic instinct kind of psycho," she laughed. "Red is awesome by the way, thanks," she said taking a sip.

"Sharon? *Really?*" she smirked. "Jury's out on that one," she winked. "Cheers!" She smiled holding her glass up to Heidi.

"Hmm that's real nice," she said smiling, enjoying the full-bodied taste.

"Great. Well take a seat, food will be a sec."

"Can I help you do anything? You seem to have gone to a lot of trouble."

"It's fine. It's literally all done. I just need to serve it," she looked back over her shoulder and smiled kindly. "How was your sleep?"

Heidi watched Anna prepare the dinner, putting plates of vegetables on the table. "Oh my gosh, it smells divine," she said, ogling the spread.

"Impatient aren't we, Mrs. Spencer?" Anna clocked and laughed. "That's honey glazed parsnips. They're my naughty food; I'm obsessed."

"Sorry," she said shyly. "And they are? I can't recall ever having these since I was at Dawn's as a kid."

"Don't be, sorry. I love it. I enjoy cooking and rarely get to do it, so having someone to appreciate it is great."

"I'll be the size of a house if I keep at this though," she said as more plates were brought over. "Is it just us two?" she asked confused.

"Yeah, sorry, not really used to cooking for anybody."

"Oh my god! Is that roast potatoes?" She could see the steam coming off the hot tray as Anna walked towards the table. "Real, hearty, English roasties. And wait, oh my... is that yorkies? Oh wow, I've died and gone to heaven. The states don't have Yorkshires; it's my biggest bug bear. I make them when I make a roast. Even though I make it like my mum made it, it still doesn't taste as good as a real, English roast," she professed. "I think it's the size of the house."

"The size of the house makes a roast not taste as good? Did you start before me?" Anna nodded her head to the wine.

"No, cheeky," she laughed. "Because I always thought part of the amazing thing about a roast was exactly like tonight, and my memories of childhood. It's dark outside, all wintery, the sound of the wind and trees. The smell is intoxicating, travelling through the entire house. Back home, I don't get that. The house is too big and airy for the smells to travel. I don't know, maybe I'm not making sense," she said embarrassed, sinking further into her chair.

Anna watched her body language change. "Then hopefully it will live up to your expectations," she said, showing off the dimple just below her left cheek.

Anna had her eyes deep on Heidi's as she walked the last two items over—homemade veg and meat juice gravy. Placing it down, she watched Heidi's eyes bulge. "Roast lamb," she set the last plate in front of them. "I called Dawn. She said it was your favorite. I hope you don't mind, I seasoned it lightly with some rosemary and mint," she said apprehensively.

"Oh my God, I've died and gone to heaven again. I may need to go and get my *fat pants* on. Holy moly this is... just wow. Thank you so much Anna for going to all this trouble."

Anna laughed loudly. "Fat Pants? Yeah because I'm sure you own a pair," she giggled again. "I can't believe you thought I didn't eat meat though. How could anyone give up a decent roast?"

"So, so true," she groaned, remembering that Anna had been winding her up again earlier, saying that she didn't eat meat. This woman was something else with her practical jokes. Heidi lifted her hands up to Anna, and smiled her politest smile.

"Um, what's up?"

Heidi watched her carefully for a moment. "We need to say Grace," she said closing her eyes and waiting for Anna to take her hands.

Anna was shocked. She hadn't ever said Grace. Grace, really? She was in England. She didn't know what else to do. She was starved, her tummy was growling, and the most famous, Hollywood superstar was at her table, waiting to say Grace. With her eyes *closed.* Anna wasn't religious, never had been. *For God's sake, this was all very dramatic,* she thought. *Note to self, no more eating together.* She took her hands.

"Dear Lord, thank you for this meal we are about to receive and even more thanks for my most awesome sense of humor and paying back Anna for screwing with me so much today." She giggled and opened one eye, waiting for Anna to react.

"You're an idiot." She threw Heidi's hands back. "I was completely confused. I have never said Grace, and Grace? It's bloody prayers!" She said, shaking her head at Heidi.

"Sorry, it was payback for today. For the, one, two, three times I believe you pranked me. Two can play that game, that's all," she smirked. "I'm not very religious. However, I am thankful for many things, and your incredible cooking skills is one of them. Cheers," she said lifting her glass.

"Cheers. Now let's eat," Anna said, filling her plate.

"I can't remember the last time I ate cauliflower cheese," she groaned.

"Thanks," she laughed. "Dawn told me I wasn't allowed to cook you that, or I had to get fat free cheese. I don't know what they sell in L.A., but over here fat free cheese is air! I figured after you said she'd been whinging about you getting fat, I'd go all out. Even sent her a pic of it all one by one and then switched my phone off," she laughed again.

Heidi laughed. "Awesome. I did the same the other night from the Indian. She called my mum. Who *does* that? She's obsessed," she laughed. "I'm glad my phone's upstairs, so I can eat in peace. Seriously though, this gravy, and the lamb—it's so tender! And the yorkies and veg. Oh, and did I mention the cauliflower cheese? What's the secret to that? My God, it's all like a piece of heaven," she groaned.

"I'm glad nobody can hear you because you're making massively inappropriate noises," Anna laughed heartily. "It's amazing how praising you are of it. I'm happy about that. Oh, I forgot to say, your shopping's over by the stairs. I moved it out of the way, so it didn't smell of roast dinner. Although, you may like that." She laughed again. "Oh, and my apologies for the clothes. I wouldn't normally eat in my work gear, but I just didn't get a chance to shower and change yet. I feel even more scruff now that you're dressed like that.

"Sorry for the noises. I really don't care though," she said simply. "It would be a sign of gratitude in some countries, so that's what I'm going with," she winked. "Thanks for the shopping. Do I owe you anything else? And please don't fret; this was the least dressy outfit I had. I felt it inappropriate to come down in my PJ's. *Not* a good look." She smiled piling more food onto her plate.

"Well not nearly as inappropriate as the attire, or lack of, that Jack saw today I believe?" Anna was laughing now.

"Oh yes. What did he say? He came in all protective and brazen and was like 'who are you' and 'what are you doing here?' Then he was like, '*I* didn't know about you, so, clearly you are an imposter.' Heidi laughed, holding her shoulders out as Jack had done earlier that day.

"Well I would've loved to see that. Yes, he can be quite the protector. I didn't mention it to him as I wasn't sure what I could and couldn't say really," Anna said seriously.

"Oh, it's fine. This is your life, Anna. I'm intruding on it. If you think he can be trusted then tell him who I am, and what I'm here for. If you're unsure, then he didn't see me anyway; I had a face mask on. I'll just hide away when he's here. It's fine either way," she said sincerely.

"He's trustworthy. He's incredibly loyal, and as much as he is a 'boys' boy, and would *love* to go to the pub with his mates and tell them how he got Heidi Spencer-Brady over her cheating husband and into her knickers, he works very hard for me and for his family. So, if I say I'll sack him if it comes out, he'll 100% keep your secret."

"I don't want you to have to threaten him."

"It's okay, we have a good relationship. It won't be like a threat as such."

"Okay, whatever you think is best. And FYI, he won't be going anywhere near my knickers, thanks very much."

"We'll see. He's quite the charmer. You never know, you could write a movie about it."

"I'll leave that to the professionals and stick with what I know—this side of the screen," she tapped the table. "Anyway, if he's such a charmer, why isn't he in your knickers?" She smirked at Anna who was now completely silent.

"That's a line not to be crossed. Employer and employee. Plus, I'm old enough to be his mother!"

"As am I!" She said confidently.

"I thought you older, Hollywood women loved the younger boys," she said with a lopsided grin.

"Maybe they do. I'm not like most Hollywood women though."

"Do you always have to have the last word?" Anna asked her, smiling.

"Pretty much, yes."

"You're quite infuriating," she smirked to her guest.

"I get that a lot. You should speak to Everett. He could go on for hours about how infuriating I am." She smiled back, suddenly realizing that Anna's demeanor had changed.

"I'm sorry. I was only—"

"Hey, don't be silly. I said it. It's fine. I'm fine with it. I personally don't think I'm infuriating, but, well, he totally did." She smiled. "But never mind," she said lifting her glass. "Here's to no men, and infuriating women who like to have the last word... oh, and awesome wine and lamb!" She said, smirking back at Anna.

*

They finished their dinner and Heidi insisted on washing up. She finally let up when Anna reminded for the fourth time that she had a dishwasher. Embarrassed at the assumption, they eventually agreed that Heidi would clear away and load the dishwasher, while Anna showered and changed.

Heidi finished the clearing up, and sat on the sofa reading her kindle. The red went down wonderfully, and she wasn't quite sure if it was normal practice to open another. She had bought lots, so it wasn't like it was *stealing* Anna's. She remembered the shopping that Anna had left by the stairs earlier and went to check its contents. Heidi pulled out two pairs of women's fitted jogging bottoms, two pairs of jeans—a light blue and a dark blue pair—an oversized hoodie, and a few t-shirts. *Perfect* she thought; *exactly what she needed.* She smiled widely at the ensemble without noticing Anna come in.

"I didn't think I'd see the day that a Hollywood superstar, owner of a multimillion pound mansion, who probably earns about 50,000,000 per year would look so excited over Asda jeans and t-shirts," she said laughing.

Heidi noticed the long, dark curls that had been hidden under a baseball cap all day. She had a flashback to when they were kids, remembering those long, black curls. She was so envious of them.

"Sorry, um, yes," she shook herself out of the stare. "I love it, I love it all. It's perfect. Surely you didn't get all of this, and the booze, and my groceries for 250 pounds though? I must owe you more."

"Nope, I think I have about 15 quid change for you. You're not on Rodeo Drive anymore, Dorothy." Anna checked her watch, noticing it was half after eight.

"Do you have somewhere you need to be? Or is someone coming over? I can go to my room," Heidi said.

"Heidi, you're a guest, and I've told you to make yourself at home. Nobody is coming over, and even if they were, you wouldn't need to be sent off to your room," she said seriously. "No, I was debating opening another bottle of wine..."

"Oh awesome! I didn't know what the etiquette was, but I was hoping you would want to," she said excitably.

"Um, okay. I was going to say I'm normally in bed by now."

"Oh right. Not to worry then," she said embarrassed, confusedly looking at her watch.

"My day starts at 4:30 am, so I'm normally in bed by this time. But seriously, as it's your first night, why not? I can ask Jack to come over earlier and help out in case I'm not up to scratch after being led astray by the nation's sweetheart," she winked.

"Wowzers, that's an earlier start than me! It's fine, I don't want you to feel obliged."

"Heidi, shut up and pass the glasses," she said laughing again.

Heidi stopped and looked away embarrassed. *What the hell was up with her? She's acting like an idiot*, she scolded herself, cringing.

"You okay to continue with the same bottle?"

"Yes, for sure," she said quietly. Heidi noticed Anna's height. *She'd always been quite tall*, Heidi thought, *but now she'd grown into that body*. Her athletic frame was clearly a result of the job she undertook. Her arms were evident of that, shown off in the black vest she wore, causing Heidi to enviously stare at how defined and toned they were.

"You okay?" Anna asked, breaking Heidi out of her state.

"Sorry," she said embarrassed, thinking of something to say. "I was just thinking, don't FaceTime your cousin. If she sees you have arms like those, she's going to make me farm every day," she said light-heartedly.

"You're great with those compliments, aren't you?" She smirked. "Um, thanks I think?" she raised an eyebrow to Heidi. "Farming is very good exercise. Very physical."

"So, I see," Heidi said without even thinking. She grabbed her glass and walked back to the couch. *What the hell was the matter with her?*

Anna smirked at Heidi's awkward nature. She was so easy to wind up; she seemed easily embarrassed. She made her way to the lounge area and sat on the armchair opposite the couch. "You want the TV on?" Anna said to a distant Heidi.

"You *have* a TV?" she said surprised.

"I don't live in the dark ages, Heidi. Yes, of *course* I have a TV." She pressed a remote opening cupboard door against the far wall, revealing a giant flat screen curved TV, which then came to life. "Very few extravagances I have, but I kinda like my gadgets. When I had the downstairs remodeled, I went with this," she said enthusiastically. "I spend so little time not working, but when I do, I like to unwind with the odd perk or two.

"Do you ever go out? Like with friends or guys? On dates and stuff?"

"No, I really don't have time. My day starts at 4:30am and finishes around 6:30pm, with minimal breaks in between. I work seven days a week and obviously that means I'm in bed normally around 8:30pm. I go to bed with a book or my iPad, not a guy; it's just my life," she shrugged her shoulders casually. "A social life doesn't really fit with my lifestyle," she said, taking a sip of wine.

"Wow, sounds lonely."

"To each their own, I guess," Anna said nonchalantly.

The chat had been continuous so far, but it was around this moment Heidi realized what entirely different lives they led.

"So, is there anything you wanna see? Do? Achieve here?" Anna asked.

"Achieve?" Heidi responded amused.

"Well I don't know. Dawn said something about sending you with manuscripts, so I didn't know if you needed to have them read or memorized or whatever by a specific time?"

"Ah, no, no. I have some time," she said distantly. "To be honest, I'm not really sure about it all. It's suddenly all become very real—my life, or lack thereof. I suppose I need to draft a list of everything we own for when he *officially* files. Or, when he *finds* me to be able to file," she said sadly. "No, I'm just here. I'm gonna enjoy some reading and stuff."

"I can get Jack to take you out if you like? Not like that, but you know, if you wanna go somewhere. A theme park? An aquarium? London? I don't know. Something that you enjoy doing," she said kindly.

"That's very kind, but I'm good. I just need to adjust. It's just very new to me. Thank you for the offer though. I would really appreciate it if you would allow me to do stuff around here too. You know, earn my keep." She laughed softly.

"Don't be silly, you're on holiday. Plus, nothing needs doing."

"Right, okay," she said disheartened. "Hey, it's late. I should let you get to bed. I'm kind of floored, so I'll take my book to bed," she said. "Good night Anna, and thanks again."

"Heidi?" Anna called, noticing the sadness in Heidi's voice.

"Yes?" she turned, grabbing her bags.

"Do you enjoy cooking?"

"Yes, I love it. I rarely get to do it, but I enjoy the relaxation of it all." She smiled back. "Why?"

"Well if you fancy it, and it doesn't make you feel like you're being used...if you really want to 'earn your keep,'" she rolled her eyes. "You can always cook us dinner tomorrow night? I have loads in and you'll have free reins all day. I'll be home around six. I mean, only if you have time," she said.

"*Really*? Yes, of course I have the time!" she said excitably. "For just you and me or will Jack join us?"

"If you want Jack to come, I can invite him," Anna said seriously.

"No, just us is good. I didn't know if he normally came over. Great stuff. I'll get on the iPad now to look for ideas," she said happily. "Good night Anna, enjoy your day tomorrow," she said again and rushed off to her room.

Anna lay her head back on the armchair. She loved cooking herself, so was it a big deal to get excitable over the prospect of Heidi cooking for them both? Of course, but it was more than that. It was the sadness behind not being able to do anything. Anna was already questioning her decision to let Heidi come over, but maybe Heidi was right. Maybe it was just the newness of the situation. As soon as she adjusted, she would easily fill her time. Maybe for the next few days she could get Jack to put in a couple of extra hours; he'd be happy with the extra money. That would give Anna some early finishes. At least then she could have a few evenings with Heidi for her first few days, and just do some normal things like playing games or watching movies.

Does a movie star even watch movies? She was so far out of her comfort zone right now; she didn't have a clue which way to turn. Refusing to ponder on the thoughts now, she decided to get some sleep. It was day one, and well past her bedtime; things would get easier, surely.

Chapter Nine

Heidi spent the better part of three hours searching for recipes. Why had she not thought to at least ask what Anna did and didn't like? How difficult would it be? Maybe she should just cook a multitude of things and hope for the best? She suddenly felt disheartened all over again. Cooking was the perfect opportunity to kill some time, or so she'd thought. No, she wouldn't let this mood bring her down; Heidi would go find Anna. She had her new clothes now. They were fine for a farm, and she'd go and ask her about food preferences. At least then she'd have a starting point.

Heidi left the house in search of Anna, but she had no idea where to start. The land was vast, and she couldn't really see anything in any direction. Heidi couldn't tell if the fencing and buildings in the far distance were part of Anna's property, but decided to first set off in that direction. *What the hell do farmers even do* she thought, looking around aimlessly. Anna had said she worked, 14, 15 hour days, but what exactly was it that took up all that time? Heidi continued the walk towards the fence. Hearing something behind her, she looked back, the loud snorts of a pig running toward her as fast as Usain Bolt. She picked up her pace slightly, but it was *fast*. It looked at Heidi like it'd spotted dinner. Heidi sped up a little more, the pig gaining distance on her. Suddenly, she remembered reading somewhere that pigs would eat a human. Literally *every* part of them. Their clothes and bones and everything. *Shit!*

She ran for dear life. She had no idea where she was running to, but all she could focus on was the fence up above. It was low, so low, she could easily jump over it. What if there was something *worse* in there? Pigs *eat* you alive. Even crocodiles don't eat every part of you. There couldn't be anything worse. No, she knew she needed to get over that fence and face the consequences later. She looked back to find the snorting pig still chasing her. Heidi reached the fence and quickly jumped over it, the pig squealing erratically trying to eat her. The next thing Heidi felt was a cold and wet substance seeping into her clothes.

"Fuck! *Fuck!*" She shouted over the still screeching pig.

"You alright there?" She heard a male voice behind her, and looked up.

"Amazing," she muttered, turning back. "Jack, hi," she said, sighing heavily.

"Hi, Heidi. Watcha doing?" He sang, holding out his hand. "*Stop*, go now!" He shouted to the pig, who was still squealing and snorting on the other side of the fence. Finally, it turned and ran back to where it came from.

"What's going on?" Heidi heard as she watched Anna running over.

Great, Anna's here now!

"Heidi! What's happened?"

Heidi wiped the mud off the side of her face and took Jack's hand. He pulled her up with such force that she almost landed on her butt. Heidi watched the smirk on his face as she looked at him with such venom, and wiped the mud out of her eyes and mouth.

"Wait...are you Heidi—"

"Jack, back to work. Go sort Poppy out," Anna said with a glare that made him leave without further words, still chuckling to himself.

"What's going on?" She bent slightly to come face to face with Heidi. "Are you okay?" Anna said shielding her from Jack's view.

"Yes," she said somberly.

"What are you doing here? What happened? And how did you end up in this state?" she said, taking one of her gloves off, and wiping off the wet mud that covered Heidi.

Heidi noticed the sincerity and concern from Anna. "I came out to find you," she sighed. "Then that stupid, bloody pig started chasing me. I thought it would be okay at first, but he wouldn't let up. So, I ran for my life. I know they eat you whole, like bones and clothes and everything. I had to run. I saw the fence to jump over, but the pig caught up to me, so I jumped so fast that I fell off and into the mud," she said sadly.

"Right, okay," she said, trying to contain the smile.

"Are you actually laughing at me?" Heidi said seriously.

"No. I promise, I'm not," she said holding her hands up. "But it *is* a little funny," she added, her smile growing.

"It really isn't. I could have died out there!" She stomped.

"Where did you get this idea from? That's Poppy; she's still quite young and thinks everyone and everything wants to play with her. She would have chased you until you turned around and started chasing her!"

"I read it somewhere; they eat everything. Or maybe I watched it somewhere," she pondered.

"Heid's," she said softly. "If they were going to eat anyone or anything, I'm sure Jack would be top of the list.

It's hardly like there's anything of you to eat anyway, is there? "She pulled at her top playfully. "Secondly, maybe hogs do that, I don't know, I've never heard such a thing, but certainly not pigs. If they did, it would be more about how they were raised. None of mine would, so you don't need to worry. What were you even out here for?" she asked, hooping her arm through Heidi's and walking her back to the house.

"I spent ages looking for recipes and was totally stoked to be able to do something, but then I realized I didn't have a clue what you did and didn't like. I was going to just cook a variety, but that seemed silly, so I thought I'd come find out," she said sadly.

"You really are very sweet," Anna said without thinking. "Sorry, probably shouldn't say that about a superstar."

"Anna?"

"Yes?"

"Would you please stop referring to me like that? I'm just a woman like you, who has a profession like you. I am just me," she said quietly.

Anna smiled at her, sensing the change in her demeanor. She should probably call Dawn as this didn't seem like it was going to work out too well for Heidi. "Yes, of course I will," she said concerned. "Bread and butter, pudding, and oysters."

"Excuse me?"

"The only things I don't eat. I love a roast as you saw last night, and I love anything spicy. Mexican, Chinese, Japanese, Indian, Ethiopian, Brazilian. *Anything*. Anything you make, I'm sure will be great," she said sincerely.

"Thanks," Heidi said glumly.

"Come on, don't be sad. I tell you what, get dinner ready for five tonight. I'll get Jack to work late and we can do something. Sorry, I don't know what you like to do yet. We could watch a movie, have a TV show marathon, play some games, anything."

Heidi raised her eyebrow to Anna. "Games?" She giggled. "What are we five?"

Anna stopped. "Oh charming, Edwards, nevermind me being kind," She said, opening the front door for her to walk in.

"Wow, blast from the past. Nobody's called me that in years." She smiled at the reference to her birth name, taking her wellies off. "Get back to work, farm girl," she said as she walked in to the serene and safe house.

"Long time since I've been called a girl!" she shouted not looking back. "It's nice that it's meant with more warmth than acrimony." Heidi watched her walk off, saddened at the prospect of anyone being nasty to anybody, let alone someone as kind hearted as Anna.

*

Heidi located a docking station in the kitchen. She plugged her iPhone in and poured herself a glass of Chardonnay. It was probably far too early to be drinking, but she didn't care. She was on...vacation, a sabbatical. *Whatever*. She loved cooking and enjoying a glass with it. It had been, gosh, years since she'd last cooked. She found lots of recipes she'd wanted to try. Since most of the food was in the freezer, she needed to wait for it to defrost and utilize what was in the fridge.

Heidi found spice rack upon spice rack in Anna's cupboards. This thrilled Heidi. The wide array meant she could make pastes, spices, and sauces to start marinating as soon as the food defrosted. She was completely in her element, and at last was starting to feel a little bit of herself again.

*

Heidi looked at the time and cursed. It was nearly 4:30. She was still messy from her earlier disasters, and needed to take a shower before preparing the food. Anna said she'd normally get freshened up before dinner, and she wanted to make sure dinner was ready by six pm, that way there was no rush or pressure. Heidi couldn't remember the last time she'd made a meal for somebody. In fact, she thought it may have been Everett when they first started dating. That, or Dawn, who used to regularly make her cook spaghetti for them both.

Heidi got out of the shower, unsure of what to wear. Why would she even worry about it? She cleared her mind, throwing on sweats, and a Nike workout vest she had brought with her. Although winter was commencing in the UK, it was warm in the house. She needed to check that Anna wasn't just doing it for her benefit though. After making her way downstairs, she made an ice filled lime soda. Giggling to herself again, Heidi took a photo and sent it to Dawn, with the words, "See I'm being a good little movie star!!"

Heidi spent ages routing through cupboards to get the equipment and storage she was searching for. Finding numerous Tupperware containers, she placed the pre-prepared spices and marinades for the coming days in with the meats, sealing them and storing them in the fridge. She loved making Indian and Thai foods, the vibrancy of the flavors and intensity of the heat made them equally her favorite foods. She also enjoyed that they took a great deal of preparation time, which made it more gratifying to cook. They were also very pungent, which *she* had no issue with. It was some of her favorite smells. She hoped Anna didn't think it was stinking her house out.

Heidi put everything away, tidying away where possible before picking up her kindle, and returning to her book as the food finished cooking.

Heidi looked away from her book, hearing the door open. Anna walked in like a drowned rat, looking less than amused.

"It's raining?" Heidi asked uncertainly.

"Yeah, it was earlier. I dried off and then had a fight with a cow in the lake. Don't ask," she said shaking her head. "This place smells *amazing*. What is it?" she asked about to take the lid off one of the pans.

"Oi! Don't you dare," Heidi reprimanded.

Anna turned to face Heidi, smirking while she leaned against her cupboards. "Well well well, look who got a tongue," she said, grinning widely.

Heidi folded her arms across her chest. "Don't mess with the chef, farm girl, or you'll regret it."

Still smirking, Anna walked towards Heidi. "Will I now?" She laughed and made her way to the stairs. "I need a shower."

Heidi giggled, ignoring the flush that appeared when Anna left. She enjoyed the banter; her and Dawn used to have it too before work took over it all.

Heidi turned the heat down on the oven and switched the griddle to a high heat. She could hear the footsteps above. Hearing that Anna was out of the shower, she started plating.

She filled another glass of Chardonnay, putting both on the table with the bottle in a wine cooler. Heidi retrieved the carafe of lemon iced water and placed that and the serving bowls between them. She filled one with some olive oil and chilli flakes, and balsamic in the other. The griddle was smoking heavily now, cutting the ciabatta in half. She poured some olive oil and sprinkled some sea salt along the top before placing it face down. Heidi removed the foil parcel out of the oven and placed it on the table on a small plate, noticing Anna watching from the doorway. "Jesus, you scared the hell out of me."

"You sure do have a fowl mouth for Hollywood's number one sweetheart. I'm sorry, I didn't mean to startle you. I was just enjoying watching you in the kitchen. Clearly Disney chose the right person. You are like the epitome of a Disney princess. All chirpy and singing; you'll have the birds helping you tidy up next," she giggled. "So, am I allowed to touch yet?" she said, sitting down and moving towards the foil wrapping.

"No!" Heidi bellowed.

"Okay okay, calm down," she smirked. "Heid's?"

"Yes?"

"Is my pan on fire?" She raised her brow.

"*Bollox!*" she spun around and quickly turned over her ciabattas, thankful that it was the heat of the pain as opposed to the bread burning.

"Disney princess with 'bleeps.' I can't wait to watch this movie," Anna laughed, watching Heidi transport the bread to the serving platter.

Heidi scowled at Anna as she cut the bread into two long strips and brought it to the table. "I guess if all else fails, you get dinner on the table every night and someone to mess with, huh?" She immediately realized the implication that could've been made. "Um I didn't mean…"

Anna smirked at her, watching as she carefully opened the foil packaging and released the garlic aromas through the air. "So, what *did* you mean? Are you insinuating I'm after you or something?" She continued smirking and started sniffing the roasted bulb of garlic. "I know you must have men *and* women throwing themselves at you, but you don't need to keep getting embarrassed or correcting things you say. You are quite safe." She was still smirking, knowing the impact she had on a seemingly flustered Heidi. "So, what have we got? It smells incredible."

"DIY garlic bread," she said simply. Cutting the garlic bulb in half, she took some, dipping a piece of bread into the chili oil, the balsamic, and then squeezed some of the roasted garlic across the top. Heidi, impressed with herself, raised her eyebrows to Anna, and took a bite. "Awesome," she said, " if I do say so myself." She relaxed and smirked at Anna.

"The princess did good it seems," she copied Heidi, groaning loudly. "This is delicious," she confirmed. "Where did you get this idea from? I've never seen garlic bread like this before."

"Oh, one of my favorite Italians back home. I like the way you have a bit of a mixture," she nodded enthusiastically. "Bread and oil. Bread and balsamic. Bread and both. Garlic bread, roasted garlic—my little piece of perfection. Plus, I'm easily pleased. I think it's kind of cool." She smiled widely.

"True, true. The girl may just give me a run for my money." She smiled holding her glass up to Heidi. "Cheers, thanks for doing all this," she said politely. "And FYI, your earlier statement… I have no intention of expecting dinner on my table every night," she stated. "I'll also not respond to the latter part of your comment," she smirked.

Heidi shook her head, ignoring the comments. "Cheers, you're more than welcome."

They clinked their glasses together.

"How are you doing after the mud bath, and near *'pig murder'* experience?" She widened her eyes to Heidi.

"Wow, just wow. You are totally wasted here, you know that? You should come back with me and do stand up," she mused.

Anna held her hands up in mock defeat. "Okay, okay. No more mocking, I promise. And seriously, if this is the talent of your cooking, then I promise to behave, if only for more food. I give you my word." She smiled. "Seriously though, this is delicious."

"Good, I'm glad you like it. I hope you like the next course as much."

"Do I get to know what it is?" she asked inquisitively.

"Do you wanna?"

"I wouldn't have asked if I didn't. I have zero patience. I don't like surprises. I like to know what I'm dealing with up front," she responded.

Heidi smiled that perfect "heart winning" smile. "See you shouldn't have told me that because now I have no option but to make you wait," she smirked and went to the stove to continue her main course. "Oh, and I'll maybe have to hide tomorrow and the next night's dinner just to stop you from peeking," she said, flicking her dirty blonde hair over her shoulder for extra effect.

Anna liked this girl; she had balls. She was a fraction of the kid she recalled spending time with, but that was to be expected given the length of time that had passed, and the elevation of her life. Heidi was genuine fun, and Anna really liked that.

"Mmm, I could get used to this. You sure you wanna return to the states?" she laughed.

"What..." she turned around, leaning against the cupboards with her arms behind her. "A Hollywood superstar waiting on you hand and foot?" She smirked, wondering why she was enjoying this.

Anna was about to say something, but refrained. "You're getting chatty," she raised an eyebrow and put the last piece of bread into her mouth without looking away from Heidi.

Bloody hell what was she doing? Heidi remained in silence as she sliced the chicken up. She put the pasta in the bowls before carefully placing the chicken breast over it and pouring the cream sauce on top. She chopped some fresh basil and garnished the dish before serving it to Anna.

"Mmm, this looks and smells phenomenal. What is it?" Anna said, taking a small taste of the creamy sauce. "Oh wow, oh wow, oh wow. Mmm," she groaned again. "God, this is like heaven on a plate. My word, I've never tasted anything so beautiful. It literally melts in your mouth. I love the sun-dried tomatoes in it. Oh hell yeah," she groaned.

"Well now who's making some, um, interesting noises?" Heidi laughed at her. "Glad you like it. It's one of my favorites. Horrendously fattening, but at least you get to work it off," she said suddenly looking up like a rabbit in headlights.

Anna laughed loudly. "Chill out, Heidi. Let's just enjoy dinner and relax," she said, returning to her food. Anna was unsure of why she kept getting flustered. She could only assume it was the lack of social skills on a normal level these days.

*

They'd spent the last hour playing Monopoly. It was something neither one of them did regularly, but Anna assured Heidi that she would spend some time with her doing normal things despite the debates about 'babysitting.'

"Would you like some dessert?" Heidi asked.

"You did dessert too? Jesus, I won't be able to lift a bale of hay if you carry on like this."

"Sorry, I got excited after the psychotic, 'poorly named' pig tried to kill me," Heidi said nonchalantly, remembering the snorts and cackles.

"Seriously, Poppy really *didn't* nearly kill you; she was playing. And what do you mean 'poorly named?' I think it's a cute name."

"Poppy, the pig? It's ridiculous. Like Lola, the laughing llama. Are all your animals named in this fashion?"

"Watch it, Edwards. You'll be sleeping out there with them otherwise," she said smiling. "So, what do we have for dessert?"

"Warm brownies. Do you have some ice cream to go with?"

"Blimey, you really don't want me to let you go, do you?"

Heidi smiled shyly. Anna requested a very small portion, solely to taste.

They carried on with the game until shortly after nine, by which point, Heidi had won. Something relatively new it appeared. Anna enjoyed her getting so excited by something so simplistic. Saying their good night's, Anna, with her tired head and full stomach, took the information to bed to consider.

Chapter Ten

The following day went by far quicker. Heidi ordered more food to cook online and Skyped her niece and nephew. She promised she'd speak to Anna and ask if they could come visit. Utilizing her time, Heidi continued the Indian cooking from yesterday, adding a few more meals to their ever-increasing array.

Last night was great, and suddenly she was starting to feel as though she would get through everything. She didn't know how or when, but today she'd spent a lot of time thinking. For the first time in a long time she felt like she was ready to start putting things back together. This was new. It resulted in a call to Dawn, which was good since Heidi hadn't seen a TV, magazine, or newspaper for nearly a week. It was something she wished she could say was normal, but unfortunately, in her world, as much as she detested it, she couldn't help but check regularly. As it had transpired, this stupid, young mistress was all over the tabloids saying that she didn't want a baby out of wedlock and since Heidi had 'done a runner,' she was preventing a wedding. Dawn said the phone rang constantly; the hills were buzzing to life about Heidi, and where she'd gone. Margherita was getting quizzed. The press had even turned up at Sofia's hospital. Dawn said the outcome was incredible. There were people digging way underground. She needed to check on her parents if the press were making it their mission to dig as deep as possible. Then of course, there were the ones that were severely broken-hearted that their Hollywood sweetheart was so distraught that she'd gone AWOL.

Heidi felt bad about everything. She wondered if Everett or his new lady friend, A.K.A. 'tramp,' would divulge about the numerous historical affairs.

Of course, Dawn was already all over that. She didn't think there was anything to worry about. Dawn worked her backside off to get a name for herself in Hollywood, *and that she had*. With that came elevated levels of trade secrets. Dawn heard through the grapevine that the new 'sweetheart' of Everett Spencer-Brady had been nominated for an award following a recent exceptional performance. However, although the award was secured, now that was no longer the case. Apparently, the deception towards "Hollywood's Sweetheart" meant that said award was unlikely to come to fruition. She'd also been pulled for two movies that she was involved with. The public was devastated for Heidi. Ev would never really be able to go public about the affairs, or he could destroy his own career too. If he was prepared to take that risk, then it was going to give her the upper hand and her career would flourish more than it already had. Heidi wasn't mean, but she wasn't too sure how she felt about this latest information. This girl, this *child* was new to the industry, and yeah, she knowingly had an affair with her husband, but this sounded like it was destroying her. *Did Heidi really want that*? Of course Dawn would say yes, but she wasn't Dawn. Dawn was built for Hollywood. Heidi, on the other hand, could take it or leave it. She loved her job, and kept her head down where possible. Well, until Ev came along. Then everything had to be big, and fancy, and public. Heidi pushed it aside for now. Anna was due home soon, giving her enough time to call her parents, and start dinner.

"Hey, Mum."

"Hi, sweetie! How's things? Are you okay?" She sounded chipper. *The press couldn't be there yet, could they?*

"Great. Anna's been fantastic. It's so, well, *different* I suppose. It's private and... well, private. Massively, so," she said. "How are you guys? I spoke to Tony and the kids earlier."

"Oh, did you? Yes, we're okay," her mum said simply.

Heidi sighed heavily. *No such luck then,* she thought. "I'm guessing from that response, and Dawn telling me about the extent to which the press is going, they're hounding you guys too."

"Don't worry about us, Heidi. It's the norm. Have you read or seen anything, though?" Her father jumped on the line too. "They're saying you've gone into hiding."

"Yes, Dawn told me. I'm sorry you guys," she said sadly, noticing Anna walking into the house. "Yes, *yes* I'm fine. No, only Anna and I. Oh, and her farm hand," she said. "I just never expected all this to happen," she said sadly. Heidi moved herself next to the bi-folding doors, taking a seat on the floor as she took in dusk over the scenery.

"What's Dawn say, dear?" Her mum asked.

"She says he won't say anything about the affairs because his own career will crash and burn. And if he does decide to, then ultimately, it would be better for me as it will get me more *'sympathy votes.'* Apparently, it'd be great for my career and me," she sighed.

"And what about the young woman?"

"Again, Dawn said she's losing out majorly—on an award, a couple roles. She's getting ripped apart out there."

"And you don't like that?" her mum said.

"No. You guys didn't raise me that way. Jesus, I'm 41 years old and taking down a 20-something year old without any control over it. This industry is awful. It's damaging and judging, and this...this kid," she spat, noticing the bare legs next to her own. Heidi looked up, seeing the sad, and concerned smile on Anna's face, a bottle of red wine in hand. Her long, dark hair was messy now, with wavy kinks in it, like she just pulled it out of the hairband that it had been tied in, tucked under her hat all day. She was wearing a pair of men's boxer shorts that sat favorably on her hips, complimenting her toned, slightly muscled thighs and legs. *They were long; incredibly long*, Heidi thought. The white vest she wore was tight and flattered her curves. She had a beautiful body; it was shapely and feminine. Odd, given she looked far more masculine when at work. *She was beautiful*, she thought as she took in the full view of her, reaching Anna's eyes, who watched Heidi observe her.

"Heidi?" she heard her mum call into the phone.

"Sorry," she said, embarrassedly looking at Anna. "This girl has been pulled into it and probably thought she'd jump the ladder a step or two, but this could be so damaging. It could result in... God, it doesn't even bare thinking about," she said somberly.

"Sweetheart, it could just result in her leaving Everett and finding the next man to jump up that ladder with. You know how fickle it is there. You've *lived* it long enough. Don't you worry about that, just concentrate on you," her dad said.

S. L. Gape

"I'm sorry, guys," she said sadly, noticing that Anna had disappeared again. She could see her in the kitchen in the reflection of the patio doors.

"Don't you be sorry, we're so proud of you. Come on, you have so much to be thankful for. Enjoy your time there and spend some of it with Anna; you always got on so well as kids. Then when you're ready, you can make the choice of what to do next," her mum said.

"Yeah, she's been pretty awesome, especially considering I've completely turned her life upside down." Anna sat back down with a plastic wallet, this time closer to Heidi.

"Good, I'm glad. I know you're in safe hands there. We'll try and get down to see you once the press goes."

"Okay. You couldn't go golf today then, no?" she said, picking at her bracelet with her thumb.

"Oh, don't worry about that, sweetheart," her father said. "It seems my game's been off for a while. I was starting to get bored of losing to everyone," he laughed, but she could hear the tension in their voices.

"I guess I should go. I'll call you in a few days."

"Take care, sweetheart. We love you."

"Me too." Heidi hung up the phone, wiping away her falling tears.

"Hey, what *happened*? Come here," Anna said, pulling her into a tight hug.

After a minute, Anna pulled away, looking down at Heidi. "What's wrong, Heids?" she asked softly, wiping the tears from her eyes.

Heidi shook her head quietly and lay back on the floor with her head in her hands. She tried to speak, but behind her hands it was muffled; Anna had no clue what she was saying.

Anna rotated her seating position, and lay down beside Heidi. She turned to face her, gently pulling Heidi's hands away from her face. "Wanna try that again?" she smiled softly.

Heidi sighed heavily and filled Anna in on the full story. She listened carefully. She allowed Heidi to get it all out before offering her words of wisdom, and making some valid points. Heidi knew everyone was right, but interestingly Anna was the one that made her see sense. She knew that because Anna was new to it all, and like herself, not equipped for purposely destroying people's lives, that she too felt sorry for the girl who was cheating with her husband.

Anna made Heidi see that irrespective of whether the other woman was single or not, she knowingly got involved with someone that could never be questioned whether he was single or not. She hadn't told him to end things first. She hadn't pushed him to call it. She continued it, knowing the whole time he was married to Heidi. That was evident in the publicity she was now gaining. Interestingly, Anna noted that there would still be plenty of interest in the "mistress" from many companies; not everyone would ditch her, just the ones with morals, maybe. She was right. Those sleazy, reality TV shows would show interest in her. Geez, Everett had asked her to do them about 40 times. The "fly on the wall" types where they follow you around. Ironic really; he would've never maintained any type of affair with cameras on them 24/7.

She was right about it all. Heidi shouldn't feel guilty over everything. It wasn't her doing. None of it. If this little 'wannabe' wants to do all of this, then she needs to take the fall that comes with it. The part Anna *really* emphasized was that she needed to make the most of her time here.

Heidi needed to stop with the communication on a work front with Dawn. She had her phone, and Google; she could check for herself, occasionally. Dawn wouldn't mind that because that was her view initially. Dawn kept telling Heidi not to worry. *That's what she paid her for*. Dawn had already prepared the press release, and was going all out with it. Her best friend and agent knew how to work the media which meant that Anna was right. Heidi could focus on some downtime back in the UK and allow Dawn to take care of the press back home.

"I'm sorry," Heidi said glumly.

"For what? We're friends, aren't we? Like they say, a problem shared is a problem halved," she said sincerely. "Fancy takeout tonight? How about Indian or Chinese? We can watch a movie together and forget about today," Anna said.

"We have Indian. I'm just being stupid. I'll go and cook that." She started to get up.

"Well…" Anna said, grabbing Heidi's wrist. Heidi looked down at where Anna's fair skin met Heidi's tanned wrist. "How about we leave that tonight, and order Chinese. Tomorrow when you're feeling better, you can cook that. I'm away Saturday and back Sunday night, so you'll have a couple days to yourself," Anna smiled sincerely.

"Oh, you are? Right, um, okay. Look, I don't want to make you leave your house. I can leave so you don't have to," she said back to Anna.

"Chill out. I was planning on leaving anyway. It's my dad's birthday, so we're all going to his place to see him. I have a train around 11am and I'll be back around 5pm on Sunday," she said.

"Well, it may be a little too late, but would you mind if I asked my brother and his family to come stay for the night? I spoke to them today and the kids were begging to come visit. They want to see the animals." She smiled. "As I said, it may be too late, but I said I'd ask to check if you minded. I guess if you're away then it makes sense?" she asked.

"Heidi, you don't need to ask; of course it's okay. If they can't make this weekend, then just have them come up when they can. We have regular field trips from local schools come over and the kids love it, especially Lola." Anna shoulder bumped her, smiling.

"Yeah, I bet. A spitting laughing camel? I mean, why wouldn't they?" she rolled her eyes. "I feel bad about dinner; I can cook the Indian. I only had one task, and that was to cook. I feel like I've ruined everything," she said sadly.

"*Come on.* Seriously, you've had a difficult day filled with a mixture of emotions. I'm fine to get takeout. I didn't ask you to make dinner *every* night, nor did I expect you to. Please, for me?" she pleaded.

Heidi noticed the long, dark lashes protecting those big, brown eyes, and felt captivated by them, by her.

"You know you really do put an awful lot of pressure on yourself. You've had a rough time, so stop making yourself feel guilty. Come on, we can have some fun tonight, open some wine for a change," she winked. "Let me treat you to Chinese and have a good night. Plus, Gordon Ramsey is a firm believer that your emotions go into your cooking, so you know what? It'd probably not taste very well. I'd like to chill together tonight and then tomorrow while I'm grafting—", she gave another wink — "you can put all your happy and positive emotions into that food," she said seriously. "Plus, how much more

S. L. Gape

intoxicating will the food be with an additional day to marinade?"

"Okay, okay. You win," she said, taking the Chinese menu from her hands.

*

"It'll be here in about 40 minutes. That okay?" Anna asked, returning with the glasses for the two of them. "I really do need to stop drinking; I've never drank as much as this. Tonight, we have an excuse though. Pour that for us?" she asked, putting some music on. Anna threw a couple of cushions on the floor where they were sat, and opened the blinds fully, revealing the setting sun.

Heidi diverted her attention from the wine pouring to the view before them. "It's so beautiful; you're lucky."

"Thanks, it was part of the reason I remodeled. It was nice to be able to relax after a long day and just watch the sun set. It'll be a good one tonight," she said, the clear, light orange sky streaming in.

"I don't think I've seen anything so beautiful anywhere in the world," Heidi said seriously, moving closer to the window, and quietly staring off into the distance.

Anna knew that Heidi had a day filled with mixed emotions. Not wanting to interrupt her, she allowed her some time to reflect.

*

Heidi sat at the window, small and childlike, holding her knees close to her chest for nearly 30 minutes before finally speaking. "So… difficult day." She smiled, pointing to the wine.

"You'd think, wouldn't you?" She giggled. "Sorry, didn't want to interrupt you. You seemed lost in your thoughts," she said handing her a glass.

"Yeah I kinda was. Thanks for earlier. You made me realize that I don't need to feel bad. He did this. Well, *they* did. I'll stop overthinking everything and just enjoy my time here," she said holding up her drink. "To new friends."

"I'll drink to that. Look, I know you and I are worlds apart, and I don't know, nor do I understand the whole Hollywood deal, but regardless of where you are, or what you do, it's still the same. He cheated on you with this girl. You either accept that, try to win him back, and work at it, or you forget him and move on. Just because the world's looking at you it doesn't change the facts. Granted, it's a factor; I get that. You're an icon and people look up to you. Kids aspire to be just like you. That, for me, is the biggie here because ultimately whatever you decide is going to be scrutinized to hell. What you don't want is people to start changing their opinion of you, the way they have with Everett. Ultimately, I think what you said is the best way to go. Keep your head down. Reflect, and enjoy your time to assess things. Better still, let those idiots keep digging themselves into a deeper hole." She smiled and there was a knock at the door.

"Dinner's here." Her eyes twinkled as she went to get it. "Are you happy for me to serve or do you want to help yourself?"

"No, go for it," Heidi said, turning back to the sunset.

Anna handed them both a bowl filled with Chinese food and filled their glasses up again. "You want to sit at the dining table or are you happy on the floor?"

"Here's just fine. I like the view," she responded, taking a bowl of food. "So, what are you doing for your dad's birthday then?" she asked.

"Does it bother you that you'll be here alone?"

"God no, don't be silly."

"Good. We're just going for dinner with all the family. Dawn's folks, a few cousins, and our grandpa. Then we'll go the pub for a few drinks. That way the kids can go home and stuff. It'll be good to see him. I speak to him regularly, but I never see him. Hence, I'm trying. Are you going to see if your brother can come up?"

"Yes, maybe. I'll call Meg tomorrow and see if they're free. It may be a little late, but if you're sure you don't mind them coming another time, I'd love to have them visit."

"Yeah, completely. Be good to have some children around for a bit. It'll be a breath of fresh air. How's the food?"

"Awesome. We have great Chinese food back home—it's only Indian and roasts I hugely miss—but this is good. And yeah, I'll get Tony and Meg to come up with the kids as soon as I can. I figure it may be best to leave it until after you return as I know nothing about the animals. They'll be pissed if I can't show them stuff on the farm."

Anna laughed. "True, pointing out 'laughing camels' and 'cannibalistic pigs' from a telescope wouldn't be their idea of fun," she winked.

She did that a lot, Heidi thought.

"You going to be okay alone?"

"Yeah, big girl now." She winked back at her. "I'm sure if I can rattle about a 16-room home alone, I'll be fine out here with the laughing camels and cannibalistic pigs," she laughed.

"You should spend some time with her. As I keep saying, Poppy is a playful pig; she wouldn't bite, let alone eat you. She is more than happy with the feed she gets from Jack and me each day. You're quite safe."

"Yeah that's what you say now. Wait until you come back, and I've disappeared and there's no sign of me. The only evidence will be when you cook her and find my diamond ring in her tummy."

"Oh my god, you're a fool. Regardless of the wealth and stardom, you're still a fool. If I remember correctly, you've always been a fool. I remember you always got me in trouble acting foolish. It always made me laugh, so I'd get told off," she scolded Heidi.

"Moi? Never!" Heidi smirked. "I couldn't help it. I remember the three of us were thick as thieves. I remember Tony crying once when Dawn's parents came over to ask if they could bring me here with them and he begged to come too. And…oh my god, we were so evil. We told Tony it was a girl's only weekend. He came down the next day to go to school, dressed as a girl, and said he would become a girl so he could come see the animals. My folks let him take the day off so they could explain to him things didn't quite work like that. They took him to the farm and McDonald's. He didn't shut up about it for weeks. When we came back, Dawn told him that your farm was 'old McDonald,' which was where McDonald's came from. We got to see the animals, go to the *real* McDonald's, learn how to make it, and eat as much as we wanted. He cried for days," she said, reminiscing.

"That's so cruel. I'd expect it from *Dawn*, but not from you," she laughed.

"I know, right? It's about all I can remember from our childhood actually, which is pretty shameful," she sighed.

"Hey, don't worry about it," she said touching her arm. Heidi looked at Anna's hand on her arm and then up at her. "It's called old age," Anna said with a lopsided grin.

"Idiot!" Heidi said rolling her eyes, trying to ignore the sensation left from Anna's touch.

Chapter Eleven

Heidi got up the following morning and felt the need to get out of the house. More importantly, she really needed some exercise. It had been over a week in Surrey now, and her diet and drinking were abysmal. Added with zero exercise, she could already feel the difference in her body and mind. She contemplated the feasibility of having a Skype fitness class with Troy. *She would just have to be creative*, she thought. She messaged Troy for ideas to help her. The property was large enough to at least get a few miles of walking done. She got dressed and left the house, hoping to avoid any laughing camels and evil pigs. The prospect of a long walk before returning to cook the Indian was fulfilling, and she was looking forward to something.

Heidi got as far as the entrance to the field where she had her first encounter with Poppy, the cannibalistic pig. *She had no idea why she kept calling it cannibalistic; even if it did eat her, that wouldn't make it cannibalistic!* Looking around, she pondered aloud which direction to choose today. She knew if she walked to the right, she'd come across Jack and Anna like she did the other day. She pondered why she wanted to bump into them.

"You alright there?" She turned to face Jack.

"You have a habit of sneaking up on me," she said looking up at him.

"I think you'll find this is my domain," he said pointing to the ground. "You keep randomly appearing in my workplace," he smirked, folding his arms, showing off the muscular definition under his long sleeve, grey t shirt.

"*Your* domain? Well aren't we master of the kingdom?" She questioned, arching her brow.

"You know what I mean. My domain as in my workplace. That you keep appearing in. I'm just here doing my day job, and then boom, just like a genie—" He clicked his fingers. "—you appear!"

"*Oh*, that's right. One moment I'm on set filming in Hollywood, and the next moment, I'm in a bathtub in Surrey, and you walk through the door. Gosh, how incredibly stupid of me."

"I knew it." He clicked his fingers again. "I could tell you secretly wanted me. You've just been wishing yourself here, haven't you?" He winked. "Come on your majesty, I'm guessing you want my boss?" he said, laughing.

"Your boss? No, why would you think I want her? I don't want her," she rambled.

Jack looked at her, confused. "Alright then," he said, turning and walking away.

God, he was infuriating, she thought, running off after him. It was his young mentality; he'd have a ball in L.A. if he ever visited.

Why would he visit? There was no reason for him to.

She was getting out of breath just walking fast. She needed Troy to come back with some advice on working out while she was here, and quick. She wondered if there was anything on the site that she could do to help keep her in shape, or Dawn would be *right;* she wouldn't get another job. The media would have a field day.

"Boss, you have a visitor!" he shouted through a big, wooden building.

"I told you I didn't want her! Why did you just do that?" she asked.

"Hi, everything okay?" Anna asked, walking out, and wiping the sweat from her brow.

"Yes fine, I didn't want you. I was just out for a walk."

"So, why did you follow me then?" Jack asked.

"I didn't follow you, I…" *Shit, she followed him.* She shook her head quickly, trying to sort the situation. "Sorry, as I said, I was out for a walk. I'm in desperate need of some exercise."

"I can help with that," Jack popped his head around the corner, smirking.

"Work!" Anna shouted, rolling her eyes at Heidi. "Come on, why don't we take a walk. Jack, you got this for a while?"

"I don't want to interrupt your work. I was genuinely just going for a walk. I didn't know how safe it would be going for a run."

"How safe?" Anna quizzed.

"Well, yeah. I didn't know if a load of animals would come chasing me if I started running," she said seriously.

"You're quite safe here, you know. Come on, I'll take you for a walk, so you can see which areas are animal free," she smirked. "You sure you're going to be okay tomorrow? I can get Jack to stay over if you like?"

"No!" Heidi snapped, noticing Anna's inquisitive glare.

"Is everything okay? Did he do or say something?" she asked concerned.

"God, no! Not at all. He's just young, and arrogant, and quite infuriating," she said looking out at to the lake. "Wow, this is beautiful."

"Sure is," Anna said, smirking a little at Heidi and her admission on Jack. "You see the wooden building back there that we've just come from?" Anna said, pointing it out.

"Uh huh."

"Well, all the way over to that fencing," she pointed to the opposite side, "And down to the lake here, all of that's free of animals. You can do what you want in this space. I have a bike if you want to cycle a few miles a day around here, or run. But there's plenty of open space here for you to utilize."

"Thanks Anna, that's awesome. I was about ready to pay for a swimming pool to be put in so I could go swimming each day." She winked to her.

"Well, as much as I'd love a swimming pool, the weather here would give me about three swims in it," she laughed. "Plus, when you've gone back to sunnier climates, I'll have no time to maintain the upkeep of a swimming pool each day," she giggled.

"This is true. Hey, I'll get Santiago, the pool boy over here. Apparently, he's very good with tubes and his hands," she winked.

"That sounds so very wrong," she squirmed. "I'm quite alright, I'm more than certain I can get by just fine without Santiago's experienced...*hands* and *tube* fixing. Anyway, moving swiftly on. Are we having the Indian tonight?"

"If you still fancy it?" Heidi asked.

"Definitely. Been a bit of a disastrous morning. I was going to have a sober night, but I could use an ice-cold Tiger, and some decent Indian food."

"Well I can't promise it will be decent, but I can deliver the rest. I guess I should get back and get to work then," she smirked. "Hey, thanks for pointing this out. It's awesome. I really feel quite yuck, so this is good for me to know. I'm kinda hoping that Troy has some ideas too on how to use the space," she said kindly.

"No worries at all. Um, do you have some free time before you go back?"

"I've got all the time in the world, Anna." She smiled. "What for?"

"I wanna show you something. No animals, I promise." She smiled, grabbing Heidi's arm. "Come with me?" she raised her eyebrows.

A few minutes later they arrived at another big building. This was more like a normal outer house made of concrete and wood.

"Come on," Anna said, pulling her excitably.

Heidi couldn't help the smile forming as she saw the excitement and sparkle in Anna's eyes over whatever it was she was about to reveal. They walked through a couple of doors, and Heidi noticed the loud buzzing, the coldness to the room. "What *is* this place?" Heidi asked Anna.

"Come on, you'll see," she said, grabbing her again.

Heidi followed Anna, who led her through a final door before arriving to lots of machinery happily whirling, swirling, and swishing away. Anna opened a little door to a big, silver machine and grabbed a box. She turned the machine on and saw ice cream fill the box. She looked at Heidi, whose eyes widened. "Here, have a taste," she held the spoon to Heidi's mouth and allowed her to taste it.

"Oh... my... gosh. That's *incredible*. You make your *own* ice cream?"

"Yup, pretty much any flavor you want I can make you," she said shyly.

"Anna, that's incredible. I can't believe everything you have, and do here. It's... it's *outstanding*. I'm so impressed." She reached for the spoon in Anna's hand.

"Uh uh uh. What do you think you're doing?" She moved it out of the way and high in the air, so Heidi couldn't reach.

"I'm grabbing that spoon and delighting my body with some more of that phenomenal ice cream. Don't mess with a girl and her sweet tooth. You best give me that right now," she said.

"Oh really? Or what?" She smirked. "Come on, what's it worth?"

"What's it *worth*? Well, what do you want?" Heidi said, raising an eyebrow and smiling slightly.

"Boss..." Jack walked in, looking at the pair who immediately looked guilty. He eyed them cautiously. "Um," he paused. "Um, we've got a problem. We've lost a couple of sheep. I think we may need to get Karen down."

"Karen? Wait...lost, missing? Or lost, dead?" she asked seriously, passing the spoon to Heidi as she followed Jack.

"Lost, dead. I think a fox got in," he said, the two of them leaving Heidi without another word.

Jesus. What was she doing, or thinking? Heidi slid down the wall to the floor. "Bollox!" she shouted, feeling the numbingly, cold floor. "Bloody hell, that's cold," she said rubbing her bottom. Revisiting the ice cream, Heidi closed her eyes and allowed the creamy, buttery flavor thrill her senses. She put the lid back on and decided to take the box as she went on her mission to try and remember how to get home.

*

Heidi walked what she figured was the long route home. Not that it bothered her—she loved walking—and although it was October, it wasn't yet freezing. She missed having seasons. In L.A., they got rain maybe five times a year, if that. And never, *ever* did it snow. No. Snow was what you saw when you visited Aspen, New York, and Canada. The sharp air was chilly, but bearable. She wore a long sleeve shirt under her short sleeve, *and* a fleece. Arriving at the house, she was instantly hit by warmth, and the strong aromas of spices awakened her senses. She'd cooked far too much, but figured it could quickly be reheated the next night when Anna was gone.

Heidi finished marinating the lamb, eagerly awaiting the outcome. Her favorite restaurant provided the recipe last week. Heidi grabbed the casserole dish and put it on a slow heat. *It would be falling off the bone when Anna got back home,* she thought.

She finished prepping and marinating. When Anna arrived home, the starters and main course were ready to go in the oven. With a few hours to spare, she decided to change into something more comfortable and check out some of the trainers that Troy suggested. He'd also sent some DVD's, so she could at least start those in the interim.

Heidi scrolled through the list. One name kept coming up. She was listed as the most expensive, but had fantastic reviews. Dialing the number, she was surprised to get an answer. *Maybe they weren't as busy as they made out?* Either way she needed to do something. Dawn would be stoked when she found out.

"Hi. Yes, my name's, Hei... Hilary, and I've seen details of your services online. I was wondering if you had some spare time," Heidi said to the person on the phone.

"Hi, Hilary. I'd love to help, but I currently have a waiting list about six weeks long I'm afraid. I can put you in touch with somebody else if you like? How regular are you looking? An hour a week?"

"Um, no, I was looking for an hour, maybe two, per day, and to be honest I really wouldn't want anybody else. My personal trainer in the states recommended you," she lied.

"An hour per day? You realize that I charge £100 per hour?" she asked incredulously.

"I do. As I said, I've been told you're the best in my area."

"Are you in Berkshire then?"

"No, Lightwater."

"Surrey?" she asked surprised. "There are people far closer to you than me."

"As I said, I want the best. I understand you'd lose out on travel time, et cetera. I'd happily pay you double time for your services. I'd like a Sunday off. However, I can adapt that should you have a day off per week. Which would mean two hours on Mondays."

"Double time? That's 1400 pounds a week. Is this a joke?"

"Nope, not at all. I'm really quite desperate, and if you need me to, I can have the money for the entire month in your account this afternoon," Heidi said nonchalantly.

"Um, can I take your number, Hilary? I'll have to consider some things. I have a few new people being trained, so I'll see if I can move things, and call you back within the hour."

"Great stuff," she said, providing her cell number and hanging up. She could just imagine what this poor woman must be thinking now; no doubt, intrigued. She pretty much guaranteed that she'd get a call back within the hour.

She opened her phone and began texting a message to Dawn.

Hey, getting a PT here to stop me from getting fat, as you requested ;) Can you send me a confidentiality agreement, swiftly? Thanks! Hope you're well and aren't pissing Margherita off too much. MWAH love you - H xx

Heidi saw the dots move immediately as Dawn responded.

I didn't say you would get fat. See attached. Hope he's hot. Have you shagged Jack yet? D xx

You're disgusting. Thanks, xx

Yes, it's why you love me. Get on it, PUN INTENDED!! ;) Hope you're enjoying yourself! All kicking off here still. Obviously, L.A. doesn't change overnight - hope to see you soon. Xx

*

As expected, Heidi received a call within the hour. *Keen, but long enough not to look desperate,* she thought.

"Hello?"

"Hi, is this Hilary?"

"Um, yes. Y*es, it is!*"

"Hi, it's Helen, the personal trainer. I could move things around slightly, and swap some new customers to other staff. When were you looking to start?"

"Ideally tomorrow. I haven't done anything for a couple weeks, so if possible, I'd like to train through next Saturday with just one hour for Monday, if that suits you. What days off do you have?"

"None. Too many of my clients like to do set days, so it's not practical. However, I do prefer, when possible, to

S. L. Gape

start and finish earlier in the day if that's convenient for you?"

"Yes, definitely. My PT's in the states come over at five am. Although, I don't necessarily need it that early; it's more for work there."

"Oh, you work in the states?"

"Yes. Sorry, I probably should've mentioned I'm here on vacation—a lengthy one—so while I'm here I need to get some training done. I'd also like to give you contact information of my current PT. I know he'll be able to give you some background info that will benefit both you and me, if that's okay?"

"Yes, absolutely fine."

"Great. There's one last thing before I get your bank details."

"It's fine, I'll give you my details tomorrow when I come. I don't want you back paying me before I speak to your PT. I can get details of your PT back home. Is seven am okay or too early?"

"No, seven's perfect."

"Great," she said, waiting for Heidi to finish.

"So, this is somewhat delicate. Before we start, I need you to sign a confidentiality agreement. I can send it straight to your phone now if you can print it off and then return it to me. Then we're good for tomorrow."

"A *what,* sorry?"

"A confidentiality agreement. It basically means that you cannot discuss me or anything about me to anyone."

"Um, Hilary, I pride myself on my trust and confidence and there's no way I would ever discuss anything to do with any of my clients to anybody. I have all manners of clients and I—"

"—I'm sorry, but this is non-negotiable. I cannot risk it, I'm afraid. This needs to be signed before I can move forward. Believe me when I say, you'll understand when you begin working with me." *God*, Heidi thought, *she was making herself out to be a monster.*

"Um, right. Well I guess you better send it over," she said oddly.

"Great, I'll send it to this number now by text. I suggest you read the entirety of the agreement. You'll notice there's no name on there for obvious reasons. Would you like the month's money in cash, check, or wired to your bank account tomorrow when you come?"

"Bank transfer is fine. I'll send the agreement back this evening. See you tomorrow. "Oh, and Hilary?"

"Yes?"

"Do I need solicitors involved? To read?" She added. "You know, review and sign on my behalf? Sorry, this is new to me."

"No, as long as you read the whole thing to ensure you fully understand, and then sign it to confirm that should you fail to comply with any aspects, you'll be subject to legal action taken against you," she said simply.

"Oh, right. Um okay, I'll read through it now. If there are any issues in relation to this or tomorrow, I'll contact you later."

"Great stuff. I'm sure there won't be; there isn't normally. Looking forward to meeting you tomorrow," she confirmed, hanging up.

Helen would no doubt be completely confused by the situation. She really hoped it'd all work out. It'd be fantastic if she could start working out with a proper trainer again.

Chapter Twelve

It was close to 5:30 and Heidi poured herself a glass of red while cooking. That would be the first thing she needed to sort. The daily drinking. She couldn't believe how much she was drinking lately. She seemed to be bored. She'd never had so much time to herself. The manuscripts hadn't been opened yet, and she needed to get on top of it. Tomorrow, after Anna left, she would get started. It'd be the perfect distraction.

Heidi put a couple of beers in the freezer for Anna, recalling her earlier words about ice cold beers and Indian. She wondered if she would still be home at the same time. There were issues with her sheep, that's what Jack had said. *What if she couldn't get back on time?* Wondering why she was fretting, she'd lower the heat until Anna came back. Opening the oven door, Heidi checked her tandoori spiced lamb shoulder. "Mmm very nice," she commended herself. She poured the curry over the meat, gave it a quick stir, and returned in back to the heat.

Heidi set the table, filling it with cutlery, napkins, poppadum's and sauces. She'd really gone to a lot of effort, and overdone it, yet again. It was still her favorite meal. She loved the time and effort that went into it. Unfortunately, that always led to huge portions.

She switched the TV on and enjoyed the remainder of her wine while waiting for Anna. Heidi wanted to buy her something to thank her, but had no idea what to get. She didn't really seem like the materialistic type. Gucci bags and purses would be a waste. She loved technology, though. Maybe she could get her something cool that had to do with that. She'd speak to Tony; he was good with technology. That way when they came up, he could see what she had or find out what she'd like. She'd call them tomorrow to see if they could come up soon.

Heidi heard her phone ping. A message from Helen.

Hi Hilary. Please find attached the read, understood, and signed confidentiality agreement. I'm slightly concerned now that I'm walking in to something with no details of you. You could turn out to be an axe murderer and nobody knows who you are, or where I am.

Heidi re-read the message. *Jesus, she lived in a town full of 'crazy people,' the poor woman was probably thinking all sorts,* she thought consciously.

Hi, I'm sorry, I didn't even think about that. Normally my manager sorts things like this for me. Okay, why don't we rearrange tomorrow? I'm staying with a friend over here. Why don't I send her to meet you for coffee? You can bring someone with you and I can get her to bring a copy of her passport, that way should I turn out to be an axe murderer (FYI I'm not) then the police have a link directly back to me :) She smiled to herself as she typed. At least the woman was sensible. She had to be older, maybe around Heidi's age.

Weirdly ... or maybe just stupidly there's something that's making me want to trust you. Or maybe it's just intrigue given all the hoops today. I will come. What's the address?

Heidi responded excitably, thanking the woman, and sending her the address. Things were finally starting to pick up a little bit. Now all she needed was Ev and his new lady friend to get the hell out of her life.

"Hi," Heidi heard from the door.

"Hey," Heidi said quietly, unsure what Anna would be like after their childish antics and she and Jack running out without a word.

"You okay? Drinking again, eh?" She smirked.

Heidi breathed a sigh of relief. She didn't know why she was still acting like she was constantly on edge. That was how she'd been over the last couple of years with Everett. "Boredom, but you'll be pleased to know I have made an executive decision and gone about changing that. And yes, I'm fine, thanks."

"Oh really? Sounds ominous. Dinner smells amazing," she said, an oddness filling her at the relaxedness of the situation. "I didn't get a chance to eat, I'm starved," she said, quickly turning to face Heidi. "I'm so sorry, I didn't mean that to sound like you're my housekeeper or cook," she said embarrassed. "It's just, I've been looking forward to your Indian for the last few days since you made it and I haven't been able to smell anything else," she offered kindly.

Heidi laughed a little. "Don't sweat it, farm girl, you can use me for my specialist cooking skills." She winked. "On a serious note though, I didn't know when you'd be home after… um, today. Hope everything's okay? I haven't started the food yet. I can put it on now; it'll be ready in about half hour, if that's okay? As you can see we have poppadum's and dips while we're waiting."

"Sacked, sacked I tell you," Anna winked. "I'm fine, I'm sorry about today, it was a pretty shit day, but unfortunately it's part and parcel of my job. I've sorted it now, hopefully. Anyway, I'm pretty sure you had a wonderful affair with my ice cream." She smirked again. "I noticed the tub is gone."

"I figured it was only fair: I provide the dinner, you provide the dessert." She winked and felt herself blush as she thought about the suggestive wording. Heidi couldn't help but notice the slight wrinkles around her dimples. She really had aged incredibly well. Heidi noticed Anna watching her with a big smirk on her face. Unable to control the heat filling her face, she quickly turned, and fired up the cooker.

*

Anna utilized the delay in food to spend a while in the shower. It had been an odd day with mixed emotions. From panic to stress to laughter. What was she *doing*? Her dry humor and sarcasm had always gotten her into trouble, but now, acting this way with a Hollywood superstar? Seriously, she would end up having a claim against her at this rate. She couldn't help but acknowledge how nice it was to have someone there though. Someone to come home to each night. Someone to eat and drink with, talk about her day with. That was wrong, all wrong. She couldn't get used to this. Heidi will have her life back on track soon enough and be gone. Anna purposely didn't do this—have friends. Her life didn't allow for it, and now look. She was enjoying the company. Maybe she should let Jack move in after all.

She heard a knock at the door, and spun around. "I'm naked," she shouted, cringing immediately as the words left her mouth.

"Um, well that's good to know, I think." She heard Heidi chuckling behind the door. "I was wondering how long you would be. Shall I start setting it up now?"

"Oh shit, yeah, sorry. I needed to pack before I showered. I'll get dressed and then be down."

"Yes, that may be wise. Sitting opposite you naked may be somewhat off putting," she laughed loudly causing Anna to roll her eyes as she fell on to her bed.

"Geez, you weirdo," she said quietly to the room. She pulled her hair from the towel and allowed her wet curls to fall over her shoulders. She threw on pajama bottoms and a t-shirt and followed the delicious aromas.

"Hey."

"Hey yourself. Can I look or are we still naked?"

"You always this funny, or is it just through the winter months?"

"Ah, on the contrary, my friend," she said, handing her the ice-cold bottle of beer from the freezer. "I haven't experienced winter in 10 plus years. It's just my natural comedy and humor. What can I say, I was blessed," she laughed as she turned to face Anna.

"How lucky I am to have you in my presence then, I suppose," she said, raising an eyebrow and her bottle. "Smells good lady, what have I got for my dinner?"

"Jesus, you sound like a dude from the Stone Age. You took long enough; I thought you were starving. Open the poppadum's if you like," she said.

"Dude? You're so American! And seriously, you sound like a nagging wife from the 70's," she smirked. "Sorry, I wanted to pack so that I'm not rushing in the morning. Which means I can have a few beers and not have to worry about a hangover. Thanks so much for the dinner though. You really don't need to do all of this. It's been great having you here and having some company for a change. I may need to hire a cook when you're gone so I can come home every night to dinner on the table," she smirked taking a bite of poppadum.

Heidi put the starters into a large bowl and turned the oven down so the curry would stay warm for when they were ready for it.

"Wow, that looks amazing. It is just you and I though, correct?" Anna said, stealing an onion bhaji. "God, this is incredible. You made this from scratch?"

"Yup, sure did. I know it's all quite naughty, but I figured, last time. As of Monday, we start eating healthy again," she stilled herself, embarrassed. "Sorry, I wasn't insinuating that you were getting fat. Jesus, there really is nothing of you other than... well, muscle. I just meant I wouldn't normally eat like this, or drink like it. I'll cook healthier options for me and then I'll happily cook you what you like," she said, focusing on the bowl and grabbing some food for her plate.

"Are you always like this? Chill out. I knew what you meant, and I'm comfortable in my own body. I don't eat fried stuff all that often. However, I do a hell of a lot of exercise in my job, so I'm confident that I can occasionally eat badly. But yes, deep fried Indian starters and Chinese food daily isn't good for my arteries, so I like the thought of a satisfying compromise," she said, dipping the starters in the dips that Heidi had made, making all manner of weird and wonderful noises.

"So, you looking forward to your weekend?"

"Sure am. Be fab to have a bit of time off and see my family. Some of my cousins I haven't seen in about five years."

"Seriously? Wow," she nodded. "I wish I'd known earlier; it would've been the perfect time and excuse for Dawn to come over. She would've loved it," Heidi said.

"I know. I'm sure there will be another time. I reckon she'll be over sometime soon," she said taking more food.

S. L. Gape

"You think? Do you know something?"

"No. Sorry, I didn't mean to get your hopes up. You just don't seem to spend time apart, so I meant, she'd start missing you soon, and banging my door down." She smiled.

"Yes, this…" she said, pointing her fork to Anna while chewing her last mouthful. "…is very true. I really miss her. Other than my honeymoon we've never spent much time apart. It's weird thinking about a potentially long time apart."

"Don't take this the wrong way," Anna said seriously. "Do you have any idea how long you'll stay for? I don't care, it's kind of nice having you here. Well, not you specifically, but just some company. Sorry, that sounded horrible. I just meant…oh you know what I mean," she said, rolling her eyes and looking up to a smirking Heidi.

"You're awesome at this social thing, aren't you? How do you like the Indian?"

Anna chose to ignore the comment. "It's awesome. I needed something like this to enjoy. It's as good as a real Indian. Where did you learn to cook Indian this well?"

"The owner of my favorite Indian. I'd love to take you some time; I think you'd love it." She smiled sincerely.

"I think it's highly doubtful I'll ever get to L.A."

"First, it's in London. I took my folks there last week. Second, you should really come to L.A. It's awesome and I think you'd like it. Additionally, I think you could do with a decent break. Do you want to wait before the main or are you okay to go straight in?" Heidi looked at her, smiling wide.

"Main? There's more? Jesus, did you think we were going to miss out on the next six meals?" Anna questioned.

124

"Funny! Nope, but obviously, if we were out for an Indian, then of course we would have a starter and a main," she said simply. "So," she said, eyes wide.

"My word, you are a hard-working lady. Shall we have a break? Have a beer, listen to some music, and watch the sunset? If the food can wait."

"Cool, awesome idea. That's fine. It's been in for around six hours. Another hour will be just fine."

Anna choked on her beer, pulling the bottle out quickly. "Six hours, are you kidding me?"

Heidi giggled. "No, I'm not. It's a slow roasted curry, hence the length of time. Let me just clean these away and you choose some music. I'll tell you about my news from today." She grinned excitably.

"Can a curry be slow roasted? Will it not have evaporated?" she asked confused, wondering how she makes curries.

"Sorry, the tandoori lamb is slow roasted. I only put the sauce in an hour ago."

Chapter Thirteen

Heidi's alarm went off the following morning, and immediately, she regretted the booze last night. She was shocked. *How much did they have to drink?* It'd been another great night. The food went down a storm. So much so, they had gone back for more at 11:30. That was about the time she remembered Anna putting on the Heart radio station which was filled with 80's classics that they sang along with loudly. It was club classics Friday and Heidi had truly missed the simplicity of having fun with a girlfriend. Her and Dawn used to do it all the time. Since she became her manager and agent though, it always turned into work one way or another. As much fun as she'd had, now she felt guilty. She put her training tights and a workout vest on and got herself together before Helen arrived. It was a quarter to seven on Saturday and still a little dark. More importantly, she hadn't done any exercise for a couple of weeks with everything that was going on at home. Now she felt terrified. This morning was going to kill her.

She finished brushing her teeth, and the door knocked louder than necessary. "Shit," she said, wanting to reach it before it woke Anna, who was enjoying her one and only sleep in. She rushed to the door, and opened it, noticing the mixed-race woman who was maybe around the mid-thirties mark.

"Hi, Hilary?" she said, pushing her phone back in her bag before looking up to Heidi. "You're not Hilary. You're Hei…bloody hell, you're Heidi Spencer-Brady. You're

Heidi, bloody Spencer-Brady. Bloody hells bells," she said dumbfounded.

"Quite finished?" Heidi said, smirking to the trainer.

"Um, yes, I'm really sorry. Apologies. I just... well I'm just very surprised. I have a few high-profile clients, but this... well, this is off the scale."

"Hence yesterday's confidentiality agreement. Are you going to come in?"

"Yes. Apologies again. I can assure you, I swear my lips are sealed. Agreement or not, I wouldn't say anything about you."

"On the contrary, I'm not so phased about people speaking about me; it's the nature of the industry. My concern is that nobody can know where I am."

"Well I get that. It's understandable. I'm sorry about everything you're going through, just saying. Okay well, enough of all that. You wanted my help, so let's get to business."

"Thank you. Troy is waiting for us to call. FYI, the time difference means it's gonna be 11pm on a Friday night back home. Who the hell knows what state he'll be in," she said seriously, as she dialed the number to Facetime Troy.

"Heeeeyyyy. How's my gorgeous Hollywood superstar?" he said, raising a martini to her.

"You say that to everyone. Okay, so I'm here with Helen, the new PT. You good to go through everything with her?"

"Yup, sure thing sweetie," he smiled genuinely, suddenly sobering himself and sitting upright.

"Hi, I'm Helen," she said to the face in the iPhone.

"Hey, Helen. I'm Troy. First and most importantly, you need to look after my girl down there."

S. L. Gape

They spent 10 minutes discussing what Heidi did, and what she now needed to focus on. Helen seemed to be incredibly knowledgeable as she reeled off things to Troy who kept throwing *"excellent's," "great's,"* and *"I love it's"* back to her.

"Right, we ready?" Helen said, after finishing the call and removing Heidi's phone completely from reach and sight. She liked this woman already. She had a fantastic body, and clearly took a great deal of pride in her career and love for fitness.

"Yes, I only have one thing. Will it be noisy? I'm staying with a friend who's currently still in bed. I don't want to wake her. We may need to go elsewhere."

"I normally use loud music as I find it gets the adrenaline pumping, but as it's your first session and we'll spend today assessing your level, we can keep it low key."

"Great stuff. I'm fine with that. It literally *is* the only day it matters. Normally, Anna is at work, but she's going away today, so she's still in bed. Normally she won't be here, so we can have the music as loud as you like."

"Great. Right, come on, we're wasting time. Unless you're only wanting to firm up your mouth, we aren't here for this," she said seriously.

Geez, she was taking Troy's okay to be firm with her to a whole other level. She was satisfied that she'd gotten the right personal trainer.

*

"Oh my god. I can't do it anymore. Please no more," Heidi said crying out.

"You need to get back on track. You're lucky, though; it's 8:15 and I really need to get going."

"Thank God."

"Excuse me?"

"Um nothing," she said, giving her very best Hollywood smile.

"Not gonna work with me, sorry. I don't care who you are, or how pretty that smile is."

Heidi dropped the smile quickly, furrowing her brows. What the hell? *Everyone bought into the smile*, she thought as she heard a giggle, turning around to see Anna leaning against the doorframe shaking her head profusely.

"How long have you been there?" she asked accusingly.

"Calm down, Hollywood," Anna said. "Hi, I'm Anna. This is my place. Nice to meet you."

"Oh hey, um, nice to meet you too," Helen said, looking between the two women. "She's all yours. Good luck. Same time tomorrow, yeah?"

"Yes, lets!" Heidi said sarcastically.

"Less of the sarcasm please," she admonished her, causing Anna to laugh again and Heidi to swing around looking like a reprimanded puppy.

"Whatever!" she slammed. "Do you have your bank details? Are you happy if I just pay the $6,000 for now as I don't know how long I'll be here for. How about we say a month, and then we can go from there?" Heidi heard choking behind her and decided against looking at Anna, who, no doubt, was shocked to hear the cost.

"Look, you don't need to double it. It's fine."

"I insist. With what you've proven in just this last hour, you're just as good as Troy and Nina. I'm more than happy to pay that. In fact, you're cheaper than them."

"Oh, that makes it all the better then. I tell you what, let's compromise. I say three, you say six, so let's go four and a half. I think I'm gonna have fun with you. And when you're back home and all the dust has settled, I can put you on my website as one of my clients." She smiled wickedly.

"Okay, that's a trade-off I'll go for. Just no details yet?" she raised an eyebrow in question.

"Of course, I've signed the paperwork, haven't I? Hey, nice to meet you Anna. Have a good day today. Heidi, I look forward to tomorrow's session," she winked and left the house.

"Looks like you have an admirer," Anna said, smirking to Heidi.

"What?" she asked confused. "What're you talking about? She's my trainer. There's no way she's gay."

"Yeah yeah, whatever. I need to get ready," Anna said, leaving the room and rushing up the stairs to her room.

Heidi shook her head profusely, unsure what the hell Anna was on about. Why would she say that? She really enjoyed this morning and she liked Helen, but now that made her feel weird. It wasn't new to her; she'd had women come on to her before. But the closeness and the physical contact between a PT and client would make it a bit weird, wouldn't it? Heidi wiped the sweat off her forehead and slumped down on the couch, choosing to ignore Anna's comments.

*

"Heid's? Heidi?" she heard distantly. She adjusted her eyes, rushing up quickly, and smashed her head straight into Anna's.

"Ouch!" they both cried in unison, sitting down, and rubbing their foreheads.

"I'm so sorry, I must have fallen asleep," Heidi said.

"No shit, Sherlock. You have a head of stone. Jesus, I'm going to look cracking tonight with a golf ball on my forehead," she said, massaging the sore area softly. "I was just letting you know, I'm leaving," she said.

"Oh right. I'm really sorry," she said again getting up. "You get yourself off and have an awesome time. Send my love to Dawn's folks. Do you want me to do anything? Do you want dinner when you return tomorrow?"

"Nah, you're good. I'll probably take my dad out for Sunday lunch and then return. So, I'll be home about four-ish?" she asked.

Heidi didn't really know why it sounded like she was asking her if that was okay. "Cool. I was going to make some soup, so if you get peckish in the evening there will be some of that. Have an awesome time, and I'll see you tomorrow. I hope the golf ball doesn't expand too much." She smiled, nodding her head to the small red mark on her forehead.

"Yes, thanks. It may have knocked some sense into me." She touched her arm. "Right, you've got my number and I know you won't want it, but I've also left Jack's on the side. Just in case. If you need anything he'll be able to help out."

"I won't—"

"Yeah, yeah I got it. You don't want to call him. He's a good guy and he knows this place inside and out. If anything happens with the animals or the machinery or even the house he'll be able to assist on my behalf. I know you have a thing about him, but you know how these things work. If anything is gonna go wrong, it'll be when I'm gone," she said evenly.

"I don't have a thing with him; he's just a kid. I don't really have many dealings with them."

131

"Fine. Look, I don't know what it is with Jack; he's harmless, and a good guy. To be perfectly honest, I can't imagine his cockiness is anything different than those of the guys in L.A. Maybe that's the problem, that he reminds you of people back home. Or maybe you secretly like him," she said, kissing her on the cheek. She left before Heidi had a chance to respond to the statement or the embrace, which had equally shocked Anna herself.

Chapter Fourteen

Heidi searched through the movies and box sets that Anna had stored on her TV. She'd cleaned, cooked, shopped, showered, and now, as dusk was settling, her MacBook was on her lap, and she chilled with a movie and some alone time.

She found something easy going, and pressed play. She opened her MacBook and found the manuscripts Dawn had sent her. She swiped through, debating what to choose before changing course and doing something different. Closing the documents, Heidi opened a new word document. Over the last few months, while spending so much time alone, thoughts had been occupying her mind. Deciding to bring them all together, she allowed the words to slowly pour out.

*

Heidi felt and heard a loud grumble in her tummy. It felt like her throat had been cut. "Jesus," she said aloud, noticing the time. She used her finger to scroll to the top. *Wow,* she thought; that was a lot of words. Having become so engrossed in the typing, hours had passed. Dinner time had come and gone, but she couldn't help but smile to herself as she looked down at her computer again. *Right, now dinner needed to be had.* She looked at the TV, realizing the show had long been finished, and was back to its normal blank screen. *She'd not even noticed that.*

133

Grabbing some bits from the fridge, the knock at the door startled her. She stopped still, looking towards it. *Who could it be?* It was after 8:30 and there was nobody around for miles. She was acting like she was the lead in a horror movie. Slowly, Heidi opened the door and looked up to see Jack standing there.

"Um, hi. What are you doing here? Please do not tell me Anna put you up to this. I really don't need babysitting."

Jack sighed heavily. "Heidi, are you always like this? Because I'm really starting to get confused. Anna talks about you and says how cool you are and that you'd never believe you were a Hollywood legend. Then every time I see you, well, you act like a snooty, up your own ass, arrogant cow," he said seriously. "I'm not out for anything Heidi. I love my job and I love Anna. She's a great boss and an even better friend. I'd never do anything to screw her over. She didn't ask me to come around; I was out with the boys. I had to run over to get some cash and I saw these," he said, holding out three newspapers with her and Everett's photo plastered all over them. "Anna said you didn't bother with the press, and given the fact that it's now spouting bullshit about potential legal proceedings, and *now,* ridiculously offering rewards, I thought I should let you know," he said, handing them to her and turning to walk away.

"Jack," Heidi said, grabbing his arm. "Wait."

Jack stopped and turned to face her. "What?"

"I'm sorry I was rude. You're right. I guess if Anna likes and trusts you then I shouldn't doubt her judgement. I shouldn't have been that way. I guess this is all just new to me, and I don't feel like I have control over my life. It's no excuse to be rude to you, but I guess…well, not an excuse, but with all the shit going down, I don't know how to deal with your...the way you are."

"Heidi, I was only ever screwing with you. Anna said that her cousin had seen a picture of me and was badgering you about hitting on me. I'm not gonna lie, I'm a 24-year-old lad—as if I wouldn't be all over that. But if I was making you feel uncomfortable, you could've just said. Or told Anna. I would have stopped winding you up and been courteous," he said.

"I was completely out of line and believe it or not, I never act that way. It's inexcusable, but unfortunately, Anna was right. Dawn did keep going on about it and I guess it just made me feel like I needed to push back. Dawn is the one that gets over one guy by getting under another and I'm just not built that way. Jesus, I'm a middle-aged woman. Why the hell would I feel the need? Don't get me wrong; I was flattered with the attention, but the last thing I need right now is more drama in my life. Dawn thinks a quick lay with a cute, young guy will make everything all better."

"But she hasn't been married for over 10 years and then publicly had her heart broken. She's unable to get over it the way I would, or Anna would, or my mum or sister would," he said.

Heidi looked up at him for the first time properly and saw the sincerity written on his face. "So, you really left your friends on a Saturday night to help me?"

"Yeah," he said shyly. "As I said, Anna's a great boss, and a great friend. Which means *she* likes you, so *I* like you. I got her back, so I now got yours," he smiled widely.

"You fancy coming in and joining me for a drink then?"

"You don't have to do that. I accept your apology, but it's fine. Moving forward, I'll be civil."

"I know I don't have to, but I'd like to. As you say, you're good friends with Anna. She's awesome, and has an awesome sense of judgement, so I'd like to get to know you. And not in a—"

"I got it, I got it," he laughed. "Sure, I'd love to. Do we need booze, or shall I go get some?"

"Nope, we have plenty. Beer or wine? Or spirits?"

"Beer's good. Oh, you were making dinner? You sure you're okay with me being here?"

"Yeah, I got side tracked this afternoon and ended up not eating all day. My tummy was seriously pissed that it had been deprived, so I was just looking for something when you came by. I don't know what to have," she said grabbing the drinks.

"We could order a pizza? They have an awesome place that delivers. If you like them?"

"You didn't eat yet?"

"Well yeah, a bit ago, but look at me," he said, holding his arms out wide and looking down at himself. "I'm a growing lad. I normally get a pizza or a kebab on the way home, but I'll eat now. And you can't beat beer, pizza, and movie night on a Saturday," he said, clapping and rubbing his hands together excitedly.

"Now, I wouldn't have taken *you* for a date boy. I thought you'd be all over the single dude lifestyle, and a free lay every night of the week. You talk like you're ready to settle down," she said, handing him the phone.

"Cheers," he held his beer out to her. "What're you giving me this for? To send a selfie to your hubby?" He winked, holding the phone.

"Backatcha," she hit his bottle with hers. "No, I thought you were ordering me a pizza."

"You? Singular? You not about sharing then, Hollywood?"

"Nope, definitely not. I've had an appallingly bad week with food. Dawn would be on the first flight out and starving my sorry butt if she knew. However, Helen fucked me majorly this morning, and will be back tomorrow for more of the same. So, I figure I can have one last naughty day."

Jack stood there, wide eyed.

"What's up?" she said confused.

"You really have no idea what you just said, do you? Okay, lemme order dinner and then you can tell me about this woman you've been fucking. What do you want on your pizza?"

"What?" she said shocked. "I haven't been fucking a woman, what the hell?"

"You said it," he confirmed. "Pizza?"

"What? *When?*"

"Heidi! PIZZA."

"Sorry. Um, I'm torn between chicken or pepperoni."

"Oh, I thought you were gonna say some shit like Hawaiian, coming from L.A. That rubbish about having healthy stuff on shit food."

"God no. Who the hell puts a pineapple on a pizza?"

"True. Okay, their pepperoni is awesome, but if you like spice then the spicy chicken is good too."

"Great, get them both. We can share," she said happily.

"Girl after my own heart."

"Yes, but unfortunately I am no longer 24 and can't carry it off anymore. I have to work my butt off these days with personal trainers, killing my body each day."

"Ah, so that's what 'Helen fucking with your body this morning' means. There I was expecting a night of sexual revelations of the hottest celeb out there," he winked, speaking into the phone to order their supper.

*

Heidi could see what Anna liked about Jack. She felt bad for giving him such a tough time. Anna was right, he *was* a good guy. He even insisted on buying her dinner to show not all men were assholes. He'd been good company, and he was nothing like what she assumed he'd be. She needed to stop judging people and assuming all guys were the same.

"What did you reckon about my pizzas, then?" he asked.

"Amazing. Seriously, they were to die for. Thanks for this, I've had a brilliant time. Who knew," she winked and punched his arm. "So, we're out of beers. You want some wine, or do you have somewhere to be?"

"Nowhere to be. I'm good here. And before you start, I don't mean like that, but yeah, wine is good."

"I know, I know. Quit it already; we've beaten that idea to death," she laughed. "Red or white?"

"Red, Anna's a major fan of Rioja, so she's bound to have a few stashed away. I'll grab some more for her tomorrow. Do you need any shopping? I can go for you if you like?"

"You're sweet. No, I'm good thanks. I did some earlier today. It's coming Monday evening between six and eight, so Anna will be in. Excellent choice," Heidi said, getting a bottle of red from the cupboard.

"So, can I ask you a serious question?" he said taking the glass. He expertly and maturely sniffed before taking a sip, delighting in the flavor.

"Sure. I can't guarantee I'm going to answer, but go right ahead. Do you know what channel this Heart station is on? We listened to it last night, and they had some awesome songs on there."

"Give it here," he said, switching the station. "Fair comment on the response. What are you gonna do? This prick is offering a reward for anyone that can help him find you. Are you gonna just stay in hiding? And if so, for how long?"

"Good questions. To be honest, I don't know. Dawn called a few days ago and gave me an idea as to what was going on back home, and what they were saying. It's always harder in L.A. as the paps are fricking everywhere, you know?"

"Well no, but if the movies and stories are anything to go by, then yeah I can imagine."

"Unfortunately, it really is the same. So honestly, I don't know. I can't stay here forever; filming will start soon. Honestly, I didn't come to hide from him or the divorce; that was an added benefit. I really couldn't give a dime or dollar to what he's saying. I came here to keep my head down, but not because of him. I came because I can't even take a swim in my pool without the intrusion of helicopters or people sneaking around my property to get dirt on me. Then all of this happened. Dawn is thrilled; not by what he's done, but by the way he's acting because apparently it's working in my favor. This girl was likely to win an award, and they've kinda retracted it. Ev's getting slated because of his actions and because of my low profile everyone seems to feel sorry for me. Dawn thinks it's doing my career great. I don't so much care about that side, but it's her career too. And what I pay her for. I suppose I feel worse for my folks. My dad can't go golfing, my mum can't go grocery shopping…it's all kinda messed up."

"Yeah, I get what you mean about your parents. I'd feel the same if the tables were turned. Dawn seems to know what she's talking about though, which is good. I know you say you don't really give a toss, but ultimately, you're Heidi Spencer-Brady. It's who you are, so you need to make the right choices. Kids, women, people all over the world look up to you. You need to make a positive contribution. Make them realize you don't need to just roll over and accept it. You can make it, *without* a guy on your arm."

"My God, for a 24-year-old, you're wise. Anna said something similar."

"Sensible woman she is," he laughed. "And thanks," he said proudly.

"Yeah, speaking of being a role model, I try not to do the whole *'celebrity'* thing. I never really look at it that way."

"Well you *are*. My niece is 11. She's at that age where she doesn't *quite* like boys yet; thank God—I'll break their necks—but slowly, her friends are getting boyfriends, and the curiosity is creeping in. She brought a teenage boy last week to Sunday lunch. I work seven days a week for Anna, but I always leave early on Sundays. We have a big family afternoon, no exclusions and no excuses," he said proudly.

"Well she had this teenage magazine and you're on the front cover. She's at the age where she thinks she's grown up. She's just started secondary school, and spouts all this stuff about you and Everett. What he's done and how it must be horrific for you, how he's degrading women. We're all like, *what*?!?! But you know, it's impacting her and so many others. Young and old. So, yeah, for me, honestly, the thought of sitting there tomorrow, or next Sunday or the Sunday after that, seeing you and Everett back on the front cover, and Mills thinking that's okay? That's *acceptable*? That someone can treat their partner so horrifically, so disrespectfully? I don't want that for my nieces, my sisters, my mum, or anybody. If you're with the right person, you wouldn't need to do that shit. If they ain't the right person, why go there in the first place? I know it's probably so far detached from the real world—my life," he said distantly. "I guess, it's different for everyone, but for me, that's *not* cool."

Heidi was speechless. For a 24-year-old guy, he couldn't have put it in better terms if he'd tried. He literally stunned her into silence.

"Sorry, I didn't mean to upset you," he said leaning forward and wiping her eye.

"You didn't, Jack. You just surprised the hell out of me. You're right. Everything you say is 100% right. He is making it evidently clear he doesn't want me back, but I wouldn't have gone back anyhow. Like you, I wasn't brought up that way. It isn't the first and it won't be the last, but I do deserve more. Equally, I've never thought of it like that. I shy away. I don't like the whole publicity thing, believe it or not. So I never really thought of..." she stopped considering how to word it. "Well, the impact I may have on people out there. I avoid the tabloids, but I see and hear that I'm in it so often. I guess logically that's because it sells. I sell papers and magazines, but you never really think of who's reading them and why. You see your picture on the TV or in a newspaper, but then you don't think about the rest—what's going on, what people are doing with that, families having dinner together, and talking about it. What they've read. Me. My life. You know?"

"I'm only 24, but I grew up quick. I'm the youngest, but act the oldest. While my friends are out partying at university or just starting their careers, I still live with my mum and my sister. I work seven days a week. I party Saturdays, partly because I know I have a short day Sunday and because I know I have the best hangover cure in the world—my family, the best dinner you'll ever eat, and kids screaming, shouting, and fighting for attention," he said smiling.

"Wow, you're a big time family guy, huh?"

"You bet. And without going on about it, that was my point earlier. I didn't want to make you feel uncomfortable. I was having a laugh, but Anna is my friend *and* my family. Albeit a different type, but she took me in when I needed it. She had faith in me and invested in me. People don't do that shit. People don't care. They have lives, and they don't care what the circumstances are, or what you're going through, or what you need. She did though, and I love her for that. Don't get me wrong, I'll hold my hands up now and say I'm drunk. God, I'm drunk," he said holding his hands up and smirking. "I would love to do shit with you, go back to the boys, and say I banged a Hollywood A-lister. Or that I shagged a 'worldy' like you. Even go to the press and make shit loads of money, and put your idiotic prick of a husband in his place by saying I was dating you whether I was or wasn't. But I have far too much respect for Anna, my job, and you. My job is everything to me. She told me if I went near you, I'd lose my knackers and my job. As hot as you are, I ain't prepared to lose either." He gave her a playful grin.

"She did?"

"Yeah. I think she realized that you aren't ready for it. Maybe like you said, you're not. You aren't Dawn, so you don't need to jump from one to another to make it all okay. I don't know, but I don't want to disrespect my best mate, nor do I want to lose my job."

Heidi held her pinkie out for Jack to take. "You are truly the most wonderful of men. I pinkie promise when all this is done and settled, I'll come see your niece. Whether it's here or at your family's house, I don't know. It depends on how all of it transpires. But I promise, I'll do this for you." She smiled sincerely.

"You're a decent person, Heidi, and as awesome as Anna said you were. Mills would absolutely love that."

"Backatcha kiddo," she said, sighing contentedly and reflecting on how wrong she had been about him.

Chapter Fifteen

Heidi woke to her phone alarm and slammed it off. Jesus, it was like deja vu. She really needed to stop drinking this much. *Christ alive, did Jack drive home?* No, she wouldn't have let him. They do it all the time in L.A. Would she have stopped him? She eased her head off the pillow and looked out the window. *Phew, his car hadn't moved.* Did he stay? Or did he go and come back again? Maybe he got a taxi. Jesus, she was a 41-year-old woman getting so drunk she couldn't even remember basic details.

Heidi felt worse than yesterday. Helen was going to kill her this morning! First off, she needed coffee. She'd run one over to Jack too. That's if, he was at work. *If he wasn't, then Anna was going to kill her*, she pondered.

*

"Good morning!" Helen said handing a fresh OJ to Heidi.

"Wow, I'm getting my dollars' worth, huh? Thanks," she said taking a sip. "This is *the* best hangover cure," she said, enjoying the ice-cold liquid.

"Woah," Helen said, grabbing Heidi by the arm. "You're hungover? Again?" she said seriously.

Heidi could see she wasn't messing. Jesus, she really was taking this whole thing to another level. She straightened her face. "Um no, of course not." She smiled sweetly.

"I know you're paying a load of money, but I'm not going to let all of Troy's hard work be undone. Equally, I don't want my reputation tarnished. Yesterday I went easy on you; today we play ball," she said seriously.

"Um, you are aware that my husband just left me for a child who's having his baby? I think I can justify drinking a little bit more than usual," she said sharply to Helen.

Helen stopped in her tracks, looking up at her.

Bonus, it worked, Heidi thought.

"I'm sorry. You're right. If that's the case, maybe this is too soon."

"No, it isn't," she said quickly, disappointed that Helen had still managed to change it. "It's a pretty shitty time, and I wouldn't normally drink this amount," she said again.

"I get it's a shit thing to go through…" she said considerably. "But don't pull that shit with me. I spoke to Troy last night and he said you'd play the sad victim. Start stretching!" Helen slammed.

"Damn it! Wait, how the hell did you speak to Troy?"

"How many personal trainers called Troy do you think there are that train celebrities in Hollywood?" she said. "Actually, scrap that. Bad example. More than you'd expect. I Googled it and there's pictures of you and him. Jesus, you literally have *no* privacy, do you? Anyway, nice diversion. Stretches," she demanded, switching the music loud enough that even if Heidi screamed she wouldn't have been heard.

*

"How you feeling now?"

"Like I've been run over by a bus. Seriously, did Troy put you up to this?" she asked, unable to get up off the floor.

"He just said that when you have a little break, you find it really tough to get back into it. That you'll try to use bribery, sob stories, and illness. Interestingly, he was spot on. You used all three."

Heidi briefly lifted her head, enough just to give Helen a dirty look. "I don't know what both of your problems are. There's no reason to bully me."

"Really not the case, is it? So, I guess I should go. Same time tomorrow?"

"Yeah, why not? The inside of me has been killed, why not the outer body too?"

"Get a grip girl. Dawn and Troy told me you'd let yourself go with the eating and drinking. Personally, I don't see the difference. But we need to get you back to working out without collapsing on the floor," she said leaning over her.

"Damn it," she said slapping the floor. "Ouch." *This woman was torturing her.*

Heidi attempted to move three times in the last maybe 30, 40 minutes, but she couldn't. This woman enjoyed killing her. *She would be famous for being the woman who killed Heidi Spencer-Brady,* she thought.

"Hiii," she heard in a slow drawl.

"Oh my god, Jack. It's you, thank God," she said, slowly lifting her head a smidge. "You need to come get me. I need you to pick me up and take me to bed. And that's not an offer before you start," she said.

"What the hell did you do? Is this from the booze last night? I figured you celebs with all your free booze and free

146

parties would make you a pro," Jack said leaning over her body.

"It's not even funny. This is not about the drinking. Although, I'm pretty sure I may have made things somewhat worse by the amount we had. She *hates* me. She hates me and I'm sure she wants me dead. She keeps saying I'm outta shape and I let myself go. I mean, *really*? That's just plain mean. Are you going to pick me up already?"

"No. Get a grip. I'm leaving; it's Sunday lunch family time. I'd ask you to join, but I have a somewhat large family, and there's no way we could keep the kids mouths shut," he said sadly.

"Oh, it's okay. I think I may just stay here for a while."

"God, you're such a girl. You're worse than my sisters," he said, picking her up and putting her on the sofa. Jack threw the throw over her and kissed her forehead, saying goodbye.

"Thank you, you're my knight in shining armor!" she shouted as he left.

"Right you have one of two choices, Heidi," she said out loud to the empty house. "You can either stay here and spend all day whining, or get up, shower, and do something," she sighed, picking her body up off the couch.

"Ouch. Ouch. Ouch. Ouch," she said, walking to her room.

Heidi put some lavender stress relief bath bubbles in the tub, allowing it to fill and bubble high. At least she wouldn't have any issues with anyone imposing on her now. She undressed, grabbed her kindle, and lowered herself into the tub. She breathed relief as she stepped in. The next couple of hours were spent blissfully, relaxing and reading in the bath. Opting for a cup of tea to assist in the healing process, she'd refilled the tub three more times, before analyzing how wrinkly she'd become. Albeit far less achy, and dead bodied. She needed to get up, and cook some food. Anna would be home in a few hours. Sure enough, she didn't know if she would want any food, but at least there would be some if she did. She'd been reading a magazine and come across a recipe for some winter favorites and Halloween cupcakes. It made her eager to enjoy some kitchen time before returning to the laptop.

*

Her hangover slowly subsided as she enjoyed some time in the kitchen. She'd made the cupcakes, decorating them with different red icing, as if it was blood, and different Halloween style sprinkles that she'd found in Anna's cupboards. She was as excited as a four-year-old over decorating cupcakes. Dancing around the kitchen, she made her way back to the couch and grabbed her MacBook. The indulging of cake mixture had given her a blast of energy. Perfectly timed, she returned to her word document.

Heidi was excited, picking up from where she'd left off before Jack came over last night. She'd been thinking about it all day, which was weird. It seemed to be taking over her mind. Her thoughts, her *life*. She needed to call Dawn. She'd promised she'd call her tonight, as it was her quietest day. Heidi needed an update on what was happening back home. As Jack highlighted last night, Ev had stupidly put out a reward. S*eriously*? Who the hell did something so ridiculous? *Of course Everett, with his stubbornness and love for young girls,* she thought aggrievedly.

Heidi pushed the thoughts out of her mind and got back to the computer. The soup would be ready soon. She'd spend time on the computer and then make a good old

American grilled cheese and soup dinner. Sighing contentedly, Heidi looked outside watching the chilly air. The low mist, and the wave and fall of the leaves was magical. *God, she missed this.* The opportunity to fully appreciate seasons. No opportunity to go for a swim or have al fresco dining 365 days of the year. *No!* Instead, she wanted barbecues in summer, long walks in fall, listening to the crunch of leaves under your feet, cozy nights in winter with candles on at 5pm, thick fluffy pajamas snuggled with mulled wine and old movies, to the fresh blossom of flowers—the scents and the re-introduction of butterflies. Heidi smiled distantly, reliving her childhood, the times they'd enjoyed as a family, relishing the things she'd so easily forgotten about. She missed them.

Heidi felt the vibration of the alarm going off next to her leg. She'd set it for dinner so that it didn't burn, especially since she was getting so engrossed. Closing the lid, Heidi gave herself a break to have some dinner. She sat at the breakfast bar with her book, thinking she needed to call Troy, and find out what he'd said to her new trainer. *She was demonic today*, she thought as she heard the door open.

"Heeeeyyyy, you're home," she looked at her watch. "And surprisingly early, everything okay?"

"Well I can leave again if you like?" Anna said, smiling. "Smells good in here. You enjoy some alone time?"

"I'm sorry, I didn't mean to be rude," she said embarrassed. "Have you eaten? Do you want something? And no, don't leave."

Anna sat down opposite Heidi. "Ah you missed me," she winked. "I haven't eaten since breakfast, no. Long story, but it's fine. Jack leaves early on Sunday's to spend time with his family, so I just wanna go check on the farm and the animals and then I'll make something. I'll literally be 20 minutes. I'm not properly working, just a check-up." She smiled, eyeing the grilled cheese that Heidi was eating.

"Here, take this half. It'll tie you over," Heidi smiled and handed her half of the sandwich. "Jack left around one-ish," she responded.

"No, don't be sil..." Anna stopped, seeing Heidi's glare. "Thanks. I'll make you some more when I come back. Did Jack come over before he left?"

"Yeah. I think he came by to check I was still alive. I *was* on the floor almost dead. But it was because of my psycho personal trainer this morning as opposed to the booze last night."

"Last night?" Anna questioned. "Who were you boozing with last night? The hot PT or the hot farm hand?" Anna said raising an eyebrow.

"The hot PT? Really? You think she's hot? I don't think I'm going to be able to carry on with her if you keep saying things like this; it makes me uncomfortable," she said cautiously.

"You have an issue with gay people?"

"Hell no. Definitely not. Troy, my PT back home, is gay. I love him and his husband, but as you can imagine, training sessions can quite frequently result in very compromising positions. If that happens while I'm facing her, I'll end up mortified and looking like I do actually fancy her."

"Do you fancy her?" she asked seriously.

"Of course I don't. I'm straight, you fool."

"That doesn't mean anything," she said, walking off and grabbing her bag.

"Of course, it does. It means everything. I'm straight. I don't fancy women. Yes, I can see Helen is incredibly attractive, but I don't fancy her!" she shouted, taking one last bite of the grilled cheese, leaving the food to follow Anna upstairs. *Why was she saying these things?* Heidi thought. More importantly, why was Heidi getting so pissed off about it?

Heidi reached Anna's room and crashed inside without even thinking. She stopped as soon as she'd realized what she'd done.

Anna, topless, spun around as she heard her door fly open.

"Shit, I'm sorry!" *What the hell are you doing,* Heidi thought, rubbing her head. She felt embarrassed as she faced Anna. Anna, who now stood in front of her, in just her jeans and bra. Having a discussion about fancying a woman when you are straight seemed somewhat odd and ironic given the impact a semi-naked Anna had on her at this precise moment.

"It's okay. We're both adults *and* women. Therefore, you have what, 25, 26 years of experience with bras," Anna said pointing to the plain, black t-shirt bra she was wearing. "And like you were saying..." she coughed questionably. "Or shouting, should I say, you don't fancy women because you're straight," Anna said smirking.

God, she was infuriatingly painful, Heidi thought. "Exactly!" she smiled sarcastically and left the room, shutting the door behind her. Heidi cringed. "You idiot, " she said to the wall as she gently head butted it.

"You okay there, Hollywood?" Anna smirked, watching Heidi head butt the wall numerous times.

Heidi jumped back. *Jesus, she just couldn't catch a break from humiliating herself.* Heidi turned on her foot and made her way back downstairs without another word to Anna. She slumped on the couch, head in her hands. She was so goofy. How had she lost all ability to be sociable these days? You'd think the job would mean she'd be an old hand by now, but she just seemed to struggle, in, well, *normal*, social situations. Like this. Refusing to overthink any more than she had, Heidi cleaned up after dinner and decided to take her laptop and some wine to her room.

"Private party?" Anna said, walking past Heidi on the hallway.

She looked up, embarrassed again. She noticed the change in Anna now. Her hair was pulled up into a high ponytail, and she had on a tracksuit. "Um, yes… no," she corrected herself quickly. "Sorry," she sighed.

"What for? You apologize way too much Hollywood. So far you've had nothing to apologize for," she said, gently squeezing her arm, and rushing down the stairs. "I figure the jumping onto the young farm hand didn't work out too well given you're drinking now," she giggled, and before Heidi had a chance to speak, Anna was out the front door.

Heidi walked into her room, sighing. In the five minutes since Anna had gotten back, Heidi shouted at her, and stormed into her bedroom while she was in the middle of changing, thus, imposing on a partially naked Anna in her own home. And *now*, Anna thought she'd slept with Jack! Or at least *tried* to. She supposed she didn't need to say anything about Jack to Anna. It *would* stop her thinking that she fancied Helen. *Why the hell was she so bothered about Anna thinking she fancied Helen*? If she carried on like this there would be stories all over the world that she was homophobic. Heidi looked at the bottle of wine, contemplating whether she really should be drinking again.

Opting not to, she grabbed her MacBook, and got comfortably seated as she continued with her project.

*

Heidi heard a knock at the door. "Yeah?" she said, checking her phone, surprised by the time.

"Hi," Anna walked in holding a glass of wine. "Peace offering?"

"Peace offering? How so?" Heidi said, closing the lid of her computer.

"Oh, sorry. I thought you'd have finished that bottle by now, hence this." She smiled, gesturing to the wine. "I figured, as you've hidden yourself away, that I must've offended you. *Again.* Look, I'm sorry. I know I'm a wind-up merchant. It's sarcasm, or a poor attempt. I'm not very good at the whole sociable thing. The last time I lived with anybody was my parents, so I'm not all that used to it. I thought I was being funny. I certainly didn't mean to offend you though," she said sadly. "I was really looking forward to getting home. This weekend's…just been a bit weird. I apologize. I know you aren't gay. I also know you don't fancy your trainer, *nor* do I think you're homophobic. Sorry," she said shyly, offering the glass of wine to her. "It's colder and fresher."

Heidi watched her demeanor. Why would she think for a second that this was on her? "Thanks. I figured I should probably curb the drinking, given how much I've drank since I got here. Plus, I can't cope with early workouts on a hangover," she mused.

"Still trying to kill you then is she?" Anna laughed, sitting on Heidi's bed.

"Yeah, a lil bit," she rolled her eyes. "I even tried to pull a fast one this morning, and play the 'victim' card, but she saw right through it," she laughed. "Look, you didn't offend me. You've been awesome. Way more than awesome. Amazing."

"Well I wouldn't go quite that far." She smiled softly. "I won't get my big head out the door if you keep telling me I'm amazing. As long as you're okay and I haven't offended you, then I'll let you get on," she said to Heidi, leaving her room.

"Are you done?"

"What?"

"Are you done now? With work?"

"Oh yeah. I was only 20 minutes. I came up because I was concerned you may have been avoiding me. Plus, I missed you…a little. Like a smidge," she smirked.

"You did?" she smiled. "Well, I best come and entertain you for a bit then," she said already feeling a flush. "Sorry you've been alone. You should have come and gotten me; I would've made you some food."

Anna chose to skip over her embarrassment for now. "I managed a long ole' time without you," she winked. "Plus, I didn't want to interrupt you. I didn't know if you were busy or sleeping. Like you keep telling me, you *don't* need babysitting, and neither do I," she said leaving.

"Oh Heid's?" she said, turning back awkwardly.

"Yeah?"

"I hope you don't mind; I stole some of your soup. I hope that's okay. It smelled delicious, and I couldn't help myself."

"How rude. Dinner on you tomorrow, then?" Heidi winked. "Yeah, it's fine. I made something light for the both of us. So…you got any more of that downstairs?" she

said, throwing her eyes to the wine. "Or have you been guzzling in my absence?" she arched a brow and smirked.

"*Cheeky!* You've been drinking me out of my own house," she raised her brows. "Good job. I brought a load more home with me. There's more downstairs, but seriously, don't come down on my account if you have stuff to do," she pointed to her computer. "You really don't need to come down to entertain little old me."

"Ever thought maybe I want to come and entertain you?" Heidi said, cringing instantly as the words left her mouth. *Not again. What the hell was wrong with her*? "Um…that sounded less weird in my head! In other news, I shopped Saturday, so the kitchen will be replenished tomorrow evening." She smiled widely, hoping to move on from the comments.

"You *are* funny. Don't worry Heid's, I didn't think anything of it. I do like watching you squirm though," she said winking, and leaving for real this time.

Heidi fell back on the bed, covering her face with her arms. *What was up with her lately*? This wasn't her. *Why did she keep making such a fool of herself*? She closed her eyes, trying to wash away the stupid comments she kept making. *Did she really want to go down there, and face her after saying that*? Heidi liked her company and had missed her.

Her mind drifted to earlier in Anna's room. Her jeans perfectly fit her tall athletic frame. She had curves as women should, but still a perfectly sculpted midriff with indents from her hips down into her jeans. She thought back to the large rose on her side. It reminded her of the rose in Beauty and the Beast. It was surrounded by foreign writing, and she was curious about what it meant. *Was it Arabic?*

"No, no, no!" Heidi said, sitting up quickly. "What are you doing?" She shook the thoughts anxiously. *Why, oh why are you thinking about this*? *What are you doing? Why are you thinking about her perfect body? And that cute tattoo? Nope, Heidi. No!* She scolded herself once more. *She does not have a perfect body. She does.* She argued with her own thoughts. Clearly farming worked her well. Anna had an enviable body. *Yup, that's it. A perfectly enviable body, with a cute tattoo on the side. Nope, not cute,* she scolded again. *It wasn't cute…it was…*she pondered. *Hmph. no! Yes…yes, it was cute,* she thought, as she imagined tracing her finger around it. Cute in the American way. Cute as in '*oh I love it'* cute. Not like the English cute, like sexy cute. "What the hell are you doing? You're actually insane," she said to the room, suddenly starting to worry about herself. She was literally going crazy. She'd go down and see Anna. Catch up and have a drink. Plus, Anna would need to go to bed soon anyway. *Then she'd call Dawn,* she thought. And Troy, to find out what the hell he'd said to Helen, the destroyer. The *lesbian* destroyer. Why did Anna think she was gay? Was she? Oh who even gave a shit?

Heidi grabbed the bottle and the wine glasses, making her way back downstairs. She walked into the lounge and noticed Anna leisurely sprawled across the couch, watching TV. She was holding a bottle of beer in one hand and playing with a ring on her finger with the other.

"Everything alright? Sorry, I didn't notice you there," Anna said, moving up the couch.

"Hey, no need to move, I'll sit on the floor. I kinda prefer it."

"You sure?"

"Sure am," she said focusing on the TV. Simon Cowell filled the screen. "What're you watching?"

"Just X Factor. Turn it off if you like. I wasn't really watching. It was on in the background," she said thoughtfully.

"Are you okay?"

"Yeah, fine," she said unconvincingly.

"That was an incredibly poor attempt at believability." She looked concerned.

"Ah, of course. Trying to act in front of the best actress in the world," she rolled her eyes. "Seriously, I'm good."

"That's a very big statement I must say. Also, clearly incorrect. But thanks, I guess. P.S. I don't buy it. I consider you a friend and I hope you feel the same, so if you wanna discuss anything, or chat, well, my door's always open. Well *your* door," she raised her eyebrows comically.

Anna laughed. "Well my door is *never* open, but apparently that doesn't matter because you'll just storm in when I'm half naked anyway," she winked at Heidi. "Thank God it wasn't thirty seconds later. I would have been starkers," she feigned shock back to Heidi, who ignored the nervous twitch forming from her words. "You're really easy to embarrass, aren't you? I don't think I've met anyone that goes red as often as you do. Luckily, the L.A. tan hides it. Well, unless you pay close attention." She smiled widely.

"You love it, I see," Heidi said sarcastically. "Embarrassing me, I mean. For the record, had I known you would be getting undressed, I wouldn't have done that. I do apologize. I really shouldn't have done that. Incredibly rude of me," she said seriously.

"God, who cares. We're both big girls. I particularly loved the way you looked traumatized. You clearly forgot whatever you were coming in to rant at me for."

"I did no… hmm," she said thoughtfully. "You're right, I did. *Bloody hell*. Well, it's done, and I can assure you, you didn't insult me. No more barging in, I promise," she held up her hands.

"It's all good. So… I hear Jack stayed over," she said, raising an eyebrow.

"Did he tell you that?" she said surprised.

"No, I don't interrupt him on his family time. We haven't spoken since Friday."

"How the bloody hell did you find that out, then? It's hardly a small village. There's nobody around for bloody miles."

"Maybe I should have said I spoke with him on the phone. He called to revive his amazing night of passionate sex with the world's most beautiful and talented bachelorette," she smirked.

"Full of these compliments tonight, aren't you farm girl?"

"I don't know what you mean, Hollywood," Anna said, keeping a very intent and deep stare on Heidi. "Well, silence speaks volumes."

"Evidently so. I knew it wasn't Jack because after properly getting to know him last night I've come to understand he is incredibly genuine and loyal, and wouldn't have done that. Plus, had it been Jack, he would've said he showed up to forewarn of my idiot husband and his worldwide appeal to find me. We bickered briefly before making up and enjoying a couple of pizzas, and *way* too much booze. He would have also confirmed that even if '*Hollywood,*' as you both seem so intent on referring to me, had even hit on him, he would've ever so politely and gallantly declined on the basis that he has the utmost respect and loyalty to his, um, what did he say?" she considered. "Ah yes, his amazing boss and best friend. And because he doesn't want to lose his job or knackers, which I hear you threatened him with," Heidi said amusedly. "You've got a lil bit of redness going on there, Anna," Heidi said, pointing to the entirety of her face and smirking.

"I didn't say that," she said shyly. "I only said not to go near you, because—"

"Hey, it's fine. It was nice to hear. And what he said about you was super sweet."

"He really said that?" she asked.

"Yup, sure did. My plans for jumping on him are now null and void it seems."

"Not even a snog? Blimey, that must have bloody killed him. Look, I won't stand in the way of a good old-fashioned bonk. I can set that up for you and inform him it's okay," she laughed.

"While I appreciate your countless charity, I am most fine without you telling a child I want to '*bonk*' them," she laughed. "I'm pretty sure it was only our grandparent's generation who would say such things," she said amusedly.

"Well, the offer's there. Happy to assist in getting you laid." She stopped, feeling a flush. "Um…"

"That sounded better in your head, right?" Heidi laughed.

"Yes," she said shyly. "But just so you know, when I stopped by the store to get some booze for us on the way home, I bumped into his mum. She said I'd been misleading her son again. Apparently, he left his mates to come to work, and didn't go home last night. Oh, and the smell of booze today was evident he hadn't been working."

"Ah I see. Yes, it appears to be a common theme recently. However, tomorrow I'm committing myself to a life of 'weekend only drinking.' Especially the way Helen seems to work me. Do *not* say a word," she pointed accusingly to Anna.

Anna held her hands up in defence. "As if I would," she smirked.

"You want a Halloween cupcake?" Heidi said, trying not to pay attention to the dimple in Anna's left cheek.

"You made Halloween cupcakes?"

"No, I nipped to the store to buy them, signed a few thousand autographs, and then came back home to enjoy some rumpy pumpy with the young farmhand," she said sarcastically, as she watched and felt Anna's mouthful of beer come flying back out with a loud raspberry sound.

Heidi amusedly watched Anna try to compose herself and contain her laughter. She seemed mortified from spitting her drink out as embarrassment flooded her face.

"Shit, sorry. That was *very* uncool. I can't believe I just spat on a Hollywood A-lister," she said awkwardly. "Hang on, will I make my millions from that?" She laughed.

"You'd get *good* money from the press."

"Great, lemme do it again," she giggled. "I like the sarcasm though. And yes, I would love a store bought cupcake please," she winked. "I'll have to start a book. Or maybe I should just barge in your room when you're half naked and see if I can get a cheeky photo. I bet I'd make loads more money with that," she mused.

"You wanna see me *naked*?" Heidi said, realizing that she had nowhere to hide after that, and praying that Anna took it in the good humor it was meant. *Oh shoot, silence.* That wasn't good. *Why did she say that?*

Anna didn't know how to respond. She couldn't say what was about to come out of her mouth. *Did Heidi really think that she was serious? There's no way she'd sell shit to the papers.* "Well as I said earlier, we're both women. It ain't like nothing I haven't seen before," she said with a poor attempt at being relaxed.

"I can assure you, after seeing *your* body today, you definitely haven't seen it all before. Jesus, when you see mine…" Heidi stopped. *What the fuck was wrong with her?* She quickly spun around already noticing the slight eyebrow raised on Anna's face. "I'm *so* shit at this. Why do you make me so ridiculously awkward? I don't know what's up with me. Everett has made me into a social car crash. Okay, let's try again. First off, I didn't mean that to sound like there would be a time that you *would* be seeing my body. Second, I didn't mean to imply like I have this phenomenal body and you don't. On the contrary; the point I was trying to make is I work my ass off *all* the time. I must watch what I eat and drink and it's still nowhere near as good as yours. My point was, you haven't seen it all before if you look in the mirror every day and see that," she pointed her finger up and down Anna's body. "If I had your body, I'd be naked all the time." *Okay, so this wasn't weird at all…*

Anna couldn't help but laugh at her. "It's fine, I was intrigued about the '*when*' you see my body. Thought I'd missed something." Anna smirked.

"Oh. I didn't mean tha—"

"I'm kidding, I'm kidding. You could have just been referring to the pool you were getting for me."

"I'm just sloping out of this conversation now. Clearly intoxication causes wider issues for me."

"Come on, I'm playing with you. Besides, you have an incredible body. You talk like you don't, and it's reflective of teenagers. You can totally tell you look after yourself. It's incredible, and if you think otherwise then that's just insane! Anyway, as you say, lets slope out of this conversation. It's all becoming somewhat bizarre," Anna said, smiling slightly.

"Yes, let's. And thank you," she said shyly.

"More than welcome. Now, where's my cupcake?" she asked.

"Oh, making me pay for my keep, huh? You need another beer?"

"Hell yeah. And yes, I wouldn't say no," she said, wiggling her beer bottle.

Heidi handed Anna a beer and a cupcake.

"Mmm, these are good. *So* bad, but so good," she said, indulging in the dessert. "You really are a great cook. That soup was incredible. The only thing missing was the grilled cheese to accompany it."

"You should've said something. I would've made you one."

Anna laughed at Heidi's gesture. "Thanks. That's kind, but I think I've had more than enough rubbish since you've arrived. Like you, I need to start eating healthier. Plus, on a serious note, you're not here on holiday from what I understand, so you really do need to get some work done and stop acting like my personal chef," she said taking another bite. "After tonight obviously."

"Obviously," she smirked. "It's okay, I'm getting loads done during the day. I'm not slacking, so Dawn won't be kicking either of our asses.

"Good, glad to hear it. Although, I'd love to see her try and kick my ass. Anyway, what did you get up to while I was away then? Other than working hard with the hot trainer, and 'cougar-ing' my farm hand."

"You're painful," Heidi said, wondering if Anna was gay, and wondering why it mattered if she liked Helen. "Are you gay?" Heidi blurted out abruptly.

"Excuse me?" Anna scoffed.

"Well, you keep going on about how hot my personal trainer is. I was just wondering if you fancied her yourself? I can set you up if you like?"

"You're an idiot. No, I do not want you to set me up, thank you very much. I do *not* fancy her in any way, shape, or form. I can appreciate a good-looking woman. She's an attractive woman who clearly wants you."

"Why do you keep saying that? I've met her twice. She's probably excited that she's training an actress. People don't seem to get that I'm just a normal woman doing a job. They don't see me as a real person, like this," she pointed to herself. "She's just star struck. I don't think she's gay, and she definitely doesn't fancy me."

"We'll see. So how's it all going with Everett?"

Heidi looked up, noticing the sincerity in Anna's look. "I'm not so sure, actually. Apparently, he's put out a reward, which is why Jack stopped by yesterday. I mean *seriously*? What the hell? Everett's such a jackass. It'll be because he wants to marry her. I don't know, I just find it all very odd. It seems a bit desperate, really. By all accounts, his life and career seem to be getting pulled through the mill a little. He apparently is having a real tough time. I spoke to my lawyer. He called yesterday as he's concerned. His recommendations are to not rush. Everett can serve me; I don't care. I'm out of the public eye, relaxing, and having some fun with a new friend." She smiled softly.

"And they're happy with that? Legally?"

"Yup, they sure are. In fact, he said stay if you can, and keep away from Everett, just to piss him off," she laughed. "I'm wondering if Dawn's been speaking to him."

"I like your lawyer a lot."

"I know right. He's cute too. I could set you up," she winked.

"Please do. We can visit each other alternate weekends," she rolled her eyes. "Seriously though, please, *please,* don't think that there is a shelf life for this offer. I wasn't lying earlier; it's been fun having some company for a change. You can stay here as long as you need to," she said seriously.

"That's kind. You're pretty awesome," Heidi said, reaching up to touch Anna's arm, immediately feeling the warmth and softness of her skin. She pulled away slowly, "I mean that."

"I know," Anna whispered. "Look, it's getting kinda late. I need to be up exceptionally early tomorrow after being away. I should—" Anna coughed a little. "I should probably go to bed." She smiled.

"Yeah, of course. I'm sorry. I keep trying to lead you astray," she said awkwardly, noticing Anna staring at her intently.

Anna went to say something, but stopped. "Goodnight, Heidi."

Heidi watched her leave, confused. *Had she offended her somehow*? She sighed heavily, pouring the last of the wine into her glass. She dialed Dawn's number, waiting for the international dial tone to connect.

"Hey! How *are* you?" I haven't heard anything from you, I was getting worried."

"I'm good, how's everything over there? Did you go and see Margherita?"

"I did. She made me dinner last night. Best enchiladas in L.A. are made in *your* home, you know that, right?"

"I sure do know that." She smiled softly.

"So, how are you?"

"Okay I guess."

Dawn went quiet. "Um Heid's, there's something you should know," Dawn said apprehensively.

"If you're talking about the rewards, I know. Jack came over last night with some British papers. He told me."

"Oh, thank god! Wait, *Jack*? *The* Jack? Farmhand Jack? While my favorite cousin was away? Ohhh, lemme get champers and you can fill me in! Hang on a moment."

"Champagne? It's the middle of the day," she scorned. *Pot, Kettle, Black,* Heidi thought.

"Yes. Tough day. So, where were we… Oh, yeah. *Jack* came over last night? I know Anna was at my uncle's 70th because I've had my Sunday chat with mum, and she said that Anna was there, and looked amazing. She was raving about you. So, you were alone with Jack? He's cute, huh? Did you get laid? *Please*, tell me you got laid. It's been four years. I bet he's huge. Is he huge?"

"I'm afraid not. And what do you mean she was raving about me? Who was? Your mum?"

"Really? He looks big, definitely like he would be well endowed," Dawn said.

"What are you going on about? Who was raving about me?" she asked again.

"You said he wasn't big—"

"Dawn!" she shouted. "I said I didn't sleep with him, not he wasn't big. I have no desire to go there. We're friends. We drank, ate pizza, and gossiped. He's nice. He's *also* a kid. Anyway, what do you mean raving about me? Your mum to Anna?"

"Oh, who gives a shit about that? Anna sat next to Mum and Dad at the table last night and Anna raved about you, saying you're an awesome cook, how you've been feeding her, and bollox. So, you really didn't do *anything*? *Nothing* at all? Nada? Niente? I can't believe that. Or are you just telling me that? You know I'd want *all* the details."

"No, I'm serious, really. Nothing happened! So, what else did your mum say then?" she asked, intrigued what she'd thought.

"Heid's, who cares? Seriously, it doesn't matter. I already know you're awesome. It's why you're my best mate. I want some gossip. I want some pure, exhilarating, *dirty*, porn star sex gossip. *Not* to talk about my cousin, and what she thinks of you!" She sighed. "I suppose if you aren't going to give me anything, we may have a quick stopgap chat. How's it going? Saw Troy last night, and he said you have a trainer. Is she okay? Troy said he spoke to her yesterday and told her all about you and that she could do all sorts."

"God, don't tell Anna that," She snipped in.

"Why, what do you mean? What does it have to do with Anna? She's always been really fit from the farm? Curvy, but fit."

"Women kill for curves like hers. And yes, she's in very good shape. I didn't mean about that. She keeps saying that Helen fancies me. So, if you tell Anna that Troy said Helen can do anything to me, she'll take that as another opportunity," she said laughing.

"*Do* you fancy Helen? Is she cute? What does she look like?"

"*What*? Dawn, what the hell is up with you? Are you kidding me right now?"

"No, why?"

"How long have we been friends?"

"37 years or there about, why?"

"And how many relationships have I had with a woman? How many women have I *slept* with? How many women have I *kissed*?"

"Oh, give it a rest. That means nothing. We are the age of pansexual. Like that even matters."

"What the bloody *hell* is a pansexual?" Heidi scoffed.

"Something about not having to choose, just being with whomever you want to be with, I believe," Dawn said nonchalantly.

"Is that not bisexual?"

"No, it's something different. I'm not quite sure."

"You realize you're not quite sure because we are *not* living in that age. 20-somethings are living in that age, *not* 40-something's."

"You're kidding, right? They covered it in Sex in the City, I'm sure. You know the Lovell's down the street?"

"Yes," she shook her head. *God only knows where this was going*. "Mrs. Lovell slept with Santiago, their pool boy. I think you told me?" Heidi questioned.

"No, that's what I *heard*, but I've since found out that's wrong. Her husband *thought* she was shagging Santiago. Seemingly, he came home and she was all fingers and thumbs, no pun intended, with the tennis coach. The female tennis coaches—they're all lesbians, those tennis people."

"Well, *that* isn't a sweeping statement, is it?"

"For real, it's all over the hills."

"Come *on*."

"No, seriously Heid's, I kid you not. This is authentic."

"So, lemme guess… it was your pedicurist's, brother's, sister's, auntie's, cousin's, dog's, mother who told you?"

"No need to be sarcastic! Anyway, the point I was trying to make is there's no such thing as straight anymore. We live in L. A. We try everything here first. I bet the person to create the word pansexual was from L.A. All I'm saying is, if you aren't going to jump on Jack and the trainer's hot, maybe see what it's like with a girl. In fact—"

"Dawn."

Silence.

"Dawn?"

More silence; she could hear the cogs turning.

"Dawn!" She screamed.

"What?"

"Do not get any ideas."

"About what? I don't know what you mean."

"*Bullshit*. I can hear them turning. Don't think you're going to come up with some weird and wonderful publicity stunt, where my adulterous soon to be, 'daddy husband' has driven me into the arms of my beautiful British personal trainer. The female trainer. That'll suddenly win the world over with a beautiful love story, spiraling the gay community into a whirlwind because the darling Heidi Spencer-Everett is swapping teams. Sides. Whatever the hell you call it," she said turning around at the sound of water running behind her.

"Oh, hey," Heidi said.

"Hey, what?" Dawn quizzed, unsure what was happening at the other end of the phone.

"Not you," Heidi said into the phone, still eyeing Anna cautiously.

"Hi, sorry I didn't mean to interrupt," Anna said apologetically.

"Is that An? Put her on."

"She's in bed." Heidi said.

"What are you doing in her bed? Is it Jack?"

"Seriously, do you come up for air! I'm not in her bed," she said rolling her eyes to Anna who stood looking at her, confused. "She went to bed. She's just come down to grab a soda. So, no, and it's not Jack either," she sighed.

"Cool, put her on real quick."

Heidi mouthed sorry to Anna. "She wants to speak with you."

Anna smiled softly. Anna gently grazed Heidi's hand as she took the phone, ignoring the how the sensation made her feel. Anna needed to park that with everything else from today. It all needed analyzing. *But when she was sober and sensible.*

"Hey cuz! How goes it? Listen, you *know* I love speaking with you, but as you're fully aware, when you start your day, I'm ending mine. I need to be up at four am, so I can't really chat right now. How about I call you back at six tomorrow for a FaceTime date?"

"You know all work and no play makes you a very dull girl."

"Thanks babes," Anna responded.

"No worries. But I'm serious. I'm concerned. You need to get laid."

"I don't need to get laid, but thanks for your concern. I need to sleep. Just like normal people."

"Dude, it can't be far after eight pm. How the fuck do you need to go to bed? Normal people go to bed for sex. 80-year olds go to bed for sleep," Dawn said.

"Okay, well, clearly I'm 80. I'm happy to go to bed for sleep and not sex babes. Sleep tight beautiful."

"You'll shrivel up!" Dawn shouted.

Heidi, who overheard her choice of words, squirmed. She'd never seen Anna look so... disengaged. "When was the last time you did it?"

Anna sighed, rubbing her temple. She loved her cousin, but it was like deja vu every time they spoke. She wasn't in the mood for this right now. "You know how long it's been Dawn—about 20 years; get over it. I'll come over soon, and fuck everything that moves," she sighed. "I need to sleep. I'll pass you back to Heid's. Love you darling, take care," she said, handing the phone back to Heidi.

20 years? 20 years since she last had sex? What the fuck? Surely, that couldn't be right.

"Hey, it's me," Heidi said. "Good night," she said to Anna, watching her hand raise behind her as Anna walked off, not turning back.

"What's up with *her*?" Dawn asked.

"You know I love you, and you're the most amazing friend and agent, but you're an ass at times."

"What the hell does that even mean?"

"You can be so inappropriate. You don't take people's feelings into consideration. You can be *so L.A.* It's taxing, and you know what? If she hasn't had sex for 20 years that's not your, *or* my business, Dawn."

"Well, obviously it's not *your* business? But really who *does* that? Who doesn't get laid for 20 *fucking* years?"

"Dawn stop, she's my friend. I don't feel comfortable having this conversation. Listen, I need to call Troy. He said he has a session in ten minutes, so I'm gonna call him. I'll speak to you tomorrow when Anna calls you."

"Oh, right, okay. See ya then," she said and hung up.

Heidi sighed, replicating Anna's actions and rubbed her temple. Suddenly, her interest in drinking swiftly subsided. She had to be up early, so she gave in, and called Troy from bed instead.

Chapter Sixteen

Heidi woke abruptly, her breathing haphazard at the detailed dream of Anna and her, together. Like together, together. Heidi was confused by the dream, but more importantly by how it made her feel. She adjusted her eyes, checking the time. It was 1:34am. She couldn't stay up, but did she *want* to go back to sleep. It was early evening back home, which meant everyone would be around. She went through her phone register, pressed call, and made her way down to the kitchen.

"*Buenos?*"

"Hola mamacita. Como estas?"

Heidi smiled, listening to the erratic Spanish yelled on the other end of the phone. She suddenly realized how much she missed Margherita. She sent her love and well wishes, and she understood more of the language than she could speak. Heidi waited for her rant to be over before she finally interrupted.

"Are you okay? I miss you," Heidi said sadly.

She could count on one hand the amount of times Margherita had spoken to her in English, and when she did, it was always when she was concerned about her.

"Que pasa, Heidi? What's wrong? You sound sad. Is this friend no nice?"

"Gosh no. *No*. Not at *all*. She's amazing. She's been so accommodating, and friendly, and stuff. I just... oh, I don't know."

"Si, you do. Don't lie to me. I know you better than this. Have you spoken to your parents?"

"No. I should, I know. I just needed to come to terms with some stuff."

"Que?"

"I don't know," she said softly. "I just wanted to say hi. It's the middle of the night here," she said sadly. She didn't know what she was expecting or wanting to say to Margherita, but in the here and now, she wasn't feeling it.

"That's okay, for now. Ti amo. I love you. Heidi, you intelligent. Don't doubt you. Por favor? Follow your heart, chica."

Heidi was unsure why she had said that.

"If you unsure then don't, but you instincts es perfecto. Por favor, follow your heart. I'll be here for always," she said simply.

Heidi listened to the words, wondering what Margherita was trying to say. Wondering *why* she was trying to say it more importantly. *They weren't on the same page.* Geez, Heidi wasn't on the same page with anyone, anywhere; not even in the same book. "I will. Thank you. I love you too. Bye, Margherita," she said hanging up.

Heidi breathed in heavily trying to quiet her weeps as she wiped away a few drops. *What was happening to her? Why did she feel this way, and what had that dream meant?*

Heidi got the hot chocolate out of the cupboard, and switched the kettle on. She broke up some mint aero and dropped it in, distantly watching the bubbles melt away. *Her vice.* The mini marshmallows were the "piece de resistance." She watched them bob away on top. Heidi smiled, thinking back to the numerous times she had made her parents bring out millions of mint aero solely for her hot chocolate concoction. Which of course, they never failed to deliver. It was her mum that used to make it for her and Tony as kids. She thoughtfully ran her thumb around the mug. She recalled the first time she had introduced Margherita to it. She couldn't help but chuckle to herself. It was in her new home and she was unable to sleep. She'd gone to the kitchen in this large house she'd never wanted, and just felt alone. *Afraid, and alone*. Heidi had been 29 years old then, and though she was on every TV screen in the world, she'd always been a closed book, walls built around her. She'd got up that night and made her drink, as the newly hired, tiny, crazed Mexican woman came in blabbering ferociously in Spanish. She swiped everything away from her; she was like the Tasmanian devil.

Heidi finally calmed her down enough to establish that Margherita, dedicated as she is, thought that if Heidi wanted hot cocoa in the middle of the night then Margherita would always get up to do that. They argued into the night about Heidi teaching Margherita how to make it. Heidi thought back to that night; it was probably when she decided that Margherita would be a permanent fixture in her new life in L.A. That night, Margherita told her all about Sophia. She didn't speak a word for two solid hours as this loving woman spoke candidly and proudly about her grandchild. It was also the first time that Margherita openly slated her in a mixture of broken English and Spanish for her choice of drink. Even still, Margherita paid incredible attention to every detail in the mint-mallow process, determined not to let Heidi see that she secretly enjoyed it.

"You couldn't sleep either, huh?" Anna said.

. "Hi," Heidi said, sitting up straight. "Sorry, I didn't mean to wake you," Heidi said concerned.

"You didn't. I haven't slept. My heads a bit of a mess." She smiled sadly. "I figured I'd just get up now. What are you doing up?"

"You can't go out now," Heidi said.

"Calm down, sweets," Anna said, squeezing her hand and looking inquisitively into her drink.

"Sorry," she whispered. "It's mint-mallow. You want some?" She held out her cup as Anna looked at her questioningly, sniffing first and then slowly sipping.

"That's better than it sounds," she said approvingly.

"I'll make you some. Here, sit," she said. Switching the kettle back on and facing Anna, she rested against the cupboards behind her. "Sorry if speaking on the phone woke you; I needed to speak to someone. I should've left it until the morning."

"You called someone at this hour?"

"Yeah, it's tea time back home. I called Margherita. She's like my states mum. As I've mentioned, she's awesome and gets me. I knew she'd talk some sense into me."

"And did she?"

"Huh?" Heidi said, putting the water in the cup and bringing the ingredients to the table. Anna inspected it concisely.

"Did she talk some sense and get through to you?"

"No."

"Oh," she said flatly. "Sorry about that. What *are* you doing?" she said watching Heidi crush a half bar of mint aero and sprinkle it into the cup. "Do they not sell mint hot chocolate in L.A.?"

Heidi looked up seriously. "Not that I've seen. Do they here?"

"Yes," she laughed. "Far easier than this process," she said, playing with her ring.

"You do that a lot," Heidi said, pointing to the ring and passing her the cup.

"Play with my ring?" she smiled. "Yeah, it's a thinking thing. It was my mum's."

"You got a lot on your mind too, huh? That's why Margherita couldn't help. I couldn't talk to her. I don't know what's up with me, but I need to get my shit together. All over a stupid dream too," she rolled her eyes.

"A dream?" Anna quizzed. "And yeah, apparently you're not the only one."

"Yes," she said blowing on her drink and taking a sip. "I had a bad dream and I couldn't get back to sleep. Actually, that's a blatant *lie*. I had a wonderful, yet bizarre dream, but… I don't know how to explain it," she sighed. "I just needed to speak to someone, but then I bailed and couldn't tell her. Do you like the drink?" She smiled softly.

"Yes Heidi, I *love* it," she said, feeling like there was maybe more meaning to the words.

"Why couldn't *you* sleep?" Heidi asked.

"Too much going on in my head I guess," she said, reaching for the cup. Anna stopped as Heidi grabbed her hand, looking up to her.

"I forgot. You can't have mint-mallow without the mallow," she said and dropped some mini marshmallows into Anna's cup. "You wanna talk about it?" she continued.

"Do you?"

Heidi pondered the question. *Did she want to? Did she not want to?* "I had a dream and I guess I just don't know what to do with it," she said seriously.

"Can't beat making a hot chocolate to get over a nightmare, huh?" Anna said, stroking the table considerably.

"True, but I wouldn't necessarily say it was a nightmare. Did you have a rough time back home?" Heidi asked her seriously, raising it for the first time since she came back.

"What makes you say that?"

"You just haven't really been yourself since returning. And not that I'm up now normally, but I'm assuming you don't normally go to work now," she worked her eyes up Anna's bare arms, reaching her eyes. "Something hasn't been right. *You* haven't been right," she said seriously.

Anna sat there silently assessing the information and considered whether she should respond. "I struggle seeing my dad that's all. It was just weird. Maybe too much time to think," she sighed. "You know how Dawn was going on tonight about not sleeping with anybody for 20 years?"

"Well I didn't know if that's exactly what was meant, as I only heard your side."

"I don't blame you for covering, but you don't need to. I heard the remainder of the conversation, Heidi; I was at the top of the stairs. I heard you say to her that you didn't feel comfortable discussing my sex life," she said softly placing her hand on hers. "That meant a lot," she said keeping her hand there. "She's right. I used to date and stuff. I had a couple of boyfriends, but when my mum died, I saw what it did to my dad. He left the farm six days after the funeral. My grandparents, his parents, bought this place when he was four years old. He grew up here. He lived here, saw the rise and fall, and raised his *only* child here. Then the love of his life died here. He couldn't do it anymore. The heartbreak killed him more than anything

177

else had," she stopped, taking a deep breath. "You know how everyone thinks us Brits are negative? That we focus on the negatives? I believe that's true. I wonder what he would've done if I were a child at the time. I was 21, an only child. We were such a close family. My mum died of cancer, and my father had to leave the only home he'd ever known. All the memories they shared together here. After she died, all he saw was pain…sadness…death. He couldn't cope, so he left. He's never been back here since. He loves me; I've never doubted that. But I see sadness in his eyes when he sees me, when he recognizes parts of her in me. It tears me apart, you know?" she said sadly.

Heidi didn't know. Heidi was fortunate enough to not know what she was talking about. She looked down, noticing Anna's hand still on top of her own and turned it over so she could hold it completely. Equally. "I'm so sorry, Anna."

"Don't be. It's life, isn't it?"

"No, it *isn't*. It shouldn't be. I'm sorry that happened to you. I wish I could stop the pain."

Anna smiled slightly. "Thanks, you're lovely."

"Not really. I like you. You've been incredible to me, and I think you deserve the best."

Anna smiled softly, looking down at their hands entwined. Her skin was delicate, and light compared to Heidi's sun kissed skin. "Thank you," she whispered. Anna looked up to Heidi reaching her eyes that nervously eyed their hands. "Tell me about your dream."

She wanted to say so much, but couldn't. "Oh, it doesn't matter," she said shyly.

"That isn't fair. I told you my stuff."

How could she tell her? She thought back to the dream, that body moving towards her, her fingers grazing the rose on her side. Her body was soft, and her hand now, felt exactly as she remembered in her dream. It was so *perfectly* soft in her dream. She wondered if it was really that soft to touch? Anna had been moving towards Heidi, wanting, a look of desire in her eyes, and Heidi seemingly wanted the same. Just as Anna reached her, and grabbed her hands, she woke up. *She bloody woke up.*

Heidi felt flush as she recalled the details. She looked down and noticed they were still holding hands, that Heidi had been gently stroking her skin. *That was awkward.* It was fine when she spoke about her family, but why was Heidi still doing it? Anna must've seen the look, as she slowly untangled her fingers. Anna moved her hand to cover her cup, watching Heidi carefully.

"I had a dream."

"So we established."

Heidi threw her a look of discontent, shaking her head. "I had a dream about something that... I guess, was somewhat inappropriate. I don't know what it meant. Does it mean that there's something wrong with me? Does it mean that subconsciously, I want that? Does it mean...I don't know. What *does* it mean?"

"Do you want to discuss the contents?"

"NO!" Heidi screeched, watching a look of confusion cross Anna's face.

"Did it scare you?" Anna whispered.

"No. Well yes, but it wasn't a nightmare."

"No, not like a nightmare. Like if it was real, it would have scared you?"

"Um, maybe a little. I guess? I just didn't understand where it came from. Mostly, I was disappointed I woke up. That's what scares me the most. I was disappointed I didn't get to see it through, see what happened. Feel it. Does that make sense?"

"Perfectly. Maybe, in that case then, subconsciously you *do* want it. You've buried it deep inside, and don't know how to deal with it. Seemingly, it wants to come out."

Heidi thought about her words considerably.

"You don't want that though?" Anna asked.

Anna's words seemed to have hidden depth. *Could she know what she was talking about?* Heidi thought, suddenly feeling her chest start to close. "I..." Heidi stopped, fearful as she contemplated her response. "I honestly don't know. That's what scares me the most."

"Sometimes, it's good to be a little scared. Sometimes it leads us to some of the most wonderful things."

"Interesting statement after what you've just said."

"Yeah, fair comment," she grabbed Heidi's hand and squeezed a little. "I think you know you want it, but you're just scared after Everett. Don't overthink everything," she said sincerely.

Oh God, she knew. Bugger, she *knew. How mortifying,* she thought. *But she was holding her hand.* "Hmmm, maybe."

"Seriously, don't. Look, it's late. Your time and your drink has made me feel like I could get some sleep. Hopefully, you'll find out what happens next in that dirty dream of yours," she giggled.

"*Wha*...? I didn't say it was dirty!"

"Don't worry, your secret is safe with me," she winked, leaving.

Oh my God, oh my God, oh my God. She needed to leave. This was so embarrassing. But Anna said to go with it. Was she trying to tell her something? Jesus, did Anna want Heidi? Is that why there was all the comments about

Helen? This was humiliating; she was bloody 41. You don't just turn gay at 41. It's a phase.

Heidi laid in bed for about 25 minutes. Her stress levels were worse than the anticipation leading up to auditions and award ceremonies. She closed her eyes, picturing Anna's toned stomach. Those defined lines on her sides. Her arms, holding herself above Heidi's body. *Okay, this was not helping.* Heidi clearly wasn't going to sleep, so she opted for her third call of the day to the states.

"Hey sweetie, what's going on?" Troy asked.

"Can you talk?"

"Yeah, wassup?"

"Oh nothing. Just thought I'd say hi," she said, suddenly unable to follow the verbal trail she'd planned.

"Really?"

"Mhmmm..."

"Doesn't much sound like it. Dawn said you'd be calling; you had a rough time with Helen, huh?" He laughed.

"Um yeah. It was no biggie. I was just wondering what you said to her. She nearly killed me!" she spat, wondering if she could get out what she wanted to say.

"Awh sweetie, if you were nearly killed, it's because you have let yourself go. I told her what she can and can't do. She has my seal of approval. She *knows* her stuff. I said I'd get her a sweet Christmas bonus if she has you back on track by Friday."

"Are you kidding me right now? How the hell are you paying for a Christmas bonus because I'm not!" She slammed.

Troy started to speak and suddenly stopped.

"Lemme guess. Dawn put you up to this, and now you're doing it on behalf of her?" Heidi said annoyed.

"Come on, darling. Disney can't be far off. We can't have you all out of shape. Plus, we have stupid jackasses selling magazines like it's going outta fashion. You need to be on fleek, baby doll."

"I know," she sighed. "I miss you guys."

"We miss you too. Why don't you come home? It's not the same without you. You don't sound so good."

"I'm fine. Pretty sure I've started fancying women, but…" she sighed again. "Aside from that, I'm awesome."

She heard Troy choke. "What the hell? You *do*?"

"Look, I shouldn't have called. It's nearly three am, and I've been drinking all night. I'll call you soon. Ignore what I said; it was a mistake," she said again and hung up, slamming her head back on the pillow. *Damn.* Now she needed to tell Dawn.

She finally admitted defeat and returned to the laptop on her desk.

Chapter Seventeen

"Yes?" Heidi said after hearing a knock on her door.

"Are you okay?" She could see Anna's tall figure with her standard jeans, wellies, and hoodie on. The navy and cream striped bobble hat carefully contained her long, black curls.

"Yes," she said, looking at her watch. "Where are you going now?"

"It's five—work time. I should be the one asking you though."

"I'm good, just couldn't sleep. Figured I'd put my time to use." She smiled softly. "Enjoy your day at work, Anna."

"Will do. Enjoy yours too," she said, leaving her room.

She hated how she kept overthinking everything. This was Ev. *He'd* done this to her, make her feel all weird about everything. She had two hours before Helen came to torture her again, and she was past sleeping. She was engrossed in her writing, and happy to continue.

*

Heidi's workout was way better today. Helen had been a little kinder. Unless Troy was right, and she *was* out of shape. Most likely the latter, especially since the workout was virtually identical to yesterday's. She desperately wanted to tell her that she knew all about the bonus, but knew it would likely offend the girl, or even make her feel like she was abusing their trust. She wondered what amount Dawn had offered.

Chapter Eighteen

Heidi opted for the cowardice approach. Anna returned to her normal finishes this week, and it'd been three days since she last saw her. Still, she continued to make her dinner. Because her training plan meant not eating past 6:30pm, and much lower alcohol consumption, she'd had the perfect excuse to keep cooking for Anna. *Or so she kept telling herself.* It was lame, and very teenage-like, but she was so confused over the situation. She just couldn't face talking about it with her.

It was weird, and a little awkward, and Heidi knew that. She also knew the longer it went on, the harder it was going to be. Tonight was different. Tonight, Anna made another peace offering, which was unfair because it meant Heidi kept making her feel like she'd done something wrong in her own goddamn house. *What was the alternative? Speak to her? 'Hey Anna, so you know how you opened your house to me, well, I know you're straight, but, well I've been dreaming about having sex with you, and I can't stop thinking about running my tongue along your rose... no pun intended. I'm referring to the tattoo, and maybe other places too. Yeah, that'd awesome!* She thought.

She needed to get out, so Anna could get her life back. Tonight, Anna brought her a bowl of ice cream. They'd had a brief and somewhat awkward conversation, but agreed to have dinner and wine on Friday, which of course, already got Heidi excited, yet a little nervous. One thing she knew:

she'd have an awesome day cooking, and majorly impress her.

Chapter Nineteen

The days came and passed, and Heidi seemed to have acquired an addictive personality. She was no longer weekday drinking, but she was also not sleeping and obsessing over work. She was up late into the night, and rising early to get back on to her MacBook. This wasn't out of the ordinary, the late nights and early mornings. It was normally when she was on set shooting a movie, not just when she was at home.

Heidi hadn't stopped thinking about Anna in days, which consequently had transpired in her paying attention to what she wore in the evenings. She tried not to make too much of an effort given they sat indoors, but she found it difficult not to. The dreams were becoming a regular occurrence, albeit she still didn't manage to get to *'the good part,'* and she was unable to detract from inappropriate thoughts occupying her mind. They'd hardly seen each other or *spoke* since Heidi had professed about the dream, and while she didn't go into any level of detail, she couldn't stop thinking that Anna knew the 'straight' movie star was now crushing on her 'straight' housemate. She wanted to try and find out if she was gay. Find out if she knew Heidi appeared to be crushing on her. Find out if she was thinking the same thing. But not too obvious; just enough to say... *What was she talking about? She didn't want to say anything. God, what was she doing? Did she even know?*

*

There was a huge turn in the weather, the temperature dropping loads, which meant Anna worked harder. Heidi decided to go for a winter dish—a lamb hot pot, warm bread and butter, and a nice bottle of red. Heidi showered and changed into some yoga pants, and a racer back vest. It was a 'slumming it' outfit, but it still managed to show just enough. *This was insane. How could this really be happening? Why did she want Anna to be interested in what she was wearing?* Heidi thought walking back downstairs.

"Hi. Oh my word. What is that? I was going to treat you to pizza."

"Oh yeah, so Helen kicks my ass again tomorrow? At least I know this isn't filled with fats, salts, and stuff. Then *I* can kick ass tomorrow," she said.

"You can tell," Anna said, smiling slightly. "Can it wait 20 minutes while I sort myself out?"

"Sure," Heidi smiled, returning to the food. She put the bread in the oven, and put some more fruit into the Spanish sangria. Normally, she made it in the sun so that she could reminisce holidays in Spain with Dawn, but red wine all night just seemed a bit too heavy. You couldn't beat a decent Bordeaux, and a bit of fruit and brandy added in for good measure, with lamb

Soon after, Anna returned. Her long, black curls dampened her bare shoulder as they fell lazily around her vest. Heidi watched as the droplets of water trickled slowly down her freckled shoulders, which she found oddly arousing. *Oh God, please don't be an idiot tonight*, Heidi thought. *Jesus, she felt like a horny, teenage boy. She was a straight woman living with a straight woman, and suddenly having sexual thoughts about her.*

Worlds Apart

*

Heidi poured two glasses of sangria and left the carafe on the table next to them. Laying out the plates of food, she noticed Anna in the corner, smiling slightly at the ensemble.

"Hey, food's up. I poured you some sangria, but if you don't like it I can get you some red."

"No, that's fine. I love it," she said taking an additional sip. "Mmm, especially the authentic stuff. Brandy?" she questioned.

"Of course; it's the most important ingredient, in my opinion. There's not many places outside of Spain and Spanish restaurants that I've found it. I miss vacations in Spain—tapas in beachfront restaurants, watching sundown over the sea as you enjoy the most aromatic, perfect sangria ever," she said reminiscently. "What are you smiling for?" Heidi asked.

"You go so American at times. I just find it odd. It takes me back to us being kids, messing around and…" They both stopped, hearing the door knock.

"Who's that?" Heidi asked concerned.

"Don't worry, nobody knows about you being here," she squeezed her hand.

Anna went to the door and opened it. "Hey, what're you doing here?"

"Shit with the family, shit with the boys. I was kinda hoping you may want another member of the drinking party?" Jack said.

"Heid's, Jack needs some playmates for the night." Anna looked in expectantly.

Heidi couldn't establish if she was happy or sad. The more she drank, the more concerned and afraid she was that

189

she'd try it on with her. If only just to see what it was like to kiss a girl.

"I made plenty of lamb hotpot and fresh bread, if you want to join!" Heidi shouted, handing him a bowl.

"Anyone up for a scary movie?" Anna smiled, holding up some DVD's.

"Hell yeah. What 24-year-old guy wouldn't love watching horror movies with two 'worldies?'"

"What exactly is a 'worldy?'" Heidi asked him seriously.

"It's what the youth of today call someone hot or fit, whatever you wanna call it," Anna confirmed.

"Yeah, what she said," Jack said, taking a huge mouthful of food.

"Right…" Heidi acknowledged the response. She got up and made more drinks as Anna put the first movie on. Setting the carafe and jug close by, she took her seat next to Anna, unsure whether she could be trusted drinking and sitting in such proximity, especially given Jack was there.

As the night progressed, Heidi could feel the brandy and red wine mixture forming in her body, feeling and appreciating the warmth and satisfaction from it. Moving her position to get more comfortable and less cold, she lay her head on Jack's shoulder, and pulled the blanket further around her, accidentally grazing Anna's bare leg underneath it. She noticed the immediate glance from Anna, and Heidi could feel her heart desperately racing. She looked at Anna's lips, and for a split second, wished they were alone so she could lean into them. It was clear she needed to stop drinking, but she couldn't stop the wanting she'd started feeling. Anna eventually looked back to the movie. She pulled her knees up to her chest, and discreetly grazed over Heidi's fingers, her breathing suddenly even more erratic.

Heidi desperately tried to stay awake. She could feel her eyes start to droop, which she wasn't happy about. She felt a hand graze her thigh with a gentle squeeze and it brought her back to life.

"Guys, it's late and I need to be up early, so I'm gonna crash," she heard Anna say.

"What? Why? We have half the movie left," Heidi said pleadingly, noticing Anna's eyes on Heidi's arm around Jack's chest. *Shit, they were l comfortably sprawled across each other and it looked like more than what it was,* she thought sadly.

"I know, but it's late. You guys finish it."

"I promise, I'll be to work on time, sweetie," Jack said, kissing her cheek and sitting back down again. "I'll make sure this one behaves," he smiled, oblivious to Heidi's obvious disappointment.

Heidi sat, unfocused on the movie any longer. Moments later, it happened again. *Was that…Jesus…that was Jack's hand stroking her leg. What the*? She turned to face Jack and the next thing she knew his lips were on hers. Heidi jumped up quickly. "Jesus, what are you doing?" she spat.

"*What?*" Jack rushed backward so fast he fell off the couch, cursing as he did. "What's wrong? She's gone now," he said confused.

"What does *that* have to do with anything?"

"It's okay. She's said it's okay. Anna said you liked me. She likes you so much; she just wants you to be happy. She was concerned I'd get hurt, but I told her I wouldn't. It would be two consensual adults," he said, still completely confused.

S. L. Gape

"She told you I *like* you?" Heidi said flabbergasted.

"Well… yeah," he said, questioning his own response. "Yeah, totally. She said you'd realized you liked me and told her the other day. She said you were unsure, and giving yourself a tough time because of it. You couldn't establish if you wanted to like me or not. She said she wouldn't ordinarily do it, but she really likes you and wants you to be happy. You deserve to be happy. I'm confused, did you not tell her that?" he said anxiously. "Look, I'm really sorry, there's clearly been a misunderstanding. Please don't be mad with her. She got it wrong, I suppose. I… oh it doesn't matter. I don't know what's gone wrong, but I really like you as a friend and don't want to lose that."

"Oh God," she said, holding her head in her hands, sighing heavily.

Anna didn't like her at all. Heidi completely misjudged the situation. "It's okay, it's… it's not your fault. Look, I need to crash. Would you mind?" Heidi said, exhausted and confused by his touches earlier.

"Um yeah, no worries," he smiled softly. "Heidi, I don't know what happened here, and I'm sorry if I fucked up, but please don't make me lose my job," he said worried.

"Don't be silly. Of course you won't. Come here," she said, pulling him into a hug. "It was a misunderstanding. I'm just confused what I've said to her to give her that impression."

Of course Anna didn't want her. She was straight and so was Heidi. Plus, she didn't want a relationship. She'd completely misread everything, her kindness. Jesus, Anna was just thinking she would get her friend a decent lay. Seriously, how had she gotten this so wrong?

*

192

Heidi had been lying awake since 4:20 when she heard Anna get up and get ready for work. She still couldn't believe she'd gotten into this situation. Getting out of bed, she changed into her gym gear and waited for Helen, who always seemed to arrive 15 minutes early. Today, she felt groggy and fuzzy headed. It was going to be a difficult one and Helen was sure to torture her for it.

"Good morning."

"Hi, how are you?"

"Seemingly better than you. Everything okay?"

"Yup, wonderful. Can't wait for my workout," she said, not completely lying.

"Blimey. Do I need to push you harder?"

"Hardly, I'm just feeling muscle strain this morning. I'm ready to work. Should we get started?"

"Are you sure you're okay, Heidi? Is there anything I can do?" Helen grabbed her wrist and looked concernedly into her eyes.

Heidi smiled slightly. "Troy was right; you're super sweet. Thanks, I'm good though. Honestly, I just need to work through some stuff," she said walking away, and starting her stretches.

*

"Hey, hot stuff," Anna said, laughing at Jack. Immediately sensing his low mood, she grabbed his arm and pulled him to look at her. "What's up?" she said concerned. "What happened?"

"Nothing. You got it wrong. She jumped up swearing when I was just…well ya know," he said shyly. "I felt like a right prick, Anna," he said ashamed. "She's right you

193

know. No disrespect, but everyone needs to keep out of her business. I genuinely don't think she wants anything other than to get through her personal issues. Or, at least not me. Dawn's getting in everyone's head and there was no part of her that was on the same wavelength as me when I tried to kiss her."

"What did she say?"

"She was pissed off. What I did was wrong. She's upset, mate. Like, sad. I've been shitting myself all night about coming in to work," he said sadly.

"Jack, don't be daft. It was me that said it. It was a misunderstanding on my part. You won't ever lose your job, Jack, don't worry. I'm sorry mate, I really got it wrong. I don't know…I'm, well, confused," she said, shaking her head. "Look, can you hold up here for a bit? I just wanna go and check on her, explain everything."

*

"Jesus, I think my lungs have spontaneously combust," Heidi said gasping for breath as she lay on the floor.

"You did bloody brilliant, lady," Helen said, holding her hand out and pulling her up with force.

"Thanks. It felt awesome," Heidi said, feeling better already.

"Good. You already look and sound better than you did this morning. You sure everything's okay? I know we haven't known each other for long, but you have a fantastic opportunity to take advantage of that confidentiality agreement. If you want to talk about anything at all, I'm a good listener," she winked, stroking her arm.

"Good thinking," she laughed. "Maybe I should get my money's worth," Heidi winked to Helen, noticing the slight wrinkles of her dark skin around her eyes. She initially thought Helen was around her own age, but looking now, she seemed older, though she still looked good.

"Well this is true. About that, I can't take it all Heidi; it's far too much. I want you to pay what I charge everyone else. I enjoy spending time with you, and you're an excellent student, but I don't want you paying more. I don't care who you are."

"We've already discussed this. I'm happy to pay it."

"It isn't up for discussion," she said sternly. "You're a lovely woman, and I'm not about to take advantage of that. For the record, your husband is a fool. What on earth possessed him to leave such a beautiful and wonderful woman? And no less for a tramp. Imbecile," she confirmed.

"Thanks, Helen. That's kind of you to say, but everything happens for a reason, and I'm not gonna lie, I'm kinda glad it happened. Things change. You grow up. Life changes and stuff. I'll be okay. I've met some wonderful people, and I'm sure I'll meet someone better one day," she said nonchalantly.

"I think so too," Helen said, touching her arm again. "It will be hard at first, and I can't imagine how it is with everything being so public, but you're doing great. You've managed all this, so just take time to explore the possibilities and continue enjoying it. It may happen, it may not, but don't overthink it. Go with it. Enjoy it," she said, forcing Heidi to meet her own eyes.

Heidi took in her words. Helen was right; this is exactly what she needed to do. Granted, last night was a bit of a fiasco. Maybe she needed to come outright to Anna. Tell her it was her that the dream was about. Maybe she'd cook dinner for them tonight and explain why she's been acting weird.

S. L. Gape

"Thanks, Helen. I really mean that," she said sincerely. "You're right. I never take risks. I'm always so worried what might be publicized that I hide from things. But you know what? Life's *too* short. Like you say, it may not happen, but if I don't try, I'll never know."

"*Really?*" Helen said quietly.

Heidi nodded slowly. "Yes," considering the prospect of her plans. "*Really.* Why not take a risk for once? You only live once," she said nervously.

Suddenly, a puckered Helen leaned in towards her. Heidi heard the door unlock at the same time Helen's lips pressed against hers. Turning quickly, she saw Anna's shocked face. She apologized and rushed out.

"*Shit!*" Heidi scolded. *Again? Really?*

"It's okay, I'm sure she won't say anything," Helen leaned in again.

"Woah, *woah.* What are you doing?" Heidi asked confused.

"*What?* What do you mean?" Helen said backing off. "You said you were going to go for it. Cease the moment. Troy said you fancied me," she said, rubbing her temple shyly. "I thought you were talking about ceasing the moment with *me*," she said.

"Troy told you *what?*" *What the hell was happening. More importantly, why the hell did everyone keep telling people she fancied them!?*

"Um, he said you called him, and told him you thought you fancied me. He said you were struggling with it because you were straight, *are* straight. He thought you'd be freaking out, but he tried to tell you not to, and just go with it," she said, reliving the conversation. "I'm sorry Heidi, there's clearly been some confusion. Troy told me all of that, and said that because you were shy I should take

196

charge. He said you'd overthink the 'gay' thing. I thought *that* was the signal—you saying *go for it*. I was just taking the lead." She sat down on the chair. "I never do things like that. I guess... I was just flattered, *surprised*. I knew you wouldn't be around for long, and Troy made it sound like you needed some fun. Jesus, I wasn't going to resist. Look at you. It has nothing to do with the fame, just...well *you're* lovely," she said sadly.

"Helen, you're awesome. I've really enjoyed this last week, and Troy's *right*. You're very cute, and lovely, but I'm afraid he got it wrong. He's misunderstood me. I *am* straight. I'm not ready for anything just yet," she said, wanting to forget everything since that bloody dream. "Troy clearly misunderstood the fun I was having with him and Dawn. Please don't feel that I was laughing at your expense, I never mentioned you and I didn't even know you were gay. They've just been going on and on about having some fun, I thought I'd string them along. I never thought in a million bloody years they'd take it to another level," she said seriously. "I really hope this doesn't impact our relationship?" she questioned sadly.

"I'm surprised you still want that."

"Of course, I do. I genuinely like you," she grabbed her hand. "Just *not* like that."

"I'm sorry for the misunderstanding."

"Me too. Are we still on for tomorrow?" she said softly.

Helen smiled at Heidi, feeling that she was upset. "You really are all that the world portrays you to be. Can't just be an asshole like all the others, eh? Yeah, I'll be back tomorrow. Same time," she said awkwardly and left the house.

"Jesus H. Christ," she said to the room. "*Really*? Really!" Only she could end up in this situation. There were only three people in her life at present. Two of them had kissed her, and neither of them were who she wanted to kiss. *What was she going to do about Anna?* Last night Anna thought she wanted Jack. Today, she'd come home and seen her kissing another woman. Heidi curled up on the sofa, head in hands. H*ow did she really end up here*?

Chapter Twenty

Heidi made dinner for Anna and herself for six pm. When she didn't show, she turned the oven down, and waited until 6:30. A little after seven pm, there was still no sign of her. Plating a small amount for herself, Heidi slowly began forcing the food down, feeling that Anna was purposely avoiding her. *She'd screwed up and didn't want to make a fool of herself any longer*. Grabbing a pen and paper, she quickly scribbled a note for her.

I'm sorry, Anna. I didn't mean to make you feel uncomfortable in your own home. I didn't want to wait up any longer, so I went to bed. There's food in the oven for you, if you want any. -Heidi

Heidi left it at that. There was nothing more she could do at this point. The reality was, she was done. *What the hell was she thinking, anyway?* She was 41 years old. You don't just start fancying women! She was clearly going through a mid-life crisis. Anna's kindness towards her, and the amount of time they'd spent together...clearly she was just a little infatuated by her. She grabbed a bottle of water and returned to the comfortability of her laptop.

*

Anna's avoidance hadn't gone unnoticed to Heidi. It wasn't that they hadn't spoken; when they saw each other, it was polite, civil. The problem was, it should've been like that in the beginning, not the end. The positive thing was that she realized she was just going through a phase. Her life was different to others. Most others have these experiences at college or in their late teens, but she'd led a different life than others. Anna was beautiful, kind, and she'd been a little curious to find out more. The dream was irrelevant, and there was a large gap between *dreaming* with a woman on a sexual level, and *being* with a woman on a sexual level. Unfortunately, it didn't stop the curiosity from increasing exactly the way the dreams were.

Heidi fell into a trap, living her life the way she did the last three years—a house shared by two people who rarely spoke. That wasn't fair to Anna, and if she was honest with herself, it made her feel like shit more than Everett had. She needed to leave Anna's; there was no other way around it. It wasn't even like she had anybody to talk to anymore. Every time she did speak to someone, they misinterpreted it. Heidi needed to get away. Be alone, with *no* stress, and decide what was best to do. Clicking the pen gingerly, she could hear her mother.

"Put it down on paper. The 'goods,' the 'bads,' the 'ugly.' Then surround yourself with positivity and good people, and it will all work itself out," she'd say. In her mother's defence, it usually did the trick. She stopped thoughtfully mid click. *That was it; that was exactly what she needed to do.*

*

A few hours later, Heidi found a cottage, a completely secluded cottage. She'd gotten her parents seal of approval, and booked it. It was perfect. A large holding that occupied game rooms, a gym, *and* an indoor pool. She missed the water so much. While she quite liked the sun—it *was* better living somewhere constantly hot, so she could swim whenever she wanted—it had always been about the water. She could take or leave the weather; Dawn on the other hand loved it. If Heidi had a pool, she had her escape. The water was always somewhere she could gather her thoughts. Her pool back home was her favorite part of the house. The shimmers from the sun dancing over the gentle waves of water always brightened her mood, and that's what she'd be looking forward to the most in the next few days. *That,* and spending some quality time with her parents. Hopefully a couple of days together in private would be exactly what she needed—to enjoy some time in the water with her mum, a few games of pool and darts with her dad, and some late night family cards with them both. Coupled with her mum's home cooked meals, it was her idea of perfection right now.

Chapter Twenty-One

Heidi packed her bag, checking she'd taken everything she needed. Given she'd only taken minimal things to Anna's, she literally didn't know where to start contents wise. Her mum would have anything she'd missed, and she was going to get some swimwear for her too. Having spent some time downloading some music and books, she was practically ready to go. She'd decided that she would go for a couple of days, and then when she returned, contact Dawn and make plans to return to L.A. She couldn't hideout forever.

Anna and Heidi hadn't seen each other the last few days, so she hadn't had an opportunity to tell her she was going away. She didn't want to be rude, given everything Anna had done for her, so she wrote a note informing her she'd be gone for a couple of days. Graham, the driver that had picked her up and brought her to Anna's originally, would pick her up. She couldn't resist getting him, especially since he'd done such a decent job before. Although, as Heidi said to her parents, it was them that were in more need of a driver than her. As soon as they walked out of the house with bags, there's no way they wouldn't be followed.

Heidi walked out of the room, hearing the front door close and footsteps on the stairs. She turned to see Anna half way up them, awkwardly staring at the case Heidi had.

"You're leaving?" she asked, almost a little too accusingly. "Sorry, that was rude. But, you're leaving? And you weren't going to tell me?" she said sadly.

"No. Yes… No…" she shook her head, annoyed at herself. "Not leaving, yet. And yes, I was going to let you know; I wrote you a note." She handed the slip to her. "I'm not going just yet. Just getting away for a few days, sort some stuff out, have some me time really. I'll be out of your hair soon though. Sorry, I…uh…just haven't seen you to tell you," she said, looking away from Anna. "I'll be back Saturday, if that's okay?"

"Heidi, I'm not asking you to leave. I've always said you can stay as long as you like, and I stand by that… I… um…" she stopped, rubbing her head.

Heidi watched her expectantly. "Yes?" she said too eagerly. *Come on Anna, what do you wanna say?* She thought.

"I…" she started, but was suddenly interrupted by the car horn outside. "I'm sorry. You better go. Enjoy your break," she said taking the remainder of the stairs, two at a time. Heidi stared at the emptiness, sighing happily that she was getting some head space and time out.

Heidi pushed it aside. She was going to enjoy this time with her family if it killed her. She opened the door to a welcoming smile. "Good morning Graham, and how are we on this fine, sunny, and wintery day?" She winked.

"Well hello there miss…" he paused, seeing the darting glare she'd given him. He smiled softly before continuing. "I'm very well, Heidi, and yourself?" he nodded, insisting on taking the bag. "Beautiful time of the year, isn't it? My favorite in fact," he said approvingly.

"*Really*? How so?" she said, getting into the car, and waiting for him to get in.

Heidi looked back to the house as the car backed up, noticing Anna staring out the window. She went to wave, but before she lifted her hand, Anna was already gone. She sighed and slumped back into the chair, not realizing that Graham had already continued talking.

"You okay, Heidi?"

"Sorry, Graham. Yes, I'm fine. You were saying? This season?" she smiled politely.

"You sure you're okay?"

"Oh yes, completely."

He nodded thoughtfully. "For me, it's the best. The trees are mostly bare, and there's this low mist everywhere," he said moving his hand out to the scenery in front of them. "Especially round here. It's always sunny, no matter how cold. Faint, bright, ever so bright clouds. I like the shapes they make. I do that with my grandchildren," he smiled, looking back at her in the mirror. There's so many planes high in the sky; it's difficult not to get transfixed on all those people, thousands of feet above, and pondering what they're doing right now or where they're going," he said, stopping momentarily, allowing Heidi to look up and see exactly what he was talking about. She smiled brightly. *He was a lovely man, and it was difficult not to feel that around him*, she thought approvingly.

"It's like a complete hidden beauty round here," she said. "My friend, who I'm staying with, has these huge bi-folding doors all the way across the back, like literally floor to ceiling, wall to wall. You can't help but appreciate it when you have that surrounding you. Fields for miles and miles, and then this beautiful lake at the bottom. It's beautiful and so very peaceful," she said distantly.

"It sure looks like a lovely place. You make sure you appreciate it before you've got to go back across the pond and only have the one season," he said, laughing at his own joke.

He was right. Before long she would be home and have nothing but sun, sun, and more sun. No seasons at all. Though sure enough, the stores still stocked the various seasonal things. Like fall fashion, which normally consisted of slightly longer or thicker tops, and decorations at Christmas. But it wasn't the same. She'd spent the last four Christmas' in L.A. as Everett would never leave. Unfortunately, the kids were starting to grow up, which meant Tony and Meg and her mum and dad didn't want to come over anymore, at least not for Christmas. They knew they were on borrowed time before the kids found out about Santa, so they wanted to let them enjoy it the authentic way—cold, wishing for snow, and many dark nights. Not having steak and ribs on the barbecue, and margaritas in the pool, still applying sun lotion at six pm. It'd been five years since Heidi last went home at Christmas, and that was because Everett was filming on location. Given everything that had happened recently, Heidi already knew she'd be back home for Christmas this year. She wanted to wake up Christmas morning and run to her bedroom window to see if they had a white Christmas. Truth was, down south it was warmer, so it was rare there was ever a white Christmas. They'd see on the news and hear from family and friends that it was or was very close to snowing for them, but rarely they got it. In fact, she could probably count on one hand the number of white Christmases she'd had, but it'd always been part of the fun for kids in the UK.

"Yeah, it is. It *really* is. The whole break has been exactly what I needed," she said, distantly allowing the words to settle, and Graham, the opportunity to notice that Heidi needed time to analyze.

*

Heidi had no idea how long they'd sat there. They were in what looked like a field as she assessed all around her.

"Don't worry, Heidi," he soothed. "We're just at the back of the cottage. See that little gate there. That's the cottage. Your parents are already in, and your mum's pulled your dad to the window three times already to show him the view," he said affectionately. "Very nice place."

"How long have we been here for?" she asked concerned.

"A while. I could see you were deep in thought, and didn't want to disturb you. That can have terrible consequences, so I just appreciated the surroundings myself. I just wish my wife was here to enjoy it too," he responded.

"You should be a therapist," she said. "Would your wife like it here?"

He laughed heartily, "Yes, she'd love it, the same as your mum. She'd be on me to retire somewhere like here. And therapists get paid far too little," he winked.

Heidi laughed at him. "Well, maybe you need to consider retiring to some place like this then."

Graham looked up sincerely. "You're a good girl, Heidi Spencer-Brady, and that surprises me immensely. I'm very happy to have been lucky enough to make your acquaintance. I do have one favor to ask though."

"Sure, what is it?"

"Can I have your autograph? My wife would love it. After I got home from dropping you off last time, she was watching one of your movies. She kept going on and on about you and it killed me. I've never lied to her, not in all the years we've been together. That's the only night in my life that I despaired going to bed with her," he said sadly.

"Why the hell did you lie to her? I don't agree with that Graham. You tell her, you tell her you were my driver. I know she wouldn't say anything about where we went," she said. "You tell her tonight, okay?" she said, writing on a sheet of paper, and handing it to Graham.

"May I?" he asked sincerely, referring to the letter. It read:

Mrs. Clarke, you have the most fabulous husband. He talks of you a lot, and I can't wait to meet you. If you want anything at all, your husband has my number. All my love, Heidi Spencer-Brady xx

"You are too much Miss Spencer-Brady," he said with a slight water to his eye.

"Only for the good ones I meet. You have fun, I'll see you in two days?"

"You will," he said, nodding his head softly, giving her the suitcase.

"Wow, you're giving me the case to carry myself?" she smirked.

"You're a strong, independent, and impeccable, young lady. Plus, I thought we'd compromise," he winked.

"I knew there was a reason I liked you," she said squeezing his hand ever so gently. "See you soon."

*

"Hi, Mum, Dad. I'm here," she said, walking through the back door. She was bombarded by her parents.

They gave her the obligatory, '*how are you, you look fab, we've missed you.*'

"I'm fine, thank you. I've missed you too, yadda yadda yadda," she said, kissing both of her parents. "So, how's things? And what's the plan?"

"Well, your mum wants to catch up with you, of course. I said you'd need some time to relax. We've just been admiring the view and waiting for you to arrive."

"Yes. Graham said you'd been ogling it."

"Whose Graham?" her mum asked.

"My driver."

"Graham, hmmm," her mum smirked. "I have the best surprise for you."

"Oh yeah, what?"

"You won't *believe* it. She hasn't stopped going on about it since last night," her dad said. "I'll take this to your room, Heid's."

"Sure, thanks Dad. What is it?" She looked at her mum confused.

"Come here," she said opening the fridge to several containers. "Turn around."

"What?"

"Turn around so I can do this without you seeing."

Heidi did as she was told until her mum said she could turn back around.

"Here, look," she said.

"Oh my god, this smells fantastic," Heidi said to the number of spices heightening her senses. "You made me my favorite!"

"Of course I didn't; I couldn't make *that*. I spoke to your restaurant manager friend, and explained that you were in hiding, that I was seeing you. I asked if I could get a takeout that would hold until I saw you. He said the girls were still going on about you and even bringing people into the restaurant in hopes they'd see you. Apparently, the least he could do was give you a good going's worth. He gave it to me fresh and uncooked and even gave me cooking instructions for our normal ovens instead of those Indian ones," she said proudly.

"Tandoors."

"Excuse me?"

"The Indian ones. The ovens are called tandoors or tandoori ovens. Mum, this is incredible, honestly. How did you get there though? Isn't it 40 minutes away?"

"How the bloody hell do you think?" Her dad strolled in rolling his eyes. "I had to take her. Want a beer love?"

"Oh dear." Heidi winked. "Yes please," she said to her father. "Mum, you're the best. Thanks so much."

"Well, I'm glad you like it. Thought maybe we could have a bit of magazine and pool time, then we could have the Indian for dinner this evening.

"That sounds great mum, I'll get changed," she said, already feeling more relaxed being here with her parents.

Chapter Twenty-Two

"So, have you decided what you're going to do yet?"

"About what?" Anna said.

"What do you think? About Heid's?" Jack responded, taking more pizza from the box.

"What can I do? She was never permanently living here. If she wants to go now, then that's her prerogative. I don't know what you're asking."

"Well, she's our friend. She ain't ready to go back yet. You thought she told you she wanted me, then she's kissing women…she *clearly* ain't ready."

"Jack, do you know how long she's been married to Everett?"

"Um no. I don't read and watch shit about celebrities. Why, what's that got to do with anything?"

"Everything. She was with him for like 10 or 11 years, I believe. You think if your wife for that length of time had cheated on you, you would be this chill? Maybe she wasn't *married*, married. How do know she wasn't always gay, and just didn't want to come out in Hollywood? Everyone's got a view. What if her marriage was a farce, which is why she isn't bothered. Now she's met Helen, they both like each other, and she's found what she's looking for. She's probably taken her away for a couple of days. She said alone time. Maybe it's just those two, relaxing, away from prying eyes. It all makes sense."

"Apart from one thing."

"What?"

"What the hell was the letter to you saying it wasn't what it looked like?"

"Privacy. Denying it so nobody ever finds out."

"I don't buy it, but what do I know? I'm a dumb kid," he said, downing the last of his beer.

"You okay? What's *that* about?"

"Yeah, I'm fine. I just...I don't know. None of it makes sense. She seemed upset. The note..." he shrugged.

"Well, she isn't going to say, 'oh I'm dating a woman,' or 'I'm gay' to me. She doesn't know me, does she?"

"She knows you well enough to come and hide here. She knows you well enough to stay up late drinking with you every night. She knows you well enough to cook for you. As I said, what do *I* know? I'll get off babes, we've got a long ass couple of days ahead of us," he said, getting up to leave.

"No worries, buddy. I'll see you in the morning," she said, waving goodbye and shutting the door behind her. Anna rested her head against the back of the door. *Was he right? Did she have this all wrong?* She couldn't get away from the gut wrenching feeling in the pit of her stomach when she saw Heidi with the case that morning. Or the sadness in her eyes when Anna ran off from her. Anna hadn't wanted Heidi to see that she was hurt or upset. She thought back to earlier, watching as she left; Anna felt bad for walking away without a wave or smile; it would have made Heidi feel so uncomfortable when she had nowhere else to go or nobody to turn to. *Except for Helen's,* she thought immaturely. The amount of money she was making off Heidi... She must have some decent place to live. *What was she doing? It wasn't Helen's fault.* The problem was with her. She *didn't* want Heidi to leave. She wanted her here; albeit, she was terrified of why she wanted that, and

S. L. Gape

the consequences of telling her. She wanted it to be like it was before, having fun, and staying up, drinking and eating dinner together. "*No!*" she said sternly to the room.

Anna knew she was in trouble; she was lying to her best friend, her family. She was still kicking herself over the incessant waffling, the compliments she'd given Heidi to her aunt and uncle. Dear God, she hoped they hadn't thought anything of it and told Dawn. Dawn would have totally told Heidi. Then of course there was the night of the dream—Heidi telling her about what she thought had been about Jack, the sincerity and compassion in Heidi's eyes when Anna spoke of her mum, the feeling of her hand in her own. She didn't understand why she relished and thought about those moments. *She was a woman.* But she'd since realized that ever since that night, every turn in her day to day life resulted in a flash of those images. Anna couldn't remember the last time she'd had feelings for somebody; it was at least 20 years ago. When her mum died, she knew she had to break it off before she completely fell in love with the guy. She didn't want to lose a love like her father had. Since then, she'd had a couple dates to satisfy her friends, but there wasn't anybody who she'd *wanted*, or *desired*. Certainly not like this. *This wasn't good...so wasn't good*, she thought.

Chapter Twenty-Three

Heidi had a fantastic couple of days with her parents. They ate the Indian last night and stayed up late playing cards. Today was spent lazing by the pool, enjoying three lots of 50 laps and cocktails with her mum before her mum disappeared to cook the mandatory family roast they'd share together tonight. She wasn't going to contest that; her mum made the finest roast. As she cooked dinner, Heidi and her father enjoyed a few beers and shot some pool in the games room. It had been a perfect couple of days together, and she was so glad they'd done it. Just the simplicity of playing pool with her dad while her mum cooked a roast was enough to rejuvenate her. Granted, not in their own home, but still, she wouldn't change any part of this for the world.

*

The dinner was fantastic, and in true fashion, her dad was sleeping on the couch. Heidi cleaned after her mum had cooked and now they enjoyed another bottle of prosecco by the pool.

"Did you know you've always had this incredible fascination with swimming pools? Since you were yay high," her mum said, holding her hand up around knee height.

"For real?"

"Mhmm. More than performing. We took you to a waterpark on holiday in Tenerife once when you were maybe four or five. You kept forcing your father to go on this incredibly high ride. He hated it, but he must have done it five times. I said to him, why do you keep doing this when you're so afraid? He was a proud man. I'd never seen him show fear before, not really. By gosh it was this tall, straight thing. It was obscene," she said smiling thoughtfully.

"So why did he keep doing it then?"

She smiled to her daughter softly. "He said you were so upset that you weren't tall enough to go on, and that no matter how scared he was for those 10 seconds, landing at the bottom, seeing you scream with laughter, and jump up and down with your big dimples was worth it. It would stay with him forever."

"Oh my god, *mum*, you're making me cry," she said wiping her eyes.

"Sorry darling, that wasn't my intention. The point was, you always lit up around water. It was like you had this weird connection that we never understood. That's why your father kept doing it," she paused. "That same day, we wandered around, and you spotted a lifeguard by one of those wavy machine pools. You quite confidently walked over, as you liked to do despite us frequently explaining you couldn't just wander off. You stood next to her proudly, looking up, and waited for her to notice you. She was so nice and luckily spoke perfect English. You asked her to explain what she was doing. The girl was very good with you, and you literally shook her hand and wandered off once again," she sighed, laughing. "Leaving us to thank her and chase after you. At lunch, you said that you thought the girl was very pretty, and that she had a nice swimsuit.

You asked if we knew she got to watch water all day, and help people if they got into trouble. You were so very innocent. It was at that point you simply told us, when you grew up you wanted to be a 'leaf' guard. We couldn't help but laugh, as you'd pronounced it the way the young, Spanish lifeguard had. You were so adamant and sincere," her mum said, looking over toward the water. "I never understood it. We didn't have that same love and passion for it as you did," she said thoughtfully. "You see, when you see the love your child has for something, you want to help them achieve that. You want to see that love shine through, that smile on their face forever."

"I can't believe I never knew any of that," she said reflectively.

"I've never seen you have that smile with Everett. I don't want to damn, or demean your relationship, darling, but I haven't. A parent wants the best for their children. And, well…Heidi, this entire break all you've done is speak of Anna. Every time you speak of her, your smile lights up the room. I love that someone could do that for one of my children. You've discussed everything, from her hard work and dedication, to her hospitality, and I don't even know if you realized it. You even complimented her dinner over mine, which has never happened," she said smiling. "I'm glad we've seen you Heid's. I was so worried, but you seem good, so I'm happy."

"Um, I didn't realize I'd spoken about her so much," she said shyly, wondering what her mother was getting at. "I'm good though, don't worry. I've had a good opportunity to reflect and assess it all. I feel better for it. Don't get me wrong, I'm still pissed with him, and I'm still gonna drag it out a little, but ultimately, I've established that I'm better off without him, you know?"

S. L. Gape

"Yes, I do and I'm glad you've realized that. You were and still are worth 10 of him. I hope you know that. The most important thing to your father and I is your happiness. We don't care what happens or what you decide, but just know we love you and will stand by you, regardless."

"Mum, what's up? You're talking like something's going on. Are you and Dad okay? The kids? Tone, Meg…"

"Calm down, everything's fine. But…while I wish it would have been under different circumstances, because we'd never want to see our children in pain, the one good thing to come out of Everett's actions is that we are able to do this. We never get to do this. I'm just happy for that fact. Sorry, darling. I didn't mean to concern you. I suppose it's just the bubbles talking." She smiled, taking her daughters hand and squeezing it slightly.

They sat there in silence for a while, each watching the lights reflecting off the ripples in the swimming pool. "It's a bit eerie actually, isn't it? I mean, being hidden away in the dark with nothing for miles. We can't even see beyond this room," Heidi said to her mum.

"Well it wasn't, no," she laughed, rolling her eyes at her daughter. "Are you falling in love with Anna?"

Heidi threw herself up off the lounger, throwing the entire glass of prosecco into the pool. "*What?* Where the bloody hell did *that* come from?"

"I was just asking," she said nonchalantly.

"*Mum*, you *don't* ask your 41-year-old straight, married daughter if she's suddenly gay. It must have come from somewhere."

"I didn't say you were gay."

"Well, you asked if I loved a woman. That, to me, says gay."

"Hardly darling, you're the era of the pansexual. It doesn't really work like that these days."

"How the bloody hell do you know what the pansexual age is?" Heidi asked flabbergasted.

"Oh, everyone knows. It's covered in the soaps and press. It's all the rage. Youngsters these days are too liberated to pick a side, so they 'love who they love and don't need to label themselves.' Good for them I say. It's nice that the world is evolving. And for the record, I'm not just saying that to get you to admit you're in love with a woman. I'm just merely stating the obvious."

"Mum, will you please cut it out with the 'being in love with a woman' thing?" she said abruptly.

"Of course, darling." She got up and walked out of the pool room.

"For God's sake, really? *Really*. The silent treatment?" She sighed. *Why the hell had she said that?*

A short while later, Heidi's mum returned with another bottle of prosecco, as Heidi watched her peeling the top away. "You think we need more?" Heidi asked.

"Yes," she said simply. "Not facing the truth will only cause further stress in your life, so maybe a fourth bottle will get you drunk enough to tell me the truth."

"The truth about what?"

"Anna," her mum smirked, slipped her house shoes off, and leaned back down into the lounger with a Cheshire grin on her face.

"Seriously, *where* has this come from? Have you read something about pansexualism or something? Or is one of the bridge women's daughters *it*, whatever you call them, and you want me to be one too so that you can talk about it?"

"Pansexuals," she said simply.

"What?"

"Pansexual. That's what you call them. You asked what they were called."

"Are you just purposely trying to annoy me?"

"No. I just don't think pansexualism is a word, and was clearing up what they were called. I'm not trying to annoy you, just make you see you're developing feelings for another woman. A woman that seems beautiful inside and out."

"How do you know she's beautiful? You don't know what she looks like."

"I saw a picture last week at bingo. Very beautiful smile. Big and dimply, just like yours," she said confused. "And those thick, dark curls… she's very beautiful," she repeated.

"Oh my god. You've gone stark raving mad. Do you *want* me to be a lesbian, so you can impress people at bridge or bingo?"

"Oh dear…" a gruff voice said. "I'll go back to sleep then," her dad said, walking in and straight back out again.

"No… Dad. *Dad!* Come here. Your wife is insane!" She shouted, feeling the effects of the alcohol.

"I told you all that donkey years ago. I'm going to watch football."

"I'm quite sure there's no football on darling!" her mum shouted.

"You know, calling your mother insane when she's fully accepting of your new lifestyle choice is really quite rude. I mean, I'm *just* saying."

"Mum, for God's sake. Why do you keep going on about this? I'm *not* a lesbian."

"Again, I never said you were. I asked if you were falling in love with Anna."

Heidi sighed defeated. "Okay, tell me your explanation, your reasoning. Why I've allegedly hit a midlife crisis and turned gay."

"You really did choose the right career, Heidi; you're *ever* so dramatic."

"Whatever. Come on, enlighten me," Heidi waited as the silence filled the air. She turned around to question her mum and saw the serious and contented look on her face. She opted to give her the space and privacy to continue with her thoughts.

"I know you've never really touched on kids. Truth be told, I don't know whether you do or don't want them. But, as a parent, you cherish the unimportant things that make your children happy, like your father and the waterslide. When you see your child talking about performing from five years old and coming home and telling you they have the lead in the Christmas Nativity, and then the lead in their high school production, the smile and enthusiasm when they get a lead character in a soap they'd spent years watching as a family, all the way to the call where suddenly, they've been chosen as a Hollywood lead—any parent would be proud. And achieving their lifelong dreams? That's just something else. Do you know the most heart-breaking thing in the world is finding out your child is leaving? Not just leaving home, but leaving the country, to go across the world. Gosh, it's demonstrably soul destroying. Do you know the one thing that gets you through it?"

Heidi was undoubtedly confused. "Um...being with someone so you aren't alone?" she asked completely confused now.

Her mum put her hand on Heidi's. "No, but close." She smiled. "Seeing *that* smile, the smile that lights up your entire world. How can you be so selfish to begrudge the love of your life their only dream? My point is Heidi, when you meet a person's partner...sorry, husband, and that smile isn't there, or it isn't like the dream they had, or the smile you know you yourself have, you question where it is. Why isn't it there? Yes, there's a smile, a great big, wondrous smile. A happy smile. But not an *'I'm suddenly a Hollywood movie star'* smile. Fast forward many years later, and after a brutally, public breakup, one of which, I wouldn't wish on my own worst enemy..." she stopped momentarily. "My point is Heidi, as a parent, you'd do anything for your child. *Anything.* When you see your child sad and hurt, the real heartbreaker is that you lead different lives. You don't quite know how to interact with the worldwide superstar that fills everyone's homes, and only our hearts. You don't know how to broach that heart-breaking time with them," she said considerably.

Heidi looked away as the tears fell. *How did she not know this? How did she make her mum feel so inadequate?*

"Sorry darling, too much prosecco. I don't want to make this a negative thing. It's far from it. I saw you marry Everett, love him, but that smile was never lit. It is now Heidi. Now, you're beaming. You're filling the house with the smile that lit up our lives, that lights up the world. I know you, Heidi. I've watched you consider the water again, and I'm taken back to your childhood," she stopped and considered her next words. "Heidi, the extremely long-winded explanation is your career and your love for water are the two things that have always lit your eyes up. Those are the only two things I can recall making that happen, until this break. Throughout this break, speaking of Anna has done the same thing to you. Every time you speak of Anna, your face lights up. Your face lights up Heidi like

I've only ever seen it light up with pools, acting, and your family. So yes, I would bet all our money *and* all your money on the fact you've fallen in love with her. I know it's not easy, but it is what it is. Yes, you've always been giddy with Dawn; I've watched it for 35 years now, but you're not giddy with Dawn like you're giddy about Anna," she stopped. "Look, you're a big girl now. We love you no matter what, and all we want is to see you with that smile that lights up our world every moment of every day," she finished. "If she does this to you, then why reject it? Why fight it? Why not see what happens? It may be nothing. You may kiss her and realize you really don't like it. But maybe, just maybe, that smile will grow and continue to get bigger and wider, and that little fizz right in here," she touched her tummy. "Will get more powerful and more exciting. You deserve to be happy honey, more than anybody. If Anna is the one to do that, then what the hell are you fighting it for?"

"Mum, you don't just turn gay at 41."

"Why are you so insistent on labeling this?"

"Because you have to. I live in a world where it's nothing *but* labels, and judgment. Can you imagine this coming out? And no jokes, please," she said solemnly.

"Okay, I don't understand your life. I hate the impact it has on us. Think of it from another approach. Forget about the people that judge. You are a huge inspiration to so many people all over the world. Think about the people too afraid to be who they really are because of religion, culture, or their country. Children who go to school and feel their lives spiraling out of control because while all their friends are talking about the opposite sex, they don't feel that way. How about you forget about the judges right now, those people who write things about you or slate you because

S. L. Gape

you're in hiding. What are they worth anyway? What about the people who idolize you? The people that see the little girl from just outside London who made it all the way to Hollywood and fought for love. They were prepared to openly love and cherish her, regardless of gender, sexual orientation, or publicity. Why not think about that, and ignore the nonsensical and bigoted people who feed off judging?"

"For an old gal, you're quite sensible."

"Charming. I am *not* old," she looked at her smiling daughter and took her hand.

Heidi lifted her knees up to her chest. "So, what if she doesn't like me back?" she said in a small voice.

"And what if she does?"

Heidi sighed heavily. "Why are you so positive about this? You're forgetting one, tremendous detail."

"Go on."

"Anna's straight."

"But you keep telling me the same. Plus, from what I hear, you don't talk about someone as much as she did at Brian's if there's not more to it," she said simply. "Heidi, you've always been incredibly analytical and sensible. You wouldn't have fallen in love with somebody if you hadn't picked up on some mutual interest, at least not somebody of the same sex."

"Well I wasn't sensible with Everett. I think you have far too much faith in me."

"Darling, this wasn't a short-term thing. You were together for 12 years. Unfortunately, sometimes people grow apart. You both have difficult lives, and to add to what I said before, you never had that fire in your belly with him."

"You're such a romantic, mum."

Worlds Apart

"No, darling, I'm just lucky enough to have met the person that puts a fire in my belly. I want my children to experience that first hand."

"Okay, so what if you're right? Then what do I do?"

"You go back, tell her how you feel, and see what happens."

"What if it's all perfect and hearts and flowers, and then I have to leave?"

"What if it isn't all hearts and flowers? What if she isn't the one? What if she is and moves to the states? What if you decided to move back home? Heidi, stop going over the *'what ifs,'* and just take it one step at a time."

"But I'm scared, Mum."

"That's the beauty of it, my darling."

Heidi didn't understand what her mum meant, but after copious amounts of alcohol she was feeling a surge in her tummy. For now, she just wanted to digest it.

"You girls stop arguing yet?" her dad asked.

"We weren't arguing. We think maybe your daughter is a lesbian."

"Mum!" she shouted.

"*What*?! I was only asleep for an hour," her father said confused, listening to his wife and daughter laugh heartily.

223

Chapter Twenty-Four

Heidi arrived back to Anna's feeling positively refreshed and relaxed. She had a great couple of days with her folks, and fun with Graham on the ride home. She decided to sort it all out, and tell Anna she wasn't interested in Jack or Helen. She wanted to make her feelings perfectly clear, and then the ball was in her court.

She got the keys out, waving goodbye to Graham, and heard a car coming up the drive. She rushed in the house and quickly went to the window to look at the car. There was a girl in the driver's side, Anna in the passenger seat. Heidi watched as they kissed briefly on the lips. Anna stepped out of the car. *Who was she, and why was Anna kissing her on the mouth?* She thought dejectedly.

Heidi felt her stomach drop. She grabbed her case and made her way back upstairs to her room before closing the door behind her. She couldn't get the thoughts out of her mind. *Anna said she was straight, but straight girls didn't kiss on the lips like that. Could she be a friend?*

Anna walked indoors and looked around for any sign of Heidi. She didn't even know what time she was due home, just that it'd be today. She needed to get her head together. She threw on her work clothes, and thoughtfully walked out into the chilly air looking for Jack. Christmas was fast approaching, and it was one of her favorite seasons. Pushing her chin deep into her jacket, her hands in her pockets, she enjoyed the crisp air and views around her. Anna thought back to last night with Julie. What was she going to do? *Did she listen to Julie, and declare her undying love for Heidi? Maybe that was overexaggerating, but she certainly seemed to be attracted to the woman. Or should she just ignore it and avoid her? She would be leaving soon. Then she didn't have to worry about getting hurt,* she thought.

"Hey boss, rough night?"

"Me? As if." She winked.

"Is Hollywood back yet? How's Jules, ready for a decent lay yet?"

"You are relentless. No, she isn't, and yeah, Jules is good. Kids are good. They kept me on my toes. How are the animals doing? How was everything yesterday?"

"All good. We may need to keep an eye on Charlie though. He was quite lazy yesterday, and has been this morning. I don't think he's feeling too well."

"*What*? Charlie? What's up with him?" she said anxiously.

"Don't panic. I'm sure he's just cold and tired as winter's coming. He's an old boy now, An." He squeezed her shoulder.

"You got it here? I need to go check on him."

"Sure boss," he said, turning back to work. "Oh, I made some more cheese yesterday. I'll get it ready and drop it off to the market tomorrow when I leave!" he shouted after her.

"Cheers," she said leaving and rushing to the stables.

"Hey baby boy, are you feeling sick?" she said making her way inside and stroking his mane. She noticed the small neigh he made; he was out of sorts. She'd never heard a low, sad neigh, not in 31 years. Anna stayed with him for a while. *He wasn't right*, she thought. Did she need to call Karen? She decided to work for a couple of hours, and later, pop back and check on him. If he was no better, she would ask Karen to come out.

Chapter Twenty-Five

Heidi woke up with a fright, unsure of the noise that had woken her. Adjusting her eyes, she nervously questioned what the noise might've been. Her phone told her it was one am. Maybe she'd been dreaming, or…*Shit, there it was again*. Heidi couldn't control her breathing. She didn't know if she was imaging in it or not. It sounded like an evil laugh from a scary movie.

There it was again. She screamed, hiding under the comforter, and covering her ears. *What was happening? Was the place haunted? And if so, why were the ghosts laughing at her*? The cackle sounded again. She was scared now, she didn't know what to do.

"I'm not going to die here like this," she said, rushing up and ignoring the haunted laughs getting louder.

She knocked ever so lightly at first. Nothing. She knocked a little harder the second time. "Anna!" she cried, trying to ignore the noise. She opened the door and saw Anna walking toward her.

"Hey, what's up? Are you okay? Are you sick?" Anna said, getting up and readjusting the bed vest she was wearing. *Well that image wasn't going to help the situation.*

"Well, no, not really. Okay, I mean… sorry, this is really embarrassing. I'm hearing strange noises in my room. I think the house is haunted," she said simply.

Anna switched the light on. "Have you been drinking?" she asked. "It's one am, and I have to work in the morning," she said confused.

"No, I haven't. I went to bed early. I didn't have a drop. I'm not crazy, seriously. There's this scary 'screaming, laugh' thing going on. I tried to ignore it, but it sounds like a clown, or a ghost. I think it might be laughing at me. It was getting louder; I didn't know what to do. Come to my room and you'll hear it."

Anna's face changed rapidly. She reacted quickly, and got up, causing Heidi to blush when she saw that along with Anna's vest was only a pair of knickers. Heidi looked away instantly, unsure why Anna was frantically looking for things.

"Heidi, what did it sound like?"

"Um I just told you, a scary, loud laugh."

"Fuck, *fuck*!" she screamed, pulling her jeans on.

"*What*? What is it?"

"That's Lola," she said. "Something's happening to the animals. That's Lola's sound of alarm. *Fuck,*" she repeated.

"Anna, calm down a second. I'll come with you and help."

"You can't help; you don't know what to do. Please call Jack and tell him I need him."

"You don't know the situation yet. You don't know that I can't help. Listen to me, I can help you. Let me just put some clothes on."

"Fine!" Anna snapped.

Moments later they were running towards Lola's screams. *Seriously, it was scarily like a horror movie,* Heidi thought.

Anna ran fast, and Heidi was by no means unfit, but she could hardly keep up with the stride of Anna's long legs. She caught up to Anna as she got to the stables. She saw Anna lying next to a big, grey horse who wailed on the floor. "Come on, Charlie boy," she heard her repeat.

"How did you know it was this?"

"Jack said he wasn't himself today and yesterday. He's not right, he's sweating," she said.

"Should I get some water?"

"Yes, just over there," she said pointing. "Come on boy, stay with Mumma. Come on, we'll get Karen, come on."

"Heidi ran back with a bucket of water for Anna. "What should I do?"

"Go through my phone." She threw her phone to Heidi. "Come on baby, come on boy. Mumma's here. The password is 9471. Go to the phonebook and call 'Karen vet.' Tell her you're calling for me, or put her on speaker. Just call her quick. Tell her it's Charlie. Come on boy, come on," she said, sponging him down with water.

"Anna, it just keeps ringing."

"Just keep trying!" she snapped. "Damn it!" she screamed, laying her body close to the distressed horse, rolling around.

Heidi kept pressing redial on the phone.

"Come on, come on boy. Please, Charlie boy," she pleaded as the tears fell freely.

Heidi felt like her heart was being ripped in two. She frantically pressed call, over and over. Anna looked terrified and heartbroken and Heidi didn't know what to do. She was completely out of her comfort zone.

"Anna, I've called nine times; I can't get through. What should I do? Should I call Jack? Or is there someone else I should call? I don't know what to suggest. Should I go get the car?"

"He's a fucking horse, Heidi, not a human!" she snapped through the tears. Heidi fell back on her feet as she sank to the ground, pained from her words. She felt the phone vibrate in her hands. "It's Karen," she said relieved.

"Hi, is this Karen? Yes, it's Hei... I'm calling on behalf of Anna. She needs you, it's Charlie. He isn't well and, well she needs you," she said. "Yes, sure."

Heidi put the phone on speaker and kept it close to Anna. "She said to give her more information," she confirmed.

Anna and Karen chatted about the symptoms, giving her direction as to what to do while she was on her way over. Anna hung the phone up, still crying as she stroked and sponged her horse.

Karen told them she was ten minutes away, leaving Anna with instructions to continue to do what she'd told her to. "You best go, Heidi. Karen will be here, and she can't see you."

"I don't mind. I don't want to leave you like this."

Anna looked squarely at her, feeling fear in the pit of her stomach. She knew she'd been awful to Heidi, but she needed to get her thoughts together. There wasn't time for that right now. "I think it's for the best," she said, turning back to the sick animal, leaving Heidi broken hearted all over again.

Heidi walked back to the house sadly. It felt like the longest walk ever, but it was sufficient time to make her realize that she needed to get out of this situation, and move back home, regardless of the consequences. For now, she just needed her bed, or at least some privacy.

*

Anna walked back to the house, the cold painful as it hit her fallen tears. It was 4:30, and ordinarily she would've been getting up for work, not just going to bed. She texted Jack to tell him she'd be in later.

Anna got in, and stripped out of her clothes, slipping into the soft bed. She lay there for a few moments staring at the ceiling, before the sobs took control, unable to stop.

She kept hearing the words in her head. *I'm sorry Anna, it looks like Charlie is Colic. There's nothing more we can do for him. He will need to be euthanized.*

Anna felt sick to her stomach. There was such a huge part of her that wanted to talk to Heidi. Apologize for how she'd treated her, and crawl into her arms so she could help her through it. But the better and wiser part of her told her she would be stupid to do that. The pain of it all came flooding back all. Her mum dying, how her dad felt when it happened, and now, the pain of Charlie dying. *Why would anybody do that? Why would anybody knowingly set themselves up for a fall?* she thought. *She'd managed everything else in her adult life alone, without a boyfriend, or husband...or girlfriend or wife, even. She would do this, alone, like she'd always intended.* She rolled back over onto her side and quietly cried herself to sleep.

Chapter Twenty-Six

"Mummy, look what I made you at school today," the little girl said.

"You *did*? That's beautiful, darling. Did you have a good day?"

"Yes, Mrs. Parsons told everybody to sing me happy birthday," she gleamed.

"Wow, that's very nice of her."

"Yeah, I know. I like her, she's definitely my favorite teacher."

"Hi, you're home?"

"Sure am. How's my two, beautiful girls?" The man kissed his daughter on the forehead and lovingly kissed his wife on the lips, whispering he loved her.

"Daddy, why do you always tell mummy you love her?"

"Because I do, sweetheart. And I love you too." He ruffled her hair. "It's good to know how someone feels. I promised her when I married her, I'd tell her every day for the rest of our lives together; and so, I will. Don't ever be afraid to show your feelings, darling. People will tell you when you grow up that it's a sign of weakness, but it's far from it. Isn't that right, honey?"

"Sure is. When you grow up, and meet a handsome man that you want to love and have your own children with, it's important to let them know. Don't ever be afraid to love baby."

"I won't Mummy, I can't wait to meet someone that makes me smile as much as Daddy makes you smile," Anna said innocently.

*

Anna woke up feeling like she was choking. She couldn't breathe and was soaked with sweat. The dream had felt as though she had taken a kick in the guts, the recollection of everything hit home. She rushed to the toilet again, vomiting excessively. When she finally stopped, she collapsed in a sobbing heap around the stall, oblivious to the cold tiles on her naked body. She felt so alone, and she knew that the dream of her youth with her family had something to do with Heidi. *How could it not?* She felt out of sorts, like she was spiraling out of control, and she had no idea what do about it.

Anna showered for a long time, re-imagining the dream and thinking about Charlie. Heidi had been incredible. She'd been there for her completely yesterday, from the moment Anna went downstairs to the moment she went to bed. Heidi had gone and found Jack, telling him Anna couldn't work, and when Anna spent the entire day crying on the sofa, Heidi lay behind her, her body engulfing Anna's, holding her tight. For days, she'd wanted it to be like that, just not this situation. *She felt completely numb and couldn't face going to work. Heidi had just been...perfect,* she thought. When they went to bed, Heidi offered to stay with Anna. They literally spent 15 hours side by side, bodies tangled together, watching movies.

Anna needed to return to work, but couldn't seem to muster the energy. Truth be known, she wanted another day like yesterday. Throwing on her tracksuit, she decided to go make coffee before she did anything.

"Hey," Heidi said, closing the laptop quickly, walking over to grab Anna's hand.

"Hi. You okay? You want coffee?" she asked confused.

"I'll get it. Sit down," Heidi said, stroking her arm. She didn't want to make Anna feel uncomfortable, but she wanted to make sure she was okay. "Would you like something to eat? Some toast? You didn't eat yesterday," she said concerned.

"I'll be fine," she half smiled.

"How about sharing one slice with me? For *me*?" she said expectantly.

"You're too good," Anna confirmed. "You look busy. You wasted yesterday on me; get back to whatever you're doing on your laptop."

"I didn't waste it," she said flatly.

Heidi put two slices of toast in to the toaster, handing the coffee to Anna.

"Thank you, Heidi. Really, yesterday, you…I don't know what I would have done without you," she wiped a tear away. "Sorry, I'll get my stuff together and be out of your hair soon."

"Anna, don't be silly. Jesus, you've gone through a traumatic time. It doesn't just happen overnight. Like any bereavement, it will take time. I'll be here any time you need me," she said standing above her seated chair. Heidi ran her hands up and down Anna's arms, affectionately. She explored further, reaching the base of her wavy curls, and wrapped her fingers around the softness of them. Heidi felt Anna's eyes on her, looking up to meet them. Her eyes darted to Heidi's lips, as she watched the increase in

234

movement through her thin vest. Anna stood up, and leaned in. Upon a loud bang, they both jumped back.

"Jesus!" Heidi squealed nervously, turning to see the toast pop out of the toaster. Heidi turned to look at Anna roll her eyes a little, and smile. *Outside of anything and everything else, at least she now knew that they were kind of on the same page,* she thought anxiously.

*

Heidi sat on the opposite side of Anna at the breakfast bar and put the two slices of toast in front of them.

"You said half," she looked at her seriously.

"Half of the two pieces," Heidi smiled. "Please, for me? You didn't eat yesterday," she pleaded, covering Anna's hand with her own.

Anna looked down at her hands again, nerves rising. "I'll try." She smiled. "Can I ask you something?"

"Sure," Heidi said, taking a bite from the toast.

"What've you been doing on your computer lately? I see you up sometimes as early as when I'm going to work. You carry it around like it's worth a million. I suppose if it's a manuscript for a top movie it could very well be," she said distantly. "I'm just intrigued, and when you slammed it down when I walked in, I wondered what's so important on it.

Heidi watched her seriously. The last 36 hours had taken a different turn, and Heidi felt comfortable with her. "Um, promise you won't laugh?"

"I would never laugh at you, Heidi," she said sincerely.

There it was again, that weird thing in her tummy. Nerves, or *maybe* something else. "No, you wouldn't. I know that. I've been writing a book," she said shyly.

"*Really?*"

"Mhmm."

"What's it about? Can I read it?"

"Um, well it's pretty stupid. You wouldn't like it…"

"How do you know?" she blurted.

Heidi watched the sadness in her eyes again, something she'd never seen before.

"I don't think it'd be rubbish. I think it'd be great. You've had so many life experiences; you must have a wonderful story to tell. I'd really like to read it."

"It's not about me. It's just a fictional romance. As I said, it's rubbish, but it's kept me busy," she said softly.

"Well, it'd help keep my mind off things," she said sadly, feeling a tear drop. Heidi captured it, stroking her cheek gently. "You should let me be the judge of whether it's good or not…" Anna sighed, moving her cheek further in to Heidi's gentle strokes. *She didn't know what she was doing, or if she could even control herself, but she was desperate to…* Her thought process stopped as they heard a knock at the door.

"Will that be Jack?" Heidi asked as Anna got up.

"No, he'd just come in," she said confused, opening the door to a couple of enthusiastic "HI's!"

"Hi?" she said to the family, suddenly realizing. *Shit!* "Hi, I'm so sorry, I completely forgot!" she said, turning to face a confused Heidi.

"Um…?" Heidi's brother, Tony, said confused.

"Come in. *Come in*! My apologies, it's been a long couple of days."

Tony and Meg reluctantly walked in, immediately seeing Heidi.

"What're you guys doing here?" She rushed over to her brother and his family.

"Aunty Heidi, Aunty Heidi!" Her niece and nephew ran to her.

"Um, is this okay?" Meg asked, noticing Anna's red eyes.

"Yes, *yes*. I'm so sorry; it's me. I'm not normally this much of a bad host. Ask your sister." She smiled sadly. "Heidi, your sister in law and I arranged a surprise so they could come and see you, and the kids could see the animals." Her niece and nephew squealed with excitement.

"Guys, guys, quieten down a little. How about you go and have a look around? Is that okay, Anna?" Heidi said reluctantly.

"Yes, sure. Hey, if you have a look around the back, you may see Lola. She might still be sleeping though."

Heidi moved toward Anna and squeezed her shoulder. "She's had some sad news," she whispered.

"Oh, I'm sorry. We should've called this morning to check. Look, we'll leave and come back another time. Or we could find a hotel."

"Meg, seriously, it's fine," Anna said smiling. "Honestly, I just completely forgot. Seriously, I can't mope forever. Some excitable little ones will be exactly what I need to take my mind off it." She smiled softly.

"Are you sure, Anna? We can go and get a hotel close by," Tony stepped in. "We'll just pop over when you're ready."

"It's fine, I'm positive. Come on, let's get you guys settled into your room." She paused. "Oh no, your *room*!" She said annoyed.

"Is everything okay?" Heidi asked.

"Yes, I just need to make the bed. I forgot to do that. I'll put fresh sheets on now."

"Where are *you* going to sleep?" Heidi asked.

"I'll just crash on the sofa. I don't sleep that much anyway."

"You can't do that. With how hard you work, you need as much sleep as you can get. They can take my room and I'll sleep down here."

"Can't you share?" Meg asked confused.

"Yes, of course. You can share with me," Heidi said, turning around so they didn't see her blush. *Oh, dear God, what the hell was she going to do now?*

"Are you absolutely sure about all of this?" Meg asked again.

"Yes, definitely. Let me get my work gear on, and I'll take the kids to have a look around."

"Well, given that I was never allowed to come with you guys when I was younger, am I able to come too?" Tony said grinning.

"Tone, you jealous?" Heidi smirked at her brother, still eyeing Anna cautiously. It had been a matter of hours since having to entertain.

"Come on," Heidi said. "I'll help you change the bedding and switch rooms," she pulled her out of the room. "I'm so sorry. Let's just ask them to go. I'll get them a hotel close by, and I'll go stay with them," she whispered.

"I don't want you to go," Anna said seriously. "I don't think I can cope with being alone right now."

Heidi looked at her sadly. "Okay, I won't leave you; I'm by your side. You know, that right?"

"I know that." She smiled, taking Heidi's hand and walking them upstairs. "You sure you're okay sleeping with me?"

Heidi spun around, shocked as she watched the awkwardness cross her face.

"Um I didn't mean like *sleep* sleep with me. Just like sharing a bed."

She nodded slowly, "It's fine, I'm kind of glad. I wanna be able to hold you tight tonight," she whispered, turning away from Anna.

*

"Are you coming with us today?" Anna asked.

"Not unless you want me to. I was thinking I may corrupt Meg, drink lots of wine, gossip," she said, widening her eyes. "Then of course make you guys some dinner."

"Oh, you have a plan?"

"A naughty plan," she said mischievously.

"In the words of Taylor Swift: I *knew* you were trouble when you walked in," Anna said, fluffing down the last of the bed.

"You have no idea," Heidi smirked, suddenly embarrassed at her words, and uncertain where it'd come from. Heidi was feeling excitably giddy yet tremendously nervous at the prospect of being so close to Anna.

Anna stood shocked as Heidi allowed the words to confidently spill out. She couldn't help but let a slight smile creep across her face. "You've gained some confidence. Well, don't misbehave too much, you need to save some of that naughtiness for later," she said walking past her. *What the bloody hell had she just said? Jesus, what did she do now?* Anna quickly turned back around to a smirking Heidi, who stood with her arms folded and eyebrow raised. "*Kids*! I *meant* the kids. You said earlier you were going to lead Meg astray, so I meant you'd be leading them astray too," she said letting the overspill of words fill the room. "I haven't slept, that's all," she said walking out of the room.

*

"Hey guys, did you find Lola?"

"Who's Lola?" Heidi's nephew asked.

"She's the farm guard. She's a laughing llama," Heidi said.

"Does she actually laugh?" Tony asked.

"Apparently so, but I've been here weeks and haven't seen or heard it," Heidi complained, rolling her eyes.

"Don't worry guys, I'll make sure you hear her before you leave. So, as your aunty has made no attempt to introduce us. I'm Anna. Very nice to meet you all," she said, holding her hand out to the little girl first.

"Hello," she said quietly.

"I'm sorry, I totally forgot. This is my gorgeous, not so little niece, Ava. You are such a big girl. Are you four, now?" she asked, scrunching her nose up. *Ava was the double of Heidi,* Anna thought. She had the same dirty, blonde hair, the same big blue eyes, even the same defined jawline.

"I know, she looks more like Heidi than us, doesn't she?" Meg said to Anna.

"God, I'm sorry," Anna responded.

"It's okay. Everyone thinks it. When people find out we're related, they all think that Heidi had her and gave her to us in some scandal," Meg laughed.

"I didn't, FYI," Heidi claimed, holding her hands up. "And this is my little seven-year-old heartthrob, Ashton," she said, putting her arms around the little boy from behind. He had the brightest blue eyes ever, and while Ava didn't have the skin tone that Heidi had, Ashton did. His dark tone and blonde hair was like a western European child. They were both adorable.

"You guys are very cute," Anna smiled to Heidi. "So, you wanna go see some animals? We can come back after and have a mini party."

"Yay!" they both squealed excitably.

"Aunty Heidi, are you coming with us?" Ava asked.

"No, sweetie. I'm going to let Anna show you, Ashton, and Daddy around; Mummy and I will cook some food for the party, and will see you when you get back."

"Awh," Ashton said disappointed.

"Can't wait for this party," Anna said raising an eyebrow to Heidi.

"In other words, kids, Mummy and Aunty Heidi are going to drink wine, and then pour some crisps in a bowl for when we return," Tony said.

"Whatever," Heidi said rolling her eyes.

"Right, are you guys ready? What do you want to see first? We have pigs, chickens, sheep, cows, goats, geese. We have a big lake out back with ducks that we could feed. We may need to leave Lola until tomorrow, when she's feeling a bit better."

"Do you have horses?" Ava asked innocently.

"Um…" she stopped, taking a deep breath. "Um…ye—"

"They're not here today, sweetie," Heidi interrupted and knelt to her niece. "But guess what we have that's a gazillion times better than that?" she said excitedly.

"*Wha*t?" she said happily buying in.

"Our very own ice cream parlor. A real one, not a store. You can go and watch how it's made and then bring some back for the party," Heidi said excitably.

"Mummy, they have their own ice cream here!" she said.

"I know. How great is that?" she said, pulling her daughter's coat in tighter and zipping her up.

"What's your favorite flavor?" Anna asked Ava.

"Strawberry," Ava said.

"Really? Mine too. Well, this is a sustainable farm. Do you know what that is?"

"No," she said innocently.

"It means that we don't just have animals; we make a living from food and drink. Like ice cream," she said smiling widely. "So we could go and pick some strawberries, then make our very own, real, strawberry ice cream."

"*Really*?"

"Wow, that's *so* cool," Ashton said.

"You have strawberries in winter?" Tony asked.

"Yeah, we have it all." She smiled. "Come on then, let's go see the animals."

"Awh, look at Av's holding Anna's hand," Meg said to Heidi as they left. "Are we *really* going to start drinking now?" she asked, looking at her clock.

"Yeah. In the words of Jimmy Buffet, it's five o'clock somewhere. We're on vacation. But maybe let's have coffee first," she said, still unable to look away from Anna interacting with her young niece.

"Works for me. It's about time your brother played Daddy for a change. So, come, sit," she said, patting the chair. "Tell me everything. How are you? God, I'm so sorry babes, I really am," she said, pulling her sister-in-law in for a hug.

"It's fine, don't you worry. I'm all good."

"Really? I must say I was surprised when I saw you. You really do look surprisingly well given the circumstances," she said confused.

"It's a long story, but it's not been great for years."

"Sorry, Heid's. So what's new? Any new boys on the go?" she winked.

"Um, nope. Not really feeling guys at the minute." *Technically not a lie.* "I just feel a bit done with it all. I'm happy having some time out."

"Understandable."

*

"Mummy, *mummy!*" they heard as the front door flew open a few hours later.

"Hi darlings. Have you had fun?"

Heidi concentrated as the excitable children spoke a million words a minute, fighting to get everything across as fast as possible.

"Blimey, they always like this, Megs?" she asked wide-eyed.

"Wow, guess you really did start without us," Anna said, handing Heidi some ice cream.

Heidi poured some wine for her brother and Anna. "Maybe you need to catch up with us," she said to Anna. "Unfortunately, little brother, you only get one as you're on Daddy duties," she smirked taking some ice cream.

"Clearly not as much as you," Anna said smirking, noticing Heidi leave.

Heidi shut the bedroom door, leaning her head against it. They hadn't drank lots, but given this morning and sharing Anna's bed later tonight, it wouldn't end well if she continued. She grabbed the gifts for her niece and nephew as Anna walked in.

"Oh hey," Anna said confused. "You okay?" Anna asked, walking into the room.

"Yes, why?"

"You're on the floor in my bedroom."

"We're sharing for a couple of days, so technically it's 'our' bedroom," she smirked. "Or, not 'sharing.' What was it you said…we're 'sleeping' together?" she raised her eyebrow.

"Do you always flirt this much after a drink, or are you just trying to make me feel better?"

"*Flirting*? You think I'm *flirting* with you?" she said astonished.

"I do, but you don't need to argue that fact." She winked. "I'm gonna get naked now; are you planning on staying?"

"What? *Nooo,*" she said flabbergasted. "Why exactly are you getting naked?"

"Because I've had very little sleep, and spent the last three hours entertaining, not two, but three children. My houseguest has drunk me out of my house, and to be perfectly honest, I want to be on the same level as you guys. I'll grab a red hot shower and come join you," she responded.

"Yes, of course. *Shower.* I'll go," she said walking away. "No, I won't actually."

"You won't?" Anna said surprised, holding her top mid-stomach and freezing.

Heidi smirked at the woman. "Don't you worry, I'm not intending on having a sneak peek. Although, what I'm seeing looks pretty good," she said, eyeing her mid-section. "I'll save that for when you're sleeping tonight," she smirked. *God what was she doing?* She returned to the suitcase, grabbing the gifts, holding them high in the air. "*Now* I'll be going," she said winking, leaving Anna in her room.

Anna fell onto her bed. Sharing the bed was going to be a nightmare. She should *not* drink. *Chances are that would make things even more difficult.*

*

"I can't believe you two just drank and didn't even make dinner," Tony said, taking a bite of pizza.

"We figured a party isn't a party without a pizza," Meg said, holding up her glass of wine and slice of pizza.

"Dad, is Mum drunk again?"

"*Again?* How often am I drunk?"

"Never, actually. I will happily stick up for you this once," he said, kissing his wife. "Guys, you need to get ready for bed soon."

"Ohhh," they each groaned. "We haven't seen Aunty Heidi properly yet!" they cried.

Ava came and sat on her aunt's lap. "Aunty Heidi?"

"Yes, gorgeous?"

"Can I come and sleep with you? I've not seen you, and I wanna come sleep in your bed."

"Sweetie, I don't have a bed here. Your mum and dad are in mine. I have to sleep with Anna." Anna coughed on her drink.

"You okay?" Tony asked.

"Yes sorry, went down the wrong way."

"I'm only small. I can sleep with you both," she said innocently.

"Sweetie, you can't sleep with them; you don't stop moving and Anna has work early," Meg said.

"Well, I will be very still, I promise. And I won't wake you up, Anna. I punch my Daddy in bed, but I promise I won't do that to you," she said pleadingly.

"Blimey, how do you ever say no to that face?" Anna whispered to Meg.

"Don't ask. Normally blackmail," she giggled.

"I wanna sleep in there too," Ashton pleaded. "Why does she get to just because she's a girl? I wanna have a sleepover with Aunt Heidi," Ashton said.

"Guys, you can't. Anna and Heidi don't want you pair keeping them up all night."

"Please, Aunt Heidi? We'll go to bed now, and be asleep when you come to bed and then we will be quiet all night," Ashton said, looking between Heidi and Anna.

Anna laughed at Heidi, shrugging her shoulders. "Guess we're having a sleepover," she said.

"Are you sure about this, Heid's? They haven't changed; they'll keep you up all night," Tony said to her.

"It's fine. Worst case, I'll come down here in the night," Anna confirmed.

"Alright, you have 10 minutes and then you go to bed. I'll put a movie on for you, and then you go to sleep," Heidi said seriously.

"Is that so you can cry, Aunty Heidi?" Ava asked seriously.

"What? *No*. Why would you ask that?"

"Mummy and Daddy said that Uncle Ev wasn't very nice to you, so you had to come here. You may be sad. We come to see you and make you happy again," she said innocently.

"You're right; you make me very happy. And no, I don't want to cry. I'm okay now, but the grownups need some time too. Plus, you need to be refreshed for another day on the farm tomorrow."

"Oh, so you can drink more wine again?" she asked, sighing and shaking her head. She ignored the adults laughing around her.

"Come on, you pair. Bed, pjs, and teeth brushing. I'll come and tuck you in," Heidi smiled.

"Okay, goodnight," the kids said, giving everyone a kiss goodnight.

"You're both going to regret this," Tony said shaking his head.

*

They stayed up later than anticipated. Heidi was happy she'd managed to cancel Helen for a couple of days. She changed into a pair of oversized pajama bottoms and a UCLA shirt from a movie she'd shot a few years ago. Hearing the tap stop, she casually and quietly waited for Anna to leave the bathroom. As the door opened, she turned to see Anna in another of her customary boxer and vest combos.

"Really?" she whispered, looking at the sleeping children. "You couldn't find anything *less* to wear?" Heidi said, walking past her towards the bathroom.

Anna grabbed her hand, watching the shock on her face. "Where's the fun in that?" she winked, letting her go.

Heidi quickly brushed her teeth and freshened up before returning to the room. "I'm not quite sure how this is going to work," Anna said with her arms folded, looking over to the bed.

Heidi picked up Ashton and put him in the airbed that Tony and Meg had put beside them. He rarely woke up through the night, so he would be fine on that. Ava was a different story. It was clearly a case of hoping for the best. Heidi maneuvered her niece carefully to the edge of the bed, trying not to disturb the little girl.

"I'm really sorry about this."

"What?"

"Having to share your bed with me and my niece," she confirmed.

"It's probably safer that way. Okay get in," she said to Heidi.

"Safer how?" Heidi turned to her.

"I think you know the answer to that."

"I have no idea what you're referring to," she said playfully.

Anna moved forward, so she was face to face with Heidi. Heidi was tall, maybe 5'7", 5'8", but Anna was still a couple of inches taller. She stared her down, considering her clear, blue eyes. "Get…in…bed!" she whispered, sterner this time.

"Hmm demanding."

"Heidi Spencer-Brady, shut up and behave. And for the love of God, get in bed before I make you get in."

Anna noticed the slight smirk on Heidi's face shone from the light outside. "I love how easy you are," Heidi whispered into Anna's ear quietly.

Anna tried not to flinch. This was *not* good. Normally, in these situations she wouldn't drink this much. She felt like she'd lost control. Thankfully, the kids were in the room. Anna was unsure of the 'good night' etiquette, so she simply muttered 'night' and tried to sleep.

Anna woke up early the next morning to the vibrating alarm under her pillow. Grabbing it quickly, she noticed Heidi's hands wrapped around her. Turning slightly, she felt Heidi's body close to her own. Reluctantly, Anna pulled away slowly, grabbed her work clothes, and made her way to the main bathroom as quietly as possible. She assessed herself in the mirror, wondering when these life changing moments had happened.

Chapter Twenty-Seven

Anna returned home just after lunch, desperate for something hearty and stodgy to help through the tireless working, the wintry weather, and fuzzy head she had.

"*Anna!*" The kids ran up excitably as she came in. She was bombarded with squeals of excitement, and questions of when they could go back to see the animals.

"They won't want to leave at this rate. Did you sleep okay? I hope they didn't keep you awake all night," Meg said awkwardly.

"No, it was absolutely fine. The wine apparently helped. I didn't wake up until my alarm went off this morning," she said. "Does anyone want anything to eat, or have you eaten already?"

"We took the kids to McDonald's to keep them quiet for an hour," Meg said, rolling her eyes.

"You want me to make you something?" Heidi asked, "I was just about to make a chicken ciabatta if you like?"

"Oh, that sounds amazing. I was craving stodgy, hangover food," she said, thanking Heidi.

*

Heidi knocked on the door to Anna's bedroom, feeling anxious.

"Yeah?"

"Hey, it's only me," she poked her head around the door. "Just wondered if you wanted cheese and bacon too," she said awkwardly.

"Oh, yes please. Are you okay?" Anna smirked.

"Yes, why?"

"You don't look it."

"Yes, I'm fine." She went to leave, but turned back to Anna. "Look, I hope last night wasn't *too* awkward. I was pretty drunk; I'm concerned I may have done or said something?" She questioned.

"No, you were absolutely fine." She smiled.

"Oh good," she sighed relieved.

"Well, outside the spooning."

"Ah... ha ha, I get it, you're messing with me again. Excellent work," she said irritably.

"Actually, no. Not this time. Calm yourself; there's nothing wrong with that and when I got ready I noticed that it was because Ava was sideways and Ashton had also gotten in sideways. We were basically clinging on for dear life. No need to fret," she said seriously.

"Oh, dear God," she said, slapping her hand to her forehead.

"Heidi, chill. If it's any consolation, I was a little bit disappointed when I had to get up and leave," she said and left the room.

Jesus why did she always do that? Why did she feel the need to say stuff, and then leave her hanging with no opportunity to respond? Albeit, what would she have said?

Heidi walked back downstairs, trying to compose herself when she walked in to find Anna entertaining her niece and nephew. Trying to keep herself busy, Heidi returned to making lunch.

"Here you go," Heidi said, putting the food down for her, and returning to Meg and Tony.

"Aunty Heidi, we think you should come with us this afternoon and let Mummy and Daddy have some alone time," Ashton said.

"Ashton, I think Daddy will be more upset that he's not going," Meg said.

"What do you mean?"

Meg scoffed at her husband. "Tony, you haven't stopped going on about it since you came back yesterday. I'm pretty sure if it was a toss-up between the animals and I right now, I'd be...well, not even a close second."

"Tony Edwards, you will not treat your wife like this!" Heidi commanded. "We will take the kids out; you can wine and dine her—put the fire on, watch the most incredibly romantic sunset ever, and have some *you* time."

"This will be very interesting kids," Anna said, taking a bite of her lunch, and raising her eyebrows animatedly to two very giggly children.

"Maybe you should *stop* vocalizing your opinions about me in front of my niece and nephew...just saying," she said, annoyed at the still giggling trio.

*

"What are we doing today?" Ashton asked, walking alongside Anna who was now suitably stuffed. The kids were appropriately dressed. "I don't know, where do you fancy going?"

"I want to feed the ducks."

"Sure thing, buddy," she said, high fiving Ashton and leading them through the long route down to the lake.

Hours had passed at the lake, and as the night drew in, even the ducks were starting to disperse. She wanted to stand by Heidi's words and give Tony and Meg some time, but they were restricted given the time and climate.

"Are you okay?" Heidi asked concerned.

"Yeah, why?"

"You seem concerned is all? What are you thinking?"

Anna leaned in to whisper into Heidi's ear.

"It's rude to whisper Mummy says!" Ava shouted.

"I'm not being rude; I just don't want to say it if you aren't allowed, that's all," Anna said, winking to the little girl who eyed her cautiously.

"Are you sure?" Heidi whispered back.

"Yes, I am. Come on," she said leading the way.

Ava held Anna's hand on the way down, continuously asking where they were going. "I told you, it's a surprise. You just have to be patient." She looked down at the little girl and winked as Heidi grabbed Anna's hand and mouthed *thank you*. The gesture sent a shock through Anna's body, which she knew Heidi felt too as she tried to release her hand. Without letting her, Anna grabbed it tighter as they continued walking.

The duration of the walk consisted of them being asked over and over 'where they were going,' and 'when they'd be there,' before Ashton noticed their entangled hands.

"Why are you two holding hands?" he asked giggling.

"Because we all are," Heidi said, nonchalantly. "We're the hand holding line."

The actress in her is good, thought Anna.

"But you aren't holding my hand," he said confused.

"That's because I figured you were too much of a big boy!" she sang. "I didn't think you'd want to hold your auntie's hand," she said sarcastically, her words hanging. She knew Ashton would soon take her hand.

Anna turned to the kids, grinning widely as she shouted, "Ready!?" and dragged them towards the stables. She was glad this was the first time she faced it since the brief period it'd been since Charlie happened. It would have been harder *without* the kids. As she established yesterday, kids were great at making you forget when sad things happened. She also knew the kids would help to pick up Jones and Mustard, who breathed an air of sadness since Charlie had gone.

Anna opened the door, and noticed it was unlocked. She immediately saw Jack.

"What are you doing here?" he asked accusingly.

"It's okay, we have visitors," she said, eyeing him carefully to ensure he knew that she was okay to be there.

"Hiya. So, who have we got here then?" Jack said, taking his glove off and putting the rake down.

"Hi, I'm Ashton. Who are you?" he asked, mesmerized by the giant in front of him.

"I'm Jack. Nice to meet you, Ashton. Cool name. So, what are you doing here? You come for a ride?"

"I don't know," he turned to look at a nodding Anna. "Who's that?" he asked, pointing to the big, grey horse. "He's really big."

"He is. This is Jones," he said, walking over and stroking the horse, who was suddenly a little more interested in the young boy. "You wanna stroke him? He's a bit sad because his best friend died yesterday," he said sadly.

Heidi immediately grabbed Anna's hand again, stroking her skin softly. She so desperately wanted to comfort her. She'd never had any connection with animals, so she didn't fully understand, but Anna was clearly upset, and that upset her.

"*Really*? Will he let me?"

"Yeah, he's dead nice. I think he'd like that a lot. Come here." Jack stood to the side ensuring that the boy was protected and so the subdued horse could get a look at the child. He knew the innocence and excitement of children would provide all the attention and love the old boys needed right now.

"Is this right?" Ashton asked. "Ava come here and pet Jones." He called his sister who slowly walked up and peeked around the corner.

"Well hello, Ava? How are you? You want to have a go too?" he asked, giving her a big smile.

"Who are you?" she asked softly.

"I'm Jack, I work here with Anna." He knelt to her level.

"Are you Anna's boyfriend?"

He couldn't help but look over the top to catch his boss's eye, and wink. "No, just friends," he smiled.

"Are you Aunty Heidi's boyfriend? Is that why she's here?" Ashton asked, getting some positive attention from the horse from his soft patting.

"Nope, I'm not her boyfriend either," he said standing again and allowing Ava to carefully walk closer to her brother and copy his actions.

"Where's your girlfriend then?" she said.

"I'm waiting for you to grow up so I can marry you," he said with that wide smile, watching the little girl giggle. "He likes you guys. He's been very sad and you've cheered him up. We mustn't forget Mustard though. He probably feels left out." He pointed behind the children's backs to the other horse, who was fully interested in what was going on next to him.

Ashton giggled. "Why is he called Mustard? That's a silly name. He isn't even yellow."

Anna let go of Heidi's hand and walked up to Mustard. "Well, every so often we have some kids or schools come up here. One year, we had a competition where the winner could name the horse. He was named by one of the children," she said, stroking the animal lovingly.

"Ahhhh, can we name one too!?" Ashton asked excitedly.

"Well I don't have one without a name right now, but I tell you what. Next time I do, I'll get you guys up, and you can come meet it, and name it. Deal?"

"Yay!" they both screamed in excitement, causing the horses to shift quickly.

"So, wanna go for a ride. We can ride by the lake and watch the sunset."

"You good to walk Mustard with Heidi?" she asked Jack.

"Oh you guys, I'm fine. You can go and take them, I trust you." Heidi said

Anna looked at her sadly, and Heidi couldn't help but feel nerves from the pull this woman had on her. "Okay, sure, why not," Anna said nodding to Heidi's gleaming niece and nephew.

*

"This is *incredible*."

"Told you," Anna said with a glint in her eye. The sunset was incredible tonight and walking along with its reflection on the lake was pure perfection.

"Aunty Heidi, why is Jack walking our horse, and Anna and Ashton don't need him to?" Ava asked innocently.

Before Heidi could allow the embarrassment to set in, Jack already interjected.

"That's because on the farms, we like to make the men feel big and strong," he said, showing off his muscle. "Ashton is taking care of them, and I'm taking care of you."

Heidi winked at the young boy—man. He really was a good guy. He'd make a million and one women happy one day. And the best thing about him was he'd happily turn down a million other women if he had the right one to love. It's a shame that Everett never shared those same values.

Making their way back after a long walk, and after plenty of selfies in the sunset, they explained that Jones and Mustard needed some food and sleep because of the happiness the kids had provided. It was getting dark and the kids needed to get out of the cold and to eat some food.

"Jack, can you come back with us? We're having a party, I think, and you could come and meet my mum and dad," Ashton said admirably.

"Oh, um, I don't know kiddo…" he started.

"Come on over, if you want," Anna said. "Have a couple of beers and grab a taxi home. I tell you what, I'll even give you tomorrow off as you've been managing everything and doing loads of extra stuff around here lately."

Jack looked from Anna to the wide-eyed, encouraging children to Heidi. "You sure you don't mind me gate-crashing family time?"

S. L. Gape

"Nope, I'd be honored. Like you, family is important to us. Plus, you have a couple of fans," she said, placing a hand on each of their shoulders.

"Are you going back now?" Jack asked.

"Yeah, you want me to follow you home and bring you back so you can change quickly?" she asked him, turning to Heidi. "Do they like Indian? I could grab one on the way back if you like?"

"Sounds good. Let's go back, and see if they're okay with that, and then we can go from there," Heidi said, grabbing the kids hands and making their way back to the house.

Chapter Twenty-Eight

The evening was filled with laughter, good food, and maybe a few too many drinks again. Jack fit in comfortably with the family, feeling a sense of closeness from the similarities of Heidi's and his own family. The biggest surprise was the normality of sitting, and drinking with a Hollywood movie star despite the odd things between his boss, and her new housemate that had discreetly gone on. The kids both seemed to like him, especially Ashton. They were blissfully ignorant to their parents while they had Anna, Heidi, and Jack to entertain them. This allowed Tony and Meg time to assess their sister's emotional state. They were happy to see that she was on the road to recovery.

Anna and Heidi discreetly flirted all night, though both were acutely aware that they were becoming less and less discrete the more wine they consumed. At least the one positive was the way Meg went on about Jack all night. It was very clear she thought something was going on between he and Heidi, but she tabled the conversation when they all retired to bed that night.

Jack left just after nine, promising to see them again soon, which caused a weird incomprehensible feeling for Heidi. She didn't like listening to them discuss a visit without her included; she couldn't think about it, at least not now.

*

Heidi finished getting ready for bed, and returned to Anna's room where Anna cleansed her face. She had a delicate and tender complexion, and as she cleaned her face, the difference of before and after were virtually identical, a desirable quality for many women.

"You okay?" Anna said, walking towards Heidi. She desperately tried not to look at her tanned legs, but it was blaringly obvious. "Forget your bottoms?" Anna asked seriously.

"I didn't actually, but this shirt is so big," she said, grabbing the middle section of the oversized t-shirt. "It's longer than some of my dresses." She folded her arms to further her point.

Anna grinned, passing her. "With your arms folded like that, I bet it isn't!"

Heidi stayed still until she heard the door shut, before finally letting out the breath she held in. "*Geez,*" she blew out heavily. She went to Ashton's blow up bed, and removed the earphones from his little ears, covering him and tucking him in. Moving onto Ava, Heidi maneuvered her from the center of the bed.

"*No,*" she cried out, rolling back over.

Heidi sighed and left her a second before trying again. "*Nooooo!*" she wailed this time, a little livelier, and rolled back over.

"*Sweetheart,*" she whispered. "You need to move over; we need you over here."

"I don't want to; I want to be in the middle," she began whimpering, still partly sleeping.

"Got a bit of a problem, have we?" Anna said quietly, leaning her body and head against the bathroom door.

"Seemingly so," Heidi turned to see a picture-perfect vision. Anna's legs were toned, and long, more so in the short navy and mint, checked boxers. Even her feet looked sexy. Crossed at the bottom with a dark grey varnish on them. The navy vest was tight, displaying the curve of her breasts, and the slight peak of her nipples. Heidi's breathing increased, and she quickly returned her eyes back to her niece. "For the record, your boxers reveal more than I'm revealing."

Anna couldn't help but laugh at her as she walked over to Heidi, softly putting her hand on her wrist. "Come on, leave her be. I'll leave the sleeping bag here, and if she gets too fidgety, I'll sleep there. I have a grueling day tomorrow, so I need to get some sleep," she finished.

"Would you like me to take her downstairs? Ava and I can go and sleep on the couch."

"Nope, not unless you don't want to sleep with me," she said seriously.

They'd been flirting all day, but now, here, virtually alone... Not that anything could happen, but the fact remained that no one could hear them now. Tomorrow they'd be entirely alone again.

"Definitely not," she said sarcastically. "I was merely asking a question. You okay for me to turn the light out?"

"You betcha," she said, getting into bed, and facing a softly snoring Ava.

Heidi also lay facing Anna, her eyes gradually beginning to adjust to the darkness. As they came to, she could see Anna looking at her, Ava's tiny body a little lower, separating them.

"Are you okay?" Heidi whispered.

"Yes, are you?"

"Yes. Sorry about this. Thanks for being so good with them. At least we'll be back to normal tomorrow, so you

can have your bed to yourself again?" Heidi said. It sounded more like a question than what she intended.

"Hmm, that's true."

They lay there in silence, eyes glued to the other, yet it didn't feel awkward at all. It seemed there was so much to say, and their worlds didn't allow for it. If the words were spoken, there was *no* going back.

"Thank you for this weekend," Heidi finally whispered. "It was the best. I miss the kids so much, and they've had an awesome weekend. I think Tony had just as much fun too."

"No worries, I think it was exactly what I needed," she said thinking of Charlie. "And thanks for today."

"What are you thanking me for? I didn't do anything."

"With the stables and horses, and just being with me. I know you aren't a fan of animals, so you probably don't get it, but I don't know how I would've been without the kids…" she stopped, breathing deeply. "Or you. It's helped take my mind off it, and Jones and Mustard really did perk up."

"I'm glad I could help," she whispered again. "And just because I've never really been a fan of animals, doesn't mean I don't appreciate pain and sadness when I see it. I clearly saw radiating from you. I just wanted to make sure you were okay. When my family arrived, I was nervous it was the wrong timing, but I'm glad you feel a *little* better."

"Hmm," Anna sighed sadly. "My dad brought him for me on my 10th birthday. The first memory I have is my mum and me riding him together. Just like today, with the kids. I love all my animals, but he was a present and he was the only animal on the farm that really bound the three of us together. I guess I always thought that he was the last part of my mum left. I know that sounds stupid…"

"It *does not!* I don't know what would make you say that. I can't imagine how that must feel, to lose a parent. And then losing something that bonded you with them. It must be incredibly hard."

Anna went to say something and stopped. "Thank you, Heidi. You're pretty much as perfect as everyone makes you out to be."

"I'm far from perfect. *Nobody's* perfect," she said.

"Maybe," she said sadly. "But in my opinion, you are. And... honestly, that scares the hell out of me," she whispered.

"*Why?*"

Anna sighed heavily. "I..." she trailed off.

Heidi carefully moved her arm over her niece's body, and stroked the back of her fingers down the outline of Anna's face. "It scares me how beautiful you are," she sighed, "It scares me that when I see you sad, I want to make it better. That when I see you tired, I want to hold you in my arms, stroke your head, and let you fall asleep on me," she said running her fingers through her hair. "And it scares me that..." she sighed again, "you're a woman, and causing me to feel things I've never felt for a woman before. But what scares me the most... is that I may actually leave here without finding out if this is all one sided."

"I...it's not," she stopped sighing. "I...I don't know what's happening. And I don't know why," she said with a nervous tone.

"Anna, don't worry. Nothing's happened. I don't want you to feel uncomfortable. I can leave..."

"Don't even continue that sentence," she responded quickly. "I'm terrified, Heid's. I've switched from being terrified of what and *why* I'm feeling this way, to what

263

happens if I fight it and deny it? Just like I've always done."

"With women?" Heidi questioned.

"No," she sighed. "That part's also new for me."

"Why have you always done that?" Heidi asked, their bodies going still as Ava turned over, whimpering a little.

"I think we need to leave this here for tonight. Maybe it's not the right time or place." Anna whispered much lower.

"Yeah, you're right," Heidi confirmed, wondering if they would ever find the right time and place.

"Catch up tomorrow night?" she asked as she kissed her two fingers, and moved them to Heidi's lips. *A small gesture for her,* she thought.

Heidi's tummy flipped. There was no way she was going to sleep now. "Yes, let's. If I manage to sleep tonight after that," she said light-heartedly. Heidi stroked her cheek one last time before taking her arm back. "Good night, Anna."

Chapter Twenty-Nine

Anna woke up at four am, happy to get out of bed. It'd been an odd night, and while she hadn't felt too intoxicated, clearly, they'd had enough. That left doubts of whether they should have said all they'd said, and what the hell would happen tonight. It was the worst night's sleep she'd ever had. She woke frequently, each time seeing the beautiful woman next to her, which of course, resulted in her lying awake, and going over everything in her head again. Then of course, there was the 'dream.' She loved what her parents had, and had always wanted that herself, but when the destruction hit her father, the impact it made on him, and how it tore him apart—that's when she decided against having the "dream."

Luckily, she had a long day ahead, and with Jack off too, it would give her ample opportunity to work through her thoughts alone. She finished getting ready, and wrote a note to Heidi's family, thanking them for a fab couple of days and promised to see them all again soon.

*

Heidi had a productive day; she'd made pancakes for the kids before they left, spoke to her parents, and even tried to ring Dawn. Interestingly, her cell was off, which it seldom was. She'd even managed to finish off her story she'd been writing. All in all, it'd been a good day. She'd finished mid-afternoon, and after receiving another shipment of groceries, she decided on a roast dinner for when Anna finished work. She felt contented that it would be a little drawn out, that she'd finally have some full one on one time with her.

She checked the time. It was just after six, and she'd not seen or heard from Anna all day. She desperately hoped she was just busy without Jack's help, and hadn't changed her mind from yesterday. Although, Anna hadn't said too much before Ava had become restless; it wasn't exactly like Heidi knew what she'd be changing her mind from. *God, she needed to stop overthinking everything all the time*. She played loud music in the kitchen as she continued with dinner, completely unaware that Anna returned.

"Hey."

"Oh hi. I'm sorry; I didn't see you there."

"It's okay, I literally just walked in. You okay? Did the guys get out okay? Sorry I couldn't be here; I left a note though."

"Yes, they got it. Look at this," she said, walking over to her with a piece of paper. "Ashton gave you his cell number, and asked if you'd FaceTime him. He said his mummy and daddy said he can't tell anyone where he'd been or that he saw me, and if he promised not to say anything, would you FaceTime him and say hi? He thinks you're the coolest person ever. I did reiterate to him that his Aunty was a *four*-time global actress award winner. Apparently, that counts for nothing these days…like, *seriously*? Ava got super upset, as she's too little to have a cell phone. Personally, I think Ashton is too, but, not my call. Anyway, Meg left her cell, so that you could speak to Ava too. I said we'd call tonight and speak to them both. If you need to sleep though, it doesn't matter. I can call them."

"Even if I wanted to, there's no way I can do it before eating; it smells amazing in here. I'm starved, I've literally had half a sandwich all day," Anna smiled. "I'm gonna go shower. How long will it be?" She stopped in her tracks, turning around. "Sorry, that sounded rude. I didn't mean that to sound like I've made you go from being a multi-millionaire Hollywood star, to a cook for a farm girl," she said coyly.

"How about we stop overthinking everything and just maybe, go with the flow?" Heidi asked seriously.

"Sounds like a plan," Anna said nervously. "I'll be back soon."

Heidi poured wine and set the table for them as Anna came back downstairs wearing some workout leggings and an oversized jumper. *Not as exciting as the last two evenings, but safety and all that,* she thought.

"Shall I plate up, or do you need a minute?"

"Nope I'm good. You want me to do anything?"

"Nah, you can sit your busy butt down. I'll come to you."

"Blimey, I need to do this more often," Anna said smirking.

"Cheeky!" She said, placing the food on the table.

"Thanks, Heidi..." she said, stopping herself. "Um, I'm sorry. Just thanks."

They sat down for dinner and Heidi poured them both wine. "Did you have a good weekend, then? Well, outside the obvious. I'm sorry, that was a dumb thing to ask," she said sadly.

"Don't do that," Anna said, grabbing her hand, squeezing it, and then quickly moving it away again. "It really was, actually. Given how it started, your family visiting was probably the best thing that could have happened," she said sadly.

"I know. I'm sorry," she said, uncertain of what to say, so instead, opted for silence.

"Your food really is incredible," Anna said after a short while. "It's so nice having a proper home cooked meal, especially after eating rubbish all weekend," she said.

"I was hoping you'd like it," she said shyly.

Anna stopped, looking at her with a small smile. "I love it," she said quietly. "What do you wanna do tonight? Or will you be writing?"

"No." She smiled widely. "I've finished it. We could watch a movie or talk? What do you fancy?"

Anna looked up at her nervously as she took a deep breath. She opted to ignore the fears for today and just roll with it. Slowly, a smirk formed on her face and she raised an eyebrow.

"Behave."

"How am I not behaving? I haven't said anything."

"You don't need to speak; your face says it all."

"I have no idea what you mean," she said smiling again. "So…can I read the book then?"

"I wouldn't necessarily call it a 'book,' it's just a story." It's *rubbish*. I'm not a writer. But I enjoyed it, so I guess that's all that matters."

"Why would it be rubbish? As I said before, you must have plenty of experiences from your job. You don't need to be a writer to write a story. I bet it's fab. I really would like to read it."

"Maybe," she said simply. "What movie should we watch?"

"You going to continue changing the subject each time I mention your book?" she laughed, knowing she wouldn't respond. "I don't know, we can decide together. What's your favorite movie?"

"Um, I don't know actually. I like the old school ones."

"What, things like *Casablanca* and *The Sound of Music*?"

"I'm not that old, cheeky. I do like *The Sound of Music* though. I mean things like *Shawshank Redemption*, *Green Mile*, *Dirty Dancing*," she said.

"Oh, I love *Dirty Dancing*. And *Grease*. They are total classics. They really remind me of being a kid."

"I know, me too. If you're okay to watch them, we could do both? As long as they remind you of good memories."

"You're cute," she said blushing. "All my memories are good Heidi; it's just sad that they are *only* memories. I'd be fine to watch both."

"Cool. Great plan. Dawn and I used to watch them obsessively as kids. We taught ourselves the words and dances," she laughed memorably.

"Dear God, you aren't going to try and make me get up and sing into hairbrushes and recreate the lifts, are you?" she laughed heartily.

"You're hilar," she rolled her eyes.

"Hilar? Jesus, you're starting to sound like a child now," she rolled her eyes. "In your defence, I think every child did that," she laughed. "Do you remember me coming to Dawn's, and the sleepover at your house?"

Heidi laughed and finished her mouthful. "Yes, I was thinking about it the other day. I kept thinking we were only six last time I saw you, but you came over a few times to our houses, if I recall? I remember always being so jealous of your hair. Still am."

"Yeah, I remember you always telling me I had beautiful hair and that you wanted it. Do you remember the kids at the field?"

"What kids?" Heidi asked uncertain.

"We'd gone to a field one day. Something happened to me. I can't remember, but they did something to me… maybe call me names or something. There was one kid you punched because of what he did," she laughed.

"Oh my gosh, yes. What did he do? Oh god, I was such a weird child. I guess I felt like I needed to protect you," she laughed.

"Apparently so. Who knows, maybe you secretly fancied me back then." Anna winked, her confidence levels increasing.

Heidi coughed in shock. "I can't believe you just said that."

"I don't know what you mean. I'm just saying maybe *that's* the reason. Maybe your crush started way earlier than you thought?"

"You think I have a crush on you? You're very cocksure, aren't you?"

"Nope, not really. I can just see the desire in your eyes," she laughed.

"Shut up," she said in response. "Stop misbehaving."

"As if I would. You finished? I'll clear up," she said, picking up the plate.

"No, you've been at work all day; you go and get us a movie to watch," she said clearing away the dishes, allowing the nerves in her tummy to subside. *Was she really going to do this*? She sighed heavily, shaking the thoughts from her mind and letting go. She downed the last of her wine, and finished loading the dishwasher before gaining the strength to broach wherever the evening took them.

Heidi watched Anna put the logs in the fire and light it. The sun was already down and she opened the blinds, lighting some candles. Heidi watched Anna, who was distantly mesmerized by the candles.

"Are you okay?" Heidi came over.

"Um, yes. I'm fine," she said embarrassed, looking away quickly.

The reality had hit; they'd flirted and made their feelings quite clear, but they hadn't been alone since those revelations. Until now. This was the first time. Two straight women. *Were they? Was Anna straight? Maybe that's why she'd never had a relationship?* This was *the* first time there had been the potential for something to happen beyond flirting. The nerves suddenly kicked in for her, and she was not so sure how to act.

"Are you okay?" Anna asked.

"Yes fine," she breathed heavily.

"Have you heard from Dawn about what's going on back home?" Anna said, filling their glasses up with more wine and sitting down on the floor.

"No, I tried to call her today actually, but it went straight to voicemail. I'll give her a call tomorrow," she said sitting down next to Anna, purposely leaving some space.

"Do you know what you're going to do?"

"Um, no, actually. I'm starting to get pretty pissed by the fact I'm acting so petulant. More so over the fact I don't even seem bothered by it. I'm thinking I may just sign the papers and get my lawyer to sort it out," she said distantly.

"I'm sorry, Heidi, I really am," she said, placing her hand on Heidi's leg.

Heidi inadvertently gasped. "Umm, don't be," she said looking away, enjoying the warmth from the touch. "I'm okay, just a bit infuriated that it's resulted in this," she said noticing the sadness cross Anna's face. "Well, obviously not *this*, but me having to run out so quickly. This—you— have made it all the worthwhile," she said quietly.

Anna smiled widely. "So, do you think you'd try and give it another go?"

"With Ev?" she spat.

"Well, yeah?"

"Hell no!" she said astonished. "It isn't the first time, you know?"

"What isn't?"

"The cheating. He's cheated on numerous occasions over the years. This wasn't the first, and it *won't* be the last, regardless of him becoming a father," she confirmed.

"Oh… I'm sorry to hear that."

"Seriously, don't be. I grieved, did the whole getting angry, crying, and smashing things many years ago. It's all over with now. I'm not hurt or numb. I'm just done, I guess."

"I get it," she sipped slowly.

"Anyway, what about you? I know you haven't dated in a while, but what's your type?"

"Random. I don't have one really. I guess it's just fizzled out of me."

"Come on, you must."

"Nope, really. I haven't looked at anyone for 20 years. How about you?"

"Um, I don't know. I like nice eyes, and a cute smile. Honesty and integrity. Go figure," she rolled her eyes.

"Hmm, true," Anna said thoughtfully.

"Come on, give me something. I punched a kid out for you back when we were kids. The least you can do is entertain me."

Anna spat her wine out in shock.

"*SHIT*! I didn't mean it like that," Heidi said, embarrassed. "Entertain me like, tell me stuff," she corrected.

"God, you are not going to let this go, are you? Fine!" She said rolling her eyes. "Um, a nice smile, and cute eyes. I'll steal that from you." She smiled. "Nice eyes, like deep blue, like… you consider them and can literally see deep-into-their-soul-blue," she added. "Hmm and a uniform. I *love* a uniform."

"Dress up, who'd have thought it? The farm girl has a naughty streak," she giggled.

"Don't you know it? "she laughed. "Oh and lastly, a nice bum. I love a nice bum," she winked.

"Oh, there's loads of cute butts in L.A., and cute uniforms too. You should totally come visit; you'd love it," she said, knowing full well that it would never happen; they were completely worlds apart.

"Sound good," She winked.

"I must say though, you can't beat a bit of uniform. Anyway, we need to stop this conversation. What movie we are watching?"

"How about *Dirty Dancing* since we mentioned it earlier? One more bottle?" she said, holding the empty bottle of wine.

"Are you going to be okay with another?"

"Yeah, you have me well trained. I typically don't drink this much," Anna laughed, making her way to the kitchen for more wine.

"Good thing you have a physical job that keeps you in shape. What would you do if you didn't do this?"

"Gosh, you're all over these tough questions today, lady."

"I know, I'm interested in your responses. Now answer."

"Ever so demanding, aren't you? Honestly, I don't know. Probably a firefighter; I've always fancied that," Anna said.

"Wowzers, you really do like those uniforms, huh?" She winked.

"To save people for a living, actually." She rolled her eyes. "Although the uniform would be a bonus," She smirked.

"Yeah, I bet. I could imagine you in that uniform. The uniform in the states is way better than the one you have here. I could see you in that uniform, all cute in those big ole boots, being all strong and stuff." She raised her eyebrows.

"So much for being good, eh?"

"It's the wine talking. Anyway, how am I being bad? I'm merely stating that my very attractive friend would suit a firefighter outfit."

"Very attractive? Wow, big words. It's only because of the hair; you told me already," she raised her brow.

"Hardly. I like that, yes, but I also like your big, brown eyes, the tiny, grey speckles in them, your dimples, that big smile, your incredible arms—well, *body*," she confirmed. "Just a few of the things," she laughed.

"Blimey, wish I'd not said anything. Now I've got a big head. Thank you, that's very kind of you to say. Anyway, what about you?"

"What about me?"

"What would you do if you weren't the biggest name to walk the earth?" she said seriously.

"I'm not really *that* much of a big deal."

"No, course not! Remind me…when did you last leave the house again?" she asked.

"*Shut up.* Are we putting on the movie?"

"Yeah, but first you must tell me what you'd be doing if you weren't acting. Or would you be the next John Grisham?"

"Hardly. The story I wrote is romance, not anything too taxing. Honestly, I don't know. This is all I've ever wanted to do. However, if I stopped acting tomorrow, I would probably go and buy a remote place in southern Italy with loads of space and have my own vineyard and make my own wine. To sell obviously, not to drink," she giggled.

"Oh yeah, I can imagine the Hollywood star, who's used to nothing but a lavish lifestyle, willingly able to give all that up to crush grapes in the sun."

"I don't deny that I've been incredibly lucky and fortunate for all of the things I've experienced, but to be perfectly honest, that's Dawn's thing, *not* mine. I love my job—don't get me wrong—but I hate the lifestyle. I hate the fact that if I need to run out for some milk, I must have a team of artists to work on me first. Or the alternative is I get bombarded. I hate the fact that I'm championing a cause which I completely disagree with; I think women are beautiful in all forms. Why should I have to get done up before I go for a run, or go grab milk? I hate that I have no privacy, and am unable to do the simplest of things. I remember before I got a big lead, I was exactly like Jack. Every Friday and Saturday I'd get a train into London. Of course, Dawn would drag us to some upmarket place and flirt with some famous athlete or actor to get free champagne. I'd happily spend the night dancing and drinking and then at 10:30 the following morning, I'd pick Dawn up and we'd go to McDonalds drive thru for a Big Mac meal and then go home to bed. Do you know how oddly satisfying that was, how many hours I've spent wishing I was still able to do it? Dawn loves it, always has, but I could lose it all tomorrow, and be happier in the end. Interestingly, I've significantly enjoyed my time here. It's made me realize a lot. So you're wrong, farm girl," she laughed, pointing her finger suggestively.

"Okay okay," she said, holding her hands up in mock defeat. "Well evidently, I've been suitably told. So, any more questions, or do I get to watch my movie now?"

"God, and you say I'm demanding? But yes, for sure. I'll press play. We may need some goodies later though. You wanna sit on the couch or are you happy to stay down here?"

"Here's fine," Anna said, banging shoulders with Heidi. She used the purpose of refilling their glasses with more wine to sneak a little bit closer.

*

The pair were enjoying the movie, singing along merrily. The alcohol was flowing, and the confidence was growing. They were relaxed. They still hadn't discussed what was going on between them, nor what had happened in bed last night, but the more alcohol that went down, the more Heidi was desperate to do something. She sipped more wine and tried to replicate the night Jack had turned up. Her and Anna had unobtrusively made contact, and she wanted to revisit that. Determinedly, changing drinking hands, she took a sip, and casually lowered her hand between them, lightly sweeping past Anna's thigh. Her heart beat fast, and she was barely able to slow her breathing down. In this moment, all she knew was desperation to see what it would be like to kiss Anna.

Anna could feel the effects of the wine. This whole situation scared the hell out of her. She stole a glance at Heidi watching the movie, noticing her chest moving frantically. Heidi moved her hand, and she thought she may have just grazed past her leg. *Did she do it purposely?* Anna wondered. She chose to ignore her doubts. *Was she going to do this? Jesus, what was she doing? She didn't do this, ever.* Anna didn't date, or get involved, least not with a woman. A *woman*? *Really*? She stopped herself again, and followed what her body seemed to cry out for. Taking a deep breath, Anna put her hand down next to Heidi's with the base of her fingers covering hers as she leaned over her legs and grabbed the bottle. "Sorry," she whispered.

Filling each of their glasses, Anna returned to her seat, but this time moved her body just a little closer. Refusing to down the drink to appease her nerves, she slowly sipped before placing her hand back to where it had just been, lightly covering Heidi's. She caught Heidi's quick glance to their hands, and noticed her chest movement begin to rise again. Anna watched as Heidi carefully moved her hand discreetly under her touch. They fixated on the TV, but softly, grazed the other's hands.

The room suddenly burst to life as the famous words from *Dirty Dancing* filled the air.

"I've been meaning to tell you,
I've got this feeling that won't subside
I look at you and I, fantasize."

Heidi heard the song and couldn't ignore the pertinent words fulfilling them.

"You're mine tonight."

Her heart raced. She had no clue how this would pan out, but Heidi couldn't hold back any longer. She turned to Anna whose eyes slowly turned to Heidi. They sat still, eyes locked, for what seemed like an eternity. Neither one knew how to take the next move.

"Now I've, got you in my sights
With these… hungry eyes."

The song lyrics played with their emotions and they lost control. Heidi rushed in, finally meeting Anna's lips with her own, finally allowing their longing to overtake them both.

The kiss intensified, and all fears and concerns seemed to deteriorate. They completely let go. Heidi pushed Anna down to the floor, kissing her harder, and pushing her hand under her top and around her waist. She pushed her other hand under Anna's rear and pulled her in closer, deepening the kiss. There was a sudden knock at the door.

"Shit!" Heidi said stopping, pulling away from Anna, and straightening her hair.

"Leave it, just *leave* it!" Anna gasped and pushed Heidi over, rolling on top of her and deepening the kiss again. She felt Heidi's leg push deep in between her thighs and couldn't help but cry out. The knock became louder, bolder, and they couldn't let it go unnoticed this time. They stopped in their tracks, their bodies intertwined, hands inexplicably placed and their breathing, accentuated. They heard the knock for a third time.

"Come onnn!" Heidi said loudly. "You've gotta be *kidding* me," Heidi sighed loudly, pushing her head in her hands.

Anna shook her head dramatically and closed her eyes as she rested her forehead on Heidi's. "I'm sorry. I'll get rid of them," she kissed the hand that was covering her head.

Heidi sat up when Anna moved away and adjusted her clothing, feeling desperately frustrated. "Damn it," she muttered under her breath as she turned to see Anna reach the door and before opening it, throw back a quick smirk and wink to her. *God this woman,* Heidi thought.

"Surprise!" Heidi heard a familiar squeal. *Please God no!*

"*Dawn!?*" Anna stuttered. "Um, what are you *doing* here?"

"What do you think? I'm here to see you guys. Fuck me An, I live in L.A. Can I come in? I'll get hypothermia out here!" She spat, pushing through the door and spotting her best friend.

"*Darling*! How are you? You look amazing," she said stroking her face carefully.

"Heeeey, what are you *doing* here?" Heidi said, giving her best friend a kiss and a hug.

"What do you think? You told me you were ready to come home. I figured you'd be ready to go to a premiere on Tuesday."

Heidi zoned out, looking at the sadness in Anna's eyes. She didn't know how to express that this wasn't what she was thinking, despite the pleading and begging glare.

"Anyway, I'm desperate to pee, so get me an invite to this party and I'll be back 'tout suite?'"

Heidi couldn't risk it going wrong, not after all this time. She waited for her best friend to leave the room and rushed over to Anna. "Please don't take that how she said. *Please,* Anna," she said pleadingly. "I texted her in the middle of the night, when the whole Charlie situation happened. You shouted at me and left and... I don't know... *fuck*!" I'm never this much of a pathetic loser. I just didn't want to overstay my welcome..."

"Bu—"

"Please stop, I have more to say. I didn't know how to handle you not liking me or wanting me, and most importantly, not turning to me when you needed someone. Jesus, what is she *doing* here?" she said as the sound of the toilet flushed. "I'm sorry. I've had the most spectacular couple of hours with you. Please don—" she whispered, cut off by Dawn's re-entrance. She turned to pour a third glass of wine instead.

"So, my two favorite people. How's everything gone? Anna, you look as beautiful as ever," she said, pulling her cousin in to a side hug. "How are you? I believe you've been treating my beautiful girl like a queen?"

"That she has," Heidi walked over and put her arm around Anna. She kissed her cheek softly; softly for impact, but not enough to make Dawn suspicious.

Anna gently put her arm discreetly around the back of Heidi. She placed it under her vest, and gently stroked her thumb over the bare skin of her back. She felt Heidi flinch.

"So, what's been going down, you guys?" Dawn said.

"Come on, let's sit down," Anna said, pushing her cousin forward softly and moving her hand slightly down Heidi's yoga pants to the curve of her bottom. Heidi gasped silently, turning to see Anna with a wicked grin on her face.

At least she didn't seem mad at her, Heidi thought.

"You both look incredible. It's scaring me how amazing you look. I'm pretty sure the promise of a ridiculously steep bonus worked on your PT; you look radiant. Clearly my idea was as awesome as me." She smiled cockily. "Apparently, some alone time with this beautiful girl was all you needed," Dawn said, blissfully ignorant to the flushes crossing each of their faces.

"Yeah, it's been awesome. So, what're you doing here?" Heidi asked again.

"Well, things have been so up and down, and then the other day, it totally took a 'down' when Ev got some fucking douchebag to come threaten to serve *me* for not telling him where you were. I mean, *really*? Give me a break!" She said, rolling her eyes. "Anyway, the day that all happened, I got home from work, and got the second request for a London premiere. I'd listened to your message about a minute later, about being ready to come home, and thought, *bingo*, let's really screw him," she stopped, taking a sip of her wine. "So, you know how my brain works," she said, smirking and raising her eyebrows frantically.

"*What?*" Heidi asked confused.

"What can I say... the Hollywood movie scene, is *in* my blood. I figured that a little bit of my beautiful bestie, coming out of hiding with... oh hell, no... *wait wait wait!*"

"What?"

"Just you wait." She ran off and pulled open the dress bag zipper, revealing the most stunning, navy fitted dress, the back completely missing and a built-in diamanté choker. The dress was probably worth more than the cottage she'd gone to with her parents last week.

"Dawn, it's incredible," she said, admiring it silently.

"I hope you don't mind, Anna, but I did the honors. I spoke to Mum. She said you're still annoying, tall, curvaceous, and athletic," she said, unzipping another bag. "Bronze is a beautiful tone. It'll really compliment your skin color, and with those enviable dark curls, you'll look outstanding. I got Jack a tux. The plan is the four of us go, and my beautiful bestie appears, preened to perfection, happy, and positively glowing with a new beau on her arm." She smiled demonically. "I've got a full crew coming over tomorrow to pamper to high hell, and then project 'Hiding Heidi' is on," she stood, taking a bow for them.

"Dawn, it's really kind, seriously, but Jack and I can't leave. I have nobody to look after the farm. It's physically impossible. Look, take Jack; he's the one you need. I can cover."

"*No!*" both women screeched in unison, causing Dawn to look at Heidi in confusion.

"Sorry," Heidi said shyly. "You've been so accommodating, Anna. If I'm going, I want you to come too. Please come?"

Anna couldn't say no to those pleading eyes, especially after what happened before Dawn arrived. "I just don't know—"

"Please, for me?" she said sadly.

Anna sighed heavily. She was doomed, well and truly. "Lemme see what I can sort out." She said, downing her whole glass of wine and sighing slightly.

"Great, that's sorted then. It's been a long ass day, and we have a hectic 48 hours, so I'm gonna go dump my stuff. Is the third room still an office?"

"Yes, you know me; I love my gadgets." She smiled warmly.

"I know, you geek. So, it's okay to share?"

Heidi and Anna both looked at each other, saying 'yes' maybe just a little too enthusiastically. They tried containing their faint smiles.

"Right then… Eenie meenie miney mo—"

"What are you doing?" Heidi asked questioningly.

"Working out who I should share with. I guess I can stay with you any time when we go back home, and I never see you, so I'll crash with you," she said, pointing to her cousin.

"Well, you've been travelling all day and night. You take my bed. I can sleep with Anna," Heidi said, trying to ignore the flustered look on Anna's face.

"No way. I'm fine; we have a pamper day tomorrow, it's all good. Plus, I want to catch up with you both," she said, kissing her cousin on the cheek.

"Well, that's all well and good, but you have half an hour and then I need to get to bed. I have to be up at 4:30, maybe earlier if you want me to leave for a couple of days."

"Still ever the bore, I see."

"We just have different lives and priorities," Anna said, annoyed with herself for being reactive.

"Hey, I'm joking. I'm sorry. You know I don't mean that, right?" she asked concerned. "You're normally equally as sarcastic."

"I'm sorry, D. It's just been a long and stressful few days. Look, I'm going to let you guys catch up. Why don't you crash with Heid's tonight? Let me catch up on my sleep as we've had her family over, Charlie happened, and then Jack's been off today. I need some proper rest, and then tomorrow we can catch up properly. Hopefully by then I've sorted out who'll maintain the farm."

"You sure?"

"Yes, definitely. I'll see you tomorrow, okay?"

"Sure," Dawn said, waiting for her to leave the room. "What's up with her?" Dawn asked, confused.

"Um, it's Charlie, the horse that her mum and she used to ride together. He died a couple of days ago.

"Charlie?!" Dawn said shocked.

"Yeah."

"Shit... no... I need to g—"

"*Don't, Dawn*. It happened, and then right after, Tone and Meg arrived with the kids. They left this morning while she was at work, and we'd *just* sat down to a movie. She literally hasn't had a chance to digest it, let alone anything else. Give her tonight, let her read a book, watch TV or sleep. Then we can give her time to talk about it, if she wants, on Tuesday," she said seriously.

"I'm glad you were with her. I don't know what she would have done without you. I hate that she's all alone. I wish she would find someone; she so deserves happiness."

Heidi ignored her comment about being here for her. "I'm glad I was too. She said she felt better that the kids had come up, that it took her mind off it somewhat. Just leave her for now and we can cheer her up tomorrow."

"Okay, cool. Dude, I've missed you *so* much," she kissed her face and pulled her in. "So, do you mind if I grab a quick shower, and then we can catch up?"

"Yeah sure. Come on, I'll show you to my room. I've been drinking pretty much all day, so I may not be up for much longer. Plus, Helen comes early. How about I bring the wine up to bed and we catch up there?"

"Oh, great plan."

"Good stuff. I'll go and get everything, and you get unpacked. Here's a towel," Heidi said. "How long are you staying for?" Heidi asked.

"Just until Friday, why?"

"Well, I wasn't sure if you were only here until the premiere, so I was gonna say if you wanna unpack, just move some of my stuff around."

"Oh, great. I'll get a few bits out since I'll probably workout with you guys tomorrow. I need silk pajamas, ASAP." She sighed.

"Awesome, well I'll let you get showered, and I'll grab the wine."

"Cool, thanks," Dawn said, walking into the bathroom, and shutting the door behind her.

Heidi stood outside Anna's room, waiting for the water in her bathroom to turn on. Once she was confident Dawn was in the shower, she gently tapped on Anna's door, knowing she wouldn't be asleep that quick.

"Yeah?"

She opened the door, seeing Anna partially covered, and reading her book. "Are you kidding me right now?" Heidi said, checking behind her and sneaking in, making sure to shut the door.

"What?" Anna said, smiling.

"You look like you're preparing for an FHM photo shoot, sprawled out in your panties and vest," she said, standing against the door.

"I have no idea what you mean; I was just hot," she said sardonically.

"You really are very *naughty*," she said, making her way towards her bed.

"Says the woman who comes into my room, and walks towards my bed while my cousin is showering next door." She raised an eyebrow.

"What? I'm merely coming to see what your book is about," she smirked.

"Really? Here you are then," Anna said as Heidi reached her side of the bed, handing the book over to her.

Heidi raised an eyebrow, skimming a page. "Sounds riveting. Seems the universe is against us getting it on, huh?" she smirked.

"Seemingly so. Although, if I'm not mistaken, we're currently alone."

"Yes, but even your cousin doesn't take that long."

"That long for what? What exactly are you expecting to take a long time?"

"Oh, you know…" Heidi said, leaning over Anna, using one arm to hold herself up and the other to tiptoe her fingers up her bare leg, watching her close her eyes. "You have no idea what you do to me. Things I cannot explain. I'm past trying to look for an explanation. I just want you, like I've never wanted anybody," she whispered in Anna's ear.

She groaned a little. "Scarily, I feel the same. The anticipation, especially when you keep coming so close, is killing me," she said.

Heidi lowered her body on top of Anna's and kissed her again, this time slower, softer, and with more meaning. It killed her that they couldn't just let go, and see what happened. *The kiss was perfect,* Heidi thought. She could feel Anna's body embrace her own as they pulled closer in to the kiss. With one arm around her lower back, and the other on her face, Heidi was completely engulfed in the moment. *Man, this woman could kiss*, Heidi thought. She knew she'd have to pull away, as Dawn would be out any moment. She was the type of woman who would happily barge in to any and every room with no forewarning.

Heidi pulled away, considering her eyes. "God woman, you're killing me."

"Touché. What is it they say about anticipation? Makes everything worth waiting for?"

"I certainly hope so given your cousin is here through Friday. That's a whole heap more tension."

"Dear God, I don't know if I can cope. We may need to get you to help me 'work,' so we can sneak off for a little bit of 'farm girl' fun," she mused.

Worlds Apart

"You realize that sounds like a porn movie, right? At this moment in time, I'm feeling as though I'm pretty much ready to do anything if it means I get to be with you without any interruptions," she winked. "I really should go. I'm pissed she's crashing with me. How much fun we could've had, sharing a bed, being sneaky, unable to make any noise," she said naughtily.

"You're a very *bad* woman. Some of us have work, so maybe that wouldn't have been the greatest idea. Anyway, *go*, let me...um, attempt, to sleep a little before tomorrow."

"You have no idea how bad I can be. Hopefully, we'll get to explore that together soon," she said, leaning down and kissing her again. Heidi didn't want this to end. She deepened the kiss a little more, and pulled at Anna's thigh, alongside her own, causing them both to groan.

"Come on! If she catches us, this will never end well," Anna stated.

"*Really*?" she said somberly. "Would it not be worth it so we can just..." she groaned loudly, "do this already?"

"Come on. Behave. It'll be far better if we can take our time, wait until we're entirely alone," Anna said kissing her cheek. "Now go. The water's stopped."

"Okay, okay. Good night, farm girl," she said, blowing Anna a kiss.

"Good night, Hollywood. Sweet dreams," she winked.

"They will be," she whispered, leaving the room. Anna was left giddily confused by the events of the past 24 hours.

*

Heidi lay on the bed, wine in one hand, kindle in the other. She'd read the same page six or seven times as her mind constantly deviated to the day's events. Her mind ran

287

amok with her, and she was confused about the whole 'girl on girl' thing. Was it possible to just turn gay? *Was* she gay now? Or did she need to have sex with her before that happened? Jesus, how would she have sex with her? She didn't know what she was supposed to do. What if she didn't like it and she realized it was just a temporary 'moment of insanity.' Maybe her mum and Dawn were right. Maybe there was such a thing as pansexual, and she didn't need to label herself. *Yes!* Why *should* she? She pondered this as Dawn came out of the bathroom in her silk pj's.

"Been a while," she said, kneeling and holding the tequila up. "I need gossip, girl time, chocolate, and tequila." She grinned wickedly.

"That's all well and good, but when I can't get up tomorrow to work out, and it's the day before the premiere, you're going to be kicking my ass because I'm too unfit and fat, and we have no time to get ready," she said sternly.

"Cut it out, you know I'm only winding you up. I'm sorry, I *was* looking out for you though. I hope you know that. Come on, chocolate and tequila. You can skip out on the workout if you need to. What did you think of the dress by the way?"

"I love it. Hopefully it will look okay."

"It will; I'm great at this. Then we just need to get everything else sorted. Tomorrow they'll start to arrive at three in the afternoon, so it should be good," she said.

Chapter Thirty

Heidi tried everything to pacify the fears and concerns following last night's escapades with Anna. Not seeing her in the morning left her with bottomless anguish that she was going to have had a mini meltdown over it all. With Dawn following her around like a small child, she was unable to go out and find her. The afternoon came quickly, and went exactly how Dawn described. She'd arranged hairdressers, pedicurists, manicurists, tanning artists, eyebrow artists, masseuses, waxers—the list was endless.

"Did you get someone to cover?" Dawn asked her cousin eagerly, once she finally relaxed a little, and began to ignore all the people in her house.

"Yeah, but I'm still unsure. I've never done this before. Jack's really looking forward to it, but, seriously, it isn't really my thing. I don't know why you don't just take him; he's the one you need."

"Anna, I'm not going to force you to come if you really don't want to, but they can often be quite entertaining., and I'd personally really like you to come with us. For *me,*" Heidi said with hidden meaning.

"What time do we have to leave?" she sighed, hearing Dawn squeal in delight.

"It'll be amazing to have you there. And, the closest I'm ever going to get you to the real red carpet of L.A." she said.

Anna ignored the comment. "What's the plan, then?" she asked Dawn.

"Well I've got separate cars for us," she said unaware of the glances between Heidi and Anna. "In case Heidi comes straight back here to collect her stuff, and not straight back with me, I didn't want them seeing you two together; you would get hounded. You have so much land, they'd swarm in," she stated factually. "I booked two cars. I figured we can go there around two, and finish getting ready in her room. If you and Jack come in the three o'clock car, I've got us four rooms all next to each other. When you guys arrive, come straight up to Heidi's for a pre-party aperitif, and final preening. Then, presto! We go down, show her face off, and enjoy the ride. You'll just be regarded as a competition couple, and they won't pay too much attention to you."

"Right, that makes sense," Anna said.

"Sure," Heidi mumbled, trying to read a distant and sad looking Anna. She felt bad. This would completely take her out of her comfort zone. This wasn't what Anna was about. They really were worlds apart.

Dawn sensed something between the two of them. They'd been acting weird last night, but she put it down to jet lag. Today, they just seemed off. She thought they'd be stoked. Well, probably not Anna. She was such a simple soul; she'd rather be in shorts and a t-shirt with a beer in her hand, and a good movie. But Heidi? Dawn and she lived for these types of things. She just couldn't put her finger on it. "You want a drink?" she asked them.

"Um, no. I'm good, thanks. I'm gonna crash.

"It's six pm," Dawn said. "I haven't even seen you!"

"Dawn, I know you think it's all excuses, but this is my business, my livelihood. Working on a farm isn't like the jobs you guys have. I can't just get up and disappear for a couple of days. It takes time, organization, which I really haven't been doing," she sighed, rubbing her temple. "I really need an early night, so I can get a good amount of work in before we leave." She could see the disappointment on Dawn's face. *Seriously, get her back to her own life,* she thought. "Look, thanks for all of this." She played with her newly cut hair.

"That's okay," she said knowingly. I'm really looking forward to having you be a part of tomorrow. I hope you know that. I'm sorry I've come in and pushed you into doing this. I just really wanted to give you one day out of work. You have no release. I thought it would be something enjoyable for you. I know you'll say it's not your thing, but you've done so much for us both. It means the world," she said sincerely, making Anna feel bad.

"It's fine. Thank you for getting me a ticket. I'll enjoy it, don't worry. It's been my pleasure; not everybody can say they had a Hollywood A-lister as their roomie," she said. "Come on, I'll have one drink with you both while I have something to eat."

"Do you want me to make you something?" Heidi asked.

"No, I think I'm going to piss my favorite cousin off."

"What do you mean?"

"I'm craving Chinese. While I did agree to tomorrow, you're not threatening me with getting fat. I'm old enough to make my own choices and I want Chinese," Anna said simply.

"Cheeky cow. Well, I best we all give them something to talk about. I could murder a sweet and sour chicken," Dawn laughed, feeling her cousin relax a little.

"Oh my God, who are you, and what have you done to my agent?" Heidi said, making a face.

"Funny. *Real* comical. Look, I know you think I'm a bitch and stuff for going on and on about the weight thing, but I never meant any of it in a bad way, Heid's. You know what they're like. You've always had a body to kill for and those are the ones they prey on. I just didn't want you to be at an all-time low with all this Everett BS, and then the press point out a tiny roll that wasn't there before. Jesus, it's traumatic enough, some of the stuff they write. You didn't come out of your bedroom for a month. I wasn't being nasty, I was trying to protect you."

"I know. We live in Hollywood; you have to go into hiding when you get a spot of acne on your face, or the world goes mad. Dawn, you *love* the place, you *love* the life; *you* adapted to it with the flick of a switch, but I never did. It's not my thing. It never has been, and that's why I hired you to be my agent. You're awesome at it, and I'll always accept you keeping me on track and telling me it as it is. I don't think you're doing anything other than managing me and looking out for me. You keep me grounded, Dawn, probably because you are so far off the ground yourself," she laughed. "It makes me realize I wanna stay firmly there," she jokingly slapped her best friend's arm. "What's going on, D? Why're you so sad?"

"I'm fine… I don't know. I just feel like I've lost you a bit. You don't seem yourself. I've missed you, and I figured it would all be good when I arrived and…well, it hasn't really," she said sadly.

"I think you're overthinking it, sweetie. There's just been a lot going on. Plus, it's all been a surprise," Heidi rolled her eyes. "Come on, let's order Chinese and have a bottle. You can fill me in on what's going on with my cheating husband," she said kindly.

Chapter Thirty-One

"I'll see you in a couple of hours, yeah?" Heidi said to Anna, squeezing her hand slightly.

"Yeah, will do. And stop with the PDA. Either Dawn's going to suspect something, or I'm gonna end up jumping on you after a couple of drinks." She pulled her face. "She's already acting like you prefer me to her."

"Well, I love her. She's my best friend *and* my manager, but..." Heidi stopped and looked around at the car in front of her, leaning in to Anna's ear. "I don't daydream about her doing things to me with those sexy arms...those *lips*...that body. I guess the point is, I really want you on a sexual level. See you shortly," she squeezed her hand, and jogged off to Dawn and the waiting car.

Anna breathed in deeply, trying to ignore what their parting words were doing to her body. *Geez, what the hell are you doing,* she thought as Jack reached her side.

"Boss, you okay? You look a bit...um, odd," he said smiling a little.

"Oh, hey. You're here. You ready to go? I've been up since three am. Our driver will be here in an hour, so we have time for a cheeky beer," she said grinning.

"Knew there was a reason you were my favorite boss. Are you and Heidi okay?"

"Yes, why?" she asked cautiously.

"I don't know. You both looked a bit odd when I was coming in. A bit secretive I suppose."

Anna took the lid off the bottles and handed one to him. "I don't know what you mean. Secretive about what? We're fine. You know me, I'm happiest in my trackie, mucking out the yard. Them making me do all this because, allegedly, I *need* some time out... it's just not really my deal, I suppose. Plus, they only needed you. Thought I'd give it one last go of trying to get out of it, *but* I suppose it's a free night."

"And a load of hot movie stars," he winked.

"Oh yeah. I'm sure they'll sit there looking at the 'countrified farm spinster' from across the room with longing glares," she rolled her eyes.

"Well if they don't, they're fools. You're one in a million. Not too bad on the eye either for an old bird," he laughed.

"*Charming*. I can still sack you, you know that, don't you?"

"Yeah, but you're not my boss today." He grinned.

"God, you're as annoying as Heidi with that whole '*sweetness and light*' thing. Very infuriating," Anna said, rolling her eyes. "So, you looking forward to tonight?"

Interesting that she's frustrated by Heidi, he thought. "Yeah, I really am. I debated bailing, though," he said distantly.

"*Really*? Why?"

"I didn't feel so great about the lies. My mum can just tell. I hate that. I'm so close to them, so lying made me feel pretty crap."

"Yeah I suppose. What've you said then?"

"I just said that your cousin was an agent in L.A. and got two tickets to a movie premiere for us. I technically wasn't lying. I just made out we were invited to a premiere because Heidi was here for it. You think she'll be around for much longer?"

"Dawn? Doubtful, why?"

"No, Heidi."

"Oh, um ...I don't know. She hasn't said anything to me, but I suspect that Dawn's probably here for a reason. I suspect they'll get the whole divorce situation moving along. Been a weird couple of weeks, hasn't it?" she said distantly.

"Sure has, beautiful. Sure has," he responded comfortingly. "We'll have a ball tonight you know? We can have a little wager, if you fancy? You know, make things a little bit exciting," he said, dancing around with his hands.

"Why do I feel like you and I are about to get into more trouble tonight than we have throughout our *entire* adulthood?"

"Because you know me better than most. Plus, you're on this little road of *naughtiness* as of late, and I'm intrigued."

"Little road of naughtiness? Am I? Fill me in. What exactly is this 'little road of naughtiness?'" she asked, hearing the door knock. Their car had arrived.

"All of this misbehaving, drinking and staying up late with a superstar, of course. What did you think I meant?" he smirked. Anyway, come on; let's do this. I'll think of something we could do," he smirked and put his arm around her shoulder. "Promise you, we'll have a ball."

Chapter Thirty-Two

"What do you think?" The stylist smiled widely. Anna turned to the mirror for the first time since her hair and makeup had been done.

"Wow… Jesus, you're incredibly talented," she said unable to recognize the woman looking back at her in the mirror.

"Well, it's far easier when you have authentic beauty to work with. You're naturally beautiful. Your bone structure, wide brown eyes, long lashes, cute dimples, and just the perfect amount of color—not too pale and not too dark. All I did was enhance that beauty," the young girl said.

"They must pay you well," she said, uplifted by her compliments. "Thanks," she said, grabbing her purse.

"You don't need to worry about that; everything's been sorted. Have a great evening," she said, walking out of the room.

Anna looked in the mirror again. Her black curls were loosely pulled into a side bun on the lower left side, which would complement the strapless dress she'd be wearing. The makeup was soft; the girl had said that because of her features they would go with low key makeup, focusing on blush to accentuate her high cheek bones and distinctive dimples. The only thing they'd been quite liberal with was eye makeup. Smoky eyes were 'apparently' the '*in*' thing, now, and she couldn't deny that the varying bronzes they'd applied really did pay tribute to her eyes.

Anna changed into the bronze dress that Dawn got her. *It was weird; she never dressed up. In fact, the most she ever did was a shirt with nice jeans at Christmas*, she thought, hearing the door knock.

"She nervously adjusted herself, slipped her feet into the heels, and opened the door.

Jack stood at her door looking like he'd just walked out of Hollywood himself, having removed the 'designer' stubble he always referred to, and his hair professionally styled for the night. He looked up from his phone. "Jesus, Mary, and Joseph!" he spat. "Bloody hell, you scrub up well," he said astonished.

"Thanks, I think," she laughed. "You look great by the way. Very dapper. I think you'll be fighting them off tonight. You've even had a shave I see. I thought the rough and rugged look was all the rage?"

"Yeah, for a farm hand. Tonight, we're big time. Seriously, hun, you look amazing. I genuinely mean that," he smiled to his friend. "You would undoubtedly be my first choice tonight," he said, kissing her hand and holding his arm out for her to take.

"You big softie. Come on, let's mess this shit up," she said mischievously.

"Let's do it," he said.

*

Heidi walked out onto the red carpet, engaging with the public and press. Oddly, she felt completely out of her comfort zone, but she plastered a smile on her face and politely avoided the questions of her whereabouts and the situation with Everett. Dawn had set everything up last night. A few champagnes for nerve control would be had before the announcement later.

"You okay?" Dawn asked.

"Yes, why? Are *you?*"

"Yes, but I know you, and this isn't you. You've been acting weird since I arrived. I feel like you don't even want me here. Then tonight you just, I don't know… turn right and smile," she said quickly as they both turned and put on their best Hollywood smiles.

"You're just overthinking it, Dawn," she leaned in and whispered to her. "We haven't spent this must time apart in 30 odd years."

"I don't think it's that. There's something else, I can tell," she said sadly.

"Of course it is," she said, holding her hand. "I've been in the public eye on such ridiculous levels, 24/7 for 20 odd years, with literally my *entire* life on show and up for public debate. Transitioning from that to suddenly hiding away is a huge lifestyle change. Don't get me wrong, I've loved it…"

"You have?"

"Yes, I have. You know me, I'm not good with change. Coming back into the limelight like nothing's changed is odd. I promise it isn't you. I'm glad you're here. How about we do a spa day tomorrow?"

"Good, I'm glad. Sounds like a plan. Let's see how tonight goes. Oh, and Heidi, you know how Troy mentioned that you might be into someone? I hope you know I love you, no matter what. If you're into Helen, I don't care. Troy could even get her work in the states, and honestly, I'd easily sort the publicity side out," she said sincerely.

"You're the best, but I don't nor have I ever liked Helen. She's super cool, and yes, very good looking, but *no,* that's not the situation at all. I'm just a little overwhelmed by what's happened recently," she said smiling.

"Can we join this party?" They turned to the male voice.

"Hey you—" *Words...words, Heidi. Jesus, stop looking and say something,* she thought. She desperately tried not to give anything away. *Unfortunately, Anna clearly didn't get the memo,* she thought, bewildered by Anna's beauty.

"Hey beautiful," Jack said to Heidi. "You look stunning. I've already offered myself to this one as I can honestly say, I've never seen a more beautiful woman. Don't you think?" he said, kissing Heidi on the cheek and looking at her expectantly.

"Shut up, Jack," Anna said embarrassed.

"No, you're right. He's right," she said clumsily. "You look beautiful, Anna," she continued calmly.

"I'd have to agree, dear cousin. You scrub up particularly well," Dawn winked. "Seriously, you look gorgeous," she said enthusiastically as she leaned in, kissing each of her cheeks.

"Um, thanks. You both look incredible," she said, unable to take her eyes off Heidi. Dawn clearly did her job incredibly well—the floor length, navy gown with the missing diamond-shaped sides, and diamante choker strap couldn't have been more perfect for Heidi if she'd tried. It was like it was especially made for her. *Maybe it was.* She had a beautiful diamond bracelet on with matching earrings. Her eyes smouldered; those beautiful, blue eyes with that eye work. Her hair was styled harshly, but so incredibly sexy. Her blonde hair was slightly shorter, and down,

299

resting at her shoulders. The top was styled and held in to a bump. She couldn't have looked more gorgeous if she tried.

"Yo, you in there?" Dawn asked the distant Anna.

"Sorry, out of my comfort zone," she blurted out.

So, young man, we haven't officially met," she said briefly to Jack before returning to Heidi. "Seriously, if you didn't shag this, you *must* be lying about this whole Helen thing."

"Charmed, I *think*. Hi, I'm Jack. I'm guessing you must be Dawn," he said, noticing Anna's confused stare at Heidi.

"You are correct. Nice to meet you, Jack. Shall we go through?" she said, leading them to the seating area.

Heidi manipulated her walk to ensure that she sat next to Anna. It wasn't like they could do anything, but she wanted that closeness. Especially when the lights went down. The closer she was to Anna, the more her senses came alive from the smell of her perfume. *The woman had no idea the impact she had on her, and all she really wanted to do was ditch this whole night and take her upstairs.*

"How're you feeling?" Dawn whispered to Heidi.

"Okay now. I haven't really seen anybody, so with any luck, I'll be fine. Press are on form, but I didn't really expect anything less. Are you okay?"

"Yes! I'm reunited with my girl, of course I am," she said, squeezing Heidi's thigh and turning to the curtain opening, revealing the screen ahead of them.

Heidi sipped her champagne quietly in the dark, listening to the sound fill the theatre. She had absolutely no interest in this movie, but being this close to Anna made it worthwhile; albeit, their thighs touching was somewhat torturous.

Anna noticed Heidi knocking the champagne back, and was concerned that she'd damage her reputation.

"Hey, you okay?" Anna whispered quietly.

"Yeah, why?" Heidi turned to her, catching her glare. "Sorry, I'm cool. You know you look beautiful," she whispered.

Anna went to speak, but stopped. "Thank you, you too. Incredible, actually."

"Stop turning this back on me," Heidi smiled.

"Why are you two talking? Watch the movie," Dawn leaned over, telling them off.

"I can't. I feel agitated. I don't want to sit still, and watch a dumb movie."

"You sound like a spoiled brat. What the hell is going on? You're never like this," Dawn said confused.

"I don't know. I guess I'm just done."

"Done with what?"

"Nothing," she sighed. "I need to use the washroom."

"You want me to come?" Dawn asked.

"No, I'm good," she said, getting up and passing by Anna.

"What's up?" She leaned over and asked Dawn.

"I don't know. I guess she's just had too much time out. She needs to get home so she can get back to normal," Dawn whispered.

"I need to go to the loo anyhow, so I'll check on her."

"Why?"

"Why what?"

"Why are you going after her?" Dawn quizzed.

"I didn't say I'm going after her. I said I need to go to the loo. You may be able to cope with not having to wee after drinking copious amounts, but unfortunately, I can't," she said getting up.

"What the hell is up with them?" she said to Jack.

"I think they're just both a bit out of their comfort zone right now. It'll be *fine*. This is new for Anna and me. I guess Heidi has had quite a bit of time in hiding, so it's like rebuilding all over again, a bit like a loss of control. She's organized and focused, so she probably doesn't know how to handle being thrown back into it. *Why* are you looking at me like that?" he whispered.

"You don't act or speak like you're only in your 20's," she flirted.

"Well, you're comparing me to spoiled, rich kids of L.A. I'm a down to earth Surrey lad," he said. "But if you heard me on a Saturday night with the lads, you wouldn't be saying that," he smirked.

"A naughty side. I *like* it! You can tell me more later. We're going to get kicked out if we all keep talking and disappearing." She pulled an awkward face.

*

Anna walked into the bathroom, and immediately noticed Heidi sitting in the chair at the far end. Distantly swirling her champagne flute, she was oblivious that she was no longer alone.

"Anybody ever tell you it's completely gross bringing drinks into a bathroom?" She walked towards her.

"Have you *seen* this bathroom? It's literally like a lounge. Anyway, what are you doing here?"

Anna got closer to Heidi, watching the way she was looking her up and down. "Maybe I wanted to see you." She leaned in close enough to kiss Heidi, but didn't. "Guess we'll never know," she said, walking into a cubicle, and nervously breathing. She felt a thrill in her bones.

"You know, I can see from your feet positioning that you aren't peeing."

"I think it's tremendously odd that you're spying on my feet when I'm trying to use the bathroom?"

"I'm not. I can just see quite easily because of the gap at the bottom. If you aren't using the bathroom, don't you wanna come out and face me?"

Anna opened the door and peeked her head around the door. "*Face you*? Face you *how*? There's nothing that I'm afraid to face you for."

"Well you ran to the bathroom and didn't bother peeing."

"Ever thought that's because you freaked me out of it. You were watching me. Maybe I'm just not a performance pee-er."

"You are very cocky in a dress."

"Touché."

"I'm sorry for walking out of there."

"Nothing to apologize to me for. Dawn may be a different story. She may see red if we don't get our asses back soon."

"This is true. Are you gonna pee? I can leave you if you like?"

"Nah, it's s fine. As they say, peeing when drunk is like Pringles," she said washing her hands.

"*Huh*? Pringles?"

"Yeah. Once you pop, you can't stop," she said, giggling. "Come on, let's get out of here," she said, opening the door for Heidi.

They walked back towards the theatre slowly. "I've come to *love* the silence, this *stillness*," she said seriously.

"Yeah, it's nice."

Heidi stopped in front of a door and looked around before opening it. She turned back to Anna, feeling mischievousness, and shoved Anna into the room.

"What are you doing?" Anna said looking up to the 'coat closet' door.

"I just feel like being naughty," she said smirking, and shutting the door behind them.

"You know you're gonna get us into trouble."

"Well, we'll just leave again then," she said, grabbing the door handle. She stopped when she felt Anna's hand over her own.

"Are you always this annoying?"

"Only when I have a woman that has got my head in such a mess. Oh, and when my manager makes me do something I don't want to do, instead of something far…*far* better," she said unexpectedly.

"Oh *yeah*? So, what exactly would you class as something far… *far* better, then?" Anna whispered running her index finger down Heidi's naked side.

"You can't keep doing this to me. You're driving me insane," she purred, closing her eyes at the touch.

"Really?" Anna whispered in her ear moving her fingertips to her bare back, listening to Heidi's groans. "You like that Hollywood?" she whispered.

"Don't mess with me, farm girl. I *will* get you back."

"Maybe that's all part of my evil plan."

"There's nothing evil about you," Heidi said.

"Is *that* so?" she said, kissing down her shoulder blade, making Heidi gasp. Anna moved up and kissed all the way down her jawline, putting her hands around Heidi and placing them on her lower back. "Still think I can't be evil?"

"That isn't evil. It's anything but. A tease, maybe, but definitely not evil," she smirked.

"That wasn't the evil part. This is," She smirked and grabbed her hand, pulling her out of the cloakroom.

"What the *fuck*? What are we doing? *Why* are we leaving? I wanna stay in there!" she pointed back.

"I know, but we'll get caught, and then we'll get in trouble. Plus, I'm enjoying being a little bit evil. *Come on,*" she said.

"Payback is a bitch; you know that, right?"

"So you keep saying. I also know that the anticipation is insane," she said arching a single brow. "Almost as insane as how beautiful you look right now. I love the hair," she whispered as they snuck back into the theatre.

"Where have you been?" Dawn grumbled.

"I told you, the bathroom. Then for a quick drink, *and* to have a word with myself. I'm good and back on form again," she said smiling angelically.

"You've become very weird suddenly."

"Thanks, I love you too," she sighed.

*

"Heidi, how are you? What did you think of the movie?" Jen said.

"At least the parts you saw," Dawn grumbled.

Heidi instantly scorned her friend. "Hi Jen, how're you? It was an incredible movie. You played your part exceptionally well," she said politely.

"Oh, thank you. I know you wanted that part, but you know what this business is like."

"I don't know who told you that Heidi wanted that role, Jen, but I purposely didn't give her that opportunity because playing the new lead in a Disney production is far more superior than a rom com. You played it well though…you know, for your level. I'm sure you'll at least get a nomination. We've got to keep rotating," she waved, dragging her friend away.

"Ouch," Anna said to Jack awkwardly when they exchanged uncomfortable glances with the red headed lead.

"Hmm, and who have we got here?" Jen purred.

"This is Heidi's new love interest. Keep it quiet though, it's still a secret," Dawn leaned over sardonically and pulled him away too.

"What the hell was all that about?" Heidi said when they were all safely hidden and replenished with more champagne.

"She's a douchebag. I mean all that hoity, toity BS that you lost out to her for this crappy role? You think I'm going to let her damage yours *or* my reputation? *As if.*"

"And the whole Jack thing? It'll be all over the—"

"Exactly. This beautiful, young face will be all over the world as the boy who has mended the heart of the nation's sweetheart," she said, clapping her hands.

"You didn't think to ask this 'beautiful, young boy's' permission *before* you screwed with his life? Jesus Dawn, you could have just destroyed his life," she said.

"Come on. When this guy's face is publicly announced as being your new bit of stuff, he'll get more offers than he ever would have had in his life. Do you have a problem with that, Jack? I can correct it, if you wish?"

"Hell no. Let the shagging commence," he smiled, rubbing his hands together, ignoring the annoyed looks from Anna and Heidi.

"Yes, indeed," Dawn raised her eyebrow and her glass to him.

"I'm going to the bathroom," Heidi said, walking off.

"What is up with her today?" Dawn asked.

"Who knows? Listen I think I may leave; this is all a bit much for me and a bit out of my comfort zone."

"*What*? No way! What the hell is *up* with everyone?" Dawn slammed.

"There's nothing wrong with me, D, this just *isn't* my thing. I've enjoyed myself. The movie was pretty good, well, until the interaction with the lead afterwards." She smiled. "But do not feel guilty. I just don't really get it—all this," she said, leaning in and kissing them both on the cheeks.

Jack stepped in to his friend knowing she was making the wrong decision. "Don't go, please. We haven't even fooled anyone yet. You owe me 20 quid by default otherwise."

"It's yours," she said opening her purse and handing him the 20-pound note.

"Hey, what's going on?" Heidi said returning.

"My bore of a cousin is leaving."

"*What? Why*?" Heidi asked stunned, unravelling the hurt behind her eyes.

"I err… I um…"

"She's bored and she doesn't like our life," Dawn said.

"That's unfair, Dawn."

"Hey Dawn, I really like this song. You fancy dancing with me? I promise I have some awesome moves," Jack said, wanting to leave Heidi and Anna alone.

Dawn looked at the women, rolling her eyes. "You betcha. I wanna know more about those moves." She smiled devilishly. Downing her champagne, she thrust the glass into Anna's hand and followed him to the floor.

"Were you really gonna leave without even saying goodbye? *Even* after the cupboard?" she said sadly.

"I just feel a bit weird, Heidi. You really don't seem happy. I haven't seen you like this. I just don't know how to make it better. I think it makes more sense to remove myself, and then there's less stress for you."

"You don't get it, Anna. You aren't the problem; you aren't the stress. The stress is that I can't just be with you. I'm frustrated to hell. I haven't done this before, and I don't know what to expect. I can't *stop* thinking about you, and the only thing that I think more about than you is that if your cousin hadn't turned up unexpectedly, what might've happened between us, where it would've gone, and what we'd be doing now. It's driving me *insane*. I can't help it. Seriously, none of this is you. The only thing you can take responsibility for is being insanely gorgeous and *that* makes me want and crave you every second of every day," she said.

Anna didn't know what to say or how to react as she listened to the words. "Meet me back at the cloakroom," she said walking off.

Heidi couldn't help her wanting stare, despite knowing full well the implications should anyone observe it. She finished her drink quickly, and made her way discreetly to the back end of the lobby where the cloakroom was. She pulled her cell out of her purse and pretended to text as two women she'd recognized from a TV show left the restrooms giggling together. She smiled slightly and waited for them to leave, checking that nobody else was around. When the coast was clear, she quickly slipped inside the cloak room, facing Anna again.

"You took your time."

"What can I say, I'm taking a page out of your book with this anticipation stuff."

"Payback is going to be delightful for me."

"What makes you think that this isn't what I'm secretly wanting? Maybe all I want *is* the payback," Heidi smirked.

"Heidi?"

"Yes?"

"For the love of God, stop talking, and bloody well kiss me."

"You are *so* lucky you're hot as hell," she said moving towards her. "You scare the hell out of me," she whispered to Anna. "I have no idea what you're doing to me, but I can't stop."

"Do you want to stop?"

"When I'm alone, and trying to think sensibly, and realistically, yes. But then I see you, whether in person, or memories of you in your bra…" she said distantly.

"Well, I'm glad you like it, but if you want to stop, nothing's really happened yet. We can just stop."

"You think I can stop now? After seeing you like this? And the kissing last night? It's already gone past being able to stop," she said contemplatively. "Anna?"

"Mhmm?"

"Do you really think nothing's happened? Is that really what you think?"

Anna took her hands. "Heidi, I haven't ever had a relationship outside of being a teenager. I don't sleep around. I don't kiss strangers. I don't do anything. It's killing me that you have completely rocked my very, very steady world. But likewise, I sit alone in bed, or at work, and realize the reality of it all. I'm adamant that I can just pull away and stop acting like a teenager. Then I see you… I see that look in your eye, that look of desire, a look that's always made me run. But I can't, not this time, it seems," she stopped sadly. "I can't stop myself. I can't control myself any longer because all I want…is to touch you, and kiss you and… um, well it doesn't matter," she said embarrassed.

"Sure it does, continue. I wanna know what else you want to do with me."

"Don't. We were discussing stopping," she said nervously, watching Heidi's eyes glaze over her own lips. "You make me lose all self-control Heidi, and I don't know how I feel about that."

"Well, maybe we both need to lose all self-control just to see what happens," she whispered. "Maybe losing self-control will be the best, most euphoric feeling either of us have ever encountered."

"Stop talking this way; you have no idea what you're doing to me."

"I think I have an idea. Maybe a flutter here," she said, touching her tummy slightly. "A crave there." She touched her lips with her index finger. "An urge…here…" Her wandering fingers moved downward, but before she could finish her sentence, Anna spun her around and pushed her up against the wall, kissing her with ferocity. They groaned heavily, hands wandering aimlessly, and their breathing heightened.

"We can't do this here," Anna said, allowing Heidi to kiss her neck fervently.

"I know, I know, but I can't stop, Anna. I've never wanted anything more," she said, pushing her against the wall a little too harshly, causing Anna to lose her footing on the coat rack. They both screamed, and instantly fell, pulling the coats down with them.

"Shit, are you okay?" Anna asked Heidi, who was hysterically laughing, piled on top of Anna and several coats. Suddenly, the door thrust open, revealing a glare from outside. A young girl dressed in all black stood facing them. She eyed Anna and Heidi suspiciously.

Heidi jumped up with an instant change to her face and demeanor. "Do you work here?" she snapped.

"Um, yes miss," she said, looking confused.

"Did you see anybody? I was getting our coats, and somebody just pushed us in here. The lack of lighting resulted in quite a fall," she said, slowly standing up and picking up the coats around them.

"It's fine, Hei... Mrs. Spencer. I'll get it. Are you okay? Do you need a doctor or some pain relief tablets?" the girl asked worriedly.

"No, but thank you." She smiled, nodding back to Anna as they both left the area.

"Oh my God, I can't believe that just happened," Anna laughed quietly.

"I know. Quick, keep walking."

"Do you think she believed us?"

"Hopefully she was too starstruck to consider anything else. Otherwise, we're screwed." She looked back at Anna. "What if she goes to the press and tells them she saw us making out?"

"*Shit!*"

"Forget it. If I have to wait any longer, *I'll* be the one outing us. It's driving me insane." She shook her head. "Come on, how about we do this whole 'smile, laugh, drink, and have fun,' thing? Soon, we'll be alone and happy, and enjoy whatever transpires."

"Yes, you said it. Come on, naughty."

"You're back," Jack said, kissing Anna on the cheek.
"I am."

"Did you get an offer you couldn't refuse?" He smirked, not giving her a chance to respond. "I'm glad you decided to stay by the way. Wanna dance?"

"You really are pulling out all the punches this evening, boy. And yeah, why not?" she said, taking his hand.

*

"You seem happier?" Dawn said to Heidi, handing her another champagne.

"I am. I'll be back in a minute," Heidi said.

"Where are you going now?"

"Don't ask," she said, kissing her cheek. "You really *don't* want to know," she smirked and rushed off.

Heidi walked over to the group of staff by the front door. "Hi, excuse me? Do you have a moment?" she asked the young girl from the coat room as the group watched on in shock.

"Um, well, it's not my break yet."

"It's fine, Lily, I got you covered," a young boy said, nodding animatedly towards Heidi.

She walked them over to a quiet corner and turned to face the girl. "Hey."

"Um, hi."

"I'm sorry about before. I hope I haven't caused any damage to the cloakroom. I just found out it was my friend. He thought it'd be funny to push me in there. I wanted to give you this by way of a good will gesture," she said handing over the cash. "There's…um, quite a lot of self-obsessed people here, shall we say. I don't want you to get in trouble for there being a speck of dust or crease in their coats," she laughed.

"Thank you, Mrs Spencer-Brady," she said softly. "You really don't need to do this."

"Say that after this lot have a mid-life crisis in a few hours," she winked. "And it's Heidi," she said leaving.

"Heidi!" the young girl called out.

Heidi turned around to face her. "Yes?" she asked.

"Thanks. Just so you know, he's an absolute tool for doing that to you. Everyone thinks it," she shrugged, leaving the actress smiling and nodding her head at the young woman's spunk.

"Where did you disappear to? Been misbehaving in that cloakroom again?" Anna winked to Heidi.

"Wouldn't you like to know?" She smirked. "Actually, I went to see the girl from the coat room. We're in the clear," she whispered.

"Oh really? Already trading me in for a younger model, eh? Hollywood, tut tut."

"Shut up, you goof," she said, bumping her shoulder. "I'll at least wait until I find out if you're any good before I trade you in," she winked.

"Is that so? Well, maybe you'll get nothing now," she said, smirking slightly.

"You couldn't resist me if you tried."

"What are you two smirking at?" Dawn asked inquisitively.

"I wasn't aware I was. We're people watching."

"Oh, my favorite pastime! Who are we discussing?" Dawn sat down as Jack indirectly assessed the glance between Anna and Heidi.

313

"Heidi, how are you?" They all turned to a voice.

"Oh my god…Ben? Hi! How are *you*?" She jumped up and hugged an ex lead she'd worked with.

"I'm awesome. You look—" he stopped, pulling away, and looking Heidi up and down, "—phenomenal. I'm glad. I was real worried given recent…well, *you* know," he said shyly.

"You can say it, Ben. The affair, the reward, the *gossip*. I'm okay. I've had the best vacation." She smiled to Anna and Jack. "You obviously know Dawn. These are my friends Jack and Anna."

"Of course, I'm still waiting for her to free up some space to get me on her books," he winked. "Hey gorgeous, you look stunning," he nodded toward Dawn, approvingly. "Nice to meet you both," he said to Jack and Anna.

"Thank you. Good to see you. You're looking as dapper as ever. Still single? Heidi may require a bit of male attention soon."

"*Dawn!*" she spat.

"Thank you, Dawn. Um, yes, I am, but you know me; I'm not about the whole L.A. thing. As much as I would be incredibly lucky to date my lovely friend, Heidi, here," he said pulling her into a sideways hug. "You know I'd rather date a normal girl, out of the public eye, so my life doesn't get picked apart, unfortunately, like it does others," he said sincerely.

Heidi mouthed "thank you" to him. *She'd always got on well with him. He was one of the few, authentic people in the industry.*

"Well, if that's the case, Anna here, is my darling cousin. She's very much a normal girl. Complete opposite of me. They've come for a night out."

"Hey, again. Lovely to meet you. Dawn's correct; you look beautiful this evening," he said, kissing each of her cheeks.

"Thanks. And yes, I'm the unfortunate one that's related to her," she eyed her cousin evilly.

"Ah, I like her. She's got the looks and the humor," he winked to Dawn playfully. "And Jack," he said, taking his hand firmly this time. "How you liking all this?" He pointed to the room.

"It's *different*. As a 24-year-old guy, you notice a lot of..." he stopped to look at his boss. "Of beautiful, young ladies," he rolled his eyes to her.

"Good save," Ben nudged him. "Yeah, I hear ya. Great for a young guy like you. As age embraces you it becomes a bit more tedious, unfortunately."

"Rubbish," Dawn spat. "It rarely does. You pair are both just old and boring," she laughed. "You're just as perfectly noble as many of the Hollywood movie stars present tonight." She glared.

"Kind," he said, turning his attention back to Jack. "So, you got your eye on anyone?"

"Honestly, I kinda feel a bit out of my depth actually. Don't get me wrong, I have no issue with pulling bird—I mean, ladies," he corrected as he saw Anna's look. "But I... well, these are women that can get anyone they want. I don't know, it's different."

"It isn't; it's all about the confidence and the arrogance. Okay, tell me. Point someone out."

"She's kind of cute, and she's been looking over a bit."

"She's twelve!" Dawn spat.

"So is *he*, Dawn." Heidi smirked, noticing the venom in her friend's voice. Dawn clearly had set her sights on him tonight.

"Just remember, L.A. girls are very different from... well, from *normal* girls," Ben said, beckoning the young blonde over with his finger. "Stick with me, dude," Ben said to Jack.

"Mercedes, how did you like the movie?" Ben said, kissing her cheeks.

"Yes, it was great, didn't you think? Hi, um, Heidi, you don't know me, but I'm sorry to hear of your situation," she said, air kissing the woman.

Ben stepped in before Dawn had a chance to get involved with her best friend's situation. He knew how protective she was when it came to Heidi, and would jump on anybody, if required. "Mercedes, have you had the pleasure of meeting Jack yet?"

"Um no, I don't think so. You look kind of familiar though," she said in an American accent.

"Well, this here is the UK's biggest new thing. He's a friend of Dawn's, and she's hoping to coax him away from British TV to L.A. She knows he'll be the next big thing back home. I was just telling him I'm really hoping to work with him. You think we could pull off father and son?" He quizzed her. "Women are *crazy* for him over here," he said seriously.

Just like that, the young woman started twirling her constructed curls around her finger. "Well how about you and I go get a shot? You can tell me all about your roles on British TV, Jack." Jack looked back at Ben concerned.

"Play along, boy. As I said, she won't give a hoot about you. That's L.A.!" He said, patting his back. "Hey, Mercedes. You need to remember that these British folks are very serious about their soap operas. He won't be able to say too much, confidentiality and all that," he winked.

"Oh, that's fine, I'm sure we can find far more exciting things to talk about," she smirked, dragging him away.

"It's scary how dumb some of these people can be. Jack's still a kid, and this is a one-time thing. Let him have some fun," Ben said.

"I think the problem is my gorgeous girl here was hoping to have some fun with Jack herself," Heidi said smirking.

"*Shut up!*" She shouted. "Anyway, I see *you've* brightened up. What, has someone caught your eye?" she said flatly.

"Doesn't always have to be about sex, D. Some of us can function without it!" she sipped her drink, watching Anna the entire time. "Besides, annoying you has always been my favorite past-time," Heidi said, winking at Dawn and acknowledging the frown on her face.

"Come on, Dawn, how about you and I go get some more drinks?" Ben said.

"Sure, you guys coming?"

"I'm going to grab that table; my feet are kind of sore. You get used to wearing sneakers and slippers for so long, and pumps actually tear your feet apart," Heidi said taking her shoe off and rubbing her heel.

"Do you really think she likes Jack?" Anna said, calling a waiter and getting two more refills of champagne for them as they sat down at the table.

"Dawn doesn't do relationships. She was totally pissed when she found out I didn't go there with him. Knowing Dawn, she probably figured that if she flirted a bit, it would be enough to convince me to fool around with him. But now she's met him herself and realized how nice, and cool he is. She's just thought, if I don't want him, she'll go there.

They've been flirting and stuff so I can understand why she's pissed," she added.

"Hmm, maybe," she said distantly.

"Are you okay?"

"Yeah, I just think I need to stop drinking."

"You *do*? Why's that? Aren't you enjoying it?"

"Yeah, but the drunker I get, the more I want to kiss you again," she said sadly.

"Oh, you do, huh?" she said leaning forward, placing her head in her hand, her eyebrows raised.

"Well, I wouldn't have said it otherwise." She smiled.

"Did Dawn fill you in on tonight's plans?"

"Um, not that I'm aware of?" she said confused.

"Chill." She grabbed her hand.

"You think that's wise?" Anna asked, looking around.

"Not when you look all suspicious," she laughed. "If you can be inconspicuous, nobody will think anything of it," Heidi confirmed.

"Hmm, that's all well and good, but what do you think hand holding leads to? I already said I want to kiss you." She rolled her eyes, smiling.

"True, true." She laughed. "Anyway, Dawn has written me a speech about Everett. You know '*I'm over him and I'm signing the papers,*' et cetera. I guess I just wanted to make you were aware. I'm pretty sure it's gonna result in some big scale 'interest.' And… well, you know how I want tonight to end, like more than anything. I just don't know that it will. But please, as soon as we get a moment alone, I promise you, I'll… um… um," she said embarrassed.

"Hollywood's gone *coy*?" She smirked. "What do you promise me?"

"You're loving this way too much. I don't *know* what I'm supposed to say. I guess I'll hopefully make it worth your while."

"You will definitely make it worth my while, Heidi. I know this is all very surreal, to say the least. Neither of us, have, um…" she stopped, trying to control her breathing at the nature of their discussion unfolding. "Um, done it before. But I think the connection has been there on a sexual level. I suppose what I'm trying to say is I have zero concerns that you will make it worth my while," she said nervously.

"Are you okay?"

"I'm fine," she said feeling her chest tighten.

"Are you sure? You've lost all your color."

"The situation just makes me nervous, I suppose. Dawn's coming back," she said, turning and pointing to a random woman so as not to look suspicious.

"What are you guys discussing?" Dawn asked, sitting down.

"Hey, you okay?" Anna nodded to Dawn. "And that girl's dress; it's beautiful. I was just saying while I'm happy on my farm and in my trackies, I kind of like being a girl for the night," she lied.

"Yes, fine. Just—" she stopped at the interruption.

"—Alright gorgeous, fancy a dance?" They all looked up to Jack holding his hand out to Dawn.

"What happened to *Mercedes*?" She rolled her eyes.

"Ben's awesome. And *so* right about L.A. women. His explanations were spot on. Not my cup of tea, though," he smiled. "She's pretty, of course, but I know *everything* about her; she didn't come up for air. Plus, her life's pretty dull. I thought I'd come back and get some more 'running around' from the woman that's been flirting with me all night," he smirked.

"I have not been flirting with you all night…" She looked at all three of them aghast as they laughed.

"Yeah, you have. Now be quiet and get that sexy ass on the dance floor," he commanded walking off to the floor and leaving her there smirking at him.

" Alright, one dance," Dawn said to Heidi. "Then we'll do this. People are starting to leave already.

"It's fine, I'll go alone."

"*What*? Heidi that's *not* a clever idea!"

"Dawn, have faith in me. Go and have some fun. I'll read it out loud," she said.

Dawn looked nervous, hesitating between Heidi and Jack.

"Go already!" Heidi said, kissing her best friend.

Heidi turned to Anna. "Look, if I leave, it isn't you; it's because of the situation, okay? "I…they will be swarming, Anna, and it won't be as easy to say what I have to say and come back like nothing's happened. They'll bribe staff to get to me. They'll bribe every last 'Mercedes' in this place with quick ways to get to the big league of Hollywood. I just want you to know, I desperately want to be with you, but it just may not happen tonight," she said sadly. *How do you explain to someone that's never had any dealing of this world, what it could be like?*

"It's okay," Anna said, "I'm coming with you."

"What? Do you think that's wise?" Heidi responded.

"Yes, I want to be with you. If nothing else Heidi, we're friends. I want to be there for you," she said.

Heidi smiled softly, and inhaled deeply. "Come on, let's get this over with."

Chapter Thirty-Three

"Huh, Hi…" Heidi began blinking back the flashes and trying to zone out the barrage of questions. She pulled out the paper that Dawn wrote for her and was just about to start reading it, hearing the memorable call of her name. Heidi's heart stopped as she heard the paparazzi turning towards Everett, striding his way up the stairs to his wife.

"Heidi. My beautiful Heidi," he said kissing her. She immediately pulled away and looked over to Anna.

Heidi's head was spinning. *What the fuck was he playing at?* She thought as she listened to the reporters calling all manner of questions to them both.

"Guys, please! Please allow me to explain. This beautiful woman here is, and always will be, the love of my life. I'm ashamed of my behavior, my actions. It was all unacceptable, but I am not leaving without my wife. I am not giving up on my wife and our marriage."

The questions about the baby came through thick and fast as Heidi watched on in astonishment—Everett giving an award-winning performance as Anna slipped off looking terribly sad.

Chapter Thirty-Four

"Are you okay?" Dawn said, stroking her best friend's forehead.

"Yes," she said flatly. "Go back, I'm fine."

"Heid's, this is a *big* thing. The whole fucking world is gonna be all over it. We need to sort through it together," Dawn said.

"D, just leave it already. *Please!*" She snapped as people moved closer, trying to catch bits of their discreet conversation.

"I'm not leaving you. For starters, I'm concerned that you're buying this shit," she said sternly.

"*Dawn!*" she snapped. "We were married a long time! When I tell the world we're over, that I'm happy with him filing for divorce, and then he decides to travel half way across the world and fess his 'undying' love. Yeah, I'm a little taken aback…"

"Oh sorry, I was just coming to see if you were okay," Anna said with sadness in her eyes.

"*Anna!*" Heidi shouted after her.

Dawn grabbed her wrist. "It's fine, leave her. She'll know you're okay if you're with me," Dawn said unknowingly.

Shit, shit, shit. What if Anna assumes that she is considering it. Double Shit. Dawn gave her an irritating glare.

Sighing lightly and admitting defeat, she turned fully back to Dawn. This was *her* world, *her* life. She'd have to speak to Anna later. "I was just… taken aback. I have no interest going back there. I don't buy any part of it. His career will hit rock bottom, and he'll know this is the only way to get it back. I also don't want to screw my life and career up by reacting too impulsively. Irrespective of what you think, *saying* or *doing* anything right then and there would've made it worse. Jesus, look at this place already. They're swarming. I don't even know how I'm going to get out of here," Heidi said sadly.

"Don't worry, I'll arrange that. I'll get everyone kicked out of the hotel if I must. Go in there, lock the door behind me, and I'll sort something," she said, pushing her into the manager's office the staff had offered.

*

Jack asked the waiter for two Jack Daniels and took them over to the lone girl at the eight-seater table. "Hey beautiful, you look like you could do with this." He sat down. "What's going down out there?" he said, kissing his boss's temple.

"I'm fine," Anna said sadly.

"Clearly," he said sarcastically. "I just heard a few mumblings at the bar, and obviously we saw the dash of people as her husband walked in. What's the deal?"

"Oh, he just professed his undying love for Heidi to the world," she said, sipping the drink and trying to act as casual as she could.

"And that bothers *you*?"

"No, why would it? It's just the whole thing. I just went to see her, and she was telling Dawn that they'd been married for years and that…well, basically, she needs to consider what he's said. I'm happy for her, if that's what she wants," she said sadly. "I just feel out of my comfort zone."

"What do you mean babes?" Jack asked concernedly.

"I was out there, like in that moment. I was there like we were…fuck, I don't know Jack. Like it was just 'us.' She's such a good friend, and that friend just told the world…the *world* about her life as her ex, no her *husband,* gallantly runs in, says it's *all* a mistake and he'll fight to get her back," she said sighing heavily. "Dude, I'm somehow living in a fucking movie," she said harshly.

Jack kept quiet, not wanting to press any further. "You want me to get us a cab and go home?"

"Definitely *not.* You need to stay and have fun. You deserve it, Jack," she said squeezing his arm.

"Would it bother you?" he asked.

"What?"

"If I um…" He nodded his head. "You know, if I got with your cousin tonight?"

"No. She's big enough and ugly enough to make her own decisions. You wanna go there? Do it. I can well imagine she has lots of fun in L.A. It's why she tells me she doesn't want relationships."

She's sexy as hell. She's a bit weird… like I suppose a bit '*Hollywood*' weird, but she's been saying stuff and I—"

"*Stop now*! She's still my cousin. I don't need to know what vulgarities she's been whispering to you. If you want to go there, do it, have a couple days off. Just remember there's no future."

"I know it's just a bang… Sorry, um—"

"Look. She will be the first to say it's just a bang, so don't sweat it," she said standing up, and downing her drink. "But Jack, I *am* leaving. Even Heidi said it would make more sense—not being seen together—so nobody knows where she's been."

"Please don't—"

"*Jack*!" She pleaded.

He stood up, noticing a sadness in her eyes he'd rarely seen before. He knew he had to admit defeat. Stroking her bare shoulder, he leaned in and kissed her on the cheek, nodding gently as he turned and went in search of Dawn. "Hey, An," he said, turning back to her.

"Yeah?"

"You look beautiful tonight."

Anna smiled at Jack, thankful that he was there tonight.

*

Anna walked back into her house just after one am feeling exhaustion in her body. It'd been a long couple of days and she was really looking forward to having her life back. Tonight made her realize that she'd been kidding herself. What the *hell* was she thinking? She was so completely caught up in this whole ridiculously absurd fantasy. Seriously, she was a grown adult acting like a teenager. She wasn't gay. This wasn't her life. She'd gotten caught up in a real-life movie, but her sense was back now. Her life was *here,* in Surrey, on the farm. Heidi's was in Hollywood, where she couldn't go out without makeup, where people pulled her apart for having a hair out of place, where she had to have a personal trainer in a time of sadness to avoid the world penalizing her for 'letting herself go.' They *were* worlds apart. What had she been thinking? *One thing she knew for sure is that she was relieved it hadn't gone further,* she thought, swallowing the bile rising in her throat. *No, she wouldn't do this. She was stronger than that. She was the strongest woman she knew, and everyone said it. She'd made it this far in her life without love, why start now?* She thought, making her way to her room.

Chapter Thirty-Five

"Hi, I was wondering if you could help me. I've been trying to call my friend in room 1326, Miss Anna Roberts? It's Heidi Spencer-Brady, and four of us came together. I can't get a hold of her and I'm concerned as she's had a little too much to drink," she said wondering why Anna wasn't answering the door or her phone.

"Miss Roberts checked out about an hour ago, madam. Anything else I can help you with?"

"*Wha*... no... no. It's fine, thanks," Heidi said hanging up the phone.

Heidi slumped onto her bed feeling the pain of her words. She sighed heavily, allowing tears of anguish to fall. How had everything gone so drastically wrong? They'd had such a special time earlier. She'd spoken to the press about her marriage and their impending divorce, but then the lying, cheating scumbag had to turn up. *What the hell was he playing at*? He'd not kept it in his pants for at least four years. 'Fighting' for her and their marriage, *really*? Heidi couldn't dismiss the sadness on Anna's face as she heard his attempt at rekindling their marriage to the world and then later, when she came to find her and overheard what she said to Dawn. It must have sounded like she was even considering it. *She'd not finished*, she thought. *She'd not finished telling Dawn there wasn't a cat in hell chance she'd go back there. Ever. She didn't want Everett. She just wasn't so sure she could have who she really wanted*. Heidi got undressed and climbed into bed, facing the prospect of losing the one and only thing that she truly believed was meant to be. *Anna was meant for her and her happiness*, she thought sadly.

*

Dawn, Heidi, and Jack returned to Anna's later the following afternoon after spending the morning in the spa, trying to cheer Heidi up. Dawn couldn't get out any information as to what was wrong with her, but her eyes were red, bloodshot, and swollen; it was clear she'd been crying.

Walking in, Heidi desperately searched the room, hoping to find Anna. She'd no idea how to do this with Jack and Dawn here. All she wanted to do was see her and explain, regardless of Everett's stupid move, that there's no way she'd go back there. Heidi told Anna about her life and her marriage, that he was a serial cheater, she'd never even consider it.

"I'm gonna go grab a bath; I'm kinda gooey after the spa," Heidi said.

"You want dinner? We'll find out what Anna wants and order something for the four of us," Dawn asked expectantly, completely missing the optimism of Anna fill her face. Heidi composed herself before turning back to the door. "I'm easy; you guys choose and I'll just have whatever," she said.

Heidi spent nearly two hours hiding away. Having unpacked and bathed, she was comfortable back in her slacks. She went back downstairs.

"Hey, you're back. We thought you'd drowned," Dawn said, looking up from the cards in her hand.

"You're playing cards?" she questioned.

"Yeah, we used to play loads when we were kids, remember? We figured we'd have a game while waiting for you two," Dawn said happily.

"You okay, Heid's?" Jack asked, placing his cards down on the floor. "Here," he said giving her a glass of wine.

"Yeah, I'm fine, thanks. I think I've had enough lately," she said, already regretting it as the nerves kicked in to the sound of the door unlocking.

"Oh, hi. You're all here," Anna said in her work overalls unable to look Heidi in the eye.

"Jesus boss, what've you been doing? Why didn't you call me? I would've come to help," he said, looking her up and down.

"Nah, it's fine. It felt like a down and dirty kinda day," she said, grabbing a beer out of the fridge.

"I could think of better ways to get down and dirty!" Dawn shouted after her, raising her eyebrows to Jack.

"Well, we all know that," Anna responded curtly, and went upstairs.

"I don't know what's *up* with her," Dawn said.

"Probably just the stress of everything lately," Jack said.

"Yeah, maybe. I suppose Heid's has been here a while. She's always kind of enjoyed her solitude. We need to get you home lady," she squeezed her shoulder.

Heidi felt sick to her stomach at the prospect of leaving, and noticed Jack watching her intently.

"Well, I guess shooting starts soon, so it makes sense," she said softly.

"I didn't mean that. I meant about Charlie. Anna has no issue with you being here, Heidi," Jack confirmed.

She smiled slightly, picking up the menu on the table. "So, what did you choose?"

"We thought pizza?"

"Yeah, I'm not really that hungry."

"What's this about pizza?" Anna said returning.

"Bloody hell, that was quick," Dawn said looking at her transformed cousin with her hair wet, a pair of shorts and an oversized t-shirt on.

"Yep, doesn't take me long."

"We were just talking about having a pizza if that's okay with you two?"

"Yes, fine with me. If that's okay with you, Heidi?" Anna said coolly.

"Um…" She noticed the civility in her voice.

"She's not hungry," Dawn said.

"Heidi, you haven't eaten all day," Jack said. "How about you and I share a spicy chicken?"

"Yeah, whatever."

"What do you want? I'll go order it," Anna said grabbing a piece of paper and a pen.

*

"It'll be around 40 minutes. Oh gin rummy! Can I join in?" Anna said far too happily.

Why was she asking like nothing's happened? Heidi thought.

"Yeah of course, come on Heid's, you too," Dawn said.

"It's okay. I'm gonna go up and use my laptop."

"*What*? *Why*? Just get your ass over here and play," she reprimanded her best friend.

"No, you can't do that. We have a top novelist in the making here," Anna smiled, ignoring the look of frustration on Heidi's face.

"What?" Dawn laughed, confused, noticing the look between Anna and Heidi. "What?" she repeated. "Is she serious?" Dawn asked Heidi.

"Why would you laugh at her? She's been through a shit time—holed up in the middle of nowhere, unable to live a normal life, or do what she wants. She's been a prisoner to her own life, and found solace in something that inspires and captivates her. She's your best friend."

"I haven't been a prisoner," Heidi whispered.

"What?" Dawn said confused.

"I. Haven't. Been. A. Prisoner," she responded to Anna. "I've been far form a prisoner, and loved every minute of it," she eyed Anna indignantly.

Silence struck the room as three of the four of them were aware that something was happening.

"You've really written a book?" Dawn re-questioned, oblivious to the situation.

"Yes, it's true. It's *nothing*. It's stupid really, just a way to pass the time. It's no biggie; it's rubbish," she said sadly, leaving the room.

"Heid's!" Dawn shouted after her. "Of course, it's not rubbish. You are so talented in so many areas. You'd be snapped up by a publisher in seconds. Jesus, I bet I could get you a book deal in the next five minutes. *Easily*. I need to read it."

"It's not worth it," Heidi said from the doorway.

"Well it is to me," Dawn said sincerely.

"And me," Anna added.

"Hell, I may as well get on board this little love train." Jack winked at her.

"What's it even about?"

"Seriously, it's nothing. Just a love story."

"Is there porn in it?" Dawn smirked.

"No, she just falls in love with a guy and that's it. End of story."

"Doesn't sound like much of a book. How many pages is it?" Dawn asked again.

"I don't know, like 300."

"300!?" Dawn spat her drink out. "Tomorrow, I demand you print it off for me so I can read it on the plane. On that note, Anna, you'll be glad to know you can finally have your home and life back. This one has decided to leave and come home with me. Not that she had much of a choice; filming starts in a couple of weeks."

Anna stared at her painstakingly before nodding her head. "Well, that's good news for you," Anna said looking away.

"Is it?" Heidi responded.

"Well, I thought you'd be glad. You can get your life back."

"Actua—"

"Actually," Jack interrupted before it could all go horribly wrong. "Heidi didn't say that. Dawn said *you* needed to get back to having your own space as she'd been here too long," he fought.

"*Right*. Well, as she said, filming starts soon. Come on then, let's have a quick couple of rounds of rummy before dinner arrives," Anna said quietly, trying to control her emotions. *Heidi looked distraught, and devastated by her words. What was she doing?* Anna thought.

*

"Heid's, you've hardly touched your food, and you haven't eaten anything all day," Jack said, touching her hand soothingly.

"Yeah, I don't really feel too great," she said distantly. "I'm gonna crash, if you don't mind. I wanna go speak to my mum," she said sadly. "I'll see you all tomorrow."

Heidi finished getting ready for bed, and climbed under the covers. She was desperate not to cry anymore, but she felt like rubbish, and it seemed she had no control whether tears came or not. Not wanting to call her mum feeling like this, she opted to wait until the morning, and go straight to sleep. She was just about to switch the lamp off when she heard a faint knock on the door.

"Yeah?" she said.

"Can I come in?" She heard Anna's voice.

"Of course. It's your house," she said immediately, regretting the harsh words.

Anna slipped into the room, noticing Heidi's damp eyes as she sat down on the bed beside her. "Are you okay? Why're you crying?"

"I'm not," she wiped her tears away.

"I'm not stupid, Heidi, nor blind."

"I'm fine, honestly. What... um, is everything okay?"

"Yes, but clearly you're not. Is it the whole Everett thing?"

"What? Of course it isn't. Why would you even say that?"

"I don't know, I just thought what he did yesterday may have gotten you upset?"

"It got me pissed, annoyed at whatever stupid ass game he's trying to play now! But upset? Definitely not."

"Well something's clearly upset you."

"What do you *think*, Anna? I can see it in your eyes. I can see that you've zoned out. You aren't looking at me the same way you looked at me 24 hours ago. I don't know what I've done or how to make it better, but nothing's changed on my part."

"You haven't *done* anything," she sighed. "I guess I've just realized...it was a fantasy. How could we have thought anything different? It was never going to work. It's better this way Heidi, before it goes too far. We're worlds apart. We would've made love, and where would that have gotten us? We'd have been broken hearted if we got any closer. I'm just saving us both the pain."

She wanted to scream to her that she was already broken hearted. "The difference is, Anna, I would've fought to avoid the pain."

"How can you, Heidi? *How*? I can't leave here; I have commitments, a whole farm to run. You spent your whole life wanting to act and you're one of the biggest movie stars of all time, so *you* can't. You can't just suddenly announce your gay, that you fell in love with a 'farm girl' from Surrey. Jesus, it's ludicrous. Everyone will think it's a phase after everything with Everett, and maybe it is—"

"—Don't do that. Don't you dare insult my intelligent or devalue my emotional state and feelings. This has nothing to do with Everett; this is about me and I how felt about you," she slammed.

"Heidi," she whispered. "I'm sorry, I am, but it's the reality of the situation," she said taking her hand. "We just got caught up in the romance and fairy-tale of it all. It's not real life. Neither of us are gay," she said again.

Heidi removed her hand from Anna's grip, trying to remember the last time she'd felt this level of pain. "Why are you so hung up on being gay? I don't give a fuck if I'm straight, gay, bi, pansexual, or anything else. I'm into you, and I thought you were into me. The fairy-tale was enough for me, and I would've done whatever it took to make it work," she said pointedly.

"Heidi, you say that now, but it wouldn't be the case. You would last six months here, without your job, without the permanent sunshine…"

"Why aren't you listening to me? None of that matters. I'm fading out of the business already. I told Dawn I wanted one last, big project and that's when it would end. On my terms, in my heyday, and then I wanted to get as far away from it all as possible. Look, it doesn't matter. I'm not going to beg you. It's irrelevant if it comes to that. I've spent too much of my life doing that and I deserve more," she said sadly. "Anna, I think you should leave now," she said rolling back over and taking in the full extent of the conversation, listening to her loud sigh, and the door opening.

"It's not about me not feeling something for you. It's because I do that I'm doing this," she said shutting the door behind her, and leaving Heidi to sob quietly.

Chapter Thirty-Six

"Are you sure you have everything?" Her mum asked.

"Yes mum, we both have everything, even the food you made," Dawn said kissing her mum's cheeks. "You realize I'm a grown ass woman, and *quite* a big deal in Hollywood," she laughed.

"Less of the cheek. I don't care how big you are in Hollywood. You'll always be my little girl. Thanks for coming and spending a day with us before you left," she said sadly. "We miss both of you so much," she said, grabbing them in a tight hug.

"I know, Mum. But you and Dad are coming out for Christmas, yeah?"

"Yes. We're just waiting on your father's doctor's advice. If all goes well, we'll book the tickets to come out for a month," she said smiling softly.

"You ready?" Heidi said to Dawn, grabbing their cases, and taking them to the car.

"Hello, Miss Heidi," their driver winked.

"Hello, Mister Graham," she winked back.

"Is the screen up to hide us?"

"Yes, well, almost fully. I figured you'd like to listen to a bit of the whinging that she's been doing for dragging her out here," he said rolling his eyes, taking her final bag.

"It's okay, I'll take this with me." She hung on to the bag.

"No bother. Is this everything?" He looked between Dawn and Anna.

"Yes, for me."

"Me too." They both smiled and stepped into the back seat of the town car.

Dawn went to speak, but Heidi shushed her so she could listen to Mrs. Clarke's moaning.

"What?" she mouthed.

"Just listen," Heidi said, pulling on her ear lobe.

They were barely out onto the road when she heard Graham's wife going on about how she needed to go shopping and do the washing and ironing, how she would miss her favorite daytime drama. Heidi couldn't do it anymore. She knocked on the screen, giggling away, and Graham lowered it, rolling his eyes in the rear-view mirror.

"Hi, Mrs. Clarke. I'm sorry to hear you're disappointed to be here today, but it was at my request," she watched the grey haired older woman turn around in her seat to face Heidi.

"Oh...my...gosh. You're...oh Graham, look who it is!"

"Yes, dear. As Heidi said, when I told her how much of a fan you were, she requested that I bring you along today."

"Oh my," she said, looking completely stricken.

"Hey Graham, how about you pull over and let Mrs. C come and join us back here for a cheeky champagne on our way to the airport?"

"Really?" she said in disbelief.

Dawn watched the old lady's happiness and surprise. "Come on, we have a glass with your name all over it," Dawn said smiling back to her.

Graham pulled over, rushing out of the car to open the door for his wife. He opened the back door, and escorted her carefully into the back with Heidi and Dawn.

337

Heidi noticed the car slowing, feeling sadness wash over her as they entered Heathrow. She couldn't believe that was it. Like nothing had happened, she was leaving the UK and returning to a home she no longer wanted, a job she'd suddenly lost all interest for.

"Are you okay, Heidi?" The elderly woman asked.

"Sorry, yes, just thinking." She smiled. "It was a real pleasure to meet you. You have a wonderful husband," she said helping her get out of the car.

"Oh, I know. It's rare these days that he can get away with surprising me, but he's certainly done it this time," she said, taking his hand. "You have a beautiful smile, dear. Find someone that puts it back on your face," Mrs. Clarke said lovingly.

"Thank you. I have one last surprise, then we really must leave," Heidi said to the woman who looked inquisitively at her husband.

"I've no idea honey." He shrugged his shoulders. "What are you up to now misses?" he questioned.

Heidi reached into her handbag and pulled out an envelope. "It's been wonderful to meet you—both of you. Graham, I'm so completely grateful for the confidentiality and your wonderful chat and humor." She smiled. "Anyway, I remember you admiring the cottage you took me to, saying your wife would love it there. I've paid for two weeks for you to stay there. You can go alone or take your whole family. There's a great games room and an indoor pool. I've made sure that the owner knows this can be redeemed in two parts, if you require. I thought you may like to have a week with family and maybe a nice break alone. Anyway, your call, but it's a gesture for the kindness you've shown me since being back. I feel truly honored that I've been lucky enough to have met you both, and if you need anything at all, please contact me. You both have my number now," she said, hugging them again. "Graham, I'll be sure to call you when I return home and need a driver," she winked.

"You really shouldn't have done that," he said. "It's my job, Heidi."

"And this is mine," she said, waving goodbye.

"You want me to try and get some privacy for you to check in?" Dawn asked as they walked towards the doors.

"Nah, I'm not really fussed. Just make sure you tell everyone that I'm not answering questions, and to leave me alone. Except kids and old folk; I'll have a pic and sign autographs for them."

Dawn gasped in horror. "Heidi Edwards, that's ageist!" She put her arm around her best friend.

"Only in a positive way." She smiled. "It's weird hearing you call me that."

"I know. I know you haven't been yourself lately, but I promise you, when we get home and see Margherita and get you back to work, you'll be yourself again in no time." She smiled oblivious to the sadness in her best friend's eyes.

They managed to get onto the aircraft with maybe only six or seven interruptions, all of which she was happy to stop a moment for. She got settled into her seat and leaned it all the way back, ordering herself a grey goose on the rocks with plenty of ice and an olive.

Chapter Thirty-Seven

Jack walked into the house and put his lunch in the oven. The weather didn't really allow for all day outdoor working, so he and Anna made a conscious effort to come in and have a heated meal. They normally ate leftovers, or just a pre-prepared meal his mum had made them both. He made coffee and went to the table, seeing two large envelopes. He saw his name scribbled across one of them and opened the package. Jack pulled out the plastic colored folder filled with paper and read the post it notes.

Ordinarily I wouldn't do this, but as you asked and have been a truly wonderful friend to me, I thought it's the least I could do! It's pretty rubbish, I'm sure. Take care, Jack, I will genuinely miss you. Hxx

He opened the cover and read the lone words across the front. '*When Winter Comes*' by *Heidi Edwards*.

He chuckled to himself, proud that she'd done it. "What a mess," he said to the room, opening the next page and beginning to read.

*

"Have you actually forgot about work?" Anna snapped as she walked into her house, causing Jack to jump out of his skin.

"Shit," he looked at his watch in fright. "Shit, *shit!*" He said surprised at the time. "I'm so sorry," he said sincerely.

"What the hell are you playing at? You said you'd be a half hour," she said considering the folder in his hand.

"Sorry, it's Heidi's book. You have one too," he said expectantly.

"Right," she said uncertainly. "Well, you're paid to work, not read. Are you going back to work, or are you taking the rest of the day off to read a book?"

"An," he pleaded with her, knowing she would be like this for a while.

"What, Jack? This is my business."

He knew it wasn't worth the fight when she was in this mood. Anna rarely had moods, which is probably why they both hit it off so well, but he'd fully anticipated this entire situation.

"I'm finished. Sorry again," he said shoving the folder into his rucksack and leaving her alone.

Anna sighed loudly to herself at her behavior toward Jack. She picked up the envelope, seeing her name on the front. She completely froze. *She couldn't do this.* Walking to the bin, Anna threw away the envelope, and opted not to eat, leaving home again.

Chapter Thirty-Eight

Heidi looked out of the window, watching the UK disappear. She sighed heavily and ignored the numbness filling her body. Dawn was fast asleep on the bed, blissfully unaware of the entire situation. She felt bad for not telling her best friend. She told her everything.

"You want one?" Heidi heard, turning to the small voice.

"Hey," she said, looking at the girl who seemed about eight or nine.

"Hey. So, you want one? It's called cola cubes, they're my favorite. I don't get them back home, only when I come visit here. I stock up." She smiled widely.

"Sure, thanks," she said, pinching a sweet. "I used to have these when I was growing up. My friends and I used to buy them on our way to school," she said reminiscing.

"Wow! You could eat candy for breakfast?" she said surprised.

"Well, probably not if my mum knew. So, do you visit the UK regularly?"

"Yeah, kinda. My dad and his new wife live there. She's British, so I gotta come back regularly. I don't mind it. She's okay, I guess. It just means I spend a whole heap of time on airplanes, and traveling alone. It's kind of a long trip for a kid," she said animatedly, causing Heidi to smirk.

"Yeah, I can imagine that sucks a bit. You wanna come around here? I have some cards if you know any games."

"For real? *Awesome*. My friends will never believe that I traveled with Heidi Spencer-Brady, *and* played cards with her…I mean, you," she said. "I only really know go fish, though."

"That's okay, we can play that, *or* we have a while yet; I can teach you a game I used to play with my family and friends when I was a kid," she said nostalgically.

"Sure, that'd be awesome." She smiled, getting comfortable in the dual seat opposite Heidi's.

"Anymore to drink Miss?" The stewardess eyed the little girl getting comfortable in the seat.

"You want a soda?" Heidi asked.

"Um, sure. I like the look of yours," she said expectantly to Heidi, the steward smirking.

"You like olives? You must be like eight."

"Nine, actually, but I'm sure I will."

"A vodka…"

"Same again?" The steward asked politely.

"Yes, and a club soda on the rocks with olives, apparently."

"Am I getting the same as you?"

"Sure are," Heidi said. "So, what's your name?"

"I'm Aubrey. What would you like me to call you?"

"You can call me Heidi. You wanna find out the rules to the game then?"

"For sure. Thanks Heidi!"

"What *for*?"

"For being my friend on the flight. I've been doing this since I was five. Normally I just get put up front and have an occasional conversation with the staff here. It kinda sucks," she said sadly.

"Well, today you have a friend for the journey," she said, holding up the glass.

"Cheers," Aubrey said and sipped a little. "This is good," she said crossing her arms casually and copying Heidi's actions with the olives. She inspected them considerably as she pulled the toothpick out and bit into one.

Heidi couldn't help but laugh as the little girl tried her hardest to enjoy it. She lost control as she spat out the olive and rapidly wiped her tongue.

"Have another cola cube; it'll take the salty taste away," she said, holding up the sweets.

"That's gross. How do you eat that? It tastes like I poured salt right onto my tongue," she said, taking two cola cubes and putting them in her mouth. "Yuck, gross!" She said, sucking harshly on her sweet. "What's this game called?"

Heidi sat up. "It's called gin rummy. Have you heard of it before?"

"Nope. Is it a grown-up game?"

"No, it's for kids too. We used to play a lot as kids."

"Oh," she said surprised.

"Why '*oh?*'"

"Because it's named after liquor, I figured it would be a grown-up game. So, how does it go then?" she asked, listening to Heidi's rules, and having a couple of practice runs first. "You used to play this a lot as a kid, huh?"

"Yeah, we did. My best friend and I used to stay in on Saturday nights," she stopped and pointed to Dawn. "She used to come for a sleepover every Saturday; we'd get a fish and chips supper and play this," she said memorably.

"My mom says that's the thing she misses the most about her and dad divorcing. The fish and chips in the UK," she said. "Is that what you were upset about before?"

"Fish and chips?" she asked confused.

"No, silly. Splitting up with your husband. Is that why you were upset before?"

"What makes you think I was upset?"

"Because I took a selfie of you earlier to show my friends, and I could see a little tear just here," she said, pointing to her cheek.

"Oh, you know you could've just asked for a photo."

"You know, you coulda just answered my question," she said, shaking her head. "Plus, I spend a lot of time flying here in business class from UK to LAX, so I see lots of celebrities here. My folks say I can't bug them no matter who they are."

"Right," Heidi said, wanting to change the tone. "You're wise for a nine-year-old, aren't ya?" She smirked. "No, that isn't what I was upset about," she said, looking out of the window.

"So, what's up? You wanna talk about it?"

"Um, I don't know that I do, but thanks. I've just got a lot going on in my head, and I don't know how to deal with it all I suppose," she said.

"Well, my mom always says that when you have a lot going on in your mind, that's when you gotta talk. Get it off your chest, right?"

"If only it was that simple."

"Well, why isn't it? Something made you sad, you find out what it was, and make it better. If it's a person, then you just need to explain to them that they made you sad and tell them why."

Heidi looked at the girl, forgetting how simple things are when you're a child. "Well I don't think they meant to make me sad. I just think they were trying to stop making themselves sad anymore."

345

"Well that's dumb," she said abruptly. "So, you're both sad and you didn't just tell each other? All you have to do is make up and then you'll both be happy again."

"I wish it was that easy, Aubrey. But the reality is, we *can't* both be happy. Not together. So, we just have to deal with it," she said simply.

"So, you're sad because you can't be happy together, but you're *both* sad apart?" She asked contemplatively. "I don't get it," she said confused. "It doesn't make sense. If you're both happy together, and sad when you're not together, then why don't you just *stay* together?"

"Why did your parents separate? Was it the distance?"

"No, my dad met another woman—my step mom. That's why he lives here now. Why?"

"I just wondered if it was the distance is all."

"Is that what your problem is? He lives in the UK, and you live back in the states?"

"Yeah, kind of."

"So, why not move back? Or why doesn't he move here with you? Bet you gotta house plenty big enough."

"Because they don't want to. They have other commitments and I have to start filming a new movie soon. I can't leave."

"So, do your jobs, and then move back home. You seem bummed that you aren't with him anymore, so maybe Hollywood isn't your home anymore. Maybe the movies aren't as important to you as he is. At least give it a go. Maybe you won't even miss being a movie star. Or you could easily get a job over there, *or...*" she sat up confidently getting into the ideas she offered Heidi. "You must make a *lotta* bucks from being a movie star," she said wide eyed. "So, maybe just do one job a year over here, then move back to England. I think you're overcomplicating it, Heidi. It's really kind of easy," she said bluntly.

Heidi laughed. "You're good company, Aubrey, you know that?"

"Well my best friend tells me that, yeah," she said nonchalantly.

Chapter Thirty-Nine

Anna returned home, trying desperately to ignore the new silence. The silence she used to adore, but now, evoked a feeling of sadness. She saw the brown envelope poking out of the top of her bin. Feeling bad for tossing it in the first place, she went to retrieve it. Anna thought back to the awkwardness between them as they'd said goodbye. *How things change,* she thought. *Where would they be if Dawn hadn't shown up? Would they have ended up in bed together? Of course they would have; that was a given. But what then? Would they have thought better of it when she had to leave? Was Heidi telling the truth? Would she have fought it...for them?* She needed to stop thinking about it all. It was done now. She couldn't change it, nor did she want to. "Everything goes back to normal," she said aloud, pushing the folder back into the coffee table drawer.

Anna opened the fridge, looking for something to eat. She'd hadn't eaten all day, and her appetite still wasn't there. She knew her job required strength, but ignorance was driving her at present. She grabbed a beer and shut the fridge door. Anna looked at the post-it-note she'd put on there earlier. Picking it up again, Anna rubbed her thumb over the writing.

Anna, thank you from the bottom of my heart for everything you've done for me. This lame book is dedicated to you! I hope you like it. I wish I could have been with you as you read it so I could have your feedback, but I guess it wasn't meant to be. This has been the most perfect time of my life. Look after yourself, Anna. I hope you get everything you want and deserve. All my love forever and always, Heidi xx

She read the message over and over, unable to stop the constant draw to the last words. *How had she managed to get into such a mess?* Leaving her beer on the counter, she switched the light off and made for bed instead.

*

"Hey darling," Jack's mum said. "What're you still doing up? Do you not have to be up for work in a few hours?"

He looked at the clock. "Crap. Yeah, I do," he said, looking at how much was left of the book."

"What's that?"

"Oh, a friend's book."

"Since when do you read books?" She laughed, sitting on the edge of the bed.

"I guess since someone I knew wrote it."

"Are you okay, love?"

Jack sighed heavily. "Yeah."

"Well it doesn't look or sound it. You want a quick cup of tea and a chat? Or do you need to go to bed?"

"I really should, but I don't think I'll be able to sleep. Come on then," he said to his mother.

"So, what's going on?" she asked, putting some biscuits on the table. "Are you okay? You're not in trouble, are you?"

"No, God no. *I'm* fine, mum, I promise. I've just got a problem with one of my friends," he said distantly before coming back around to his waiting Mum. "Mum..." he said, squeezing her hand. "I promise," he contemplated. "Look, I have a friend that I think may be gay," he said sincerely. "I think she and my other friend want to risk losing any chance of happiness rather than just admitting it. I don't want them to do that. I wanna make them see it's messed up, but without embarrassing them over something I know nothing about. I just don't really know what to do," he said, seriously.

"Well, what makes you think this?"

"I saw them together, and then I saw them apart," he said withdrawn.

"You're a sweetheart. You'll make a lovely husband and father one day. You've always been a complete romantic," she said, stroking his hand. "If you genuinely think this, then why don't you approach them and ask? It may be that they're scared of telling people around them because of how people will react. Raise it first."

"Hmmm, I don't know how that would go down. I suppose it's worth a thought. I think I have another idea though," he said thoughtfully.

"Care to share?" His mum requested.

"Not just yet, Mum. I'll reveal all soon," he said, kissing her cheek. "Thanks Mum, you're the best. I need to crash. I gotta be up very soon," he said, grabbing another chocolate biscuit.

Chapter Forty

Heidi woke with a start, feeling her sweat on the pillow. She lay awake and stared up at the ceiling thoughtfully. Four years ago, she found out her husband had been cheating on her for about eight months. She thought back to that night, as she lay there in the same manner, realizing the problem and surprise of *this* situation felt *far worse*.

Heidi couldn't contend with another night of tossing and turning, *or* overthinking and crying. She made her way to the kitchen and switched the TV on, while making herself a mint aero hot chocolate. Having forgotten how celebrity focused the channels here could be, she was surprised to see the revelation of her husband's antics all over it.

"Miss Heidi, que pasa?" Margherita said sleepily.

"Hey Margherita, what are you doing up? It's really late."

"Si, por—"

"Es possible en ingles? Soy cansada."

"Si. What's the matter? You never tell me to speak in English. You sad? Why *you* sad? You want Senor Everett back?"

"No. Definitely not," she confirmed. "I'm fine, just jet lagged is all."

"You been home too long to be jet lagged senorita. Plus, you look very sad."

"I'm fine," she said filling her cup with water. "You want some?"

"No, gracias," she said turning her nose up.

"Café con leche?"

"No, puedo… okay okay. Si, por favor."

Heidi smiled and made her coffee. "So, how is Sophia? All good at the hospital?"

"Si, si. She is. They very happy with her. She told me so," she said proudly.

"Awesome, you think we should go visit? We could take a little vacation. She could show us the sights?"

Margherita looked at her carefully. "Si, possible," she said. "So, how was your break? I know see you much. You look well. Sad, but well. What's Dawn's cousin like? She was nice to you? Look after you?"

"Yes, she was. Very kind in fact. It's weird, in the thirty years of not seeing her, she was exactly how I remembered. She was very accommodating, which was nice given how I must've put her out."

"Put her out? Por que?"

"Well, yeah, of course. She lives alone. She's up most mornings at four am, and works right through to six pm. She comes home to a quiet house, and is in bed by eight. Then I come along; I can't do anything, or go anywhere. Not only was her home invaded, but she had to stay up late and entertain me. Even had to shop for me."

"Why you no shop on the online?"

"I did," Heidi smiled, squeezing her hand. "But she did it for me first."

"And she looked after you? You no have problems with animals?"

"Yes, she did. She *really* did. My first day she made me a good meal," she groaned loudly. "She's an awesome cook."

"Si?" she said questionably.

"Nearly as good as you're cooking," Heidi winked.

"Good comeback, senorita." She laughed. "So, she worked all day and then cooked you dinner? This nice girl, no?"

"She was lovely. She made me a good meal, and then she nearly fell out of her chair when I told her I could cook. Since she was so perfectly hospitable, letting me stay and stuff, the least I could do was cook for her. Every night, she came home and I cooked for her. We drank too much, I'm ashamed to say, but we ate good food, drank good wine, and talked a *lot*. We laughed a lot, and just did normal stuff." She smiled.

Heidi and Margherita were there until the sun came up, having dissected everything from her break away, to the people she'd met. From the ridiculous farce of Troy thinking she'd fancied Helen, and everything in between. Having kept her up all night, Heidi demanded Margherita go to bed, and not to work. After a good 20 minutes, and a compromise of fresh made pancakes and OJ's, they finally dispersed to their own rooms, and caught up on their sleep.

Chapter Forty-One

Dawn looked at her phone, instantly alarmed when she saw the international number. She knew her family's numbers by heart, plus caller ID showed the name, but she still worried whenever she saw a UK number.

"Edwards Talent Agency, Dawn Edwards speaking."

"Hey good looking. How's tricks?" The male voice came over.

Dawn barely recognized Jack's voice. "Well, you clearly know me if you're calling me good looking, but what makes you think I know *you*?" She sipped her chai latte, smirking in the California sunshine.

"Well, you knew me pretty well last week. If I remember correctly, there was even a '*oh my god, don't ever leave my life*' in there." He chuckled.

"*Shut up.*"

"What? It's true."

"I was in the moment; I say that to every guy."

"Hmmm yeah yeah, I bet you millions you don't. So, how you doing?"

"I'm awesome. I've just got another big contract, so I'm out interviewing a couple of kids to mold into mini me's," she scoffed.

"God help us!"

"*Whatever*, you loved it. So, how's things there? How's my cousin? You looking after her?"

"Of course, don't I always? How's my favorite movie star? You looking after her?" he asked inquisitively.

"Hmmm trying. I think Everett messed with her head."

"*Really?* What's happened? Has he come back to her?"

"God no, nothing like that. It's just *weird*. Like, she's constantly pissed off. I don't know, maybe she's having a midlife crisis. It's kinda the norm over here," she chuckled.

"Dawn, have you read her book yet?"

"Yeah, did you read it? It's kinda cool. I've sent it to a few different publishers. There's no way we won't get at least half a dozen offers. Jesus, it's Heidi Spencer."

"Yeah, easily I'm sure, but did you notice anything about it?"

"Like what?"

"Dawn, the book is about Anna."

"*What?*" *she asked* confused. "Are you drinking? What are you talking about? I don't know what you were reading, but Heidi's book was about a girl and a guy falling in love. His name was Tom, not *Anna.* It has *nothing* to do with a farm. What were you reading?"

"Dawn, the boy is her. How have you not noticed this?"

"*What?* It's a boy—Tom—I just told you. What are you going on about?"

"Dawn, it's Anna," he tried again.

"Why the hell would it be Anna? You realize you're making absolutely no sense."

"Dawn, they're in love with each other, and now they're pining for one another. I'm sorry, but it's the truth. The description of the character... of Tom... it's Anna."

"You're mental. How are they *pining* for each? How the *fuck* are they in love? They're two straight women."

"Fuck me, are you always this impossible?" He sighed. "Dawn, what does it matter if it's two women? Jesus, they've fallen in love. Why do they need to label

355

themselves? More importantly, why do *you* need to label them? No wonder they didn't tell you."

"What do you mean they didn't tell me? Are you saying they told you over me that they're in love?" She questioned.

"No, but I was here, in the throes of it. I watched it all unfold."

"Are you kidding? Jesus, can you imagine if the press got a hold of this?" She dismissed him. "They'd have an absolute field day. She could lose Disney. Do you know how many celebs do that now? Pretend they're gay…"

"They're not pretending; they're in love. Jesus, *you're* a nightmare. Who gives a shit what the press thinks? I don't think she'd be broken hearted over a role because she's already broken hearted they're apart. I know nothing about your careers and Hollywood, but as far as Disney goes, this is the 21st century. They can't be far off from putting a gay character in one of their movies," he stormed. "If they denied that, I'm pretty sure all hell would break loose. I don't think they'd want that on their shoulders. It's *discrimination*," he said.

"Okay, slow down a minute. Let's get this straight with a more understandable explanation. You say this man in the book is Anna, and you think that's why she's in love with her?"

"Do me a favor, Dawn. Go to page 21, 74, and 189. They're all very '*descriptive*' characterizations. Then call me back," he sighed, hanging up.

"What…the…actual…fuck?" she said aloud. *What's he going on about? She can't be in love with a woman. It's a woman. And her cousin. Wait, Troy said Heidi was into Helen. He said that Heidi had physically told him she fancied a woman. What the…* she thought confused. Dawn lifted her sunglasses up, noticing the artist across the street. Finishing her drink, she rushed over to him, dodging the hideous L.A. traffic.

"Hey, you busy?" she asked the street artist.

"Do I *look* it?" He tutted.

"Do you actually *want* to earn money?" She spat. "Can you draw normal things or just copy stuff?"

"Lady, I'm an artist. I can draw anything you want me to. You, your dog, your home. Your favorite movie stars. A s—"

"Yeah yeah, I got it, Michelangelo. Can you read?"

"Are you for real, lady? Look, stop wasting my time." He stopped, seeing the wad of dollars in her hand. "I mean, sure I can."

"Good, I need you to read this." She circled the descriptions on the pages Jack mentioned and ripped them out. "Then draw the characters based on the description.

"Lady, you high?" he said confused.

"You want the business or not?"

"You know, you brits are normally pretty polite, but y*ou*... not so much."

"I'm not here to make friends. I have business to sort out. If *you* can't do it, I'll get someone who can. If you can, and want the business, how much?"

"Whatever. 30 bucks," he said.

"You said you can draw anything, so get started. When you've done that, I need you to do another with hair. *My* hair. Got it?" she said.

"You're crazy. Yeah, I got it. But that's two pictures, lady. 30 bucks a piece makes 60 bucks total," he said, holding up two sheets of A1 paper.

"Really? They don't need to be full pages. Can't you just put them on one?" She snapped.

S. L. Gape

"Fraid not," he smirked.

"Fine. Just hurry up already!" She snapped. "60 bucks on two bloody pictures, just to prove a point to a stupid bloody kid." She threw three 20 dollar bills at him, and sat on the bench opposite the artist.

"Lady, you really gonna sit there the entire time? I'll be done in an hour; come back then," he scorned.

"You're quite right I'm gonna sit here!" She said, returning to her emails as she waited.

*

"Lady, I'm done here!" he shouted across to her.

"Great," she said, pushing her cell back into her handbag as she walked back to him.

"As per the description," he said, holding the paper up, and watching her face change. "You okay lady?"

"Yeah. *No,*" she stopped, noticing the similarities. "Sorry, yeah, I'm okay," she shook herself, understanding Jack's words. "Um the next one," she said quietly.

"Sure thing," he said, holding up the picture.

"Ah!" she said, moving her hand for something to grab on to. It hit her. "Holy fuck," she said, rubbing her head. She grabbed her phone out of her bag and started running towards her car.

"Lady! *Lady*! Your pictures!" She heard after her. "Crazy ass lady," he muttered to himself.

"Hello?" a familiar male voice picked up.

"What the fuck did you do to my best friend!? She's gay!? You *turned* her into a lesbian!? You were supposed to bang her. I sent her there to fuck you, and you *turned* her *gay*?"

"Seriously? Would you give up with the 'gay' thing, Dawn? I tried to sleep with her. Believe me, when she first arrived, I wanted to. I can't help that I wasn't the one she was into. Look, now that you're up to speed, what do we do? I reckon we have one of two choices. We sit back and ignore it, or we do something about it."

"And what exactly do you propose we do?" she asked exasperatedly, her mind filled with the new information. "Wait... is this the reason she hasn't slept with anyone in 20 years? I always thought it could be she was gay," she said.

"*What's* your obsession with being gay and labels? She's fallen in love and that's all that matters. You wanna know the reason she hasn't slept with anyone in all that time?"

Dawn stopped considerably. "*Why*? How do *you* know? I just thought maybe she was interested in women and didn't want to upset her dad. What is it?"

"Dawn, the reason she hasn't done anything is because she saw how broken hearted your uncle was when her mum died. Anna had a couple of relationships before she died, as people do, but when that happened, and her dad left the farm and never came back, she swore to herself she'd never have to go through it. Whenever she sees him, she still says he's completely broken hearted. Anna didn't want to ever put herself through that. She's happy just to have her life here on the farm. Don't get me wrong, I've forced her on a couple of dates over the years, as have some of her friends, but when it gets to them wanting a second or third, she backs off entirely and we're back to square one. I asked her about eight years ago if she was a lesbian and told her I knew a friend of my sister's was gay; I could even set them up. But she was adamant she wasn't. I don't think she's ever been into a woman. Not until now. I think they've just

fallen in love. I don't know about you, but I can't deal with
the moods and the sadness. I'm not prepared to sit back,
and let them walk away from a happiness that they both
deserve," he said loyally.

"Dawn? *Dawn*, you still there?"

"Yes," she sniffed.

"What's up? Why are you upset?"

"She's always been like my sister, Jack. We've grown
up so close. I can't believe I didn't know any of this. I can't
believe that after all this time she's talked, not only herself,
but another wonderful person out of love. I'm just so sad
that anyone would think this is the better option for their
life," she said sadly.

"Well, let's sort it then."

"Right," she said, pulling herself together. "What's the
plan? You seem like the romanticist here. I serial date; I'll
be rubbish. Jack, on a serious note, what happens if it
doesn't work? We could do all this, and it might logistically
fail. By that point, they're in too deep, and end up worse
off," she said.

"We can only do what we can, which is make them
realize how happy they made each other. Neither of them
are...were gay, so that's gotta be an enormous amount of
pressure for the situation, especially given Heidi's life.
Throw in the *'logistics'* as you say, that the world has eyes
on them, and it's gonna be hard. But if it's meant to be, then
love will find a way. It's up to them to make it work. And if
it doesn't, it might just be enough to steer them in the right
direction with their love lives. You in?"

Dawn went quiet for a while. "Are *you* gay?" She
laughed.

"Only you would make a joke out of something
serious." He rolled his eyes.

"Sorry, it's a vice, and you do sound all girly and shit with your grand, romantic gestures," she laughed. "Thanks though, *seriously*. Listen, can you pick me up from the airport?"

"*What*? You're coming here? *When*?"

"Yeah, I think Uncle Brian needs a little visit. I'll call you soon with the details, okay?"

"Sure thing. This is proper exciting."

"Seriously? Are you sure you aren't gay?"

"Three times, Dawn…three times," he smirked, pressing call end.

*

"Penny for them?" Jack asked, leaning against the barn door, watching Anna.

"Oh hey, what're you doing here?" she asked, wiping her eye.

"I work here, remember?" He felt pain as he saw a tear roll down her cheek. "Wanna share?" he said, handing her half of his bacon sandwich.

"I'm fine."

"Clearly!" he said sarcastically.

"Fine," she snatched some of the sandwich from him, taking a bite. "Happy now?"

"Not really. You should know better. We need to keep our strength up in this job. More so this time of year. I know you're sad she's gone, but you have to eat babes."

"What do you mean, 'I'm sad she's gone?' Who?" She tried to act confused.

"Anna, don't insult my intelligence. I'm more of a girl than you when it comes to love and romance."

"I don't know what you mean," she reconfirmed.

"Okay," he sighed. "No worries. I'll let you get on. I need to get back to work, anyway," he said sadly.

God, why did she just keep pushing all the time? She fucked it up with Heidi because she was too scared. It left her feeling broken—the exact thing she was trying to avoid. Now she was lying to her closest friend.

Anna scarfed the last of the bacon sandwich, realizing how much she enjoyed eating. She rushed to the cold barns, and made a container of ice cream. Taking some spoons, she made her way out in search of Jack.

"Knock, knock." She watched him transfer the milk around with a brief look to her before

returning to the job. "I come bearing gifts," she said, holding up the ice cream.

He looked at her, giving a stony nod without a word. *Not making it easy,* she thought.

"So, you knew, eh?" she said, looking down at the hay she was kicking with her foot.

"Knew what?"

"You know what," she said again.

He looked up to his friend and could see the awkwardness and sadness all over her. He turned and sat down on the seat he'd used for milking earlier. "Yeah, I kinda figured it out," he said, opening the ice cream and pulling his chair closer to the haystack.

"How?"

"Honestly, the way you looked at each other. That wasn't unrequited love; it was lust, passion, want, desire. It was love, Anna. I started playing this game when I saw you both. Who could get the bigger smile and twinkle in their eyes when speaking about the other?"

"Shut up," she said shaking her head.

"Unfortunately, you think I'm joking. It was nice. It was cute," he said taking a spoonful. "I loved listening to her speak about you the way she did. I *loved* it. The same goes for you. I'd never seen your eyes light up or known your smile to be as wide as when you spoke about her. But now there's an enormous difference, a gap. You seem sadder than when Charlie died and I don't know how to help you. I see a woman who refused to ever love anything more than an animal transform to a woman who was happy, and giddy, and excited to get home. A woman in love. And on the other side, I saw a woman who came here because her husband cheated on her. She feared animals—was scared to death on numerous occasions—but still faced her fears just to see you. Jesus, she got up in the middle of the night to help you with your dying horse, Anna. If all that isn't love, then I don't know what is," he said impatiently.

"You're talking like this is all… *normal*? How can it be? I'm a woman. She's a woman. We're not gay."

"Oh seriously, mate, get a grip. How do you *know* you're not gay? You haven't ever had a boyfriend *or* a girlfriend. And what even *is* gay? What does it mean? Not everyone wakes up at 10 years old and realizes they want to kiss somebody of the same sex. Not everybody *must* make a choice. Some people are happy that they're lucky enough to have experienced something so wonderful and magical in their lifetimes, regardless of whether it's the same sex or not. They wouldn't dismiss it based on gender. I don't see a woman loving a woman. Well, bit of a lie; I mean, you're both fit," he winked, trying to lighten the situation a little. "Seriously though, I see a person, a beautiful person at that, inside *and* out. And I see a funny, gorgeous, caring, honest, maybe a little wired, person; that must be an L.A. thing as she's nowhere near as wired as your cousin," he smiled, nudging her shoulder. "Look, my point is, all I'm seeing is a beautiful person who's fallen in love with another beautiful person. To be perfectly honest, I'm, well, jealous. Two amazing people who are lucky enough to have found something so wonderful."

"This is all well and good, but you are completely incorrect…" Anna stopped as she stuffed a spoonful of ice cream into her mouth.

"For fucks sake. Just admit it! You love her as much as she loves you, and you're heartbroken she's left," he said.

Chapter Forty-Two

"Hola, como estas? Dande esta, Heidi?" Dawn said.

"Hola. Bien bien, et tu? No Trabajo?"

"Who, me or her? I was interviewing... shit, my *interview*! *Bollox*. Lo siento, Margherita," she apologized for swearing. "Momentito?" she said and quickly called the young interviewee to apologize. She confirmed that something had come up, and that she'd be in touch when she returned from the UK.

"Aqui," Margherita handed her a cup of coffee.

"Gracias," she said taking a small sip. "Are you okay, Margherita? You look tired. Do you want me to speak to Heidi about some extra help?"

"No, no, no. Bien. Cansada. I didn't sleep much."

"Ah, right, I see," She smirked, pointing her finger teasingly.

"Loco chica. I no like you, Miss Dawn," she said, sipping her own coffee. "No, Miss Heidi was no sleeping. We came and speak until morning."

"Is she okay? She hasn't been herself since we returned," she said.

"That's because she found love, and she doesn't have love aqui."

"She told you about Anna?"

"No senorita, her words and her smile told me about Anna."

"Really?" she said sadly.

"Si... que pasa?"

"Nada," she responded. "I'm gonna get a flight home to get this sorted," she said.

"*Home*? This is your home."

"My English home. I need to see if we can get them to realize they've made a huge mistake. They have an amazing chance of something beautiful. They can't deny it just because they're scared," she said coyly.

"You are loco, and rude sometimes—Hollywood rude—but you love Miss Heidi. If anyone can do this, it's you, " she said kissing her on the cheek.

"Gracias, mi amor," she said, dialing her travel agent and leaving Margherita.

Chapter Forty-Three

"My God, I can't believe I've done this to my girl," Dawn's Uncle Brian said with his head in his hands.

"Brian, how could you have ever known?" Dawn's mum said. "Like Dawn, we just thought she was too busy or she might be gay, and didn't want to admit it."

"Look Brian," Dawn's father said. "We all would've gotten involved if we'd known, but we didn't. We can change all that now though. She's apparently fallen in love with someone who seemingly feels the same way, so let's not dwell on the past. Let's fix it," he said, pointing to them and Heidi's parents.

"Brian, I spent a weekend with my daughter a few weeks ago, and she talked about Anna the entire time, to the extent that I basically confronted her. She's clearly *that* smitten with her. I don't want my daughter to get hurt, but if Anna feels even half of what my daughter does, then I think they may be each other's soul mates," she said softly.

"They're on an even par," Jack said. "I've spent time with both of them, together *and* apart, for the last month. It happened quickly, but they're consumed by each other. I've never seen a brighter glow, or a more loving glance than when they're together, and I've never seen a sadness more prominent since they've been apart," he finished, looking up to Dawn who mouthed 'gay' to him.

"Right, well, no time like the present. I'm going to see my daughter. Who's coming?"

Dawn watched them all stand up, mumbling their confirmation. "We won't all fit in Jack's car. We'll follow straight behind you and ride with Heidi's parents," Dawn's parents said.

*

Jack pulled up to the farm, waiting for Dawn's parents who followed close behind.

"Are you okay, Uncle Brian?" Dawn whispered, noticing him eye the farm that's been in his family for three generations.

"Yes love, I'm good. It's just odd being back here after all this time," he said sadly.

"You're doing the right thing," she squeezed his arm.

"I know. I need to get my daughter back on track. It saddens me she's wasted 20 years without ever experiencing love because of me."

"Don't be silly. You're taking a massive step now. You really haven't been here at *all* since Auntie Ann died?"

"No, I haven't. I suppose you're right. I just hope it works."

"Have faith. She's got this incredible and wonderful belief of love. You guys instilled that in her. That belief is so strong, it's scared her. But now she's had a taste of it, so just believe. She's finally found what you guys had. Let's focus on that."

"You really think that?"

"That's what I keep hearing." She smiled and took his hand.

"You ready to do this Mr. Roberts?" Jack asked sincerely.

"Call me Brian. Come on, let's sort this out," he said, knocking firmly on the door.

*

Anna heard a knock at the door, wondering who it could be. She wasn't in the mood to see anybody. In fact, she wasn't in the mood for anything these days. Remembering that Jack had a doctor's appointment today, she answered the door, in case it was him.

"*Dad? Dawn?* What are you doing back? Auntie Nora, Uncle Pete? Jack, why aren't you at the doctors? And..." *No, it couldn't be*. She recognized them from the press. *Was that Heidi's parents?* "What's going on? What are you all doing here? Dad, what…you haven't been here since Mum died. *Shit,* has someone died? Oh my god, *Heidi. What's happened*?" She screamed erratically.

"Anna, calm down. Nobody's died or is hurt," her dad said, pushing her inside and allowing everyone else to follow.

"Told ya," Jack said to Dawn discreetly.

"What's going on? What are you all doing here?" she said again, still looking concerned.

Jack went to the fridge and got out a bottle of wine, pouring a glass for her. He offered more to Aunt Nora and Heidi's mom and made coffee for their dads.

"Anna, sweetheart, sit down. I've been informed that this is what is known as *'staging an intervention,'*" he said proudly. "I'll go with that, in light of what I've heard today. I hope you don't mind speaking about this in front of everyone, but what I will say is that everyone is here because you and Heidi are both cared for."

369

"*Heidi*? What's Heidi got to do with this? Is she here?" She immediately looked to the door expectantly.

"No, darling. She's back in the states. She doesn't know I'm here either," Dawn said sitting next to her and taking her hand.

"Dad, what are you doing here? You haven't been back since Mum died. You haven't even come for a birthday or Christmas, not in 20 years. I don't understand."

"I know," he said sadly. "Just give me a minute," he sighed, nodding his head sadly. "Anna, I'm sorry, love. So very sorry. I have ruined your life, and had absolutely no idea I was doing it."

"*What*? No, you haven't. What do you mean?"

"Please just let me finish. I've been a silly, old fool, and never once thought about the impact it would have on you—my leaving. Your mother would be so disappointed with me and that breaks my heart. Anna, I never once questioned why you never brought home a boyfriend or anyone to meet me. I always assumed that you were either too busy, or just too embarrassed to talk to me about these things. Honestly speaking, I guess I wouldn't have known how to handle those conversations. But I'm your father, and at no point should I ever have accepted that. I heard today that family members thought you were gay because you'd always stayed single. Again, that's wrong. Not that they thought that, but that I failed to pick up on it. Worst of all is that I found out the reason behind you staying single all this time was because you were afraid of love," he said sadly. "That *I* made you afraid because you saw me break apart when your mother died. I should've never ran away like I did. I acted incredibly selfishly, and I've sat back all these years. I'm the proudest father on the planet that you simply got up, and made the farm work. You bought it, evolved it.

By God, you've been so incredibly innovative and done things I wouldn't have even thought about. And because of that, you accomplished *all* of this," he said, pointing to the room. "It looks fantastic by the way," he nodded approvingly. "But Anna, this isn't right. I'm sorry I scared you beyond embracing love. That was so wrong for me as a parent. Darling, you are an amazing, young woman, and seemingly have an equally amazing, young woman who loves you just as much as you love her."

"Wha...bu—" She didn't get to finish.

"Don't deny it, sweetheart," he said, walking over to her and holding her face. "Don't. *You're* sad and *she's* sad, and yes, maybe eventually it would ease a little, but regrets *never* fade. I've nothing but regrets for everything I missed out on—this place, spending time with you. Even more so after what I've heard today. You can't leave this, Anna. I won't let you; you deserve what me and your mother had. You should face your fears like I have, coming here today. Once you do, you'll realize, there's nothing to be afraid of. It's a leap of faith that will open so many more possibilities and opportunities for you, love," he said sincerely.

"Dad, I don't know what you think you know, or who's spoken to you, but..."

Mrs. Edwards walked towards Anna. "Can I ask you one question?" she said seriously, looking directly into Anna's eyes.

"Um, yes," she said nervously.

"If you don't love my daughter, why did you react the way you did when we arrived? You thought something had happened to her."

Anna could feel the woman's eyes bore into her, and she didn't know how to answer without lying. She also knew, they'd all see through her lies. "Because we're friends. I wouldn't want any of my friends—"

"Right, okay then," she interrupted. "I guess we've all wasted our time here. Heidi's aware I'm here, and waiting for an outcome. Clearly you don't feel the way she does, so I'll let her know she's wasting her breath," she lied.

"*What?*" Dawn mouthed to her behind Anna's back, watching her shrug her shoulders.

"She feels something for me?" Anna said questioningly.

"Of course, she does. Would we all be here if she didn't?"

"So, why didn't she come here? Why are you lot here instead?" she asked.

"*Work!*" Dawn and Jack shouted in unison.

"Actually, no. That's not entirely true. The truth is she doesn't know we're here. I bluffed, but I'm glad I did. If you didn't love her as much as she loves you, you wouldn't have even cared if she were interested or not. The fact of the matter is, you were the one that pushed her away, Anna, and said you *couldn't* do it. She'd already tried to fight for you, in her mind; she didn't want to keep begging you. Nobody would. So, you see, you're the only one who can change it," Heidi's mother said while holding her hand.

"Are you *insane*? *You* sent her packing!" Jack scorned her. "*You* pushed her away. The only person ever to make you smile the way she did and *you* pushed her away. I can't believe you did that. I thought it'd been a mutual thing, that you just lived too far apart, or, I don't know!" he slammed.

"What the *hell* were you thinking?" Dawn added.

"She *told* you that?" Anna asked sadly, seeing the hurt fill her father's face.

"She couldn't not, love. She's been completely broken hearted. It was evident, and as such, she had no other alternative but to tell me everything."

"I didn't mean to hurt her," she said, allowing the tears to fall. "We'd had an amazing night at the premiere, and then her husband showed up, saying he was going to fight for her. I didn't want to stand in her way. I just realized that we would never be able to make it work. We're too different. And…I thought, if I end it sooner rather than later, we wouldn't get hurt."

"Well, that clearly worked," Dawn spat.

"We know you never meant to." Heidi's mum smiled. "After hearing what I've heard today, believe it or not, I get it. We all get scared. But you need to look at the pros and cons and establish which outweighs which," she said.

"What if it doesn't work? We'll both get hurt."

"You're already hurt, darling," her father walked up to face her. "What if you have a lifetime together, like your mother and I did?"

"You didn't though, Dad; she died. It was cut short."

"Only for me, darling. Your mother spent all her adult life with me, her beautiful daughter, the animals she loved to hate, and our perfect world. So, you see, my darling, you only saw my hurt and my pain. You forgot the happiness we shared for 27 wonderful years. Look, if you don't want this, and you're happy here with just you and the animals, watching the world go by, then, darling, that's what you must do. But if you love this woman, and she was prepared to risk her career to fight for you, then go after it. Anna Elizabeth *go* and fight for what you both deserve before it's too late."

"You okay?" Dawn asked her.

"What am I going to do about this place? I can't leave Jack here alone," she questioned.

"Why not?" he said.

"Darling, you don't need to. I did this for over 40 years. I may be old now, and a bit out of shape, but your grandfather was still working at my age. I have this young man who knows what to do nowadays. He can tell me. We can manage, darling. Come on, when did you last have a holiday? Go and have a couple weeks in the sun with Dawn."

"A couple of weeks? I can't do *that*."

"*Why not*? You don't trust me?" Jack asked.

Anna's head spun. *Was she considering this? It was insane.*

"Don't panic," Jack hugged her. "Everything will be okay here, I promise. I'll call you every day with an update if you need it," he said.

Anna sat down. "Am I doing the right thing, honestly?" She looked around the room and watched the smiles and nods cross their faces. "What the hell am I supposed to say?"

"Babe, you'll know exactly what to say when you're together. Which is a good thing because I booked us flights for tomorrow night," Dawn confirmed.

"Are you *kidding* me? Dawn that's absurd. That isn't enough time. I need to do too much."

"Sorry kiddo, can't run the risk of you bailing. These four can go back tonight. Your dad can stay here, and between him and Jack, you guys can go through what needs to be done. Then you and I can get you packed, have a few beers, and tomorrow, Jack can take us to the airport via your dad's house. He can grab some stuff while Jack drops us off and then bring your dad back. It's a dynamite plan."

"It's all too quick. I don't have enough time to get organized."

"How about I go back with them? You three young'uns can have a few drinks tonight, and stop her from stressing anymore. Darling, I don't need you to make a list for a job I did all my life, and you don't want me spoiling your party. It'll give me a chance to get my things together," her dad finished.

"Dad, can we have a word for a second?" she asked, walking to the front door.

"What's up, sweetheart?"

"Are you sure you're okay to do this? You're not leaving tonight because you can't face it, are you?"

"I'm fine, Anna. I got this far; the rest will be fine. I know I'm an old man, but Jack will have it all covered. I'll just help, the same way you did it all by yourself," he said seriously. "I'm fine babe, you just do this for me *and* for you."

"Am I doing the right thing, Dad? I'm a woman…she's a woman. How is that even possible?"

"I don't know, darling. The heart wants what the heart wants. You've fallen in love. Go get her. This is the fun part."

"I can't believe I'm doing this."

"Nobody deserves happiness more than you, darling," he said, kissing his daughter's forehead and saying goodbye.

Chapter Forty-Four

"Are you okay?"

"No, I feel physically sick. I have no idea how I got here."

"Aer-o-plane," Dawn said, grinning widely.

"Shut up!" Anna scolded. "I don't know *what* I'm doing here. I don't know if she'll even want me anymore. I don't know what to do."

"The girl is a movie star. Do you *know* how many love stories she's filmed over the years? More than I can remember. So tell her you love her, that you can't stop thinking about her, and you want to make sweet, mad, passionate love all night long," she said smirking.

"You're painful."

"Well, someone in the family needs to be. You wanna go the house, or to the studios?"

"Studios? God no. The house is fine."

"The house it is."

"*Wait!* What if she kicks me out? At least at the studios she won't make a scene in front of people."

"Okay, the studios it is."

"*Wait!* What if she goes mad because people get wind of me, and I *out* Heidi Spencer-Brady to the world?"

"For the love of God, Anna, make a *freaking* decision."

"Home," she said sadly.

"Come on, chill out. Don't worry, you can meet Margherita since we don't know when Heid's will be home.

Plus, she doesn't know I'm back yet," she said trying to calm her down.

"I just don't know if I can do it. I don't know what to do."

"Tell her you love her and be done with it."

"Oh great, amazing words there," she said. "Holy shit!" She burst out. "Please tell me this *isn't* Heidi's."

"Yes, it is, why?"

"Oh, Dawn, I definitely *can't* do this."

"Babes, chill out. *Come on.* She isn't in. One step at a time, eh?" She squeezed her shoulder as she drove up the driveway. "*Come on.*"

"I think I'm going to be sick," Anna said.

"Probably because you're dressed for winter in 74-degree heat. I think you need a neat vodka," she said, pressing the doorbell and listening to Margherita's feet, flip flopping across the floors.

"Buenos Dias mi amor, como estas?" Dawn watched the elderly woman's eyes cast over her before spotting a nervous Anna and moving towards her quickly.

"Anna? Dulce, *dulce* Anna," she said, grabbing her face in both hands.

"Um, what's she saying?" Anna asked awkwardly, looking down at the woman, who stood on her tiptoes and cupped her face.

"She says you're sweet. She clearly doesn't know you like I do. Margherita, Anna no entiendes. Solo ingles?"

"Since when did you speak Spanish?"

"Since my best friend's housekeeper refuses to speak in English," she rolled her eyes to Margherita. "Oh, and since she used to speak about me in Spanish." She looked at Margherita disdainfully.

"Solo ingles… Si? Nada?" She spoke to Anna.

"Oh Jesus, what's she saying now?" She slapped her arm. "Ouch, what was that for?"

"We don't blaspheme."

"Oh gosh, I'm so sorry."

"S'okay, senorita. I forgive."

"Why do you forgive her and not *me*?"

"Cos, you do it many years to annoy me. Come Anna, what you like? Café con leche? Agua?"

"You realize that we speak nothing but English back home? She needs wine *or* vodka."

"Nada? You speak no Espanol?"

"Well, in the UK we don't really have a requirement like you guys have for it. We have a small amount of Spanish, but they're mostly people who travel. They tend to go to London." She smiled. "As opposed to here, where you share a piece of land with South America, most of which are predominantly Hispanic."

"Brains as well as beauty. What happened to you?" Margherita smirked to Dawn.

"Graciosa!" she scolded. "I was *sarcastically* calling her funny before you ask," she said, grabbing a bottle of wine from the fridge.

"Are you okay? You look like you're going to be sick," Dawn said to her cousin.

"Yeah, I think I am."

"Chill, seriously. You need a drink," she said. "So, what are we going to do? Hey Margherita, do you know what time she'll be home?"

"Why you worry, Anna? You love her, no?" She questioned, pouring them both some wine. "All she says is late," she said looking at the clock on the wall.

"Well, it's just after seven now. Should be anytime in the next few hours, I guess."

"I'll cook some dinner for you, then you go unpack. This will work better than Dawn's advice of drink. Drink doesn't help everything," she scorned Dawn who rolled her eyes.

"Unpack? I'm not staying *here,* am I? I thought I'd be staying at your place," she said nervously.

"Well either or, but Margherita is right, maybe you should stay here. That way, you'll be here when she returns. Also, I'm at work first thing tomorrow, so this probably makes more sense. You can chill here with Heidi and Margherita," she confirmed.

"I don't know. What if she doesn't want me here? You can't just stay at someone's house without their okay."

"Listen, between Margherita and I, we have enough clout to say you can."

"Why she wouldn't want you here? She loves you; of course she want you here. She want you in her bed," Margherita said, wriggling her eyebrows comically.

Oh, dear God, Anna thought. *Her housekeeper was talking about them having sex, what the hell?*

"Why wouldn't she want you here? She's head over heels in *love* with you," Dawn said, watching the transformation on Anna's face. "What?"

"You really think she *loves* me?" she asked softly.

Margherita put her hand on Anna's. "Sweet Anna, Heidi loves you. She be very happy to see you. This I know," she said stroking her face softly. "She very sad without you."

Chapter Forty-Five

Heidi came home just after four am, and Anna still hadn't slept. It was a little after eight now and she was stressed *and* jet lagged. She felt incredibly uncomfortable for being in someone's home who didn't know they were there. Equally, she couldn't stop worrying about what Heidi was going to say or do when she saw her. Dawn had given her keys to her place in case she wanted to go there. Of course, she could just go straight back to LAX. Heidi wouldn't have ever known she was there. This felt like a very appealing option now. Unable to stop her mind running away with itself, Anna decided to get up, and get out before Heidi woke up. She'd go to Dawn's, and work out what she was going to say or do when she saw her. She freshened up, putting her jeans and a t-shirt on, and left the room as perfectly as she'd found it. Quietly, she made her way down the center staircase. It was bigger than her entire house. She couldn't imagine the woman who'd spent so long at her house lived somewhere like this. Anna stopped still, suddenly feeling sick to her stomach as she could hear Heidi's voice. She was singing a song she didn't recognize, the same two lines over and over. *God, she missed her*. Anna was convinced Heidi would hear her uncontrollable breathing, but she simply couldn't resist the pull to her beautiful voice. Anna stood at the side of the door, and felt her belly flip as she watched Heid make a fresh OJ, moving her hands to the song she was singing. She was so fixated that she didn't notice Margherita sneak up behind her and push her into the kitchen with a scream. Losing her footing, Anna crashed onto the floor. *What the?* she mouthed to Margherita, who looked apologetic before hiding when she saw Heidi.

"Anna? What the *hell*? Shit, are you okay?" she asked, confusedly pulling her up.

"Yes, fine, though seemingly your housekeeper has something against me," she said, getting up and rubbing her shoulder.

"What were you doing? What are you doing here? What's going on?" Heidi said.

Anna stood there in silence, completely dumbfounded by the entire situation.

"Hablar! Hablar!" They heard.

Anna looked back to Heidi even more confused.

"She's telling you to speak. Margherita aqui! *Ahora*!"

"Si?" she came in sheepishly.

Heidi and Margherita had a conversation in Spanish, confusing Anna immensely. She kept noticing Margherita pointing to her. She needed to say something, but she couldn't get a word in.

"I love you," she blurted and watched in slow motion Heidi's OJ drop to the ground.

Margherita ran to the broken glass and began picking it up.

"I'm sorry. I don't speak Spanish, and I didn't know how to stop you both because I couldn't understand and… sorry, I'm rambling," Anna said, looking down to the floor.

"So, you *didn't* mean it?" Heidi asked sadly.

"No…yes…*Jesus*. Can we go somewhere to talk please?" She looked down at Margherita who eyed them fervently.

"Yes," she said, leading them out.

*

Heidi walked into her bedroom holding the door open and eyeing Anna cautiously as she took in the expanse of the room. "Blimey, you have my entire lounge in your bedroom alone," Anna said, looking at the positional wall separating the biggest bed she'd ever seen, and the lounge. She spotted the floor to ceiling windows looking out to one of the best views she'd ever seen, leaving her completely breathless and mesmerized.

"So, I'm guessing you didn't come here just to look at the view from my bedroom," she interrupted Anna's evaluation of the area.

"Well, yeah. You guessed right. How are you?" she asked interestedly.

"Okay, I guess. Yourself?"

"Um, I've missed you. *A lot,*" Anna surprised herself by the words.

"You *have*?" she asked surprised.

"Yes, loads."

"When did you get here? And *why* are you here? In my house, no less."

"I hope you don't mind. Dawn and Margherita thought it was best for me to stay here last night. I didn't think it was right. Margherita said you wouldn't be home until late, and Dawn had work this morning, so I went with it. Sorry," she said twisting her ring on her finger.

"You've been here all night?"

"Um yes. I didn't really think it was the best idea to get up at four am to come say hi. I thought you'd probably be wrecked."

"Yeah, I was, but I would've loved to see you. It's been a really long day."

"That's nice to hear. So, you're not *mad* at me?"

"How could I be *mad* at you? You didn't do anything. I get it; you're too scared. I can't blame someone for that, at least not when I'm fully aware of the reason behind it. I'm upset, I'm not going to lie. I feel a little disappointed that I wasn't enough for you to overcome that fear, but in your defence, I can't honestly say I wouldn't have done the exact same."

"Right," she said softly.

"So, how come you left the farm?"

"Unfinished business," she said looking to Heidi.

"Unfinished business? How so?" she asked confused.

Anna breathed in deep. *It was now or never...* "Because I stupidly let the woman I love leave without telling her, and because I let fear control me."

"So you *do* love me?" she said with a slight smile.

Anna smirked at the woman walking towards her. "Yes, I do. Not quite sure how, or why, but I do. Seemingly, everyone knew but me. They all think I'm far less happy without you."

"Everyone?"

"Oh yes, *everyone." She smiled.* "Wait for this; you may want to take a seat," she said walking towards the bed. "Hmm, maybe we should go over here?" she said awkwardly, redirecting them to the lounge area, and filling her in on the details of the 'intervention.'

"Your dad really came back? And he's there now?"

"Yeah," she nodded her head surprisingly. "He was devastated he'd made me too scared to face love, and even more upset that he'd never realized. He's there now with Jack while I get a two-week holiday," she said shyly.

S. L. Gape

"You have two weeks here?" Heidi asked astonished.

"Well, I have an open return. If you'd like me to stay for two weeks, I will. I didn't really know how this would go down, so I figured the open ticket was probably safer."

"Do you want to stay here for two weeks?"

"Well that depends."

"On?"

"On whether you'll forgive me, so we can continue where we left off."

"*Really*?" she said, raising an eyebrow wickedly.

"*Naughty.*" *She smiled.* "On a serious note, I am sorry, Heidi. I never meant to hurt you. I thought given that every time we...well, got close, something got in the way. It was like the universe was telling us something. I just thought it was a sign telling me not to do it, that I'd end up broken hearted the way my dad was. But like my father said, I focused all these years on when she died, and the aftermath. I'd forgotten about the perfect and beautiful times they shared. More importantly, I never realized I'd be so broken hearted when you left. I hated not having you there every day. I still can't quite fathom what this is," she said confused. "I can't explain why suddenly I'm attracted to a woman, or what's going to happen when we..." She stopped. "Sorry, if we...well, you know, do stuff. The point is, I don't know what or why this happened. I don't know if your fame will tear it apart, or if you'll run as soon as people start questioning it. If it worked out perfectly, I don't know how we'd make it work with you here, and me back in the UK. If I'm honest, I don't know much, but I do know that somehow, somewhere along the way, I've fallen in love with you. A woman, a Hollywood megastar. I have, and even if you said, no, you didn't want me, it's like my father said: regretting it would be far worse than never knowing," she said nervously.

"I don't know the answers to any of those things, Anna. I know my husband cheated on me four years ago for the very first time, and has since left me a little while ago I didn't hurt anywhere near as much as I've hurt since not being with you. I've never loved anyone as much as I love you. I have fallen, and fallen hard," she sighed. "I wish I could say that none of those things will be an issue, and that we can *make* it work, but I don't know that for certain. I'm happy to go with it though, and see what happens over the next two weeks. If it's as good as what it was before I left your house, then we go from there," she said expectantly.

"You mean it?"

"I mean it." She smiled. "You left your home and your job to travel a couple thousand miles just to tell me you love me. You think I'd let that go unnoticed? Plus, you are hard to resist in that shirt," she smirked.

"*Really*?" She looked down to the navy V-neck t shirt she was wearing.

"*Really*. Those arms, that cleavage… err, yeah," Heidi said.

"Is that so?" Anna said, walking towards the couch Heidi sat on, and pulling her up.

"Uh huh, sure is," she said facing her. "God, I've missed you so much." She stroked the back of her fingers to Anna's cheek. "So, you love me, huh?" Heidi started giggling.

"*Shut up,*" Anna rolled her eyes, picking her up in one swoop, walking her to the bed and gently laying her down.

"Watcha doing?" Heidi sang, raising an eyebrow.

"Something I should've done a long time ago," she said, straddling her and laying her arms on either side of her head. "I'm making love to you, my beautiful, Heidi Edwards." She leaned down, and gently pushed her lips against Heidi's, groaning as it deepened. Anna pulled away carefully. "Are you okay with this?" she asked nervously.

Heidi nodded shyly. "I think so. You make me feel like everything is perfect around me, sending shocks through my body with a look alone. I'm pretty sure that while it may be new to us both, our bodies will guide each other," she whispered.

"I haven't slept with anybody in over 20 years," Anna confirmed. "That scares me a bit."

"I haven't slept with anybody in over five years. It's been a long time for both of us, but none of that matters. We're in love, and we want to make love to each other. That's what counts. If you're not ready, I don't want to pressure you."

"You're wrong. You know I'm desperate to be with you on a sexual level; I'm just concerned is all."

"Well how about we not overthink it then? I think it's fair to say, we're both scared. We don't need to do this right now. Although, I'll caveat that with I may need to go take a quick shower to alleviate some stresses," she smirked.

"Woah, fighting talk," she said, leaning her head into Heidi's. "You really are the most beautiful woman I've ever met. You absolutely take my breath away every time I look at you," Anna said sincerely, stroking her blonde locks.

"Um, thank you. I feel the same way," she said, looking down to Anna's singing and vibrating leg.

"It's just a text," she said, getting her phone out and seeing Jack's name come up.

"Oh, it's Jack. Read it!" Heidi said, snuggling into her.

"No way. We were kind of in the middle of something."

"Come on, it may be the farm. You should check."

"If it was urgent, he'd call me," she said, rolling her eyes and opening the message.

Anna read the message and quickly threw the phone back down on the bed, horrified.

"You *wrote* me a poem? Let me hear it!"

"I don't know what he's on about," she said shyly.

Heidi turned her flushed face over to face her. "I love that you've done that. It's incredible. *You're* incredible. I'm not letting this go FYI. How about we listen to the song he sent?" she said.

"He's so soppy. I can't believe he's sent me a song to give to you to win you over," she chuckled.

"Only if the poem didn't work," she pointed to her. "And FYI, the poem already did," she said, watching Anna find the song "Far Away" by Nickelback. She pressed play as they both quietly listened to the words.

"I wish I had a kind, beautiful woman for him. He's so adorable, I can't believe he sent that," Anna said, looking up at Heidi. "Hey, what's up? Why're you crying?" She turned rapidly to face Heidi.

"I'm not, I'm fine."

"You clearly aren't. I can see the tears."

"I just can't believe that all these people are rooting for us. I can't believe how perfect you are. I can't believe you wrote me a poem; nobody's ever done something like that for me. I can't believe you left home *and* the farm—which you *never* do—to come and tell me how you feel. I can't believe how perfect you are," she said, using her sleeve to wipe the stray tears. "Idiotically, I feel like I'm in one of my movies," she chuckled.

"I'm not perfect, I'm far from it," Anna said.

"You're *my* perfect."

Anna smiled to her, gently caressing her face. "I love you," Anna said, kissing her again.

Heidi pulled away, smiling wickedly. "Enough to read me my poem?" She raised her eyebrows.

"Soooo, sex?" Anna said laughing. She squealed noisily when Heidi started tickling her, and pushed her onto her back, mounting her.

"Sex? *Sex*? *Really*? I don't want sex. I want mad, passionate, beautiful, love-making," she said seriously. "Seriously though, I love that you wrote me a poem. Please let me read it," she said sadly.

"You need to stop. You're making this out like it's this wonderful thing and it's crap. I don't have your artistic talent, so—"

"I wouldn't care if it was 'roses are red, violets are blue, you are hot, and I wanna fuck you.' The fact that you've done it is beautiful in my opinion."

"Bollox, why didn't I think of that?" she said, pulling her in and kissing her softly.

"Baby, puhlease!" Heidi pleaded.

"You're painful with those puppy dog eyes. Look, I was just trying to pass the time. It's stupid. I've never done this, so it's no good. And it's private. Jack knew I wrote one, but nobody else. He hasn't even read it," she said, opening her phone to the notes page. "You sure you wanna put yourself and me through this hideousness?"

"More than anything in the world," Heidi smiled softly. "I love you with all my heart, Anna Roberts. I don't know how, or why this has happened. I don't know what I'm supposed to do next, or how somebody falls in love with the same sex without even having sex, but when my 67-year-old mother starts telling me about pan-sexuals, then clearly, I'm beyond overthinking it. I just want 'us,' and what we'll be together. I love the innocence and I love the normality of us. You make me feel normal, and *me* again," she said shyly.

"Me too, baby." She kissed her nose. "As promised," she sighed, quietly looking up at an anxious Heidi.

Tonight, I woke, I saw you there,
A picture perfect without a care,
I thanked the lord for all he'd gave,
Ignored the fear and embraced the brave.
As captivation overtook my all,
The sincerest notion began to fall.

Abruptly here, awoken and battered,
I question to whether your own heart was shattered?
Astonished I failed to put up a fight,
I delight in the perfection which made life so bright.

Always in life I've been graced with affection,
Until meeting you, a different connection,
Endeavouring to confront two worlds apart,
Understanding that True love had captured my heart.
Your beauty, your honesty and positive view,
The way you complete me. Prohibits a life. Without
you.

"Oh my God, Anna, that's amazing. My gosh, you're...I love you, with everything," Heidi said emotionally. "Did you really write that for me?"

"Yes, but—"

"Anna please don't make light of something that means everything to me," Heidi said, noticing Anna's awkwardness. "Shall we call Jack real quick?"

"Okay." She smiled. "Why do you want to call him?"

"It'll be fun. Plus, he can see us happily lazing here together and we can say that we love his song," she said excitably.

"You're as much of a hopeless romantic as he is," she said, holding her phone up to them as the FaceTime dialed out.

"Hey, you okay?"

"Yes, we're awesome. How are you doing?" Heidi said into the phone.

"Get in!" he shouted. "You know I could make millions off you pair looking all hot in bed together?" He raised his eyebrows animatedly. "So, how are you both? Guess things are back on?"

"We are happy *and* yes, together. We love your song, thank you," Heidi said, "I miss you, big guy."

"Well, you need to get your backside back here then. I miss you both too," he said waving erratically. "You bang yet?"

"We're hanging up now," Anna said.

"*What*? Dawn said she originally sent Heidi to get laid, allegedly by me, but in fact she was more drawn to you," he laughed. "One of us has to do her."

"Bye, Jack," Anna laughed, ending the call, and throwing the phone to the side. Anna pushed her to the middle of the large bed. "So, Jack's got a point. One of us has got to help you get through stuff," she said straddling her with a wink.

"Well, if it'll help with the pain and distress…" She smirked.

"Good point," Anna said, slowly lifting Heidi's top up to reveal her bra. Her breathing heightened.

"You enjoying yourself?" Heidi laughed.

"I don't know what you mean," Anna responded, keeping her eyes on Heidi's body.

"Sure, you don't. I can't believe you're here, and we're like this. I love the way you touch me, so delicately. I love just looking at you like this," Heidi said.

"You do, huh?" Anna rolled onto her side to stop and look at Heidi. "I feel the same to all of the above and cannot believe how beautiful you are. Your body is driving me insane."

"It is?" Heidi asked. "Well, it's all yours," Heidi said, pulling Anna back on top of her and groaning contentedly.

Anna leaned down, kissing around her bra. She cupped her hand around the area and Heidi's breathing buckled.

"You sure you're okay?" Anna asked.

"I couldn't be better," she whispered softly. Heidi lowered her head to the pillow, stretching out to allow Anna to explore her body.

Anna still felt unsure about the situation, but Heidi's groans provided her with much more direction. She removed her clothes and couldn't stop looking at the black matching underwear set that Heidi sported. She was desperate to remove the bra, yet the idea got herself in to a state of panic. Sure, she'd taken a bra off three million times in her life, but she'd never taken somebody else's bra off before. That wouldn't be quite so easy, and what if she *laughed* at her? *God, why was everything so stressful?* She thought. Anna ignored her fears, and continued kissing down her body, taking a deep breath. She maneuvered Heidi onto her front, feeling a sense of accomplishment as she inwardly praised herself for the excellent idea. Better still, this was quite possibly an even better view of her. Anna kissed down her back as she tenderly unclasped her bra, pulling the sides down with ease. Kissing along her back, she heard her prominent groans. Anna, completely lost in the moment, became transfixed by Heidi's body. Unable to wait any longer, she rolled Heidi back over and softly caressed her nipples with a playful squeeze, causing Heidi to gasp. She had no idea how she seemed to know what to do, but she was going with her instincts, and her instincts told her she wanted her, every part of her. So that's what she was doing—exploring every part of her. Anna quickly moved her mouth to her breast. She kissed it softly, hearing her cries. She ran her tongue around it, circling in small motions. Anna carefully cupped her breast and lightly bit the tip of her nipple.

"*Oh my God!*" Heidi cried out with pleasure.

Anna couldn't remember ever being this turned on before and wondered if Heidi was as close to coming as she felt herself. *How was that even possible*? She braved the move, hoping that what she was about to do was okay. She ran her nails slowly down her tummy, slowing as she reached her knicker line. Hearing Heidi gasp, she continued. She teased a little, running her finger around the top of her underwear as she sucked and pulled her nipple between her teeth. Anna softly stroked the area, feeling the smoothness beneath her underwear, engaging in this new and unfamiliar contact. Anna heard cries emerge from Heidi and continued her mission, making her way further down. She felt Heidi lift her lower body up to accommodate Anna's roaming hand, and could already feel the heat. Anna entered her slowly and carefully, putting a little bit more pressure on her nipple. She was stunned that already her body was starting to react to her touch. She continued the motions as Heidi's body rippled erratically and listened to her repetitive cries.

"Jesus, Anna. *Oh my God,*" she said, pulling her up next to her. "For someone that's not done that before, you sure as hell know how to please a woman."

"Stop, you're embarrassing me. You seemed ready anyway. I'm not gonna lie, that was probably the most nervous I've been in my life," she said shyly.

"I wouldn't have guessed. That was… wow."

"Stop, please," she said awkwardly.

"I'm sorry, I didn't mean to make you feel uncomfortable. I just didn't expect it to feel as amazing as that. I've never been so turned on. And I've never come that quick, or intensely."

"I guess I just don't really know how to deal with this."

"You don't need to deal with anything, Anna. Just be yourself and I'll do the same. And if you want to, we can occasionally make love. For the record, I really want to," she smirked. "*Really* want to," she gasped.

"I *also* want to, just saying." She eyed her and kissed her lips again.

"Well that's fantastic news then." She pushed Anna on to her back and kissed her with a passion neither had experienced before. Heidi couldn't wait any longer. They had plenty of time to explore each other; now, she just *needed* her. She wanted her fully, and in this moment. Heidi kissed her harshly, feeling and hearing the groans from Anna. She stopped and tried to catch her breath, as she considered Anna's eyes. "I'm sorry, I'm rushing," she said out of breath.

"I don't care, I can barely hold on. I need this… I need you," she said hurriedly as she opened her legs, and felt Heidi's body drop between them. She pushed harder into the kiss, feeling a hand slip inside her jeans. Anna could tell how aroused she was, and clearly, it was something pleasurable to Anna as she heard her excitable groans when she found Anna's center. Anna rolled them over, pulling herself on top of Heidi, forcing her fingers to go deeper inside her. Their kisses became harder, and faster. Heidi used her thigh to push her deeper as she felt waves come over Anna. Anna groaned loudly, over and over as the experience left her. Anna fell on top of Heidi in a breathless heap. She maneuvered her hand so she could pull her into a closed hug and delight in the moment.

"So, do you regret waiting 20 years for that?" Heidi whispered giggling.

"I regret waiting all this time for sex with you," she said, running her nail over the tip of Heidi's nipple.

"Easy girl," she said, moving away a little. "As much as I'd love to spend all day in bed with you, I do unfortunately need to head into work. I'm already late," she said sadly. "Now that I know you're here, I can try and get a couple days off. Why don't you come with me today, though?"

"Can we misbehave on set?"

"Of a Disney movie? That's so wrong," she laughed. "You want to come? Or you could always stay with Margherita?"

"Yeah, I'm not feeling that idea."

"Why? Do you not like her?" she asked concerned.

"No, I do. She's fantastic, but I don't know if I could face her after we've just done that. Especially not after your screams."

"I did *not* scream," Heidi laughed.

"Oh, but you did. Big, loud ass shrills," she giggled.

"Well, that's your fault. You did it to me." She kissed the tip of her nose and jumped up, putting her clothes on.

"Spoil sport. I was enjoying the view," Anna said, leaning on her elbow.

"Well, consider yourself lucky. At least you got a look." Heidi bent down and pulled at her t-shirt, kissing her softly. I promise you, my love, I will work my butt off today, so we can get an early finish. I'll tell Margherita to have a night off. Then we can do this maybe a little bit slower, and longer… and louder." She winked, kissing her again. "Come on, we need to go," she said, holding her hand out for Anna to take.

*

Anna spent the day being waited on hand and foot by the staff on set. She ate lunch with Heidi, who promised her they'd have a couple of days together with nice restaurants to dine in. Today, they ate a buffet on set so she could rush through the shoot to get home and finish where they'd left off.

Anna sat quietly, watching as Heidi read lines into a microphone. It reminded her of the video to the song Band Aid, where varying artists sang into it the way Heidi did now.

"Hey cuz, how's it going?" Dawn walked in and kissed her cousin on the cheek.

"Hi, what're you doing here?"

"I figured you'd be here. I just finished work, so I thought I'd pop in to see if you fancied going for a drink until she finishes."

"Umm, she said she—"

"Calm yourself, you love bird. I won't be taking time away from her. I'll speak to the director and find out how long she'll be. She can either meet us there, or I'll have you back before she's done. Unless you want to watch someone speaking into a microphone for another six hours."

"Six hours?" Anna asked incredulously.

"Chill babes. You'll be back fucking her brains out in no time," she whispered.

"Dawn, do you always have to be so vulgar?" She scolded.

"Ahh sorry, make beautiful love to each other into the night," she said, sticking two fingers into her mouth, pretending to gag.

"*Whatever*. How do you know how long she'll be?" Anna asked ignoring her cousin.

Dawn waved to Heidi, and walked toward a guy sat in a chair with 'Director' written along the back. They had a brief discussion as Dawn checked her watch, and blew a kiss to Heidi.

"Come on. Best case, two hours. Given how much she's putting into it, he reckons three max. Check out my little cousin, the 'hot shot' lay. You're so good she's desperate to get out of here," she smirked. "Come on, I'll treat you to a few expensive cocktails, and some celeb spotting in the fancy parts of L.A. We could always go to West Hollywood. There's a great gay scene there, which is apparently more your thing now."

"Do you have to be an ass all the time?"

"I'm sorry," she said, pulling her in to a hug. "I'm stoked for you both. I *really* am. I just wanted to wind you up a little bit. I've never seen you smile so much; it suits you, gorgeous. How about we drop my car off real quick, and then get Heidi to come meet us with her driver? She can have a beer with us, or if you guys wanna get off—no pun intended—before you start, I'll just stay out."

"Sure," she said, waving to a confused looking Heidi.

"Come on, think of it logically. She will get much more done without you there to look at. We can text her and tell her what's going on."

*

"I think we're going to get bed sores," Anna said, tickling Heidi and kissing her neck softly.

"Most likely. We haven't gotten out of this room for two days."

"That's technically not true. We've showered and bathed together," Anna said wickedly. "A lot."

"Good to stay clean," Heidi murmured, stepping her fingers slowly down her tummy.

"Again? *Really*?" Anna said, groaning loudly, and allowing Heidi to continue what she'd already started.

"What can I say? I'm making up for lost time," she said, rolling her back over again.

Chapter Forty-Six

"Are you regretting it?" Heidi asked concerned.

"No, why?"

"Because I can already see you leaving me. Your eyes have a different look," she said sadly.

"That's sadness, Heidi. I haven't done this before, remember? I've had the best two weeks ever with you, and now I have to leave. I don't want to be away from you. I don't want to have to return to a house that has memories of you without you in it. I don't want to look at Jack, who now reminds me of you. He's gonna want to know details, and I have to talk about how wonderful and perfect everything was, and go back to being in bed alone. Nobody to kiss goodnight, nobody to snuggle into, nobody to wake up to. It just hurts a lot, that's all. I guess I'm being selfish; I just want what normal people have."

"And we will," she said.

"How can we? You're a Hollywood movie star, and I'm a farm girl from Surrey."

"Anna, I told you. I don't care about that anymore. I can act in the UK if I want to, but I'm not so sure I even want to act anymore. I just need to finish this movie. I loved writing that book, and now it's being published. They even want a sequel. Jesus, your cousin is even trying to get a movie deal from it. The point is, I really *enjoyed* that. I don't want to phase out of Hollywood like so many others. I want to go out with a bang. I don't care if I have to move back to the UK with you, or anything else, if you'll have me."

"But you don't want that. Your dream is to live in southern Italy with a vineyard. You said it," she said.

"Dreams change, baby." She kissed her lips. "I have a different dream now, and that can be anywhere in the world if the woman I love is there with me. Granted, the vineyard is how I once saw my life going, but I don't care if it means I can spend my life with the woman I'm in love with. Please stop, Anna, you're scaring me. Don't run from me, not again. We only have three weeks apart and then I'll back for Christmas. After that, we'll see what happens."

"*Really*?" Anna asked surprised.

"Really, what?"

"You want to spend Christmas with me?"

"Hell yes. I already know what to buy you; I saw it a couple days ago. I want to wake up with you on Christmas morning, make love to you for hours, make breakfast together, open our gifts together, have our families over and cook together, and then have a big Christmas night party, with Jack and his family and friends. I want it all, and I want it with you," she said. "But you have to promise me one thing."

"What's that?"

"Even if I can't get there until Christmas Eve, you cannot decorate the tree without me. We do that *together* with mulled wine."

"I can handle that," she said, snuggling into her lazily. "Oh, and in Christmas P.J.'s."

"Of course. See, baby, we already have our own traditions," Heidi said, tapping her nose.

"Do you think it's stupid?"

"What?"

"Talking about traditions at our age?"

"*No*. What relevance has age got to do with it? You really do overthink a lot, don't you?" She laughed. "I think it's great we're doing these things. I don't think it matters if we're 15, 41, or 92. Love is love. Plus, it's private to us. It's not like we're going to tell everyone our private things, is it? Personally, I think it's lovely. It means everything to me, just like you do."

"I do love you, you know that? And yes, unfortunately, I overthink everything," she sighed.

"I know, yes. Your overthinking is part of what I love about you. I know you're scared, but we have three weeks. I suggest you make the most of it because chances are, you'll never get a night alone thereafter," Heidi smirked.

"Promises, promises. Anyway, I guess we should probably make a move now," she said sadly.

"No more sadness. We'll FaceTime every day when it's convenient for each other. We'll text, email, WhatsApp, Facebook, messenger, any or all of them. Oh, and I got you this," she said, handing her an advent calendar.

"You bought me an advent calendar?" She laughed.

"Yes. It's the countdown to me coming back to get my girl again as opposed to a countdown to Christmas," she said. "Eat from it as you please, but make sure you have 21 chocolates because that's how many sleeps you have without me."

"You know, you really are as soppy as Jack," she said.

"This is only the beginning, beautiful. Come on, we need to get you to the airport. Look at it as it's one step closer to being together properly."

"Charming, you sound like you want rid of me," Anna said stifling a grin.

"Don't think that," Heidi said quickly.

"I'm kidding. Come on, one last shower?" Anna raised her eyebrow.

"Um nope. Last one here, maybe, but the first of many," she giggled, pulling her up quickly.

Epilogue

"Only four days left, eh?" Jack smirked to Anna.

"Sod off, idiot, and get back to work." She punched him playfully.

"Oi, that's bullying!"

"Well, I'm your boss *and* Human Resources, so you're screwed buddy," she smirked. "*Plus,* no Christmas bonus if you keep on." She laughed at him.

"Charming, even after I stepped up for two weeks *and* got you with the love of your life," he laughed. "On a serious note, I bet you can't wait."

"Too right. It's been so hard, and I'm completely ready to see what happens next, you know?"

"Yeah, have you had any thoughts or discussions? Or are you not prepared to say at this stage?"

"Don't be silly, you're my best mate. Honestly, I'm not too sure. She lives there, and has this huge career, which I know she says doesn't matter. She says she'll come here and write, but I'm worried it just won't be enough for her. She told me she wanted to eventually retire to a barn house in the south of Italy with a vineyard, and hide away from the world, making wine. I don't know, I feel like it's all one sided. I don't want her to regret being with me because of all she's given up. And just because she says it's enough, that I'm enough, well, how does she know that'll be enough forever?" She pondered.

"And how do you know it won't?" He said back.

"You really are wasted being single. Thanks mate, and hey, listen, don't worry about anything. Whatever I decide, I'll make sure you're *not* impacted," she said, kissing his cheek softly.

"It'll be fine. I love you, and want you to be happy. I can get a job elsewhere if I need to. I have savings; I may even see if I can put it towards a small holding. Do like you did, and grow a place with my own stamp on it," he said proudly. "Why don't you come to family lunch today? We've got roast lamb. Come on, Mum would love it."

"Thanks for the offer, but I'm all good. It's your family time, Jack, and your early finish. You don't need to be looking at your boss's ugly mug," she winked.

"Maybe, just maybe, I like my boss's ugly mug," he said. "Come on, for me? You can't speak to Heid's, so just come to dinner. We can sleep in tomorrow, have a few beers, and play some games."

"Thank you, I do love you. Honestly, I'm gonna skip this time. I wanna have an early start and just chill with some online Christmas shopping."

"Ahh, sexy Christmas undies for Hollywood, eh?"

"Home, now!" She pointed to the door, laughing.

*

Anna finished work later than she wanted that night. It'd been a long and tough day in terms of work, but as Heidi kept saying, she was one day closer to their being together. Heidi was right; it was far from great, but they spoke all the time, and discussed their future. It was the next best thing to being together. Heidi instilled every confidence in her that she was all in. It was a wonderful feeling, but God, she couldn't wait to have her back in her arms again. Anna opened a beer, and put the ready meal in the microwave. It was quick which allowed more Christmas shopping time. She'd already gone mad, but she literally couldn't stop. *She couldn't believe she'd wasted all those years missing out on this, on love.* Heidi missed her call, which disappointed Anna, but she'd explained that would likely be the case while they were finishing off the movie. Refusing to loathe in self-pity, she'd have a couple of bottles of beer in her comfies, order the Christmas food, some daft Christmas PJ's, and more presents for Heidi.

Anna finished her meal and grabbed herself another bottle, dancing around happily to the radio in the background. At least if they were snowed in there was enough food and drink to keep them going until about summer. Giggling at the prospect, she heard the door knock. She instantly cursed Jack for not listening to her when she'd said she'd be fine alone.

"I'm fine, why do you…." she stopped after thrusting the door open. *It wasn't Jack, not this time.*

"What are you doing here!?"

"Surprising my gorgeous girlfriend, what does it look like?" Heidi said rushing in to kiss her.

"Girlfriend, eh?" Anna said, pulling back and stroking her cheek. "When? Why? How? I don't even care. You're here. You're *really* here!"

"I am, baby. I've climbed hell and high water to get to you, so let me bloody well in," she smirked. "You like your surprise, baby?"

"Yes," Anna said, pulling her in and grabbing her cases. "Jesus, are you moving in *now*?" she asked, looking at all the bags around them.

"I can leave again," she said, raising an eyebrow.

"Um, *nah*. I'm happy with this arrangement," she said. "Now give me a kiss."

"Just a kiss? It's been almost three weeks, lady, you best get your butt up those stairs," she said. "Or maybe we can start over there," she nodded towards the table, and chased a squealing Anna.

"Stop, stop! I can't take it anymore!" Anna said, trying to control her hysterics and breathing.

"I don't know what you mean," Heidi said, smirking. "So, you missed me?"

"God, more than anything. *So much,*" she said sadly, walking into her arms.

"Well, no more sadness, angel. I'm back. I don't want to be apart again anytime soon. Which means you're going to have to put a bit more faith in Jack when we go to the worldwide premieres of my new movie," Heidi said seriously. "I always knew I'd miss you, but my God, I didn't think it'd be anything like this. I've been pulling 20 hour days just to get finished. I'm kind of glad I have a bit of time before Christmas because I need to sleep," she said.

"Well, I don't know how much sleep you're likely to get this evening, but as soon as I go to work, you have all day," Anna smiled. "I missed you, baby."

"Me too, gorgeous."

"Good. Well in that case, I'd like to give you a gift," she said seriously, grabbing a wrapped present.

"But it's not Christmas yet. Let's wait."

"I know, but this is an '*us*' gift. You have plenty of Christmas gifts." She smiled shyly.

"I do? Well, I guess I need to go Christmas shopping tomorrow then. Ohhh, how very *normal!*" she said.

"You don't like that?" Anna quizzed.

"No, I *love* that."

"Good. In that case, this is for you," she said, breathing heavily.

"Are you okay?"

"Yes!" she snapped. "Mhmm," she said slower that time.

"You sure? Are you sure you want me to open this?"

Anna closed her eyes, breathing heavily. "Yes, Heidi. I really do."

Heidi opened the large envelope, pulling out two more envelopes. She looked back to Anna and raised an eyebrow. She opened the envelope that had a number one written on it, pulling out a picture.

"What's this?" she said, inspecting the paper.

"Open the second one before you say anything."

Heidi went to speak.

"Please Heid's?" Anna pleaded.

Heidi did as instructed and opened the second envelope, pulling out another picture. This one was of the farm, with a 'For Sale' sign on it.

"You're selling your farm!?" she shouted.

"Well, I thought if you were serious about leaving L.A., *and* your job, then it was only fair we compromise. Hence, the Italian barn," she said, flipping over the first piece of paper and showing her. "It was more for the gift as opposed to this one. There's loads out there. I figured maybe a cheeky month over there, researching the vineyards before we buy may be worth a thought or two," she smirked.

"Oh, you do?" She smiled kindly. "Look Anna, I don't think you should leave here. It's your family home. This… this here, is *my* dream," Heidi said seriously, holding out the picture.

"What's your dream is my dream. Why shouldn't I sell it? I've loved it here, but we can have some animals over there, I'm sure. I'll make it worth your while," she smirked.

"Oh really? Well I guess I can allow that," she laughed, still unsure of what Anna was proposing.

"Not that I need an excuse, but look, I wanna be with you, and I like the idea of it. If I sell this place, then we can afford to do it."

"You don't need to though."

"I couldn't afford to without selling it."

"You don't need to because I can—"

"Heid's, don't even go there. Don't damage this before it's begun. I don't need your money."

"I'm not saying you do. Look, please just hear me out."

"No way, I'm not having this conversation."

"Anna, please. I've done this job for a long time. If you really want to be with me, like I want to be with you, i.e. forever, then honestly, please just hear me out. If you really don't want me buying it, I get that. You're a proud woman, but please, I just have one thing to run past you."

"Fine, but I'm not agreeing to anything."

Heidi smiled sincerely. "Thank you. That's a new thing for me, so thank you," she sighed and took her hand.

*

"You really wanna do this?" Anna asked, concerned.

"I really do. I think it's the perfect solution, and I couldn't think of a better thing to do. Nor for a better person. If you aren't sure, we can leave it for now."

"No, I just can't believe we're going to do this."

"You want to wait until you're sober? In case you don't want it? Or give *us* some time together in case we don't um—"

"Heidi," she interrupted. "I love you, and want you...forever. You and me forever, baby," she said.

"Well, let's do this then!" she said, squealing a little bit.

Anna rang the doorbell to Jack's house. She smiled at Heidi as they heard laughter from inside.

"I can't wait for that," Heidi smiled softly.

"Kids?" She choked as the door opened. They covered their eyes as the young girls screams filled the entire street. Jack came speeding and sliding to the door, skidding into it to see Anna and Heidi.

"Mills, what's up with you?" he began, laughing. "Are you going to stop screaming if I let you go?" He asked, kneeling next to her and watching her head nod.

"Okay good," he said, removing his hand. "Millie, these are my friends. You remember Anna, and this is my friend, Heidi, who I'm guessing you already know."

"*You* know Heidi Spencer-Brady?" His mum and sisters asked him.

"No, I know Heidi Spencer. Or Heidi Edwards."

"Good to see you guys," he said, kissing them both. "Hollywood, you're back on home turf. Good to see you again, gorgeous," he said, pulling her into a big hug. "Glad you guys could stop by."

"Well actually, we aren't staying. We just wanted to talk to you."

"Oh alright," he said concerned.

"Can't you stay for just a little bit?" His mum asked pleadingly.

"Um, not tonight. Heidi's just arrived, so she's a little jet lagged. If the offer's still on the table, we'll come next Sunday, or maybe between Christmas and New Year's," Anna said to Heidi.

"For sure." She smiled to the little girl, who stood looking at Heidi mouth wide open.

"You got a minute?" Anna asked again.

"Yeah, come on in," he said quietly, knowing what was coming. He opened the door to the lounge, allowing them to walk in, and shut the door behind him. "So, let me guess. You're selling up and leaving?" he said sadly.

Heidi went to speak, but Anna stopped her. "Let me ask you something. If I didn't work here, would you still want to?"

"What d'ya mean?"

"Exactly that. If I wasn't there, would you still love it as much? Would you still want to come to work every day?"

"Yeah, of course. I mean don't get me wrong, it's partly you that makes it as great as it is, but I love it. I love the farm—the animals, the job, the ice-cream making, the cheese making—all of it. Why?" He questioned. "Look, don't worry about me. I don't want you to think you have to look out for me. Don't try and guarantee a job with the sale, mate. They'll always get around it with solicitors. I'll be fine," he said.

"No, I haven't, but I made you a promise that I'd look after you. Look Jack, we decided we want to give it a go in the south of Italy. Start up our own vineyard, and take a few of the animals from here."

"Right okay, so you're—"

"But," Anna stopped him. "Heidi made a very valid point. What if *we* don't work out?"

"I didn't say that, FYI," she winked to him.

"What *if* we don't like Italy? And more importantly, what about my childhood home? My memories, my heart, my love."

"Right?" he said uncertainly.

"Well, after many arguments—"

"That's why we're not staying—make up sex," Heidi winked.

"Will you behave?" Anna said.

"Jesus, *alriiight*. She's becoming a nagging wife already."

"Look, we've decided that I'm not going to sell the farm. At least, not just yet. We're going try it out in Italy for a bit, but we'll need someone trustworthy to take care of the farm."

Jack had the biggest grin on his face. "You're gonna let me run it?" He jumped up, clapping his hands. "*Really*? Anna, I promise I won't let you down!" He said excitably.

"I know you won't because I know you won't let your own investment go."

"What?" he asked, confused.

"You know that Christmas bonus?"

"Yeah."

"Well this year, I'll be thanking you for all of your hard work over the year, as well as…what was it you said today…getting me the girl of my dreams? I'm giving you 50 percent of the farm, Jack. It'll set you up for life, and for when *you* have a family. I can still do the books from my new home, but basically, you can move into the house, and you'll be running it. You'll need to employ a new member of staff to do it with you, but you'll be here. And since the place is half yours, you can interview and decide." She smiled.

Jack looked at them seriously. "Guys, that's a…an amazing gesture, but there's no way I can take that. Jesus, I was made up with the prospect of being manager," he said seriously.

"Jack, you've made such a massive impact on my life, and I know you mean everything to Anna. I don't want her to lose this place; this is her *life*. You deserve *all* of this. This will set you up for your life, but more importantly, we know that you'll love it and nurture it as though it was your own. Half of it will be. This is a gift from both of us, something that each of us truly knows you deserve," she said.

"I don't know what to say," he said with tears in his eyes. "I don't know how I'll ever be able to thank you."

"Just promise me you'll get a co-worker equally as good as you, so that you can rely on them when you come visit us regularly," Anna said, pulling them into a group hug.

THE END

About the Author

S.L. Gape enjoys writing, cooking, travelling and photography. She lives in Cheshire with her partner Jen, and currently splits her time between writing and her day job as a Regional HR advisor.

She gets a lot of inspiration from travelling and her experience as a holiday rep for seven years, where she was lucky enough to have lived and worked in Spain, Greece, Bahamas, Egypt and Lapland. She finds writing as a tremendous stress release for her job, and loves to live through the escapism. *Worlds Apart* is her third novel.

Follow her on Twitter: @louise_7uk and Facebook: S.L. Gape

Other Titles Available From
Triplicity Publishing

Castor Valley (Law & Order Series Book 2) by Graysen Morgen. Jessie Henry is torn when she reads about the capture of the Doyle brothers, two young men who were part of her old gang. Unable to let them hang for a crime she's sure they didn't commit, Jessie leaves her wife and the Town of Boone Creek behind, and sets out on a journey back to the one place she thought she'd never see again, *Castor Valley*. Ellie Henry watches the love of her life leave, not knowing if she will ever return. When she gets an odd telegram, nearly a week later, she fears Jessie is in trouble. With no other choice, she goes to the one person who can help her.

Close Enough to Touch by Cade Brogan. Joanna Grey injects the deadly poison into the chamber of the syringe—time after time. She's murdered before and she'll do it again. She's intelligent, educated, and beautiful. Rylee Hayes is a respected homicide detective. Her best friends are her grandparents, her coonhound, and her partner—in that order. Kenzie Bigham is the single mom of a thirteen-year-old, a church secretary, and a woman who's struggled much of her adult life with her own sexuality. Their paths will cross when Rylee's new investigation involves members of Kenzie's congregation. Will Rylee have what it takes to meet the challenge of a serial killer who's proven herself to be a more than worthy opponent?

Fight to the Top by S. L. Gape. Georgia is a forty year old, single, Area Director from Manchester, UK who is all work and definitely no play. Having no time to socialise or spend time with her family she prides herself on being fit and well-polished. Erika is an Area Director for the same company, but in the United States. Whilst she is concentrating so heavily on the promotion she has been fighting for, she's starting to feel like her life outside of work is falling apart. The two women are exceptionally different, and worlds apart. Both of their lives are turned upside down when their jobs are snatched from under their noses, and they are suddenly faced with being thrown together by their bosses for one last major project...in Texas.

Boone Creek (Law & Order Series book 1) by Graysen Morgen. Jessie Henry is looking for a new life. She's unknown in the town of Boone Creek when she arrives, and wants to keep it that way. When she's offered the job of Town Marshal, she takes it, believing that protecting others and upholding the law is the penance for her past. Ellie Fray is a widowed, shopkeeper. She generally keeps to herself, but the mysterious new Town Marshal both intrigues and infuriates her. She believes the last thing the town needs is someone stirring up trouble with the outlaws who have taken over.

Witness by Joan L. Anderson. Becca and Kate have lived together for eight years, and have always spent their vacation in a tropical paradise, lying on a beach. This year, Becca wanted to try something different: a seven day, 65-mile hike in the beautiful Cascade Mountains of Washington state. Their peaceful vacation turns to horror when they stumble upon a brutal murder taking place in the back country.

Too Soon by S.L. Gape. Brooke is a twenty-nine year old detective from Oxford, who has her life pretty much planned out until her boss and partner of nine years, Maria, tells her their relationship is over. When Brooke finds out the truth, that Maria cheated on her with their best friend Paula, she decides to get her life back on track by getting away for six weeks in Anglesey, North Wales. Chloe, a thirty three year old artist and art director, owns a log cabin on Anglesey where she spends each weekend painting and surfing. After returning from a surf, she stumbles upon the somewhat uptight and enigmatic Brooke.

Blue Ice Landing by KA Moll. Coy is a beautiful blonde with a southern accent and a successful practice as a physician assistant. She has a comfortable home, good friends, and a loving family. She's also a widow, carrying a burden of responsibility for her wife's untimely death. Coby is a woman with secrets. She's estranged from her family, a recovering alcoholic, and alone because she's convinced that she's unlovable. When she loses her job as a heavy equipment operator, she'll accept one that'll force her to step way outside her comfort zone. When Coy quits her job to accept a position in Antarctica, her path will cross with Coby's. Their attraction to one another will be immediate, and despite their differences, it won't be long before they fall in love. But for these two, with all their baggage, will love be enough?

Never Quit (Never Series book 2) by Graysen Morgen. Two years after stepping away from the action as a Coast Guard Rescue Swimmer to become an instructor, Finley finds herself in charge of the most difficult class of cadets she's ever faced, while also juggling the taxing demands of having a home life with her partner Nicole, and their fifteen year old daughter. Jordy Ross gave up everything, dropping out of college, and leaving her family behind, to join the Coast Guard and become a rescue swimmer cadet. The extreme training tests her fitness level, pushing her mentally and physically further than she's ever been in her life, but it's the aggressive competition between her and another female cadet that proves to be the most challenging.

For a Moment's Indiscretion by KA Moll. With ten years of marriage under their belt, Zane and Jaina are coasting. The little things they used to do for one another have fallen by the wayside. They've gotten busy with life. They've forgotten to nurture their love and relationship. Even soul mates can stumble on hard times and have marital difficulties. Enter Amelia, a new faculty member in Jaina's building. She's new in town, young, and very pretty. When an argument with Zane causes Jaina to storm out angry, she reaches out to Amelia. Of course, she seizes the opportunity. And for a moment of indiscretion, Jaina could lose everything.

Never Let Go (Never Series book 1) by Graysen Morgen. For Coast Guard Rescue Swimmer, Finley Morris, life is good. She loves her job, is well respected by her peers, and has been given an opportunity to take her career to the next level. The only thing missing is the love of her life, who walked out, taking their daughter with her, seven years earlier. When Finley gets a call from her ex, saying their teenage daughter is coming to spend the summer with her, she's floored. While spending more time with her daughter, whom she doesn't get to see often, and learning to be a full-time parent, Finley quickly realizes she has not, and will never, let go of what is important.

Pursuit by Joan L. Anderson. Claire is a workaholic attorney who flies to Paris to lick her wounds after being dumped by her girlfriend of seventeen years. On the plane she chats with the young woman sitting next to her, and when they land the woman is inexplicably detained in Customs. Claire is surprised when she later runs into the woman in the city. They agree to meet for breakfast the next morning, but when the woman doesn't show up Claire goes to her hotel and makes a horrifying discovery. She soon finds herself ensnared in a web of intrigue and international terrorism, becoming the target of a high stakes game of cat and mouse through the streets of Paris.

Wrecked by Sydney Canyon. To most people, the *Duchess* is a myth formed by old pirates tales, but to Reid Cavanaugh, a Caribbean island bum and one of the best divers and treasure hunters in the world, it's a real, seventeenth century pirate ship—the holy grail of underwater treasure hunting. Reid uses the same cunning tactics she always has before setting out to find the lost ship. However, she is forced to bring her business partner's daughter along as collateral this time because he doesn't trust her. Neither woman is thrilled, but being cooped up on a small dive boat for days, forces them to get know each other quickly.

Arson by Austen Thorne. Madison Drake is a detective for the Stetson Beach Police Department. The last thing she wants to do is show a new detective the ropes, especially when a fire investigation becomes arson to cover up a

murder. Madison butts heads with Tara, her trainee, deals
with sarcasm from Nic, her ex-girlfriend who is a patrol
officer, and finds calm in the chaos of police work with
Jamie, her best friend who is the county medical examiner.
Arson is the first of many in a series of novella episodes
surrounding the fictional Stetson Beach Police Department
and Detective Madison Drake.

Change of Heart by KA Moll. Courtney Holloman is a
woman at the top of her game. She's successful, wealthy,
and a highly sought after Washington lobbyist. She has
money, her job, booze, and nothing else. In quiet moments,
against her will, her mind drifts back to her days in high
school and to all that she gave up. Jack Camdon is a
complex woman, and yet not at all. She is also a woman
who has never moved beyond the sudden and unexplained
departure of her high school sweetheart, her lover, and her
soul mate. When circumstances bring Courtney back to
town two decades later, their paths will cross. Will it be too
late?

Mommies (Bridal Series book 3) **by Graysen
Morgen.** Britton and her wife Daphne have been married
for a year and a half and are happy with their life, until
Britton's mother hounds her to find out why her sister
Bridget hasn't decided to have children yet. This prompts
Daphne to bring up the big subject of having kids of their
own with Britton. Britton hadn't really thought much about
having kids, but her love for Daphne makes her see life and
their future together in a whole new way when they decide
to become mommies.

***Haunting Love* by K.A. Moll.** Anna Crestwood was raised in the strict beliefs of a religious sect nestled in the foothills of the Smoky Mountains. She's a lesbian with a ton of baggage—fearful, guilty, and alone. Very few things would compel her to leave the familiar. The job offer of a lifetime is one of them. Gabe Garst is a police officer. She's also a powerful medium. Her work with juvenile delinquents and ghosts is all that keeps her going. Inside she's dead, certain that her capacity to love is buried six feet under. Anna and Gabe's paths cross. Their attraction is immediate, but they hold back until all hope seems lost.

***Rapture & Rogue* by Sydney Canyon.** Taren Rauley is happy and in a good relationship, until the one person she thought she'd never see again comes back into her life. She struggles to keep the past from colliding with the present as old feelings she thought were dead and gone, begin to haunt her. In college, Gianna Revisi was a mastermind, ring-leading, crime boss. Now, she has a great life and spends her time running Rapture and Rogue, the two establishments she built from the ground up. The last person she ever expects to see walk into one of them, is the girl who walked out on her, breaking her heart five years ago.

***Second Chance* by Sydney Canyon.** After an attack on her convoy, Marine Corps Staff Sergeant, Darien Hollister, must learn to live without her sight. When an experimental procedure allows her to see again, Darien is torn, knowing someone had to die in order for this to happen.

She embarks on a journey to personally thank the donor's family, but is too stunned to tell them the truth. Mixed emotions stir inside of her as she slowly gets to the know the people that feel like so much more than strangers to her. When the truth finally comes out, Darien walks away, taking the second chance that she's been given to go back to the only life she's ever known, but she's not the only one with a second chance at life.

Meant to Be by Graysen Morgen. Brandt is about to walk down the aisle with her girlfriend, when an unexpected chain of events turns her world upside down, causing her to question the last three years of her life. A chance encounter sparks a mix of rage and excitement that she has never felt before. Summer is living life and following her dreams, all the while, harboring a huge secret that could ruin her career. She believes that some things are better kept in the dark, until she has her third run-in with a woman she had hoped to never see again, and gives into temptation. Brandt and Summer start believing everything happens for a reason as they learn the true meaning of meant to be.

Coming Home by Graysen Morgen. After tragedy derails TJ Abernathy's life, she packs up her three year old son and heads back to Pennsylvania to live with her grandmother on the family farm. TJ picks back up where she left off eight years earlier, tending to the fruit and nut tree orchard, while learning her grandmother's secret trade. Soon, TJ's high school sweetheart and the same girl who broke her heart, comes back into her life, threatening to steal it away once again. As the weeks turn into months and tragedy strikes again, TJ realizes coming home was the best thing she could've ever done.

Special Assignment by Austen Thorne. Secret Service Agent Parker Meeks has her hands full when she gets her new assignment, protecting a Congressman's teenage daughter, who has had threats made on her life and been whisked away to a Christian boarding school under an alias to finish out her senior year. Parker is fine with the assignment, until she finds out she has to go undercover as a Canon Priest. The last thing Parker expects to find is a beautiful, art history teacher, who is intrigued by her in more ways than one.

Miracle at Christmas by Sydney Canyon. A Modern Twist on the Classic Scrooge Story. Dylan is a power-hungry lawyer who pushed away everything good in her life to become the best defense attorney in the, often winning the worst cases and keeping anyone with enough money out of jail. She's visited on Christmas Eve by her deceased law partner, who threatens her with a life in hell like his own, if she doesn't change her path. During the course of the night, she is taken on a journey through her past, present, and future with three very different spirits.

Bella Vita by Sydney Canyon. Brady is the First Officer of the crew on the Bella Vita, a luxury charter yacht in the Caribbean. She enjoys the laidback island lifestyle, and is accustomed to high profile guests, but when a U.S. Senator charters the yacht as a gift to his beautiful twin daughters who have just graduated from college and a few of their friends, she literally has her hands full.

Brides (Bridal Series book 2) by Graysen Morgen. Britton Prescott is dating the love of her life, Daphne Attwood, after a few tumultuous events that happened to unravel at her sister's wedding reception, seven months earlier. She's happy with the way things are, but immense pressure from her family and friends to take the next step, nearly sends her back to the single life. The idea of a long engagement and simple wedding are thrown out the window, as both families take over, rushing Britton and Daphne to the altar in a matter of weeks.

Cypress Lake by Graysen Morgen. The small town of Cypress Lake is rocked when one murder after another happens. Dani Ricketts, the Chief Deputy for the Cypress Lake Sheriff's Office, realizes the murders are linked. She's surprised when the girl that broke her heart in high school has not only returned home, but she's also Dani's only suspect. Kristen Malone has come back to Cypress Lake to put the past behind her so that she can move on with her life. Seeing Dani Ricketts again throws her off-guard, nearly derailing her plans to finally rid herself and her family of Cypress Lake.

Crashing Waves by Graysen Morgen. After a tragic accident, Pro Surfer, Rory Eden, spends her days hiding in the surf and snowboard manufacturing company that she built from the ground up, while living her life as a shell of the person that she once was. Rory's world is turned upside when a young surfer pursues her, asking for the one thing she can't do. Adler Troy and Dr. Cason Macauley from Graysen Morgen's bestselling novel: *Falling Snow*, make an appearance in this romantic adventure about life, love, and letting go.

Bridesmaid of Honor (Bridal Series book 1) by Graysen Morgen. Britton Prescott's best friend is getting married and she's the maid of honor. As if that isn't enough to deal with, Britton's sister announces she's getting married in the same month and her maid of honor is her best friend Daphne, the same woman who has tormented Britton for years. Britton has to suck it up and play nice, instead of scratching her eyes out, because she and Daphne are in both weddings. Everyone is counting on them to behave like adults.

Falling Snow by Graysen Morgen. Dr. Cason Macauley, a high-speed trauma surgeon from Denver meets Adler Troy, a professional snowboarder and sparks fly. The last thing Cason wants is a relationship and Adler doesn't realize what's right in front of her until it's gone, but will it be too late?

Fate vs. Destiny by Graysen Morgen. Logan Greer devotes her life to investigating plane crashes for the National Transportation Safety Board. Brooke McCabe is an investigator with the Federal Aviation Association who literally flies by the seat of her pants. When Logan gets tangled in head games with both women will she choose fate or destiny?

Just Me by Graysen Morgen. Wild child Ian Wiley has to grow up and take the reins of the hundred year old family business when tragedy strikes. Cassidy Harland is a little surprised that she came within an inch of picking up a gorgeous stranger in a bar and is shocked to find out that stranger is the new head of her company.

Love Loss Revenge by Graysen Morgen. Rian Casey is an FBI Agent working the biggest case of her career and madly in love with her girlfriend. Her world is turned upside when tragedy strikes. Heartbroken, she tries to rebuild her life. When she discovers the truth behind what really happened that awful night she decides justice isn't good enough, and vows revenge on everyone involved.

Natural Instinct by Graysen Morgen. Chandler Scott is a Marine Biologist who keeps her private life private. Corey Joslen is intrigued by Chandler from the moment she meets her. Chandler is forced to finally open her life up to Corey. It backfires in Corey's face and sends her running. Will either woman learn to trust her natural instinct?

Secluded Heart by Graysen Morgen. Chase Leery is an overworked cardiac surgeon with a group of best friends that have an opinion and a reason for everything. When she meets a new artist named Remy Sheridan at her best friend's art gallery she is captivated by the reclusive woman. When Chase finds out why Remy is so sheltered will she put her career on the line to help her or is it too difficult to love someone with a secluded heart?

In Love, at War by Graysen Morgen. Charley Hayes is in the Army Air Force and stationed at Ford Island in Pearl Harbor. She is the commanding officer of her own female-only service squadron and doing the one thing she loves most, repairing airplanes. Life is good for Charley, until the day she finds herself falling in love while fighting for her life as her country is thrown haphazardly into World War II. Can she survive being in love and at war?

Fast Pitch by Graysen Morgen. Graham Cahill is a senior in college and the catcher and captain of the softball team. Despite being an all-star pitcher, Bailey Michaels is young and arrogant. Graham and Bailey are forced to get to know each other off the field in order to learn to work together on the field. Will the extra time pay off or will it drive a nail through the team?

Submerged by Graysen Morgen. Assistant District Attorney Layne Carmichael had no idea that the sexy woman she took home from a local bar for a one night stand would turn out to be someone she would be prosecuting months later. Scooter is a Naval Officer on a submarine who changes women like she changes uniforms. When she is accused of a heinous crime she is shocked to see her latest conquest sitting across from her as the prosecuting attorney.

Vow of Solitude by Austen Thorne. Detective Jordan Denali is in a fight for her life against the ghosts from her past and a Serial Killer taunting her with his every move. She lives a life of solitude and plans to keep it that way. When Callie Marceau, a curious Medical Examiner, decides she wants in on the biggest case of her career, as well as, Jordan's life, Jordan is powerless to stop her.

Igniting Temptation by Sydney Canyon. Mackenzie Trotter is the Head of Pediatrics at the local hospital. Her life takes a rather unexpected turn when she meets a flirtatious, beautiful fire fighter. Both women soon discover it doesn't take much to ignite temptation.

One Night by Sydney Canyon. While on a business trip, Caylen Jarrett spends an amazing night with a beautiful stripper. Months later, she is shocked and confused when that same woman re-enters her life. The fact that this stranger could destroy her career doesn't bother her. C.J. is more terrified of the feelings this woman stirs in her. Could she have fallen in love in one night and not even known it?

Fine by Sydney Canyon. Collin Anderson hides behind a façade, pretending everything is fine. Her workaholic wife and best friend are both oblivious as she goes on an emotional journey, battling a potentially hereditary disease that her mother has been diagnosed with. The only person who knows what is really going on, is Collin's doctor. The same doctor, who is an acquaintance that she's always been attracted to, and who has a partner of her own.

Shadow's Eyes by Sydney Canyon. Tyler McCain is the owner of a large ranch that breeds and sells different types of horses. She isn't exactly thrilled when a Hollywood movie producer shows up wanting to film his latest movie on her property. Reegan Delsol is an up and coming actress who has everything going for her when she lands the lead role in a new film, but there one small problem that could blow the entire picture.

Light Reading: A Collection of Novellas by Sydney Canyon. Four of Sydney Canyon's novellas together in one book, including the bestsellers Shadow's Eyes and One Night.

Visit us at www.tri-pub.com